THE FAKE DATE

L. H. STACEY

Boldwood

First published in 2018. This edition published in Great Britain in 2023 by Boldwood Books Ltd.

Copyright © L. H. Stacey, 2018

Cover Design by 12 Orchards Ltd.

Cover Photography: Shutterstock

A CIP catalogue record for this book is available from the British Library.

Paperback ISBN 978-1-83533-062-3

Hardback ISBN 978-1-83533-057-9

Large Print ISBN 978-1-83533-058-6

Ebook ISBN 978-1-83533-055-5

Kindle ISBN 978-1-83533-056-2

Audio CD ISBN 978-1-83533-063-0

MP3 CD ISBN 978-1-83533-060-9

Digital audio download ISBN 978-1-83533-054-8

Boldwood Books Ltd
23 Bowerdean Street
London SW6 3TN
www.boldwoodbooks.com

For my wonderful friend of over 30 years, Kathy Kilner.
You've been an amazing friend for over thirty years and above all else, you've always supported me in everything I've done. Thank you x

1

'Nine hours and eleven minutes,' Ella whispered as she stared continually at the watch that lay beside her. Its face was cracked. Its leather strap was broken. It was just close enough to see, but far enough away to prevent her from touching it. She had counted each time the second hand moved, watched the luminous dial as each minute had clicked forward and then quietly sobbed as the minutes slowly turned into hours.

The minute hand clicked forward. Nine hours and twelve minutes. That's how long it had been since she'd felt the first blow, the first agonising pain, the constant barrage of punches that had rained down upon her from every direction and then, once the onslaught had ended, had come the realisation that she'd been left for dead; lying dirty and broken in the muddy undergrowth of the North Yorkshire moors, waiting to be found.

She tried to reach for the watch – but her hand didn't respond. Her fingers were twisted in a peculiar shape and she tried not to look at them for fear that the sight would make her vomit. She tried not to move at all as bile rose in her throat and nausea assailed her each and every time that she did.

Strangely though, she realised that she could just about wiggle her toes. They moved awkwardly, slowly and made a dull squelching noise as she eased them back and forth through the cold, slimy mud. Until, without warning, something sharp caught against her toe, which for a moment made her stop moving. But then she thought about the pain, and slowly moved her toe back and forth again, taking a strange pleasure in the fact that she could feel anything at all.

Her shoes? What had happened to her shoes?

It seemed an odd thought, quite irrelevant given her current state. She had no idea why the shoes would concern her so much. They should have been the least of her worries. But they'd been expensive, and she'd really liked them. Unlike her dress, which was a typical, little black dress. One of the only going out dresses she'd possessed and, if she were honest, it hadn't been nearly as flattering as she'd have liked. She knew that it was ruined, but she didn't care. What she did care about was that the remnants of the dress now hung from her prone body, leaving parts of her naked and exposed.

It was October and the rain had poured persistently for days. She'd trembled relentlessly throughout the night, and at times the trembling had turned into violent shudders that had passed through her whole body. But for some reason, at that moment in time, she no longer seemed to feel the cold, nor did any part of her seem to hurt. Every inch of her had become numb and if it hadn't been for the shaking, she'd have actually thought it all a horrendous nightmare, one that she couldn't wake herself up from. She no longer felt anything, except a deep, disturbing sadness, a longing for what she'd had. For what she hadn't had. For what she'd left behind and for those who would grieve for her, if or when her body was ever found.

Ella thought of her parents. She tried to picture their faces. They were the two people who'd always been there for her. They were the people she'd relied upon the most and she fondly remembered the hours that she'd sat on her father's knee. He'd read the same books to her, over and over again. Then, in direct contrast, she thought of the snuggling with her mother. Of how they'd repeatedly watched the same musical films, one after the other, every Sunday afternoon. They'd both giggled and sang at the top of their voices, not caring if the neighbours could hear; a fond smile crossed her lips. Those times had been her happy times. Her parents had always given her a life full of love. Even though they hadn't always been able to give her everything she'd have liked, she knew that she'd had all that they could afford. And for that Ella had always felt a deep sense of gratitude and had known never to complain. Yet now, lying there in the dirt, the mud and the rain, she suddenly realised that although they hadn't had much money when she was growing up, they had been rich in so many other ways. Ella's mind drifted to the many Christmases, birthdays and happy days they'd shared. The Christmas carols they'd sung. The picnics. The football, rounders, cricket and Monopoly they'd played. Her father's overwhelming competitive nature and the way her mother would always try to help her win.

Looking deeper into her childhood, there had always been Sarah too. She was practically family, the closest she'd had to a sister and had lived next door since preschool. From the minute she'd moved in, they'd become inseparable to the point that Ella couldn't think of a single day that they hadn't spoken, texted or communicated in some way or another.

A deep, disturbing sob suddenly left her throat. The memories made her heart thump wildly. The violent trembling once again began to overtake her body and, even though she was lying on the ground, her mind began to rotate like a fairground ride, which spun at speed and wouldn't stop.

Ella tried to take control and took in a deep breath. 'Focus,' she tried to whisper as she glanced up and towards the sky. She'd prayed all night for daylight, yet even though it had been just about an hour since the sun had fully risen and the rain had stopped, all she saw were dark, depressing clouds that swirled unpredictably above her head, making her wonder if the darkness had been preferable. Between each dark cloud she noticed small, clear patches of sky, as diamante sparks of daylight tried to force their way through. Each sparkle of light gave her a moment of hope; each tiny glimmer of daylight gave her just a little assurance and each minute she stared at her dirty, cracked watch was another minute she'd survived and another minute she hoped that she was closer to being found.

A small, black, slimy beetle crawled over her fingertips, making her immediately try to flick the fingers that refused to move. She hated the thought that something could crawl over her and she had no power to remove it. She tried to scream. But couldn't. Her mouth was dry, her lips had begun to split and the taste of congealed blood had settled on her tongue. Spitting, she felt a globule of blood drop unceremoniously down her cheek, making her retch repeatedly, causing a new, and more intense pain to sear through her body. The numbness had suddenly gone; once again everything hurt. She was now too afraid to move, but began to sob into the dirt until her stream of tears began forming her own mini puddle in the wet, cold mud. Her clutch bag lay in the distance. From within it she heard her mobile spring to life. It was the first real noise she'd heard for hours and she closed her eyes as she listened to the tune. She wished it were close enough to be answered. But then she began to wonder who would have called her so early, especially on a Saturday. 'Please let it be someone who realises I'm missing,' she thought as she allowed the corner of her mouth to lift, just a fraction. It was an attempt at a smile as she tried to be brave, but then she closed her eyes and tried to imagine that she could have answered the call. That she could have shouted for help and that someone, somewhere, could have tracked her phone in order that they might find her and save her life.

Ella cursed inwardly as her breathing became shallow. It was so shallow that her chest barely moved with each breath, and she wondered if she should panic. But panic was far from her mind. Her heart rate slowed and it suddenly occurred to her that death might follow quickly.

Was this how it felt to die?

She mentally shook her head; she was only twenty-eight years old. She couldn't die. She still had everything to live for, yet fate seemed to disagree. She swallowed hard and breathed in as deeply as she could in an attempt to force her lungs to take in the air. Then she opened her eyes as wide as she could, stared at the watch and continued to count every second that flicked past. She was determined to stay conscious. Determined to live and determined to understand the events that had led to her current situation.

Why had she done it?

Because it had been her job, that was why. Her

job had always come first, yet she'd disobeyed the most important rule she'd ever learned since becoming a reporter. She'd gone undercover and had followed a lead alone. Which had been the biggest and most stupid thing she'd ever done. Her reporter's intuition had been so strong. She was sure she'd been onto a big story. She was sure that Rick Greaves was guilty of murder. He'd been married twice. Both wives had died, both suspiciously. Greaves had been a suspect; the police had been sure he'd been involved. Yet, on both occasions, he'd been cleared and released without charge. But Ella was sure that there was more to his story, was certain that he'd been involved and just couldn't believe that a man could be so unlucky that he could have lost two wives in such awful circumstances. And both before the age of thirty-five. She'd found herself gripped by his story. She'd been researching it for months and had even joined the gym that he owned to ensure that she was in the right place at the right time. She'd found ways to chat to him, to understand his side of the story. But he gave nothing away and she couldn't believe her luck when, out of the blue, he'd asked her out on a date – which she'd agreed to much too quickly. Rick had no idea who she was or what she did. To him she was just another pretty woman to chat up. But she'd seen the date as her chance. It was her way to get to him. After all, all she had to do was to have a drink or two and wait until he opened up. She remembered how she'd crossed her fingers in the hope that he'd slip up, say something he shouldn't and give her a new and intriguing angle to work on.

But had getting to the truth been more valuable than life itself?

She'd worked her way up at the Filey Chronicle since leaving school. She'd seen men like him so many times before and, with his history, she should have been aware that he could have been dangerous. So, why, why had she done it? Why had she gone on a date with the biggest womaniser she'd ever heard of? Especially when every instinct in her body had warned her against him. And why, oh why, hadn't she told Sarah?

'Because Sarah was far too sensible. She was in the force, did things by the book and she wouldn't have let you go,' Ella whispered to herself.

From the moment she'd met Rick Greaves, she'd allowed herself to fall under his spell. She'd watched him chat up other women, the other gym members, and the staff. In fact he'd chatted up every woman who'd allowed it. He hung around the female staff and Ella had often thought that he looked just a little too close to them to be their boss. She'd worked out what he was like at an early stage, yet she'd still loved it when he turned his attention in her direction. She'd loved the compliments, the cheeky smiles and the discreet touches as he'd assisted her with equipment. And she hadn't discouraged him. It had all been part of her plan and it had only taken him a few weeks before he'd asked her out.

The date had been organised by Rick. He'd suggested that they might meet for dinner in a remote gastropub, which was miles from town. They'd sat in a high-backed leather booth. They'd chatted, laughed and joked and Rick Greaves had been fun and attentive. But he'd given nothing away and, at one point, she'd thought he'd been about to kiss her. His face had been just millimetres from hers, their eyes had locked, but at the last moment he'd pulled away and, much to her surprise, he'd suddenly left the room and hadn't returned.

She tried to think of the conversation that had passed between them. Of what had been said before he'd left. But she couldn't. Her whole memory of the date had turned into a fog, from the moment she'd arrived, to the time after Rick had disappeared. She couldn't even remember how long she'd waited before she too had finally left the pub.

The only thing she vividly remembered was the sudden jolt of pain as she was being dragged from a car. A deep blue vehicle. It was one she hadn't seen before and didn't know why or how she'd come to be in it. She remembered trying to look around, trying to work out where she was, but there had been no street lights for what seemed like miles. The only light had come from the moon. It had been late, dark and she'd felt drowsy and confused and she'd knelt there in the mud, as excruciating pain thundered through her. One blow was followed by the next. A sharp, piercing pain tore through her scalp. Her hair was torn from its roots and then she remembered hitting the floor. It had been a vicious, cruel and inhuman attack. A weapon had been used, something hard, solid and unyielding, but she had no idea what had hit her, or whether more blows would come. She seemed to recollect screaming, begging and pleading for her life. Then the attack had stopped as suddenly as it had begun and she'd opened her eyes to see someone casually climbing into the car. She saw a black hoodie with a flash of gold embroidery. It was an item of clothing she'd recognised, but couldn't place. Then she remembered the fear she'd felt as the car had spun around: she could see the headlights shining at her; she could hear the tyres spinning. For a few moments she thought the car would be aimed at her, but watched in relief as it spun back around and sped off into the distance. Then her body sank into a deep and overwhelming darkness.

She'd then begun the biggest battle of all: the battle to stay alive as consciousness had come and gone. Each time she'd opened her eyes, another hour had passed and she'd prayed for daylight. But then, when it had come, she'd begun focusing on the watch face with its tiny luminous hands. It was much easier now that the sun had risen; she didn't have to concentrate quite so much, and she stared at it with hope that someone, anyone or anything would come to her rescue.

Ella let out a sigh and once again began to feel her breathing slow down. She forced her eyes open and tried to focus in a desperate attempt to keep herself alert.

'Ten hours, twenty-seven minutes and one, two, three, four, five, six...!'

The rain that had threatened began to fall. She'd dreaded the raindrops, but now each one that fell felt soft and strangely refreshing as they landed on her face.

Each tiny droplet gave her cracked, split lips a small but welcome amount of moisture as each one dripped into her dry, swollen mouth.

She closed her eyes and began drifting into sleep. But, then, what was that? Was there a noise? She was sure she'd heard something. It came from behind her, or did it? Her eyes sprang back open and she held her breath for just a second, while she listened intently. She was sure she'd heard a rustling, something moving towards her through wet moorland heather. And then the unmistakable panting of a dog.

Using every last ounce of energy, she let out a noise. It was a shrill, gurgling noise, one that she barely recognised, but knew that somehow it had come from somewhere deep within her own body.

'Here, boy, Benny boy, come here. It's raining, come on, time to go home.' A man's voice bellowed as Ella felt a soft, wet nose run itself across her face, into her ear and then back across her cheek until it stopped at her nose. It sniffed in, long and deep and was followed by a soft, whining howl as the tiny, liver and white spaniel, with ears that were far too big for its body, once again sniffed at her face, before nestling into her, bringing her body some much needed warmth. Ella tried to smile as the puppy continued to lick her face; its tongue was rough, ticklish, yet oddly pleasurable and welcoming.

A sob left her. She felt exhausted, happy, relieved, and devastated, all at once. She was alive and had an overwhelming desire to do a happy dance, if only she could move.

She once again breathed in deeply, desperate to fill her lungs, desperate to stay alive. There was still hope, just so long as the puppy stayed with her and so long as the man didn't call it away.

She glanced back up to the clouds and to the small shafts of light that still tried to break their way through. 'Thank you,' she whispered as the spaniel once again looked up and licked at her face.

'What you got there, Benny boy? Come here, I...' The man's footsteps got closer. Slow, heavy thumps at first, and then much faster as he began to run. Ella knew by his gasp that he'd seen her and she cringed for just a moment, knowing that her dress was badly torn and that her body was almost certainly exposed. But what did it matter? She'd have streaked along the River Derwent if she thought that by doing so she'd get normality back, that she'd see her friends and parents again and that her life would go back to the way it had been before.

But deep down, she knew that nothing would or could ever be the same as it had been. Not now. She was under no illusion that she wouldn't have many hurdles to jump before she'd once again be well. But when she was, she knew she'd have a burning need to find out what had really happened to her and maybe, just maybe, she'd get to the truth. The one thing she did know was that someone would pay for hurting her so very badly, starting with Rick Greaves.

My mind is spinning on an axle. My heart beats wildly and I don't know what to do next. So, I pull the car to a stop and I sit and I wait. I take in one deep breath after another as my fingers trace the VW badge that's central to the steering wheel. I stare at the luminous digits of the dashboard clock and note that it's still only just after ten o' clock at night. It's cold outside but I have the heater blowing on my feet and I kick my boots off to enjoy the warmth.

With the heat on my feet I'm now beginning to feel far too warm and I pull the hoodie over my head and discard it on the seat beside me. Another deep intake of breath makes me decide that I ought to move the car. I need to take it to the safe place and ensure it can't be found. But, for a moment, I consider going back. I want to make sure that she is dead. I want to see my handiwork up close and, besides, they always say that a killer goes back to the scene of the crime, don't they? So maybe I should.

I can feel the laughter bubbling up inside me. No one knows, but I've killed before. The first time I did it, I sat for a whole hour at the murder site, making sure the deed was done. But tonight I feel so very tired that my eyes have become painful. They're hot and burning and I feel the need to press against them with something cold. The adrenaline is no longer coursing through my veins, and I have an overwhelming desire to curl up and sleep.

I try to think rationally. Tomorrow I have to work. I have no choice, I can't stay at home. So, while I'm there I'll put the radio on and I'll listen to the local news. I might even go for a drive after work and see if she's been found. I look out of the car windscreen across the moors. By this time tomorrow the whole area will most probably be full of police, of CID, and of reporters. Every inch of the surrounding moors will be searched and I smile at the amount of work I've caused. I laugh out loud. They won't find anything. I don't leave clues. I make sure that all the evidence leaves with me and the small amount of evidence that I do leave behind is left on purpose. I look down at the hoodie. 'And you, you will be my trophy.'

I can't help but smile. I've thought of everything. Yet still I feel my head shaking from side to side. You'd think that killing someone would be difficult, wouldn't you? Well, it is at first. At first there's a deep feeling of loss. A part of you dies too. But this time, the fourth time? This time was fun; unexpected... but fun.

2

SEVEN MONTHS LATER

Ella shuffled from one foot to the other. She looked down at the cracks in the footpath and then used the edge of her fur-lined leather boot to scrape a weed out from between where the slabs joined together. She wished wholeheartedly that she could go back to her own cottage and restart her life, without having to hurt her mother's feelings.

'Mum, please don't get upset.' Ella placed a hand on her mother's arm. 'I'd stay forever if I could; it's just not practical, is it?' She paused and glanced over to where her friend Sarah sat in the driver's seat of her car. She smiled at Ella, then pulled her mobile from her pocket, checked it for messages and pushed it back into her pocket.

'Ella, are you coming? I have to be on shift at eleven,' Sarah shouted as her foot began revving the engine.

'It's time I looked after myself, Mum. You know it is and you know what Sarah's like, she'll be round every two minutes checking on me, my very own protection detail.' Ella looked down at an old sports bag that was by her feet, unzipped it, and rummaged inside to check its contents. Without thinking, she grabbed at the handles and lifted it, making her face contort as pain immediately shot through her shoulder as she unceremoniously threw the bag towards the car.

'Here, I'll sort those.' Sarah jumped from the car, picked up the bags, the two bottles of red wine and the box of books and placed them all securely in the boot of the car. 'Now, we really need to go. The boss, he hates it if we're late.' She looked up at Ella's mum. 'Sorry, Carol.'

'I know you're a grown-up and have a need to look after yourself,' Ella heard her mother say in a whisper. 'I just kind of got used to you being home again and I liked having you around. Nothing wrong with that, is there?'

She rubbed her hands down her apron and pointed to the semi-detached house that stood behind her. It was the house where Ella had grown up, the house where she'd played as a child, the house where all those Christmases, birthdays and story times had happened. It was the house she'd been brought back to after leaving the hospital, six weeks after her attack. It was where she'd lain for the weeks that had turned into months, while her battered, confused and broken body had healed.

With very little money, but lots of support from friends, her parents had worked miracles to make the house suitable to accommodate Ella's needs. A single bed had been brought downstairs and placed in the dining room. The traditional furniture had been removed and a dressing table and wardrobe had taken their place, along with a television, iPod player and the essential hoist, crutches and wheelchair. None of it had been glamorous, but unfortunately all of it had been necessary. Her parents had done their best, made the room homely and had surrounded the makeshift bedroom with items from her childhood, along with fresh, brightly coloured flowers that they'd placed by her bedside. Her father had even created a temporary ramp from old paving slabs to make it easier for them to get her in and out of the house in the wheelchair.

'Oh, Mum. I bet I was a right cow when I first

came home, wasn't I? I'm so sorry.' Ella pulled a face remembering the hours of self-pity she'd gone through. 'At least you can... you know...' She pointed to the front of the house. 'You can get rid of the ramp now, put the dining table back where it belongs and get your house back to some sort of normality.' She smiled.

'Oh, Ella, you were not a cow. I won't have it said.' Her mother tried to laugh and held out her arms. 'Should we just say that you might have been a little bit more demanding than usual at times? But I didn't care; I was just so happy that you were... you were still... you know... still... that—'

'Okay, okay, don't say it. I know,' Ella whispered as she rocked her mother back and forth in her arms. Carol Hope had always been so strong, and positive. But since that night, the night Ella had been attacked, she had noticed that her mother always looked fraught. She seemed constantly worried and anxious and there wasn't a moment during any part of the day that she hadn't looked at the point of bursting into tears.

Kissing her mother lightly on the cheek, she hugged her once more. 'Give Dad a kiss for me when he gets home from work,' she said, before smiling and climbing into the front passenger seat.

'Right, we really have to go,' she said as she shut the door and wound the window down. 'It's good of Sarah to help me and I don't want to make her late.' She locked eyes with her mother, choked back the tears, swallowed hard and nodded at Sarah, who waved a goodbye and released the handbrake. Ella didn't look back, concentrating on the road ahead, the road that led to her home.

* * *

'So, are you excited, you know, about going back to your own house?' Sarah asked with her normal happy go lucky attitude as she turned into Common Lane.

Ella nodded. 'A little apprehensive too. But it's time.' She pushed her long auburn hair back from her face. 'Look, there's Bobby.' She pointed to the local farmer who'd already spotted her and was waving enthusiastically from his tractor.

Sarah laughed. 'He seems a little, well, over friendly. How well do you know him?'

Ella waved back. 'Not too well. And, yes, he is friendly, in a puppy dog sort of way.' She blushed. 'He's always smiling, cheerful and he always seems to be around when I need something doing.' She paused. 'Last year when all that turf was dumped on my front drive, he dropped everything and moved it all for me. I tried to pay him, but he wouldn't take anything. So, I'd say he's harmless. I owe him one.'

Sarah pulled the car to a halt. 'Ella, after what happened to you, no man is harmless and you owe him nothing. Understood?'

Ella sat back in her seat. 'All right, copper, stand down. You're not on duty today.' She looked at the new watch her mother had bought her for Christmas. 'Well, not yet anyhow.' She tapped the watch face. 'You still have an hour.' She smiled, then looked back across to where Bobby still waved. Sarah was right. He really did look happy to see her.

'Seriously, Ella. You don't think he could have got a bit infatuated, do you? I mean look at him. I'll check him out when I get to the station.' Sarah's hand rested on Ella's. 'Any idea if they looked into him during the original investigation?'

Ella shook her head. 'Sarah, leave it. You're not supposed to be working on my case, you know the rules.' It was true. As Ella's friend, Sarah wasn't allowed to work on the investigation into who had attacked her, but that hadn't stopped her trying to get to the truth.

'I know,' Sarah whispered, 'but if I catch whoever

did this to you, I swear to God...' Her hands screwed up into fists and she thumped the steering wheel. 'Look at him, Ella. Don't you think he looks a bit weird?'

Bobby had always looked the same to Ella. He had a wild and unkempt look about him, straw-like golden hair, muddy jeans and he wore an overcoat that always looked far too big for him. He was nice, smiled a lot and he obviously had a huge heart, but he did remind her of a beaten-up scarecrow, one that children may have lovingly made to sit with on a street corner, collecting money for Guy Fawkes Night. Once again, she waved back at him, smiled and watched as he happily drove away towards the bottom field, the one where he normally took the horses to graze.

Ella opened her car door and stepped out to look up at her house. It had been little more than a derelict shell when she'd bought it a couple of years ago. Not a window or door had locked – replacements had had to be ordered immediately – and the garden had been an overgrown jungle. But Ella had loved it and slowly, a little at a time with each pay cheque, she'd lovingly restored each room, along with another few feet of garden.

She'd arrived outside her house like this at least

a thousand times before yet, for some reason, every-thing looked different. It all looked brand new and oddly she felt just a little detached, as though she were looking at it all for the very first time. She closed her eyes and opened them again in the hope that when she did, it would all go back to how it had been. Of course, the structure was the same. At the front of the house was a door and two windows, one directly above the other. The door led straight into the front room and even though visitors sometimes used it, Ella never did. She always went down the drive to the door on the side, which led into a small hallway that separated the staircase, kitchen and downstairs bathroom. She shrugged off what Sarah had said about the attack. Being here, right now, was all that mattered. She turned and looked over her shoulder to the farm land that lay beyond the road. The view was stunning. It was so calm, so beautiful and was a view she just knew she'd never tire of, even if it did sometimes have Bobby in it as he trun-dled across his fields, riding on his tractor.

She'd really missed being here. So why did she feel a little apprehensive at the thought of being here alone?

'You're being silly. Why would you be afraid?' she whispered to herself, her mind thinking back to the last time she'd been here. She'd been with her parents. It had all seemed like a good idea at first, but she'd soon realised that the wheelchair wouldn't easily go up the step; with no ramp, she'd had to sit outside and cringe inwardly while she listened to her parents rummaging through her cupboards, her drawers and through her private and most intimate things. Her frustration had risen as she'd heard door after door slam shut.

'I can't find them, Ella. Where did you say they were? Try that cupboard, Patrick?' She'd heard her mother yell at her father, before another door had opened and, once again, she heard them rifle through her belongings.

She'd shrunk down in the wheelchair, wishing that the ground would open and swallow her. Most of all she hoped that no one she knew would see her, but her wishes were not granted, as one by one, each neighbour had walked past, spotted her sitting outside and had made their way over to her. Bobby had jumped down from his tractor and ran across the road so fast he'd almost tripped, then had asked so many questions that she hadn't wanted to answer. But the worst part had been when he'd spontaneously hugged her in a way that had sent new pain searing through her body. She knew he'd been pleased to see her, but for the first time in her life, she felt fragile and out of place.

It had been just a few weeks after Bonfire Night; she'd been cold and she'd wanted nothing more than to go inside and take sanctuary in her tiny, oak floored lounge, light the log burner and curl up before it on the rug. But she couldn't and a small part of her heart broke in two with longing.

The whole visit had been strange and from then on, she'd found it easier to stay away. She'd hidden herself in that one room of her parents' house and had tried her best not to burden them while she healed.

But her road to recovery had been slow. Ella had spent weeks in hospital. Her left leg and ankle had been broken, along with her left arm. Muscles had been torn and haematomas emerged, along with an aneurism that had been caused by the first strike she'd taken, not to mention her fingers that had also been broken. She hadn't been allowed to move at all for the first few weeks; she had known it was bad when doctors would mutter under their breath, looking sideways rather than at her and had taken meetings with her parents, which would result in her mum returning to her bedside with bloodshot eyes.

Ella was a fighter. She'd been determined to survive, and as soon as the doctors had said she could, she'd worked as hard as her beaten body would allow. She'd pushed herself to the limit with the physiotherapists and remembered crying with the pain, but had known that it was the only way she'd ever be well. Once the casts were off, she'd tried her best to walk as often as she could. She had to build back the muscles, some days with the crutches, some days without. Even though the pain had been intolerable, it had been better than the alternative; she'd hated the wheelchair, she hated leaving the house in it and hated the fact that it was so heavy that her mother could barely push it.

Outings had been a nightmare. The 'well-wishers' they'd bump into would look at her with pity, with questioning eyes and had spoken above her. They seemed to direct the conversation towards her mother, as though being in a wheelchair had stopped her mental ability to speak for herself. When they did speak to her, they normally said or did the most inappropriate things. She'd lost count of how many strangers had felt the need to hug her, squeeze her or pat her face or her head like a lost puppy that needed to be loved.

Shaking her head, Ella brought herself back to

the present. She walked down the side of the house to the back door and looked up at the pink and purple flower baskets that hung there, the patio pots that stood by the gate and the perfectly tended garden before her. 'Thanks, Dad,' she whispered. She'd always loved her garden and the flowers by her door and she took a moment to take in their beauty.

She stepped forward and lifted her hand to the basket. Each one was equally filled with three types of flower, each a different colour and height. Realising that it was the simple things that now made her smile, she breathed in deeply and took in the fresh smell of lilacs, geraniums and pansies.

She turned to the back door and hesitated before taking the key from her bag. Pressing it between her fingers, she rubbed the shiny silver metal before placing it in the lock and turning the key.

'Come on, slow coach, are we going in or not?' Sarah questioned, her arms full of bags and boxes.

Ella shook her head. 'It's okay. Just put them down there. I... I kind of need to do this on my own.'

She felt her heart begin to thump loudly in her chest; the vibration echoed throughout her like a base drum, making her suddenly realise that the moment she went in would be the first time since that night that she'd be totally alone. Ella paused and reached up to carefully stroke the doorknob. It was brass, shiny, and immediately she knew that her mother had used that cleaning cream. The one that had the odd smell, but was a necessary evil if she wanted the brass to shine like a mirror. She picked the brass ring up and stared at her reflection. But the reflection was odd and distorted with the curves of the ring and reminded her of the time she'd played around the fun mirrors in Blackpool Tower. She smiled at the memory.

For the second time Ella put the key in the door and turned it, but she halted, too nervous to go in. She stepped back and held her hand flat to the door as though making peace with her home. She looked up at the windows and felt the warmth that came from within.

'Look, let me open the door and put the boxes inside while you go for a walk in the garden. Then, I'll go to work and you can, you know, take your time.' Sarah looked directly at her. 'Besides, the reason I came was because you couldn't lift the boxes and I just want to check the house over before you go in.'

Ella reluctantly passed Sarah the key and stepped away from the door. She looked up the road towards the farm and over the fields in the direction Bobby had gone on his tractor. Everything was as it should be. Nothing had altered and life had carried on without her. Only the season had changed. It was May, the start of summer; the trees were full of leaves and blossoms, and the garden was full of roses, peonies, geraniums and lilacs. The clocks had gone forward over a month ago. The evenings had begun to stretch out just a little more each day and she looked forward to the nights when she could sit in the garden and watch the sun set late in the evenings.

She walked back down the path to where Sarah was putting the last of the boxes in her hallway. 'Well, I'd best leave you to it then,' she said as she looked down at the floor. 'If you have any trouble, if anyone upsets you or if that farmer man comes any-where near, you phone me, right?'

'He won't, but right,' Ella said as she felt herself being pulled into a bear hug. 'Now, go on, go to work.'

Sarah stepped back and smiled. 'Fine, I know where I'm not wanted.' She turned back to her car. 'I'll be off then, but my phone is on. If you call me, I'll have a fleet of cops here within minutes, you got that?'

Ella once again hugged Sarah. 'I've got that, copper, I promise,' she whispered before letting go. 'And Sarah...' She paused and caught her friend's eye. 'Love you, hun, thanks for today.'

They walked together to the gate. Sarah gave her one last smile. 'I love you too, Ella. Take care, sweetie.' She wiped away a tear and climbed into her car. And with one final wave, she was gone.

Ella stood for a moment, not knowing what to do next. She looked up and down the road, taking in her surroundings and getting used to the thought of being alone.

It was then that she realised that she really wasn't alone. She was surrounded by people, and it could have been absolutely anyone that had hurt her. The other houses on the street showed signs of life; cars were either parked on drives, or drove up and down the road. Ella noticed an old man walking towards her. He had a walking stick in one hand, a fluffy white dog on its lead in the other. He raised his stick up above his head, waved it around in the air and shouted hello. The postman passing by on his bike also lifted his hand and waved at her. Then he jumped off his bike and began to push it along, leaning it on gateposts as he ran up and down the paths of the houses and posted letters through the doors. Patricia from the corner shop strolled down the road with her brood of five young boys; all looked to be under ten years old. They all seemed to cling to her legs like over excited baboons, apart from the eldest, who ran ahead with the dog. Ella wondered how Patricia ever managed to walk. The eldest child kicked a ball up and down, allowing the jet-black Labrador to chase it as it bounced off any wall or fence that it hit.

'Peter, stop that,' Patricia had shouted as she'd waved. 'No one wants you bouncing the ball on their walls.'

Patricia once again wore a maternity dress, which made Ella laugh and shake her head. 'Oh, my goodness, for Patricia's sake, please let this next one be a girl,' she whispered to herself, before walking back down her drive and to the back door, which now stood wide open waiting for her to enter.

3

Will Taylor swung his scythe to a stop. He dropped it to the ground and looked up at the morning sun which now hovered to the east of the copper birch, meaning that it must still be before midday, but he checked his watch, just to be sure.

Picking up a bottle of water, he lifted it over his head and poured the water over his face. He then sipped at the remainder of the liquid, pulled his damp T-shirt over his head, wiped his face dry and laid it over the wooden bench that stood in the corner of the old, cracked and broken patio. The sun shone directly at the bench and Will knew that the T-shirt would dry within minutes. He turned away and looked back at the job in hand, picked up the scythe and began swinging it through the overgrown jungle that would soon become his new back garden.

Every bush grew randomly, with branches striking out in multiple directions, along with every kind of weed and nettle that could possibly grow in between. Everything was overgrown and most of what once would have been someone's pride and joy now towered high above his head. The bushes met somewhere in the middle of the garden, bowing together like a natural arch. The grass that had once lain down the centre of the garden as a lawn was now yellow, and so full of weeds that it would all have to be dug up and re-laid. Will sighed as he spied apple, cherry and pear trees, all of which he hoped he could save; he looked forward to the fresh produce each tree might bring later in the year.

Will's eyes searched between the overgrown bushes. Each swing of the scythe brought new excitement, along with a new view of what his garden might eventually look like, especially once he discovered what may or may not be salvageable and where the perimeter fences might start or end. The only view of the garden he'd had since buying the property had been from the upstairs back bedroom window. He'd noticed all the old broken fencing down one side and newish fencing down the other; he was under the impression that the garden was narrow and long, with what looked like a shed somewhere near the bottom. With every swing of the scythe, the number of overgrown bushes that still needed to be removed began to dwindle, though he still had no idea how much more there was to cut down before he'd finally get to the bottom of what condition the shed would be in when he finally found it.

He looked up at his cottage. It was looking good. His new double-glazed windows had been fitted a couple of months before. The rendering had been renewed at the back and he'd painted it white. He'd hung flower baskets by the door to brighten up his mood. He smiled; he liked them. They made it look just a little homelier, but he knew he still had a lot more work to do before he could really call it home. The new kitchen still needed fitting and would be, just as soon as it arrived. Each day brought a new delivery date, just a few days later than the one he'd had before. It should have arrived weeks ago and with the delivery date having been confirmed, he'd torn the old kitchen out in anticipation. He now realised what a hasty mistake he'd made because the kitchen now lay in a hundred pieces, smashed and broken in a skip by the back door, and the room which had been his kitchen now stood empty of usable units.

He glanced through the back door to where an old paste table was pushed under the two taps that hung from the wall. Their bare copper piping bent in an outward direction, to ensure that the taps hovered over an old plastic bowl that balanced precariously on top of the paste table. He laughed as he looked at his makeshift kitchen. It was a mess and very primitive, but he decided that in the grand scheme of things it hardly mattered.

He'd already come to the conclusion that it was a good job his work often kept him away from home. He spent most of his time rushing from one job to the other and some days the chances of cooking and eating a full meal before being called back to work were slim.

He looked over the newer fence to the house that was joined to his. It had been empty for the whole of the six months since he'd first looked at the house. He hadn't seen the neighbour once, yet the gardens were obviously looked after; the grass was well maintained and new hanging baskets had been put up, making it obvious that someone had been there.

Everything looked clean and tidy and he just wished that his house looked the same.

He dropped the scythe, wiped his hands down the denim of his old cut-off jeans, lifted his arm to shield his eyes from the sun and once again reached for the bottle of water that he'd left perched on the arm of the bench, as he admired his handiwork in the garden. He'd been up since daybreak and hard at work for hours, so he sat down on the wooden bench, lifted his feet up and lay back to rest.

Will closed his eyes for a brief moment. The golden glow of the sun reflected like rippling water behind his eyelids, shining through as deep orange, yellows and reds. The warmth made him sleepy; it reminded him of the Caribbean holiday he'd had just a few years before. He allowed himself to drift into a distant dream of white sand, rum punch, sugar cane and palm trees.

The beautiful dream of waves lapping against the shore, the sound of crickets rubbing their wings together and the soft reggae music that taunted his mind was disturbed by a sudden noise. It woke him; he could hear footsteps as they crunched across a path. He took in a deep breath, brought himself back to reality and for a moment he lay there on the bench with his arms still hugging himself, his eyes half closed. Then there was the sound of metal on metal as a key entered a lock next door.

Will sat bolt upright, shook his head and inhaled. He could hear voices. Female voices. 'Fantastic, I have neighbours,' he whispered to himself and moved off the bench. His mind still felt fuzzy, but the reporter in him was inquisitive. He wanted to know who was there, what they were doing and, what's more, why after six months they were suddenly making an appearance. He crouched down beside the fence and tried to peer through a space where one of the panels had slipped.

He was far enough down his own garden that he could see the two women as they walked from the front of the cottage down the drive and to the back. He gasped. 'Well, helloooooo!' he whispered as he admired the view. He noticed one woman with long, dark auburn hair that hung just below her shoulders. She was dressed informally in a pair of torn jeans and a T-shirt, both of which looked too big for her petite frame. She turned and looked towards the fence. It was as though she knew someone was there; her eyes sparkled in the sunlight as she stared directly at where he was hiding, before turning back towards the door. He watched as she hesitated with the key, stepped back from the entrance and paused.

But then, the other woman stood behind her, a box in her hands. She was taller than the first woman, with blonde hair that was tied up in a bun, and was dressed in a pristine white shirt and straight, jet-black trousers.

Were these the neighbours he'd never met? What's more, if they were his neighbours, he approved. In fact, he really approved. He weighed up the situation. He thought he'd seen both of them before but didn't know where. For a moment he took notice of their interaction, wondering if they might be a couple.

He watched as the auburn haired one appeared to leave her key in the door, step back and walk back towards the front gate, while the other woman walked back and forth with boxes. The woman with the long auburn hair stood deep in thought as she looked up and down the road. There was an exchange of words.

'Love you, hun, thanks for today,' he heard one say to the other and he pondered for a moment. They seemed grateful, almost dismissive and not really the words said between a couple. He then heard a car door open and close, a car engine started and the car drove away.

Will felt relieved, but he didn't know why. He

just knew that two women had arrived, one had left and the really attractive one had stayed behind. He saw her lift her hand twice. She waved to a farmer and the postman. He noticed her laugh, a sweet amused look that lit up her face, as a woman and a group of children walked by. She then turned again and walked back down her drive and around the conservatory to a bench that stood in the corner of her back garden. Her hand stroked the bench in a gentle and compassionate way before stepping up and onto the grass. She seemed to stare at each bush, plant or tree in turn. She stroked the leaves as though saying hello for the very first time. Every movement, touch or step was taken with care. She walked, glanced and smiled, making every look one of wonderment, pleasure and appreciation. If Will hadn't witnessed her familiarity with the neighbours, he'd have almost thought she'd never been there before. He felt guilty for spying and cringed at his own behaviour, but being a reporter made it his job to watch people. Besides, he was mesmerised by her and enjoyed watching the pleasure she took in the beauty of each and every little thing that she saw.

Will looked back towards where his own car was parked on the drive, at the side of the house. He really should make his presence known, at least slam the car door and pretend he'd just come home; he knew that if he stood up now and introduced himself, he'd look bad for having hidden in the first place. He hovered in the same spot, barely daring to breathe.

He felt nervous; his hands grew more and more clammy, and his legs began to shake. Crouching behind the fence, he leaned against the apple tree. He tried to rationalise the situation and make sense of how he'd explain watching her, should she spot him. But each time he thought about it, the worse the situation seemed and the more he realised how creepy his actions would look.

Should he give himself away? Should he try and explain why he'd been crouching in the mud? He waited quietly, deciding what to do. The sun now shone high above the copper birch and Will knew it was now easily after midday. He looked over at the bottle of water, which still stood beside the bench, and thought about reaching for it to take a drink, but he suspected that the water would now be almost boiled and he pulled a face, knowing how bad it would taste.

Go on, neighbour. Go into your house, give me

the opportunity to get indoors. It would make this so much easier for both of us.

He continued to crouch, leaning against the tree. A small bush stood to his side and his hand went out to use it for balance, just as his calf began to cramp and he dropped onto his knees in an attempt to relieve the pain. He immediately cringed as an old twig broke beneath his knee. He knew she'd have heard and, just for a moment, he closed his eyes and held his breath as pain seared through his calf.

'Who goes there?' he heard her shout. The words made him snort and he began to wonder how much Shakespeare she must have had to endure as a child, or how many history books she must have read.

He held his head in his hands, knowing that it would only be moments before she looked over the old, broken fence and discovered him crouching, hiding. 'I could ask the same,' he shouted back as he pulled himself back to his feet, stretched the cramp out of his calf, checked his knee for cuts and peered over the fence that stood between them.

'You seem to be in my neighbour's garden. Do they know that you're here? Cause I haven't seen them around lately and I was just about to call the police,' he said, giving her a cheeky wink, but then he noticed the look of confusion on her face.

'What? Why would you call the police? This is my house, I live here.' He saw her look back at the house. She tipped her head to one side as though checking it to make sure that it really was the right house and that she really was in the right garden.

'Excellent, I was just checking. For a moment, I thought you might be a burglar. I'm Will Taylor. Your neighbour.' He watched as she took a step away, caught her foot on a stone fairy and fell backwards.

'Argh,' she screamed, grabbed at her wrist and squeezed her eyes shut as she appeared to grit her teeth.

'Don't move. I'm coming over,' Will shouted and, using his hands for leverage as he placed a foot on his bench, he leapt over the fence without waiting for a response. A sharp tearing sound echoed around the garden as the cut-off jeans that he wore split in protest.

* * *

'Bloody hell!' Ella shouted as she cowered beside the bench. 'Don't you know how to use a gate?' Her eyes looked up to the tear in his jeans and then to his partially naked body. 'And I think you might want to get dressed,' she added as her finger pointed him up and down in a wand-like fashion. She swallowed hard. Her eyes and hands searched for a weapon just as the palpitations began; she gasped for breath and felt the tingling in her already painful fingers begin. She looked around her, grabbed at a piece of wood, began to panic and took in a deep breath.

'Wow. Stop, I'm – I'm not going to hurt you. Are you okay?' Will asked as he stepped forward. His hand shot out, making Ella swing her legs underneath her and she knelt before him, swinging the wood in his direction.

'Come any closer and I swear...!' she screamed and began to tremble as though waiting for an onslaught to begin.

'Okay, okay, please, I thought you were hurt. I was trying to help.' Ella watched as he jumped backward and away from where she knelt. 'I – I'm so sorry.' He grabbed at his torn jeans, looked back at the fence, and began to take steps back towards it. 'I shouldn't have jumped the fence, I see that now.'

Ella opened her eyes, could see the shock on his face and began taking shallow, inward breaths that didn't nearly fill her lungs. She felt faint as she watched him look up and down the garden; she thought he might be looking for a way to pole-vault himself back over the fence or make a simple escape from the crazy lady who appeared to think he might attack her. This had happened to her once before. She knew it was irrational, but couldn't help the overwhelming fear. She tried to control her panic, staring at the floor and once again beginning to drag deep breaths into her lungs.

'I'm sorry. I thought... I thought... Oh Jesus.' She caught her breath and continued, 'I thought you were going to hit me. I'm so sorry. I know it's irrational.'

'Why the hell would you think I'd do that? I kind of live here. Well, I do live here, well, actually – I live there.' He pointed at his cottage next door, looked down and pulled the two halves of his shorts back together. 'Err, sorry. I seem to have...' He looked embarrassed and even though Ella had painfully slid herself off her knees and onto her bottom, managing to keep the bench firmly between them, she then looked up at his face and began to laugh.

'Okay. Don't just stand there looking at the crazy lady, help me up.' She held out her hand to his. 'Please.' He looked tentative and she knew that he was probably waiting for her to freak out for a second time. She hesitated as he finally held his hand out to where she sat. The getting up and down still hurt and she held onto his hand for support as she pulled herself to her feet.

'You okay?' he asked.

Ella smiled and then nodded. 'I am, but, Will, you know how to make a bloody entrance, don't you?' she said as she looked him up and down. 'Couldn't you have walked round, knocked on the door and introduced yourself properly like normal neighbours do?' She raised both eyebrows. 'Or is fence jumping a bit of a party trick?'

Will laughed. He saw the irony; he looked down at the tear in his shorts and shrugged. 'Obviously, it's not a very good party trick. If it were, I think I'd have worn better shorts.' He turned his body away from hers, as one hand continued to grip the two halves of his shorts together. 'Do you mind me asking... You look just a little familiar. Have we met before?'

Ella knew he'd have recognised her from the papers. Everyone did. Everyone thought they knew her, without being quite sure where from. Now she knew she'd have to explain what had happened to her that night.

'I'm Ella Hope. I doubt that we've met before, but you might have seen me in the papers, or on the television. I...' She tried to continue, but the words wouldn't come out.

* * *

Will moved to the bench and sat down. 'You don't mind, do you? It's kind of easier to hold the shorts together if I sit down. I can push the edges under my leg, save me from, you know, flashing my underwear at you.' He tried to glance at Ella's face, taking in her features and after her comments about the papers, he now realised who she was. It had been his job to report on the case, but being in Kent a long way south of here, they'd only covered it in a small way. Little had he known then that when he moved to Yorkshire, he'd end up buying the house next door.

Now, her cowering behind the bench made complete sense. After all she'd been through, no one would blame her for feeling nervous of strangers and especially nervous of men who seemed to pole-vault into her garden.

After all, hadn't he had issues of his own? Hadn't he moved to Yorkshire to escape his past and in the process left every single person, every school friend, family friend, and colleague behind, just because he couldn't live with the guilt?

'Will, are you okay?' The sound of Ella's voice brought him back to reality.

'Ella, yes, I remember the story. I'm so sorry

about what happened to you. I kind of know that doesn't help, but...' He couldn't tell her how much he understood, couldn't tell her about his own life, his own tragedies, and, what's more, he knew that what happened to her would live with her for her whole life; the nightmare of it all would never disappear. Did she have friends? People who she could talk to? He hadn't, he'd been alone through it all. He made a silent promise to look out for Ella, to be a good friend and neighbour, if she ever needed one, and to attempt to show her the empathy that he wished he'd allowed friends and neighbours to give to him.

'You remember the story? Wow, what are you a reporter or something?' The look on her face told Will that this wouldn't be a good thing and he laughed.

'I take it you don't like reporters?' He didn't want to lie and avoided answering the question.

'Well, to be honest, I'm one of them. I work for the Filey Chronicle, but that doesn't mean that I like them. I'll never forgive them. They hounded me like a dog when I was in hospital.' She flicked the hair back from her face. 'They're vultures, nothing more, nothing less. They wait to swoop when you're most vulnerable and I'm not sure I want them as friends.'

She nervously pulled at the hole in her jeans. 'So, in answer to your question, no, I don't like them very much.'

He nodded in agreement. What she said was true; reporters were like vultures, they did swoop in, but that was the nature of the job. He had no idea what he should say or do next. Should he just blurt it out, admit to her that he was a reporter, or did he leave it and allow her to get to know him as a person first? If he waited, then maybe, just maybe, he could convince her that not all reporters were the same and, eventually, she might just realise that he was one of the good guys. He chose the latter.

'Look, I know they're not all bad, it's just that they were supposed to be my friends and I felt a little let down,' Ella continued.

'I don't know your circumstances, but it doesn't sound like you've had much support. I'm only next door. You know, if you have any issues, if anyone starts hounding you. All you need to do is shout, scream or bang on the walls. I'll do whatever I can to help.' He didn't know why he was offering – she barely knew him – but knew that if she felt anything like he did, any offer of help would be gratefully taken.

Ella smiled and perched on the miniature wall

that stood before the bench. 'Thanks. I do have support, but I appreciate you saying that.' She smiled. 'Do you live there alone?' She pointed to the house next door.

Will grinned. 'I do, I doubt anyone else would want to live there at the moment; it's barely habitable. I don't even have a kitchen, a cooker or a fridge.' He held up both hands and shrugged. 'Do you live alone?' he asked, treading carefully but still interested to know who the other woman had been.

Ella nodded. 'Yes. I do. I've been staying with my parents while I recovered, but felt that it was time to come home.' She pointed to the area behind the bench. 'My friend, Sarah, who was here earlier, she helped me bring my stuff back. But after that display, I think I should probably just get in my car, go right back and curl up on my mum's sofa. You know, allow her to baby me for a year or two longer.'

Will shook his head and smiled. 'Oh no, don't do that I kind of like having a neighbour.' He placed a hand on his heart, a gesture to show he was being sincere.

Ella laughed. 'Why do you like the idea of a neighbour? Personally, I used to quite like it when next door was empty. No loud music, no men leaping over fences, no one asking if I'd loan them a bowl of sugar, a cup of flour... Do you get the drift?'

Will shook his head. 'Ouch, I'm hurt.' He flashed her another smile. 'As though I'd ask if I could borrow sugar, come on, I wasn't going to ask for any of that.' He once again wriggled in his seat and pulled the seams of the shorts together. 'I was, however, going to ask if maybe I could throw a pizza in your oven?' he asked with a cheeky smile. 'But not borrow sugar, oh no, definitely not sugar. I mean, who in their right mind would ask a neighbour for sugar? I mean, come on, seriously? Chocolate or wine maybe,' he said, laughing, 'but never sugar.'

* * *

Ella stared at Will's trainers. It wasn't that she didn't want to look at his face, but from where she was sitting on the small wall, she would have to look past his torn shorts to look at his face; even though he had his knees pressed tightly together, she didn't trust herself not to stare. She came to the conclusion that even though Will Taylor had made quite an entrance, he seemed nice and genuine, and she quickly decided that she liked him. He was funny, quite good looking and what's more, he lived right next door, which had made coming home really interesting.

Ella tried to control her breathing as she inhaled deeply and tried to think more clearly. After all, after what she'd been through, she still had to be careful. She needed to weigh men up more before putting herself in vulnerable situations. The trouble was, she couldn't decide what it was it about Will that she really liked. He was a stranger; he had a strange accent and she had no idea where he'd come from, except that he sounded a bit southern. In fact, all she really knew about him was that he'd bought the house next door. She tried to think logically. He should be harmless and, as far as she knew, he didn't look or act like a crazy psychopath, except for the fact that he pole-vaulted fences. He seemed really friendly, albeit he'd been really embarrassed about tearing his shorts, and he certainly didn't come across as a guy that was dangerous. Then again, except for the fact that he had two dead wives, she'd have said that about Rick Greaves. He'd also been good looking, friendly and charming; they'd chatted on numerous occasions at the gym and she'd often wondered what had happened that night for him to change so very much.

She thought for a moment longer before

standing up from where she perched on the wall. 'So, you don't want wine, chocolate or sugar, but you do want me to cook your pizza.' She raised her eyebrows. 'Let me think about that.' She paused and put both of her hands on her hips. 'What am I, your mother?' She laughed. 'What's wrong with your own bloody cooker?'

He flashed a cheeky smile. 'Ah, that's the point. As I said, I don't have a cooker. I should, but...' He lifted his hands to his crew cut, strawberry blond hair and rubbed at the top of his head. 'I ripped the cooker out, you see...' He rolled his eyes. 'The kitchen units and appliances should have been delivered yesterday and I had a guy booked for today to start fitting it, but the delivery date was changed last minute to next week. So, I have a pizza, you know, in anticipation of having a new cooker. But now I have nothing to cook it in, nor do I have a fridge to store it in. So, it's just sitting there, on the paste table, looking at me. And, what's more, I'm really, really hungry.'

Ella pulled a face and stuck out her tongue. 'Well, it looks like you're going to be really hungry for a good while longer then, doesn't it?'

'Oh, come on, that's mean. Especially after I tore my shorts trying to help you.' He jumped up from the bench, realised he'd let go of the said shorts and grabbed at them quickly. 'Come on, I'll make you a deal. How about if I share? Do you like pepperoni, wild mushroom and mozzarella?'

Ella pretended to think for a moment. 'Well, that is tempting. But I had my eye on a Caesar salad, with bacon, chicken and anchovies.' She looked up into his face. His blue eyes stared back. 'Apparently my mum left me supplies in the fridge.'

Will looked disappointed and Ella noticed how he turned his face away from hers and looked towards the bushes for something to do.

'Okay, I'll make you a deal instead,' she said as she walked back towards the house. 'You go and put a shirt on, cover your body up, change your shorts, preferably for some that are not torn, and then, and only then, bring the pizza round and I'll be a good neighbour and throw it in the oven for you.' Ella stopped, turned around and smiled at him. 'Oh, and while it's cooking, you can sit on the bench.'

'So, you're not going to share the Caesar salad with me then?'

She pursed her lips and caught sight of his quirky smile. 'Let me think. Err, nope. Oh, and when you leave, do you think you might use the gate this time? I don't think that fence could handle you jumping over it a second time.'

* * *

My heart thunders in my chest as I slam my fist into a wall. Everything that happened, everything I planned has gone so very wrong. I made mistakes and I have no idea how that happened. The biggest mistake was that you survived. But I don't know how. How could anyone have survived that onslaught? And now, now I'm enraged. I don't normally get things wrong. I feel a need to repair the damage, I need to alter the course of events that will no doubt come and somehow, I need to put right what I got wrong.

I wonder how you are managing to live after the injuries you sustained. How you're managing to walk, dress yourself or brush your hair. The damage I did should have left you unable to do anything at all, yet from what I read in the papers, you're doing okay. It seems that you're getting well again and that you're working with the police to bring your attacker to justice. But that won't happen. If it's the last thing I ever do, I'll make sure that that won't happen.

4

'Okay, tell me all that you know about her,' Will Taylor barked as he made his way through the newsroom of the Scarborough Star. He walked past reception, the countless rows of bench desking, the meeting pods, and the people who sat at them. The whole room was alive with excitement. Editors and reporters were on telephones; photographers manipulated their pictures; and fingers flew over keyboards at over fifty words per minute as the whole office chatted relentlessly while working.

Josh, on the other hand, almost ran behind Will. He juggled the two cardboard coffee containers in one hand, a clipboard and briefcase in the other.

'Who? The new totty that lives next door?' Josh

awkwardly placed the coffee down on Will's desk, dropped the briefcase on the floor, sat down in the chair and watched as Will pushed the office door to a close behind him.

'Do you need to be so damned disrespectful, Josh? Her name is Ella Hope.' He dropped his car keys into his desk drawer and began attacking the keyboard on his laptop at a speed that would have probably created a new world record. 'She's the woman who was savagely beaten last year, left for dead, half-naked in a field. Remember?' He tapped his finger on the desk. 'She didn't ask for any of that to happen, so be nice about her.'

Josh pulled a face, raised an eyebrow, picked up his coffee cup and sat back in his chair. 'Okay, okay, I was just saying.'

'Well, don't. You need to think before you slate someone. Especially someone you've never met.' His eyes followed the words on the screen, before he looked satisfied with his findings, sat back and stared at Josh. 'You did run the story up here, didn't you?'

'Of course we did. Happened on our doorstep. Now, what do you need to know?' Josh was sulking. He turned his attention to his coffee, removed the lid and blew at its content.

'I need to know everything.' Will opened his filing cabinet, pulled out a file and dropped it on his desk, where the coffee cup wobbled precariously and both he and Josh watched it for just a moment before sighing with relief.

'Well, I guess you already know she works at the Filey Chronicle? Her stories are amazing and you should see some of the photos she takes.' Josh pushed his chair just far enough away from the desk, put his feet up on the table, shuffled himself into a comfortable position and ran one of his hands though his floppy dark hair. 'They're first class.' He held his coffee in his other hand and continued to sip at it, making Will raise his eyebrows at the young journalist's actions.

'And your point is...?'

'Well, if you haven't noticed, this is the Star. We're the Chronicle's opposition. They're just eight miles away.' He looked up, raised the cup and lifted his arms in the air as though Will should fully understand what he meant.

Will shrugged. 'So, why is that a problem? And what makes you think distance is relevant?'

'Come on, Will, round here there are three sheep and a cow to every human being. We have to fight for every reader we can get,' Josh answered as he continued to sip at the coffee and cheekily tipped his head to one side. 'Besides, this all happened over six months ago. If there were any new angles, they'd have it all sewn up by now; she's bound to have given them an exclusive, or sold it to one of the big guns. Right?'

Will shrugged his shoulders, lifted his hands and massaged his head with both hands, while staring intently into the computer screen. 'I think there's more to her story – some little things that she said – it makes me wonder what really happened, and, if I'm honest, I'd like to know a bit more about her.'

'Did she give you any info, anything we can use?' Josh sat forward and now looked more interested in what Will was about to say.

'No. She gave me nothing, and I'm serious when I say that.' He paused and held a finger in the air. 'You print nothing unless I approve it and sign it off. Have you got that?' Will raised his voice; he suddenly felt protective of Ella. He sat forward in his chair to keep scanning the news bulletins that flashed up on his screen.

'Hey, all right, all right, calm down.' Josh laughed. 'Bit protective, aren't we?'

Will stopped typing and turned away from the computer. 'Josh, seriously, I don't want her being hurt by the press. You should have seen her. She fell over, I thought she'd really hurt herself, so I jumped over the fence to help her and she looked terrified, threatened me with a lump of wood and then practically cowered behind the bench. She really thought I was going to attack her.'

'You jumped the fence? Seriously?' Josh paused. 'Actually, don't tell me. Nothing you do surprises me.'

Will ignored Josh's taunts. He looked determined and once again turned to the keyboard, dropped his hands and tapped the name 'Rick Greaves' into the search engine and began poring over the pages, looking for clues. 'There has to be something in here. This man's been on remand now for a good few months. The court case is coming up in two weeks and I need to know why he did it. I need a new angle, a new twist on the story. Didn't his first two wives die suspiciously?' Will stood up and stretched before picking up the coffee, taking a sip and sitting back down. 'How did he get banged up for this, anyhow? Was there any proof?'

'Something to do with some sort of trace evidence in his bedroom and the fact that your neighbour identified him.' Josh reached for a newspaper, sat back in his chair and began flicking through the nationals. 'So, are you wanting the dirt on her or on him?' he questioned. 'She is your neighbour, it's all a bit too close to home and all that shit. Why don't you look into something else?' He pointed to an article. 'This looks interesting. How about we follow this up?' He passed the clipboard he'd been carrying to Will. 'It's a company in Whitby, and they're trying to get planning permission to dig a new ash mine. There's going to be a few protesters. Could be a bit of a bun fight, we could get a few good photos for the front page.'

Will shook his head, slammed his hand on the desk and stood up. 'Seriously, Josh. The nationals have already done it; we did an article on it last week. If it's gone this far, they'll already have permission.' He threw the paper down on the desk. 'The meeting will be to appease the locals, you know, make them think they've had a say in it all.'

Will leaned across the desk and once again picked up his coffee, sipped and pulled a face. 'Have you put sugar in this?'

Josh shrugged and leaned back in his chair. 'So, what do you want me to do?'

'Well, for a start, you could try getting me coffee that I can drink, especially when I've paid for it.'

Josh stood up, took the lid off Will's drink and

began sipping at the contents. 'It tastes all right to me.'

Will glared. 'Get back to work.'

'Sorry.' Josh sat back down, and then stood up again and then sat back down. 'Do you want me to get you fresh coffee?'

'What I want, Josh, is for you to do some work. I want you to find something juicy for the front page; go speak to the others, see what we've got already. I want a front page with impact and, what's more, I want you to find me as much information on Rick Greaves as you can.'

'No problem. I'll get right to it.' Josh raised his eyebrows. 'Will, are you okay?'

Will nodded while he continued to search the internet. 'Josh, there's something about her that drives me a little crazy. If you'd seen her, you'd understand what I mean.' He paused and shook his head. 'Seriously, man, I've never seen anyone react like that. She was so vulnerable, so very... Oh, I don't know... defenceless. She made me want to pick her up, take care of her and make everything right.'

'So, you like her then?' Josh put his coffee down on the desk. 'I take it she's hot?'

Will thought about the question. Everything about Ella Hope was susceptible, yet she was brave and determined. How many other people would try to carry on, try to move forward, even though they still had so many fears?

He thought of how she'd taken the pizza from him, pointed to the garden bench and then walked into the house, closing the door behind her, only to come out just a few moments later with two glasses of wine. 'Here, time for a quick one, while the pizza cooks,' she'd said as she'd sat beside him on the bench. She'd been friendly, even though it had been more than obvious she'd been nervous of him. She'd barely spoken and had continually checked her watch for the whole twelve minutes it had taken for the pizza to cook.

He nodded. 'Yeah, I guess she's hot.'

Josh smirked. 'Oh, cool. Are we talking hot, as in fiery? Or hot as in...' He used his hands to outline a woman, stuck his tongue firmly in his cheek, pushed his glasses back up his face, winked and gave Will the look of an overgrown puppy. Will shook his head. 'That, my friend, is why you will always be single.' He pushed his chair away from the desk, stood up and walked out of the office, down the corridor and into the kitchen. He switched on the kettle and walked over to the fridge that stood in the far corner. He opened its door and lifted the milk from the shelf. Sniffing it suspiciously, he considered the thought of coffee without milk, before risking the content and pouring it into his drink. He then studied the contents of the fridge.

'Okay, today for lunch we have a pot noodle, a dried up tomato, an equally dried up bit of cheese, milk that smells a little suspect or four cans of lager. Do you northern lot ever have real food in your fridge? Or just bottles of beer?' He lifted a bottle from the fridge, waved it in the air and then placed it back on the shelf. 'Not what I expect my staff to keep in the work fridge.'

Josh once again pulled a face. 'I think, my dear friend, you need a lesson in the art of shopping. Food only gets in the fridge if you get in your car, go to the shop, put food in a basket, pay for it and then bring it here and place it in the fridge. Then, and only then, can you call it your lunch and eat it. It's really easy; remind me to show you how it's done.'

Will laughed. 'Okay, okay, don't be insolent. You made your point and I'm not your friend, I'm your boss.' Will opened his wallet and pulled out a ten-pound note. 'And with that in mind, can you go down to the deli and pick me up a decent sandwich?'

Josh grabbed the note. 'Keep the change, did you

say? And hey, who's the chick?' He pointed to Will's wallet and to the small picture of a young woman.

'None of your damn business,' Will snapped as he shut the wallet and pushed it back into his pocket. He walked back towards his office. 'Get me a large tuna mayo, with salad.'

'Okay, okay, I'm going,' Josh shouted. 'But if you've got some bit of skirt back home, I think it's only fair you tell me about her.'

'She's NOT my bit of skirt.' Will stared at the door, stuck out his pet lip and exhaled.

'Fine, in that case, do you mind introducing her to me? She's cute. I wouldn't mind taking her for a bit of a spin in the old passion wagon.'

Will glared, walked into his office and slammed the door behind him. He watched through the glass as Josh made a dash through the outer office full of people and headed towards the stairs.

Pulling the wallet back out of his pocket, Will removed the picture from behind the plastic screen. He stared at the photograph of his sister thoughtfully and just for a moment allowed his finger to stroke it gently.

Deborah was another piece of his life he had to hide and another of his memories that he had no intention of sharing. Especially with Josh.

5

Will pulled up outside his cottage. He looked down
at the carrier bag that he'd placed on the passenger
seat and tutted at himself. Why had he been to the
shop and why had he bought two steaks, ready-
made salad, salad dressing and a disposable BBQ?

'Not once did Ella Hope indicate to you that
she'd want to eat with you, so why, when you have
no fridge, did you buy enough food to feed the
street? For all you know she might have already eat-
en,' he barked at himself and looked up the cottage.
He took note of the windows and door. 'Okay. You
need to clean those,' he whispered to himself. It had
been a job he should have done before, but his pri-
ority had been knocking the place apart, making

sure he had a working bathroom and a clean bed-room, before ensuring the kitchen had been stripped and the place had been made ready for the new one to go in. Which still hadn't arrived.

'I could have washed them on so many occasions, only to watch them disappear under a cloud of dust ten minutes later,' he said to himself as his mother's words rang in his ears. 'You have to keep on top of things, otherwise it will all end up being too much work.'

He looked between his and Ella's cottages. Ella's looked perfect. It looked clean and tidy. In fact, if it hadn't always looked so immaculate for the past few months, he'd have begun to wonder if anyone had really lived there at all.

Will turned off the car engine, grabbed the carrier bag and walked towards the back of the house. 'I reckon it's time to burn some energy and spring clean the windows,' he said as he entered the makeshift kitchen, dropped the bag on top of the paste table, pulled off his jacket and ran upstairs to change.

Once back in the kitchen, he picked up a bucket that he'd left sitting beneath the table, turned on the tap and wiggled his fingers around in the water, testing the temperature, before picking up a large yellow sponge and a squeegee. 'Not ideal, but they'll have to do,' he chuntered to himself as he walked back to the front of the house, bucket in hand. 'Now, windows first, then the door.' He looked up at the upstairs window and shook his head. 'So, are you Spiderman or do you think you're going to need some ladders?' He put the bucket down and looked around. 'Okay, cleaning windows isn't as easy as it looks.'

Will looked across at the farm. The farmer was normally around most days, but typically not today. Which brought his thoughts back to Ella. She was the only other person he knew, but he wasn't sure if she'd have ladders or not. Would Ella clean her own windows, or would someone come in and do them for her? She'd mentioned her father the night before, said he liked to help and Will assumed that if the windows were cleaned, he'd probably have called in and done them for her.

Will waited for a few minutes and then knocked on Ella's door. He turned his back to the door, smiled at two women who rode past on horses and felt a sense of disappointment flood though him as he waited and waited, but got no response. He looked to the side of the house. Her car was there, which he presumed would mean that she was home, but then again it had been parked on the drive for over six months and for a moment Will wondered if Ella was allowed to drive, or whether she still wasn't well enough. Again, he knocked. And again, he waited. And then, eventually a sleepy-looking Ella opened the door and leaned on the frame, rubbing her eyes. 'This had better be good,' she said with a slight, sleepy smile.

'Sorry, I woke you,' Will apologised and pointed to the bucket and sponge. 'I was wanting to clean the place up a bit, but...' He pointed at the upstairs window. 'I don't have any ladders, and I thought—'

'And you thought that along with the pizza cooking services, I'd have a window cleaning service too?' There was a hint of amusement in her voice as she ran a hand through her hair, tossing it over her shoulder. 'You might find some in the shed. I think Dad left some down there. It's at the bottom of the garden. Help yourself,' she said as she yawned. 'And use that.' She pointed to the gate.

Ella walked back into the cottage, slamming the front door behind her and making Will wonder how much of a bad mood he'd just put her in. He shook his head as he went through the gate. 'Well-handled, you idiot.' He walked past the back door, the conservatory and kitchen window, where he heard Ella tapping on the glass.

'You want some coffee?' She waved a kettle in the air. 'Now you've woken me up, you might as well join me.'

* * *

Ella stood in her doorway and watched Will climb the rickety wooden ladder. He'd already been climbing it for the past few minutes and still hadn't quite got to the top. He'd wobbled, yelped and had almost slipped, which was when her nervous giggles had begun and hadn't stopped.

'Will, what the hell are you trying to do to my dad's ladder?' She bit down on her lip, picked up her coffee mug and took a sip.

'You can laugh, but I'm really not too fond of heights.' Will reached upwards with the sponge. 'And what's more, there should be health and safety laws about climbing ladders.' He briefly looked down and winked.

'What, like in parliamentary laws?' Again, Ella began to laugh.

'Yes, and lots of them.' Will once again wobbled on the ladder. His arms and legs were as close as they could get to the woodwork and the hand that held the sponge only left the ladder intermittently as he made wide rapid swiping movements at the window.

'Go on then, what laws should there be?' she asked as she continued to sip at her coffee while trying her best not to laugh.

Will turned on the ladder and once again made a swipe at the window frame. 'Well, the first law would be "Don't climb ladders". The next law should be that if you really have to climb a ladder, there should be a really big bouncy castle underneath it, just in case you fall.' He smirked and took another swipe at the window. 'At least then it might be fun.' Again, the ladder wobbled. 'And, if you hadn't already noticed, a man should keep at least five points of contact with the ladder at all times. No more, no less. Don't ask.'

Ella laughed and almost spat out the coffee. Her mind began running away with itself as she tried not to think of what the fifth body part might be. 'Do you know what, Will?' she said, still laughing. 'It was almost worth being woken up, just to watch you perform your circus act on a ladder.' Ella placed her mug back on the windowsill and then stood for a moment trying to stop her giggles.

'You're not funny.' Will once again swiped at the window.

'But, Will...' She paused and innocently pointed to the upstairs window. 'Why didn't you just go upstairs, open the window and spin it around? They have those really expensive pivots, you know, the ones that make cleaning easy.' Ella ducked as the big yellow sponge flew past her ear. 'I can't believe you didn't tell me that before!' Will shouted. 'If I fall off this ladder, it'll be all your fault.' He pulled the squeegee out of his back jeans pocket.

Ella shrugged. 'Hey, you bought the damn windows, not me. You should know this.'

'Hi Ella. Wait there, I'm coming over.' Bobby's Yorkshire tone stopped the game as he pulled his tractor into the farm yard opposite and jumped down like an overenthusiastic puppy. For a moment he just stood and looked up at Will. 'What are you doing?'

'I'm cleaning the windows. I might as well finish them, now I'm up here.' He flicked the soapsuds in Ella's direction making her once again burst into laughter. 'I mean, I can't have Ella's house cleaner than mine, can I?'

Bobby crossed his arms. He looked thoughtful

and his glance went from Will to Ella and back again. 'Ella's house is always clean,' he said.

Ella pursed her lips. 'Well, that'll be because I have a wonderful daddy who came around while I was poorly and cleaned everything. Looks like he even cut the grass for me and kept the garden tidy. Wasn't that really nice of him?'

Bobby gave a half smile and nervously stepped from foot to foot. And then, his hand went halfway up into the air, like a child asking for permission to speak.

'Miss Ella. That would have been me,' he whispered. 'It was me that did it. The cleaning and the garden.' He blushed and nodded at the same time.

Ella stepped back, the smile dropping from her face. 'Oh my God, Bobby, really, I... Err... Thank you, but why, why did you do that?'

He stared at his boots. 'I was so sorry you were hurt, Miss Ella. Yes, I was, and I'd watched you all last year. You worked really hard at getting the house nice.' Again, he paused, and glanced up nervously to where Will still hovered on the ladder, but then returned his gaze to the floor. 'I just wanted it to be perfect, for when you got better.'

Ella felt shell-shocked and stared open-mouthed at Bobby. For a moment, she had no idea what to say, or do. For the whole seven months since she'd been attacked, Bobby had been letting himself in and out of her garden. He'd been washing her windows, cutting the grass, pruning the trees, and keeping it tidy for her. And, yes, she had to admit, it did look perfect.

'Did you do all of it, Bobby? The hanging baskets, the tubs?' She pointed upwards but had to grab at the doorway for support as Bobby enthusiastically nodded his head. 'Bobby, I – I don't know what to say. Except, well, thank you.'

She looked at Will for reassurance. She didn't know whether to hug Bobby, or offer to pay him. After all, apart from the odd wave, the turf moving expedition and the odd rush across the road to help her carry shopping, she barely knew him. He'd always been keen to shout a hello, and on that day that she'd had to sit outside in the wheelchair, he'd tried to hug her just a little too much. But other than that, she'd barely had any contact with him at all.

Bobby moved a step closer. 'You don't have to say anything. I'm just so glad you're better, Miss Ella. I really am.'

Ella felt uneasy, took a step back and sat down on the step. The news that Bobby had been doing the garden had thrown her and for a moment she felt a little afraid that her legs would give way. Especially as Sarah's words of warning came thundering back to her.

Bobby looked anxious. He didn't seem to know what to say next and Ella noticed him shuffle inch by inch back towards the farm. 'I got a field to plough and three horses to muck out.' His whole face lit up as he listed his work. 'I get to drive the tractor all day today.' He sounded proud of himself as he pointed at the huge beast of a machine. 'I'll... I'll see you later...' He strode back to the farm, where he climbed aboard the tractor and gave them both a wave.

Ella couldn't move. Her thoughts were running away with her; she could hear her heart pounding in her chest. It was then that the trembling began.

6

Ella wandered along the lane, with her camera in hand and her rucksack on her back. She was all set for an hour or two of photography and had set off for a short walk down one of the windy lanes that led off from the edge of her village.

She stared up at the sky; it was pale blue with a hint of sunshine. It was a promise of what was to come and although it was still early morning, the air was crisp and hazy, and she hoped that the afternoon would be warm enough to sit in the garden, where maybe, just maybe, she'd spot Will over the fence, hacking away at what remained of the overgrowth. After all, it was Saturday, the start of the weekend, and if Will worked nine till five, then she hoped that today might just be his day off.

It had been just over a week since she'd watched him wash the windows, after which Will had invited her to share a meal of steak, salad and wine. He'd offered to cook on a disposable BBQ he'd bought but his garden was still such a mess that in the end he brought it all to her house and, like the pizza, she'd cooked the steaks. Then they'd both sat on the bench with wine, until the evening sky had turned to dusk.

Since then, she'd spent her evenings at her parents' house or with Sarah, and most nights she'd got home well after dark, meaning that even though Will's lights had been on and she'd presumed he'd been home, she hadn't seen him, not once. She had, however, noticed a huge delivery van parked outside a few days before, which made her wonder if his kitchen had finally arrived. A sudden sense of disappointment hit her as she realised that the nights of him needing her cooker were probably over. Ella screwed her nose up as she pictured his face. The image was as clear as a photograph. She could see his strawberry blond crew cut, the dimple in his chin, the lightly freckled face and his bright blue eyes that sparkled when he laughed. She thought of how they'd chatted and laughed that evening, about nothing and everything. All the time they'd talked, she'd watched his eyes, watched the way his lips turned on a half-smile when he was joking and the way he used his hands automatically while telling a story. The whole evening had been fun, but the night had drawn in and Will had gone home, leaving Ella to wish she'd had the courage to ask him inside for coffee. But her nerves had stopped her. Something deep inside her still felt a huge sense of anxiety. She knew she needed to trust, and knew that for her life to move on she had to escape the fear and isolation she'd felt that night. But getting over being cold, alone, and broken wasn't easy and, on some days, she felt that the fear would never go away.

She took in a deep breath. 'Seven months, that's all it's been.' She knew she had to give it time, but really wished she could turn back the clock, even if that were only so that she could remember what had happened.

Ella knelt down on the grass verge and then sat with her feet pointing into the hedgerow. Everything was coming into bloom. The trees had turned a deeper shade of green, and the birds were busy flying back and forth to their nests. A small robin bounced around beneath the hedge; it landed on an old prickly blackberry creeper and pecked at the foliage around it. Ella sat and waited patiently, knowing that the longer she sat there, the braver the robin might become and, eventually, if she waited long enough she'd get to snap the perfect moment that she wanted to capture. Her mind cast back to other photographs, to the ones she'd used in the papers, and the pride she'd felt, whether they were scenic, news or portrait. She rolled onto her stomach, and positioned herself away from the random prickles, whilst holding her trusty Nikon as steady as she could.

Even though the day was promising to warm up, it hadn't been warm enough for her to leave her coat at home and for a few moments she felt grateful for the extra layer that pressed itself between her body and the cold ground. A sudden memory of that night passed through her; the ground had been hard, cold and brutal. There had been no padding beneath her and she remembered how she'd wished for a coat or for grass, for some form of comfort to cushion her broken body. She closed her eyes and tried to think back to that night, to what had happened. She clearly remembered the colour of the car, but had no idea why. She remembered the hoodie, and she remembered watching the car as it had driven away and tried to concentrate her memory on the driver, but couldn't.

'Why, why, why can't I see him?' she screamed. A tear dropped down her face and she stared down at the grass. 'You have to think. You have to remember who hurt you,' she chastised herself, knowing that she had to put the jigsaw back together. She had to find the parts that were missing, the broken pieces that had eliminated themselves from her memory. 'Rick Greaves, it just had to be him,' she said as she pushed herself into a sitting position and looked up at the sky. Ella took in a deep breath. 'Who else would I have happily climbed into a car with, especially in the middle of nowhere?' Ella looked through the camera's viewfinder to see that the robin had gone. She sighed and replaced the lens cap before pulling the rucksack from her back and throwing it unceremoniously onto the grass.

Pulling a carton of juice from the bag, Ella sipped at the contents and for a few moments took in the beauty of her surroundings. She'd always loved the countryside and even though she'd been alone on the moors that night, somehow being surrounded by the heather and hedgerows had given her comfort. Until of course the beetle had crawled over her fingers. She hadn't been scared of the beetle, but she hadn't liked the fact that her body had failed her and she hadn't been able to flick it away. The thought made her look around where she sat and without thinking she jumped up from her seat on the grass, grabbed at the bag and the camera, and once again began walking along the lane.

'Hello,' she shouted as Patricia's eldest son, Peter, came into view. He was out walking their Labrador puppy and looked as though the walk was more of a punishment than fun. But then again, she hadn't met many ten-year-olds who wanted to do anything but watch television or play computer games.

'Hello, Ella. My mam, she had her baby,' he announced. 'Another boy, called him George, that makes six of us now.'

Ella tried not to laugh. 'Oh dear. I mean, that's lovely. Is your mum going for the football team, or is this one the last?' she asked as she threw her rucksack onto her back.

'Who bloody well knows, she's always having another one, isn't she?' He stroked the dog's head. 'And now it's my job to walk him. You know, till my mam's back up and about.'

Ella bit her lip. She couldn't believe that a boy so young could swear so easily and she tried not to laugh by busying herself and making a fuss of the dog. He was jet-black with charcoal eyes and looked up at her with the hope of a treat. 'Oh, I'm sorry, boy. I don't have anything for you.' She looked up at where Peter stood. 'What do you call him?' she asked as she stood up and flicked the lens cap off her camera. 'Can I take his picture?'

The boy shrugged his shoulders. 'Whatever, and he's a she, she's called Cookie. Mum was insistent that she had to have another girl in the house.' He moved to one side. 'You can walk her if you like, it'd save me from bloody well doing it.' He dropped the lead and sat his ten-year-old self on the grass while Ella played with Cookie, got her to lie on the grass and took her pictures. She loved dogs, always had and since that night on the moors when the puppy had saved her life, she'd thought how nice it would be to have one. It'd be a good companion, good protection and someone to love, someone who wouldn't let her down. 'When I've developed the photos, I'll drop one off for you,' she said as once again, the lens cap went back on.

Peter stood up. 'Okay,' he said as he began pulling on Cookie's lead. 'But who the hell develops stuff these days?' Ella smiled. 'Well, people like me. I develop stuff; in fact, I tend to develop and print quite a lot.' Her camera was digital. Even though she could see all the pictures on a screen, she still liked to physically see them. She thought of how many she normally took and printed in a year. Of how she'd use them to lead a story and how the whole wording of the story had been based on how the picture had turned out.

Peter and the dog headed back home and Ella turned and looked down the lane. Bobby's tractor came into view and she immediately ducked behind the hedge, her feet dropping into the ditch as she peered between the branches. She watched the tractor move from one end of the field to the other as she hid in the dirt in the hope that his tractor would disappear to somewhere over the horizon. The last thing she needed today was for Bobby to come over and talk to her. She certainly didn't want him to call her 'Miss Ella' again, it was creepy. She began biting down on her lip as she wondered what to do next.

'When in doubt.' Ella picked up her camera, poked it between the branches of the hedgerow and began taking pictures of Bobby. If what Sarah said was true, she needed pictures, something to study, something that would help with her story, until her memory returned. But Bobby's tractor suddenly stopped in the middle of the field and she could see him, sitting there, staring towards where she hid. Ella held her breath.

What if he'd seen her? What if Sarah had been right? What if he was a little bit infatuated? After all, he'd kept her garden for months and she still didn't know if he'd been being nice, or as Sarah had said, 'a bit weird'. What if... what if...

The sound of a car broke the silence and it began to slow down, making Ella duck further into the ditch as she tried to peer over her shoulder.

'For God's sake, Ella. What the hell are you doing crawling around in a ditch?'

'I... Err... Sarah, what... Oh thank God you're here.' She jumped up from her hiding position, but continued to crouch until she managed to climb into Sarah's car, where she slumped as low as she could into the passenger seat, still hiding from Bobby.

7

Ella sat in the corridor of the law courts as, one after the other, people of all shapes and sizes walked past. Most looked quite normal and she wondered which camp each person fell into: visitor, criminal or barrister? With the majority of people, it was quite obvious which they appeared to be, but in some cases they looked neither criminal nor barrister and Ella wondered if these people were the friends or families of those here on trial or, like her, a victim simply fighting for justice.

There was an overwhelming smell of different perfumes, aftershaves, and body odour that all blended into one, making her feel light-headed and nauseous. The overstimulation of her nasal passages made her head boom in rhythm with her heart, giving her the feeling that an overpowering migraine might soon develop. She reached into her handbag, took out the painkillers and popped two in her mouth, along with a sip of water from the Styrofoam cup that she held precariously in her hands. She tried to stare at the floor in the hope that no one would recognise her, start a conversation, or ask her questions. After all, she was the woman everyone had called a miracle, just because she'd survived, and she'd already come to resent the description. She was the one person every reporter had wanted to interview. They'd followed her, chased her and camped outside the hospital for days. One reporter from a newspaper in York had gone as far as posing as a florist. He'd turned up at the hospital with a bouquet of flowers in his arms, asking if he could give them directly to her. No doubt he'd thought he'd get a scoop, a photograph of her with her arm and leg in plaster, a pained, miserable look on her face. But the nurses had been on the ball – she was after all the victim of an unexplained attack – and security had been high.

'Okay, Ella. Things are about to start. I'm going to take you in and quickly show you around, just so you don't get nervous once you're in there.' Prosecuting barrister, John Burgess, spun around, his long black cloak flowing behind him, and he marched off towards the courtroom door, beckoning to her to follow. 'Come, come, we have to be quick. There isn't much time,' he said as he turned to look at her.

Ella had known John forever. He'd been one of her dad's closest friends since they'd both been boys. But the white wig that balanced on his head changed the look of his face. It made him look much sterner, older and more distinguished than his years and, for the first time in her life, she thought he looked like a stranger.

Ella inched up behind him. She tugged her black pencil skirt down and brushed her hand over the shoulders of her jacket to move a stray hair that had fallen. As a reporter that covered the community, she wasn't used to attending courts or wearing suits. Nor was she used to the high heels and perfectly styled hair. It all felt very unnatural to her and now she wished that she'd gone against her barrister's brief and worn something just a little more comfortable, especially the shoes.

She peered nervously around the courtroom as John pointed to the seat where the judge would sit. It was a little higher than everyone else in the courtroom, ensuring that everyone in there would have to look up to where he sat.

'The seat to his right is where his clerk sits, and the desk directly in front of him is where the court officials will be.' He pointed to the table. 'And there, to the side of the room, sits the jury.' He indicated to two long benches that reminded her of the pews in a church. 'You got that?'

Ella nodded. 'And there?'

'That's where the ushers sit, and behind them is the press box.'

The two areas were directly in front of where she'd be. The thought of the press being so close made her shudder and she glanced towards the back of the room. 'And what about there?'

'That's the public gallery,' John Burgess added. 'That's where your parents will be. You'll easily be able to see them should you need their reassurance.'

Ella took in a deep breath and quickly wished she hadn't, as her lungs were assaulted with the smell of beeswax and brass cleaning polish. She thought of her door knocker back at home. Of how it smelled when her mother had polished it. She even thought of how she'd always disliked the smell. But today it seemed worse and added to her already nauseous state.

'You'll be standing here,' her barrister, John, explained as his hand tapped the brass that surrounded a cube-shaped area.

'Will I even be able to see the judge, if he'll be right over there?' she asked, tipping her head to one side as she looked up and tried to work out how far to the right of the judge she'd be sitting. 'What if he speaks to me and I don't hear him?'

'Don't worry, you'll hear him.' John laughed and then walked further into the room. 'I'll be here. Keep your eyes on me; I'll ask you questions first. Just as we practised. Keep eye contact with me, I'll try and help you. But you know I'm restricted. I can't lead you.'

Ella tried to work out how quickly she could get out of the room, should she decide that she needed to bolt. The door was right at the back and she'd have to get past a lot of people. But then again, the fact that she could if she wanted to pleased her. And as everyone had already said, it wasn't as though it was her that was on trial, was it?

'All courtrooms are different,' he began explaining, but Ella's eyes focused on the area right at the side of the room, next to another door. 'Behind that door is the staircase that leads to the cells.'

'That's where he'll be, isn't it?' She felt her legs

go weak, her mouth dry and she began to twist her hot, sweaty hands together; without looking at John for his response, she knew that she was right. Rick Greaves would come through that door. He'd stand right there. Right before her.

* * *

Ella tried to focus through the fog that now took over her mind. She once again sat in the courts' corridor. Her feet felt like lead, her hands were once again hot and clammy and her throat grew dryer by the second. She sipped at her water and waited for her turn to go into court. She suddenly felt as though she were breathing through mud. The hundreds of people who'd walked around earlier had gone and the corridor was now practically empty. For the first time since that night on the moors she felt totally alone. She picked her phone up and thought about calling Sarah, but John had insisted she switch it off and she stared at the unusually darkened screen before placing it back in her bag.

'Ella Hope. Court calls Ella Hope.' The shrill voice of the court usher shouted out and Ella felt her heart miss a beat. Standing up, she took a last sip of the water before throwing the Styrofoam cup in the trash. She then turned and inched towards the court doors.

'Keep calm,' she whispered to herself. 'Keep calm, what's the worst that could happen?'

The heavy oak door was opened for her and she stepped inside. Everyone went silent. Everyone except for one person who seemed to inhale sharply, making Ella spin around on the spot, her eyes desperate to see where Rick Greaves sat.

Nothing had ever prepared her to stand up in court. Or for what it would be like to face Rick Greaves. Giving evidence against him would be brutal and she physically began to shake on the spot. As she took the Bible in her right hand and looked up to where the judge sat, every one of her internal organs vibrated, twisted and squeezed together.

The man who stood before her smiled kindly. 'Repeat after me.'

Ella tried to nod, but the nod came across as a violent shake of her head and she gripped onto the Bible as tightly as she could for fear of dropping it in front of everyone.

'I swear by Almighty God that the evidence I shall give...' He looked at her as the trembling words automatically fell from her mouth.

'...shall be the truth, the whole truth and...' Ella closed her eyes. 'Sorry, what did you say?'

The usher glanced across at the judge. '...nothing but the truth, so help me God,' he repeated the words and smiled as Ella stuttered through the words. 'Are you ready?' He pushed a glass of water towards her. 'This is for you, should you need it.'

Ella glanced around the room. Her eyes became fixed on where Rick Greaves sat, glaring in her direction. She swallowed hard and forced herself to look back at the usher. 'Yes, I'm ready,' she whispered back, as he turned to the judge and nodded.

The room once again went silent as the prosecution barrister, John, stood up. He looked serious and for a moment stayed silent, but then one by one he asked the questions that they had practised. He smiled each time she gave the right answer and nodded reassuringly as the last of his questions was asked. 'Well done,' he mouthed, before taking his seat and looking to his right to where the defence barrister sat.

Ella took a deep breath as the man stood up. He wore a black cloak, an ivory wig, and a stern glare. His poker face didn't move as he lifted a heavy black lever-arch file onto the table and dropped it with a bang. He looked directly into her eyes with no emotion, then looked down at the file before him and began to read. He then pushed a pair of glasses up his nose before looking back at her, his face solid and without feeling, as though he'd been injected with Botox.

'Miss Hope,' he bellowed. 'It is MISS, isn't it?'

Ella took in a deep breath. She was determined that he wouldn't intimidate her. 'It is,' she replied in the same flat and unemotional tone. She needed to stay calm. She made the mistake of taking a moment to glance across to the public gallery, where both her mother and father sat. Her father's lips formed a thin line, his eyebrows were pulled together and for a man who'd never raised his voice in temper, he had a look of vengeance. He glared at Rick Greaves, before glancing back in her direction. He then forced a smile and gingerly and discreetly held a hand up to wave in her direction. She noticed that her father's hand then gripped tightly onto her mother's and Ella knew that today would be especially hard for them both. Since that night, her mother seemed to have taken everyone's worries upon herself and Ella was pleased that her father was with her. He always seemed to be the strong member of the family, the one who always looked after everyone else and it suddenly made Ella wonder who looked after him. Who did her father turn to when he needed a hug, to cry, or just to vent his anger?

'So, Miss Hope. I wonder if you could remind me? How did you meet my client, Mr Greaves?'

'I was a member of his gym,' Ella replied. 'I used to attend two or three times a week.' She looked beyond the defence barrister and across to where the press sat. She'd hated the tricks that reporters used and she wondered what they were thinking. At least twenty reporters sat crowded into rows, all with their heads down and pencils and pads on their knees. All were at the ready to write down any juicy parts of the story, all of which they'd manipulate later. She tried to concentrate on who they were, but all the heads were bowed and the images of people all blended into the next.

'I see. So, as a member of the gym, you got to know Mr Greaves quite well, is that right?'

Ella looked up to the ceiling and wished she could be anywhere else in the world except in this courtroom. 'Yes, I got to know everyone at the gym, not just Mr Greaves.'

'Just yes or no will be sufficient, Miss Hope.' The defence barrister looked pleased with himself and Ella tipped her head to one side and studied his

face. It was a face that looked so smug and so right-
eous, yet so poker- faced that she'd have happily enjoyed slapping it just to see if he had any other facial
expression.

'So, Miss Hope. You're a reporter, is that right?'
He stepped backwards, rested his hand on the table
before him and flicked a page in the binder.

'That's correct.' Ella picked up the glass of water
and took a sip. Her mouth was getting drier and
drier, her stomach quivered nervously and she could
feel herself trembling from within.

'That's very interesting, Miss Hope. So, could you
tell the court, as a reporter, were you using the gym
as a way to meet people, or were you on the look-out
for new stories?'

'As I said, I was attending the gym as a member. I
like to keep fit.' She'd ignored his earlier demand for
yes or no answers. 'Sorry, I used to enjoy keeping fit.
I can't use the equipment any more. Not since that
night.'

'Miss Hope. Why did you feel the need to get to
know Mr Greaves?'

Ella glanced across at the jury and wondered
how many of them were remotely interested in the
case. One man wrote down every word, but another
seemed half asleep making her want to poke him

and tell him to listen. But then, in contrast, a woman in her late thirties continually looked at her watch and Ella wondered where she needed to be.

'I didn't need to know him,' Ella answered. 'In fact, I barely knew him at all, but he came and spoke to me. I found him interesting so I didn't discourage him. As I said, I'm a reporter. Talking to people is what I do, it's part of my job.' The moment the words left her lips, she regretted them.

The barrister pulled back his shoulders in a determined manner. 'So, on the night in question, Miss Hope, would you say that you were on a date or working?'

Ella nodded. 'Rick, I mean Mr Greaves, invited me out on a date. We were both single. I didn't see any reason to refuse.'

'Were you working?' His voice became raised and Ella took in a sharp breath.

'I'm always working. Every conversation can turn into a great story.' Again, she regretted the words and looked at John, her barrister, who had closed his eyes and was looking down.

'I see.' The defence barrister cast a look up at the judge and then looked back at her. 'Is it normal for reporters to interview people over a dinner date?'

Again, Ella shook her head. 'I'm not sure that

talking to someone over dinner can be classed as an interview.'

'Earlier, Miss Hope, you said that you barely knew Mr Greaves. Might I ask, did my client know that you were a reporter?'

'I don't know, you'd have to ask him.' Ella felt herself tremble; she felt weak and was pleased that she'd been allowed to stay sitting down throughout the questioning. She opened her mouth to take in air, closed her eyes for a moment and then once again picked up the glass of water for something to do with her hands, just as she felt her left eye begin to twitch with nerves.

'And you didn't think to tell him?'

Ella began tapping her foot. It was all she could do to count time, to help control her breathing. 'No, I don't think I mentioned it.'

There was a gasp from somewhere within the room, a rattling of chair legs and someone, a man, stood up from the public gallery and left.

'So, on the night in question, you were working. Is that right?'

'Yes, no... It depends. As I said, I like to talk to people, so I'd say that I'm always working.'

He held out his hands. 'Is it a yes, or a no?'

'I don't know, it's complicated.' Ella ran a hand

through her hair; her stomach turned and she quickly realised how easily she could answer the question wrong. 'I wasn't intending to look for a story, if that's what you're asking. But, I have to be honest, if I'd found one, I'd have written it,' she admitted.

'Could we see exhibit one, please?' He turned and looked at the jury as he asked the question and held his hand out to a clerk, who passed him a clear plastic bag. 'Might this be the remnants of the dress you wore?' The bag was long and flat and a small, black, torn dress had been arranged on a coat hanger so that it could be clearly seen.

Ella cringed when she saw it. It really was badly torn, making her wonder how much of her body had been exposed. 'I believe it is.'

'Not exactly the sort of dress you'd wear for work, is it, Miss Hope?' For the first time his upper lip moved upwards and he mimicked a laugh, a high-pitched sound that pierced Ella's mind. She lifted her hands to her ears in protest and looked up at the judge. 'Did I see you shake your head, Miss Hope? Please, answer yes or no for the benefit of the court.'

'I didn't actually say that I was working. It was a date. As I said, Mr Greaves had invited me out and I didn't have anything else I could wear. I don't tend to buy too many dresses.'

'Let me remind you, Miss Hope, in your own words you've admitted that you are always working. You arranged to meet my client for dinner, and you wore a dress that barely covered your body. Is that right, Miss Hope? Yes or no?'

Ella looked across at the public gallery for support, but the sight of her mother sobbing made her turn her attention to where her barrister, John Burgess, sat. He bowed his head discreetly in a nod.

'Yes,' she said as she stared at John for some answers, some clue as to how she should answer.

'You did. Thank you for admitting that.' He looked at the jury to ensure they'd noted his words and once again he waved the dress in the air. 'Let me put it to you, Miss Hope, that the night in question didn't go exactly as you planned, did it? You went out with my client, Mr Greaves. You wore a short and revealing dress in the hope that my client would either answer all of your questions, or he'd fall for your advances, Miss Hope. Is that right?'

'What? No...!' Ella shook her head. 'That didn't happen. It wasn't like that.' She panicked and once again looked at John Burgess. Her eyes pleaded with him for help. He'd warned her about the questioning; he'd told her to answer carefully and had also warned her that by the time the defence barrister had finished, he'd ensure she felt guilty for having survived. But this was different; he wasn't making her feel guilty, he was making her feel responsible.

Why did she feel responsible?

'Objection, your honour.' John Burgess jumped up from his seat. 'My learned friend is leading the jury; Miss Hope has already explained that she had met his client for dinner and a drink. In her opinion, it was a date. She never once admitted to any advances being made by either party.' He caught her eye and held her gaze. She had no idea how to act, how to answer or how to defend herself in a courtroom environment. And for a few moments she looked at the press box and wished that it had been part of her job to sit there, to listen to the cases, the questioning and the way the truth was easily twisted. At least then she'd have been prepared for what was happening. But working the courts had never been a part of her job; she'd always preferred the great outdoors, the stories that affected the villages, the neighbourhoods, the community and she'd always grabbed those stories first. Never in a million years had she thought she'd be standing here, having to defend her own actions, as though she were the guilty one.

Ella prayed that it would be over soon, that she'd be asked to stand down and that Rick Greaves would get what he deserved.

The judge nodded. 'Mr Kent, you may continue.'

Ella could only just see the judge. He seemed to write something in a journal and then crossed his hands, silently waiting.

'Could I ask, Miss Hope: what perfume were you wearing that night?'

'Why is that relevant?'

'Please, Miss Hope. Answer the question.'

'I don't remember.' Ella tried to think, tried to recall what she'd worn. It could have been any of four different scents, they were all lined up on her dressing table and she normally just chose one randomly.

'Then, let me remind you, Miss Hope. I believe here in your original statement...' He flicked through some paperwork as though pretending he didn't already know the answer. 'It says here that you said that you were wearing Chanel. Isn't that one of the most expensive perfumes, Miss Hope? I take it that Chanel would be something you'd normally wear for – well, for what you say was a date.' He paused. 'Or are you that extravagant for work?'

'Err, well, I don't know how much it cost. It was a gift.'

Mr Kent once again paused. He looked pleased with himself before turning a page in his binder and again with no emotion began to talk. 'Did you drink any wine that night, Miss Hope?'

'Yes. I had a glass of red wine.'

'Was it just the one glass of red wine, Miss Hope, or more?'

'Yes, just one.' She once again allowed her gaze to travel down the side of the courtroom and to the area of the court where her parents sat. She recognised three or four of the staff that worked at the gym. All were watching, glaring and waiting for her to trip herself up.

'Might I say, Miss Hope, that according to the restaurant you attended, a whole bottle of red Merlot wine was ordered?'

'Maybe it was. It doesn't mean that I drank it. I had a glass, maybe a glass and a half, at the most, if that.' She glanced back at John Burgess who closed his eyes, crossed his hands before him and looked as though he were deep in prayer.

'Do you normally drink a whole bottle of red when you are working, Miss Hope?'

Ella stumbled over her words. 'I... I didn't say that I drank a whole bottle of red.'

'But you were working?'

'I didn't actually say that.' Ella shook her head at the accusation. In truth, she couldn't remember what she'd drunk. She remembered having a glass, but then everything had gone fuzzy and that's when she'd begun to feel so light-headed. 'I had a glass. I wouldn't have drunk more because I was driving, so, at worst, I'd have had just one or two really small ones... Yes, that's right, small ones.'

'You're really not that sure, Miss Hope, are you? Was it one drink, two drinks, small glass, large glass, or a whole bottle?' He looked arrogantly at the jury and then turned back to her.

'I... Err...'

He slammed his hand down on the table. 'Which was it, Miss Hope? It's not a difficult question.'

Ella felt confused. She closed her eyes. She was in court, she couldn't lie. 'I can't remember.'

'So, once again, let me put it to you. You were on a night out... Let's say a romantic night out, which is why you were wearing a very revealing black dress, with Chanel perfume and red stiletto heeled shoes, wasn't it, Miss Hope?' He paused and smirked. 'You were out to seduce my client; you wanted his story. You ordered wine, you drank too much and this alone is why you can't remember what happened, Miss Hope, isn't it?' He paused. 'You have no idea what you drank, or how much you drank, do you?'

'It wasn't like that. You're putting words in my mouth.'

He once again looked down at the file. 'What time did you leave the restaurant, Miss Hope?'

Ella thought of the watch, she remembered looking at its luminous hands for hours, but couldn't for the life of her remember leaving the restaurant, never mind whether she'd have checked her watch or not.

'You have no idea, do you? Again, let me ask, had you drunk more than you should have?' His hand dropped heavily onto the desk.

Ella stood up and spun around on the spot, gripped the brass surround and looked across at the judge. 'It wasn't like that.'

The defence barrister continued. 'On the night in question, Miss Hope, and remember, you are under oath, can you wholeheartedly and honestly state that on that night my client, Mr Rick Greaves, attacked you? Do you remember getting into his car, Miss Hope? Do you remember my client attacking you?'

'I, err, yes... I remember getting in a car.'

'But, Miss Hope, might I again remind you that you are under oath. Was Mr Greaves driving the car?'

She nodded her head. 'The car. It was blue,' she confirmed. Again, she looked at the jury; not one of them held her eye. Not one of them looked directly at her.

The barrister raised his eyebrows. 'I'll ask again. Was my client, Mr Greaves, driving it?'

Ella sat back down. She felt defeated and stared into space. 'Miss Hope, can I put it to you that on that night in question, you were in fact so drunk that you have no idea who drove the car? IS THAT RIGHT, Miss Hope?'

Ella had begun to hate the grinding sound of the barrister's voice. It reminded her of a food mixer, whizzing round with a constant, repetitive, buzzing motion. There was nothing she'd rather do than pick up his lever-arch file and push it firmly down his throat. She wanted to bring the noise to an end and she desperately searched the public gallery, looking for her parents.

'Yes or no, Miss Hope?'

Ella held her breath and closed her eyes. 'No.' The whole room began to spin and she held onto both her chair and the polished brass rail for support.

* * *

I had fun today. I sat there, watching you stumble over your words. You really don't have any idea what happened, do you? You can't remember a thing and everyone knows that, including the jury. They won't be fooled by you. They won't be lied to. They won't even look you in the eye. You noticed that, didn't you? I watched you as you tried to keep their attention, but they barely looked at you. And why didn't they look at you? Because nothing you've said resembled the truth, nothing pointed to who attacked you and I've sat there, watching, listening and laughing at you, the whole time you were speaking. The defence barrister, he made you look stupid. Like the fool you are. You really think you can win this, don't you? But you won't bring me to justice. You didn't see me that night, and you definitely can't remember who attacked you. Well, I can't wait for the jury to come back in. For the 'Not Guilty' words to ring in my ears. I can't wait to see your face or for you to wonder what went wrong and what's more, you'll be looking over your shoulder for the rest of your life, just in case I'm standing there, waiting to strike.

* * *

8

Ella stared at the solid oak door. It was the door behind which the jury had gone to reach their verdict. Soon the door would open and from behind it would walk in the twelve people that had the ability to alter her life. They would have talked about her, judged her, criticised her and, ultimately, they would deliver their verdict on what they honestly believed had happened that night.

She sat, silently, waiting. Her breathing had fallen into a rhythm, one much faster than normal and from time to time she opened her mouth and breathed in really deeply, knowing that if she didn't she'd most probably start hyperventilating and end up in an undignified and unconscious heap on the floor.

'In, out,' she whispered to herself in an attempt to control the frustration and anxiety that was building up inside. She jumped nervously as a door opened and both barristers returned. They were followed by ushers, solicitors and probation officers, who took their seats and chatted amongst themselves. And then, as though in slow motion, the public gallery began to fill up. Her mother and father were sitting right at the front. Their eyes fixed with hers and her mother held out a hand in an imaginary hold, something she'd done many times at the school gates. A secret sign they'd shared for years. Then, that precious loving moment was lost as Rick Greaves was led in, his face stern, his stare piercing. He looked directly at her, caught her eye and even though Ella's heart began to beat wildly, she refused to break the stare first.

A sudden noise broke the stand-off. Rick looked away and Ella saw his attention turn to the door behind her, to her right. The oak door opened and the jury began to file into the courtroom. One after the other, they shuffled along the pews, and sat down. The court was full of chatter, of people trying to guess what would happen next, but then the usher stood up and an eerie silence overtook the room.

'All rise for Judge Johnson,' the usher shouted out. The whole court went quiet and stood in unison, including the twelve jurors. One or two looked sympathetically towards where Ella now stood beside her barrister, John. But others looked away, and Ella felt that it was more than obvious that they didn't want to make any eye contact with her. She tried to swallow but couldn't and she held her breath as the judge walked in and took his seat.

'Court be seated.' The usher walked across the courtroom and stood beside the jurors. 'Will the foreperson please rise,' he said, and a middle-aged man got to his feet. 'Members of the jury, have you reached a unanimous decision?' the judge asked, while his pencil tapped his journal.

'We have your honour,' the man said. His lips were pursed, and he glanced across at Rick Greaves with a slight, but obvious smile.

'Do you find the defendant guilty or not guilty?'

The jury foreperson looked straight ahead and without flinching he said, 'Not guilty, your honour.'

* * *

'So that's it, he walks?' Ella screamed. Her legs felt wobbly and she stared across the courtroom straight into the piercing glare of Rick Greaves. He looked angry, tearful and relieved all at once. He stood up, shook his defence barrister's hand and chatted to the people around him. 'How can that happen?'

Ella's thoughts exploded into a million questions. She'd waited for this day; she'd hoped that Rick Greaves would be locked away for years. But here he was smiling, shaking hands, going home and, what was worse, he was about to carry on with his life as though nothing had happened.

'Court adjourned,' someone from behind her shouted and everyone turned as the judge stood up.

Ella spun around. She could see the judge more clearly from her chair and could tell that within a moment he would leave the court and disappear into his chambers.

'Judge, please, can I speak to you? I – I need to speak to you.' She held up a hand in an attempt to gain his attention. 'Please, you can't let him walk,' she screamed. 'Did you see what he did to me? Did you see the photographs?' She reached across John Burgess, grabbed the pictures that still lay on his table and began clawing her way over the benches. She tried to pull herself towards the witness box where she'd previously stood. But pain shot through her arms and legs, making her stop and scream.

The judge kept walking. The door to his chambers opened and closed behind him and Ella watched as he disappeared out of sight. The noise in the courtroom exploded. Everyone began chatting, laughing and hugging all at once. But all Ella could hear was the distraught, hollow squeal that appeared to come from her mother, who still stood in the gallery.

The hands of her barrister, John Burgess, grabbed her carefully by the shoulders and she felt herself being physically eased back and into a seat.

'It's over, Ella. Please. You have to sit down. Do you hear me?' John Burgess moved forward, crouched down before her and stared into her eyes, making Ella take in numerous rapid deep breaths. 'You ever do anything like that again, young lady, and you'll end up being in contempt of court. So please, sit down.' She sobbed while looking over his shoulder and towards where Rick Greaves stood. Waiting to be released.

'THIS WILL NEVER BE OVER, GREAVES. DO YOU HEAR ME? NEVER!' Ella screamed, but then immediately looked up at John and whispered an apology. Ella turned and searched the public gallery;

she needed to see her parents. She needed the comfort of seeing them, and needed to know they were okay.

'Let's take you home,' Carol Hope mouthed as she dabbed at her eyes with a tissue and made an attempt at smiling. Ella held her gaze and once again held out her hand in an imaginary hold. She then glanced at her father who once again looked strong; his arms surrounded her mother and, for just a moment, the whole room blurred and there was no one else in the room but Ella and her parents.

Tears filled her eyes, but Ella stared through them as one by one each person began to come back into focus. The courtroom was still full of secretaries, barristers and solicitors who now packed away their files into huge suitcases, which they pulled behind them as they began to file out of court.

The room seemed busier than it had before and, looking up at the public gallery again, the number of women who were sitting alongside her mother suddenly struck Ella. They were all dabbing at their eyes, all showed some form of emotion that ranged from happy or sad, to relieved or indifferent and Ella wondered how many of them were friends, girlfriends, family, or soon to become lovers of Rick Greaves. On the front row were his staff. Michelle, the tall one with short blonde hair who smiled incessantly, looked like she would begin bouncing around the courtroom at any given moment. And then there was Tim, the gym's manager and Rick Greaves' former business partner, who sat with his arms crossed, his biceps bulging and his teeth practically grinding as he continually seemed to monitor everyone else in the room. No emotion crossed his face, but Ella came to the conclusion that he didn't look very happy. And then there was the young one, Nina. She was slim with long dark hair. She stared at an area beyond where Rick still stood, as though she were looking right through him with her eyes filled with tears. All of these people had befriended her in the past. All had helped her with equipment at the gym. They'd jumped on rowing machines by her side, chatted endlessly, laughed, joked and had shown her how to get the most out of each piece of equipment. Yet here they all were, all on Rick's side, as though he was the victim. None of them had been in touch with her, not once. So how come none of them, except Michelle, appeared to be happy about Rick's release?

The courtroom continued to empty.

Ella's eyes ran across the other faces, many that she'd never met and probably would never see again. But then she caught sight of Will Taylor. He stood by the door and smiled, noticing that Ella had seen him and lifted a hand in acknowledgment.

Had he just walked in or had he been there the whole time? Surely he hadn't sat through the whole case? She was sure that she would have noticed him; she tried to think of the times she'd looked over to her parents, to the public gallery and felt positive that she'd have spotted him in the crowd, especially if he'd been sitting within a few feet of both her mum and dad. But, then again, she supposed it was possible that he might have just popped in to hear the verdict.

She mentally kicked herself. How had she not known who'd been in the room? She was normally so very observant. The last time she'd seen Will had been two whole weeks before, when he'd sat in her garden sharing his steaks with a cheeky grin. But today he looked different. He was wearing a dark, expensive suit that made his short strawberry blond hair stand out vividly against it. His hair could easily be as auburn as hers, should it have been allowed to grow and Ella tried to imagine what he'd look like with longer hair, just as Will moved from his position by the door, stepping to one side to allow one of the court officials to pass, which gave Ella a better look at his angular face. His piercing blue eyes caught hers and once again he waved, stared and smiled for what seemed like an eternity, and then left the court without turning back.

Rubbing her eyes, Ella blinked repeatedly. Once again, the whole room had turned foggy and everyone had become blurred. She looked back at the gallery, but only the shapes of people remained and most of those people were now being ushered from the room.

'We'll be in the coffee shop over the road,' her mother shouted. 'We'll wait for you there.'

Ella nodded. Something else was said, but now the voices seemed distant, almost like an echo and she stared at the floor, wishing for the feeling to pass.

'Okay, Ella. I need a word? Privately.' John Burgess stood up from where he'd been sitting. He continued to pack the reams of paperwork, evidence, and stationery into a briefcase. 'Let me just finish packing this lot and we'll use one of the rooms at the back of the court.'

Ella nodded and stood up from her seat. Her legs buckled and she quickly sat back down. 'He walked,' she whispered. 'You said he'd go away for years.' She heard the words that came from within her, but deep down she felt as though someone else had said them. 'The police must have thought him guilty; why else would they have kept him on remand?'

John Burgess dropped his briefcase to the floor and grabbed Ella by the shoulders. 'Look at me.' Ella could see the emotion in his jet-black eyes; he obviously hated the loss as much as she did. She looked down and away. She couldn't bear to see his pain, no more than she could bear to show him hers. 'I said look at me.' Ella waited momentarily, before looking up. 'We'll find a way,' she heard him say. 'I'll bring him to justice. Trust me, I promise.'

Ella bit her bottom lip. 'You can't do it. It's impossible,' she growled and pulled herself out of his grip. Breathing in as deeply as she could, she dug deep within herself for strength, but couldn't stop the tears that had suddenly begun to flow. 'He almost killed me. Did you see what he did? Did you see the photos? Of course you did.' She held onto his arm. 'I'm sure you've already packed the photos away, in there, in your great big, fat file.' She stood up, walked towards the exit and pointed to the suitcase that now stood by his side. 'He punctured my lung, broke six of my ribs. My left leg and ankle were both broken. My arm,' she said, waving her left arm in the air, 'was broken, my fingers, broken. I had muscles that I didn't know existed torn from my body and I had a bloody aneurism that kept me flat on my back for weeks. They thought I would die, John. No one expected me to live and if I had lived, they expected me to be damaged. It's a bloody miracle that I'm here. But it wasn't just my bones he broke, he broke everything about the world that I knew.' She wiped her eyes with the back of her hand. 'How do I even begin to get over that, knowing that he's back out there?' The tears continued to fall and she grabbed at the doorway to steady herself. 'What if he comes after me? What's stopping him from having another go? What's stopping him from finishing the job?' She blurted out one question after the other, then turned away, kicked the door and felt her barrister push her unceremoniously through the corridor and into a small room that lay beyond.

'Ella, keep doing that sort of thing in a court of law and I've already warned you, you'll end up getting yourself arrested.' He paused and slammed the door behind them. 'You have to realise there was nothing more we could do. Not today.' His voice was stern, making Ella cower away. Confrontation made her nervous and she looked at the closed door, looking for a way to escape.

'But... but... It's not fair. What was it they said? They had trace evidence.' She held her hands up in a shrug. 'They said that it proved that he'd been on the moors.'

John Burgess shook his head. 'Listen to me. The trace was just a tiny particle of soil they found in his house. The soil matched the soil where you'd been found. All that meant was that at some point in the days that led up to your attack, he'd been up there. But it didn't conclude that he'd attacked you. There are still too many unanswered questions, Ella.' He ran his hand through his hair. 'I did warn you that there might not be enough evidence to convict him. He had reasonable doubt and, between you and me, except for the fact that you'd been with him and that you did a positive identification right after the attack, nothing else pointed to him apart from that trace. We were relying on your positive identification, but as you saw the barrister did his job and got you to admit that even you don't remember what really happened. Let's just thank God that you are still alive.'

'But he had one of those hoodies, it was in the dustbin. Why would it have been in the dustbin?'

'Again, not proof. That hoodie was identical to hundreds of others. They sell them at his gym; every staff member, gym member or even visitor to the shop could have bought one.' He lifted his case onto the desk and began rummaging inside.

She began clutching at straws. 'They should have tested me for drugs, he must have drugged me.'

John Burgess once again placed a hand on her shoulder. 'Ella, we've gone over this. It was too late. It was ten hours or more after the attack. If you had been drugged, they'd have been out of your system. It was more important at the time to stabilise you. It was imperative that you got the treatment that saved your life.'

Ella stared at the walls. 'But he had no alibi. That's why they locked him up.'

John's voice softened and he suddenly turned from being a tough barrister to long-time family friend. 'You're right, Ella, there was sufficient evidence to have initially locked him up, but only because you said you saw him, you gave a positive identification. You said it had definitely been Rick Greaves that had attacked you and that with the trace and the hoodie in the bin meant that the evidence pointed to him. But ultimately it had to stand up in court. And it didn't. You just admitted that you couldn't be sure. You didn't see his face.'

'But—'

'No buts, Ella. Both you and I know how little you remember. It could have been anyone who attacked you. The only thing that put him away in the first place was the fact that you recognised a sweatshirt, you told them that without a doubt it was Rick and they found the trace. I'm not really surprised at the outcome. I did warn you that this might happen, didn't I?'

There was a silence between them as Ella paced up and down the room. She kicked the wall, yelped and then grabbed at her foot.

'Ella. Stop. I've said I'll find a way. I will search for the truth and when I find it, I'll enjoy every moment of that court case.' He now walked over to where she stood, held a hand out to her and manoeuvred her back towards the table and chair. 'I know you wanted him put away for life and I know you are sure that it was him that hurt you, but even if convicted he'd have only got a minimum sentence of five to seven years.' John paused. 'He'd have only got more than that if and only if he had previous convictions.' He took her by the shoulders. 'So, you see, he wouldn't have got life.'

'Life is the minimum that he should have got. He has history. His two wives both died suspiciously. I've studied him, read the accident reports and Rick Greaves...' Her voice broke with emotion. '...Rick Greaves just has to be guilty, doesn't he?' she whispered, her voice now barely audible, even to herself.

'If you thought he was guilty of killing his wives, why the hell did you go out with him?'

Ella shook her head. 'I thought I could look after myself.' Her shoulders dropped, she felt defeated and looked around the room. Its plain cream walls, a table, three chairs, tinted windows and a water cooler showed it to be a typical interview room, just like the ones she'd sat in on so many occasions after the attack. On each occasion, she'd gone over and over her story. She'd repeated all that she'd known, all that she'd remembered and at times she'd wondered which one of them was going on trial.

'I wanna throw up,' she suddenly shouted as she reached out, grabbed a waste bin and held it in her arms, hugging it like a child with a giant teddy bear.

'You okay?' John looked around the room as though trying to find a fast escape, but finally walked towards the water machine, filled a Styrofoam cup full of water and passed it to her.

Ella took the cup in one hand as she held the bin

in the other, while she stared into its depths. An empty can, a crumpled up crisp packet and various torn up pieces of paper lay in the bottom. Her eyes fixed on one tiny piece. The word 'truth' could still be made out and it jumped out from the page.

'I'm going to find the truth.' She nodded as she drank the water. 'I'm going to find the truth if it kills me.' She kicked the table leg, dropped the waste bin to the floor and threw the empty Styrofoam cup towards it. 'I'm going to find out exactly what happened that night, John. I'm going to find out what he drugged me with, because for me to have forgotten so much, he just had to have drugged me. And not only that, John, there's his two wives that both died. Two of them. Don't you think that's just a little bit suspicious? Because I do. I don't believe that anyone is quite that unlucky.' She took in a deep breath. 'I just don't know what his motives were or why he married them, only to get rid of them. But when I do find out, I'm going to take great pleasure in putting that bastard away – for life, like he deserves.'

* * *

Your face was a picture. In fact, I can barely believe the not guilty verdict. I knew they wouldn't listen to you, after all you didn't sound too convincing and half of me wants to laugh out loud, but half of me isn't sure that the verdict is a good thing. Because it won't stop there, will it?

They'll keep looking for answers, searching for the truth and digging up the past. And as for you, Ella Hope, I know you won't let it drop, so I have to put another plan into place. I have to ensure that the truth is never found, and that my involvement in the deaths of so many can never come to light. I try not to think of the three that I did kill. I try to keep them buried deep in my mind, because they are the ones that didn't speak, fight back, or cause a fuss. For me, they were the perfect murders and in the future I'll ensure that all of my victims die at the scene, or that they are never found, just like my first who still lays hidden and still to this day, who no one knows is dead. I find myself nodding in affirmation, while staring into the courtroom that's now emptying of people. I sigh and stand up, while all the time trying to decide on what I should do next.

9

'I've asked the taxi to wait,' Sarah shouted as she burst in through the back door, her blonde hair hanging loosely down her back. She wore a sequin covered dress, which was far too short. It seemed to imitate a glitter ball and could have easily passed as a very broad and shiny belt.

'Hells bells, Sarah. Do you ever knock?' Ella sat down on the bottom step of the stairs, and pulled her long, fluffy dressing gown tight across her body like a protective cloak. 'You could have at least warned me you were coming. You'd have frightened me to death if I hadn't seen you jump out of the taxi like Flash bloody Gordon.'

'Seriously, Ella, when did I ever knock or announce my arrival?' She smiled, made her way through to the kitchen and picked up a mug of Ella's cold coffee and took a sip. 'Besides, I've warned you about leaving the doors unlocked. Do you know how many criminals I lock up every single week for breaking and entry? Do you?'

Ella pointed to the wall above the cooker. 'And that's why I keep my old school hockey stick right there.' She smiled. 'It was the stick I used that day I won the championships, but it's also the perfect weapon if anyone should burst in and surprise me.'

It was true; Sarah had never knocked, she was always bursting in and surprising her. But she was also a policewoman, and had lectured Ella constantly for years on home security.

'Ella,' Sarah said, putting on her stern voice. 'It'd take you an hour to get it off the wall.'

'Okay. I guess you have a point. So, come on, spill the beans. It's Friday night, so what's going on? What do you want, and why are you dressed like this?' Her finger pointed at Sarah and waved up and down. 'And why is there a taxi waiting?' She fired the questions like bullets.

'Come on, he's on the clock.' Sarah looked at her watch.

'Come on to what? Where?' Ella didn't like the

enthusiasm that Sarah appeared to have. A giddy, bouncing enthusiasm that normally meant that Sarah was on a mission, and Ella normally ended up agreeing to do whatever she asked.

'We have to go out, Ella. Don't you ever read the texts I send you? I did text, didn't I?' She began flicking through her phone. 'Besides, it's my duty as your best friend to get you out of this bear pit and back into the real world. You can't hide yourself away from the world forever. It's not healthy.' She crossed her arms across the low cut sequin dress, gave Ella a stern look and leaned back against the kitchen unit. 'I'm not taking no for an answer.'

'It's only three weeks since I moved back home. And since then I've endured a court case, so you can hardly accuse me of being a hermit, can you?' Ella inched her way up a step, pulled the dressing gown even tighter and looked towards the security of her bedroom door. She'd hibernated for the last couple of days, ever since the court case. She felt safe at home, sheltered from the outside world and she'd actually begun to enjoy being hidden away. It had been the time she'd needed to lick her wounds. Again, Ella moved up another step.

'Not a chance, don't you dare try and escape up there. Besides, you need to come out with me. I need to go to the beach party. This cute guy is going and I kind of need to bump into him and it's your duty as my friend to help me. No one else will go.' Sarah held out her hands as though in prayer. 'Please, Ella. I need you.'

Ella sighed and inched herself up another step. She was only three steps away from where her bedroom door stood, waiting. 'So, you asked everyone else first and I'm the only one of your friends that, up to now, didn't say no.' She raised her eyebrows as she watched her friend's tortured face. 'Well, guess what, Sarah? I don't want to go either.' She could tell that Sarah was trying to decide what to say next. It's what Sarah did; she'd put her foot in it and then she'd put things right.

'You... you're always my first choice, Ella. But you have been kind of distant lately and beach parties down at the gap are always fun, you know that.' Her policewoman negotiating skills suddenly fell into place. 'Besides, it'll be a good night. There's a BBQ and you like having fun. You like to be with me, don't you?'

Ella shook her head, but Sarah was right. She knew that she'd been distant. It had only been a few days since the court case, but she knew that hiding forever was totally out of the question. She also knew that the first time that she did go out would be the worst and the sooner she got it over with the better. But her heart began to beat rapidly at the thought. Ella was scared. Not just scared, terrified. She had felt nervous of everyone and everything ever since she'd moved back home and half of her wondered why she hadn't taken the easy option and stayed at her parents', in the safety of their home. At least until after the court case, like her parents had wanted. She didn't feel ready to face the world, but knew that given the choice, she probably never would.

'So,' Ella began cautiously, 'if it's a beach party, why are you dressed like you're going to Ibiza?' Ella looked outside. The bright amber indicator of the taxi continued to flash outside the window. 'Not your typical beach outfit, is it?'

Sarah brushed her hand down the sequin dress. 'Oh this, just something I pulled out of the wardrobe. It's nothing special. Besides, my normal outfits tend to be my work clothes these days and there's nothing like a copper showing up to ruin a party now, is there?' She laughed. 'So, nowadays I try to ensure that the last thing I look like on a night out is a cop.'

'I see your point.' Ella thought about what to

wear. She didn't really wear dresses. The black one she'd worn to meet Rick Greaves had been her only posh dress. She had no intention of ever going out wearing clothes like that again. From now on it was strictly sensible clothing.

'Come on, Ella. I have to bump into Josh tonight, I think I love him.' Sarah still pleaded, making Ella sigh, smile and then shake her head. Sarah fell in and out of love with someone new every day of the week and Ella had lost count of how many times they'd had this exact same conversation one week, only to have the 'I hate him, he really doesn't understand me' conversation the next. It had been like a twenty-odd-year-old merry-go-round that had begun in primary school. Sarah had gone from happy to sad on a weekly basis and just when Ella had begun to wonder if she'd ever recover, she be back to being happy Sarah: smiling and totally in love again, with someone completely new.

'Okay, okay, but the question is, Sarah: is he aware that you love him? Does he love you back or are you being a bit of a stalker?' Ella raised an eyebrow. 'Because if you are, I think you'll find it's illegal. You should check your little black book of rules; you know the one that they give you when you join the police.' Ella pulled her dressing gown cord tighter around her. 'Besides, if you are on a bit of a stalker mission, I'd rather stay here, curl up on the settee and watch crap on the telly.'

'Ella, he's the one. I just know it.' She smiled seductively, and held her hand over her heart. Ella sighed, stood up and reluctantly walked up the stairs.

'Okay, fine, fine. I'll come, but it's a beach party and I'm wearing jeans.'

* * *

Ella pulled on the jeans, accompanied them with a satin top and tied her hair up in a band before walking down the stairs to a waiting Sarah. 'Is this okay? I put a different top on first, but it was a bit revealing.'

Sarah looked her friend up and down. 'Oh yes. You look mighty good to me, girl.' She stood back and put her hands on her hips. 'It's a good job I'm straight, or you could have been in a whole heap of trouble tonight.' She laughed at her own joke, opened the door and indicated to the taxi driver that they'd soon be out. 'Now, can we go?'

Ella laughed; the comment was typical Sarah. 'I still think I'd rather stay home. It's just...'

Sarah waved her finger in the air. 'No excuses. It's been too long since you went out. At some point, Ella, you need to start your life again. Besides, I've told you, I have to see Josh and I need you to keep me company. Please.' She pushed out her pet lip. 'You know I hate going to parties without you.'

Ella looked herself up and down in the full-length mirror by the front door.

'Come on, Ella. Everyone's waiting at the beach: Jenny's made hot toddies; Simon's got the fire beacons going; and Josh says he's taking a bottle of vodka or schnapps for all of us to drink.'

'Fire beacons on Hunmanby beach? But it's June. Is it cold enough for fire beacons or are we trying to attract a few passing ships? And who is all of us?' Ella looked back down at her top, hoping it looked appropriate. Her hand rubbed over the soft satin material and she unconsciously pulled at the sleeves in order that she might cover her scars. 'I need to change this top, the arms are too short, it's far too revealing. Besides, it's bound to get cold on the beach,' she suddenly announced as once again she ran up the stairs and began pulling jumpers out of the wardrobe.

* * *

Ella jumped out of the taxi, walked across the car park and looked over the cliff edge while Sarah paid the driver. Just as promised, there were fire beacons, music and a crowd of people who she wasn't sure if she knew or not.

'Okay, I'm just going to nip into the loo to check my lippy and I'll be right back,' Sarah announced as she stepped into a portacabin, leaving Ella to stand outside where she took some pleasure in watching the fire beacons as they danced in colours of bright red, orange, blue and gold. It was still daylight, but that didn't stop groups of people from dancing to the regular beat and rhythm of reggae music, the sound of which was almost drowned out by the crashing of the waves as they rolled up and onto the beach. The flames flicked up from the base of the fire cage and shot towards the sky as more and more wood was thrown into its centre. The air was full of a thick smoky odour, making Ella pleased that the breeze was thankfully blowing seaward.

Sarah emerged from the portacabin, mobile phone in hand. 'Okay, we just have to go down the steps and wait at the bottom. Josh is on his way, he'll meet us there in ten.' She smiled, and grabbed hold of Ella's arm. 'Tonight's going to be so much fun.'

Ella followed Sarah down the wooden steps that

led to the beach. 'Okay. What are you up to?' she asked as Sarah giggled, making Ella feel suspicious, but still she pulled her boots off, and threw them down on the sand beside her. She loved the feeling of her feet being free and allowed the sand to run through her toes. It reminded her of that night in the field, the feeling of soft mud that had squelched under foot. It was a memory she'd have thought she'd rather forget and it surprised her that now she felt completely at ease with it. She sat down on the sand, stretched her legs out, pointed her toes towards the warmth of the fires and then noticed people in the crowd looking in her direction, pointing and whispering, making Ella pull the polo neck of the jumper higher up, in order to hide her face from their view.

'Hey, what are you looking at?' Sarah shouted. 'Keep your eyes to yourself, sunshine.' She stood in front of Ella, shoulders back and arms crossed. Ella smiled at the sight of Sarah all dressed up, yet still ready to go into work mode in defence of her friend.

Ella tried to ignore the people and concentrated on the crashing waves that systematically rolled further and further away from her. The tide was retreating and she hoped that the evening darkness would soon close in. For some reason, she preferred the night. It was as though it shielded her from view and gave her back her privacy.

'How long did he say he'd be?' Ella asked as she patted the sand. 'Why don't you sit down?'

'What, in this dress? Not a chance.' Sarah turned and watched the steps that led from car park to beach. 'I don't think he'll be much longer, he said he'd be here by eight. I can't wait for you to meet him.' She bounced up and down with enthusiasm and looked at her watch. 'It's ten to eight.'

'Maybe you should have worn jeans,' Ella added as she looked down at the sand, picked up pebbles that lay beside her and tossed them towards the water. One or two people were paddling up to their knees just to her right, and their screams of laughter could clearly be heard. She felt a surge of sadness run through her. It had been so long since she'd really laughed. She missed the feeling of laughing, of not being able to stop and laughing so much that tears would run down her face.

A cluster of fireworks shot upward, fizzing and banging as an array of colour lit up the sky. A whoop went up from the people to the side of them and Ella stared into the crowd, wishing that Sarah would sit down and relax.

Ella looked up. 'I thought you said that Jenny would be here? I can't see her.'

Sarah shifted uneasily and began pacing up and down. 'She, err... She should be around somewhere.'

The cliffs loomed up high behind her and all Ella could see was the lamplight that came from three tiny houses; each one was perched precariously on top of the rocks, so close to the edge that Ella wondered if one day they might fall off and topple right over into the gap. She looked at her watch and wondered if she should go home. All she really wanted was to be there, behind her locked door, curled up and cosy.

'Josh,' Sarah squealed and immediately wrapped her arms around his neck. 'You have to meet my friend. This is Ella... Ella Hope. She's been my friend forever.'

The tall young man stepped forward, pushed his overgrown dark hair backwards, and held a hand out to shake Ella's hand. But it was the man behind Josh that Ella's eyes were fixed upon.

'Hey, Ella?' Will Taylor suddenly appeared from behind where Josh stood and looked between her and Sarah.

Ella looked from Sarah, to Josh, to Will. She initially didn't put the three together, but then Sarah interjected, 'Oh great, you two already know each other. That makes life easier.'

Ella nodded and watched as both Sarah and Josh shared a knowing smile. 'Sarah, this is Will, my fence jumping next-door neighbour. Will, this is my policewoman friend who tonight is trying to get the world record for wearing the shortest and most sparkly skirt on a beach.' She paused and turned to Sarah. 'But then again, I'm guessing that you already knew that, didn't you?' Their eyes connected. 'I knew you were up to something.'

'Funny, Ella, really funny.' Sarah snuggled into Josh. 'Well, seeing as you two are already acquainted, you don't mind if Josh and I just catch up for ten minutes, do you? We'll just pop along the beach and look for Jenny and those hot toddies.' She moved close to Ella. 'That's okay, right?' she whispered, her hand placed on Ella's shoulder. 'I won't go if you're not happy.'

Ella assessed the situation, took in a deep breath, caught her friend's eye and nodded. After all, being on a crowded beach with Will was probably just as safe as sitting in her own garden with him, wasn't it?

Will was now sitting on the sand. He turned on his knees towards where Sarah still stood and shook her hand. 'Well, it was nice to meet you for all of two minutes,' he said to Sarah and laughed. 'You two go for it. Enjoy the hot toddies.' Then, for just a moment, he seemed to think about his options, before unrolling a blanket and throwing it along the beach. 'Ella, you don't mind, do you?' he asked, pointing to the space beside her. 'Looking at those two, we could be here for a while.' Will was asking for permission to sit beside her on the sand, which made Ella laugh, especially after he'd already pitched his spot, put his blanket in position and seemed to be making himself just a little more than comfortable.

'Sure, make yourself at home. It's as much your beach as it is mine.' She pointed to the blanket. 'Do you always make an interesting entrance?' Her eyes continued to search the crowds, nervously wondering if she should have made a run for home while she had the opportunity. Sarah now had what she came for and even though she knew she wouldn't abandon her, Ella wasn't sure whether to feel set up or like a spare part.

'Of course I do,' Will said, 'especially if there's a chance that someone might feed me. And there's room on this blanket for two.'

'Thank you. Being fed seems to be a hobby of yours. I take it you're hungry?' She laughed and watched as his gaze landed on the beach BBQ that stood in the distance. A group of people worked on ensuring the embers were glowing in the upturned half oil drum that stood on the sand and Ella wondered if they'd ever get it hot enough to cook the steaks.

He began to laugh too. 'I'm always hungry. So... you're here with Sarah?' he asked, while staring at the sea.

Ella nodded. 'Well, I was... But—'

Will chipped in. 'I was bribed into coming with Josh. He insisted that I had to be here tonight.' He turned and looked to where Sarah and Josh moved between friends, chatting as they went, still entwined. 'And now they've left us and disappeared behind that cockle stand.' He pointed along the beach, as Sarah and Josh were lost from view.

Ella pulled a face. 'Really? What for? What are they doing behind there?'

Will raised his eyebrows, then looked back out to sea. 'Well, by the look of them, I doubt they're making sandcastles. I guess I did tell them to go for it; I just didn't think they really would.'

'Nooooooo, seriously? You mean they're... Why would they do that?' Ella blushed and shuffled around as she got comfortable on the blanket. 'I mean, how old are they? Sixteen? Haven't they ever heard of a bedroom?'

Will laughed, then shivered and zipped up his leather jacket. 'I doubt it. I have tried to tell him. But then again, I'm not his dad. It's nothing to do with me what he does, is it?'

'So, Sarah insisted that I come and Josh insisted that you come. And now they've disappeared for a while.' Ella tipped her head to one side. 'Do you get the feeling that we've been just a little bit played?'

'It wouldn't surprise me.' He pulled a rucksack open and pulled two cans of lager from it. 'Want one? They're still kind of cold.'

Ella felt cautious. It wasn't Will that she felt worried about, it was all men, especially those with drinks on offer, and she hesitated before taking the can from him. The last time she'd been given a drink she'd ended up being beaten and fighting for her life in a desolate part of the moors. She found herself automatically checking the can for signs of tampering.

'Thanks.' Ella checked her mobile, flicking through the screen till she found Sarah's name. 'Shall I phone Sarah, see what those two are really up to?'

Will smirked. 'Well, I doubt she'd be very happy if you do. Besides, they've probably gone by now.'

Ella spun around on the sand. 'Why would you say that? Sarah wouldn't leave me!'

'Well, I don't think many women would wear a sequin dress to the beach. Not unless they were going straight to a party.'

Ella's phone bleeped.

Honey, I'm just along the beach. I'm sitting to your right if you need me. Hope you and Will are having fun Xx ps I love you

Ella jumped up and passed Will her phone. 'Okay, so it definitely looks like we were played.'

Will got up too and read the text. 'I knew it, they're trying to set us up.' He paused. 'I should have known that Josh was up to something. He never insists that I go anywhere with him outside of work.' He tipped his head comically from side to side.

Ella sighed. 'Why would they do that?' She took the phone back from him.

Will smiled. 'Look, I admit, I might have mentioned you once or twice in the office. Said that we'd had a laugh the day I cleaned my windows. I have a feeling they've decided to play matchmaker,' he said.

'I'll have a word with Josh. He should never have put you in this position.' Will's fingers touched her arm. 'I'm sorry he did that.'

'Sarah shouldn't have put me in this position either.' Ella kicked at the sand with her toes and tried to ignore the warmth that was spreading upwards from his touch.

'So, what shall we do?'

Ella was puzzled. 'What do you mean?'

'Well, we can either get annoyed with them or we can play them back at their own game.' He raised an eyebrow and winked. 'We could pretend they've done a good thing, let them think we're really happy about tonight and then maybe, just maybe, they'll leave us alone and get on with their own relationship.' He moved a strand of hair from her face as he caught her eye. 'If you'd trust me, I could give you a lift home.'

Ella's eyes opened wide. 'But...' She wriggled on the spot, half with nerves, half with excitement. 'I – I don't know...'

'I'll be a perfect gentleman, I promise. Just a lift straight home and I'll even make sure you get into your house safely, before I go into mine.'

Ella stared at the sea. She had to give Will a chance, had to allow him to prove to her that he was a good person. But still, she felt the nerves that began trembling at her bare toes and didn't stop until they reached her fingers. She rubbed her hands down her jeans and nodded.

'Okay, let's show them.' She locked eyes with Will and felt happy that Sarah had insisted on the night out. They both sat back down on the blanket and it was nice to sit on the beach as the darkness began to surround them. The evening looked as though it could end up being more fun than she'd initially thought and, if she was honest, she really did feel that she could trust Will to take her home. She watched as he turned to watch a group of people who lingered on the beach before them. They stopped and stared, and then another couple stopped in their tracks, and pointed at Ella.

He patted Ella's hand. 'Ignore them.' His voice was soft and kind and Ella took in a deep breath, wishing she could crawl under a rock and hibernate until Christmas. Or at least until everyone stopped talking about what had happened to her.

She looked up and down the beach, her eyes searching for Sarah. She turned her attention to the mobile.

Sarah, where are you and why have you disappeared on me? xx

She held the phone in her hand until it bleeped a response.

Don't worry. I won't leave you. And we only disap-peared because you've been talking about Will all week and, apparently, he's been talking about you too. So, Josh and I decided that it was time that you two spoke to each other. Xx

Ella handed the phone to Will and allowed him to read the text as she stared at the crowd. She'd begun to feel nervous again. She barely knew Will; she hadn't seen him since that night in her garden when they'd eaten his steaks. Since then her life had been busy, but she couldn't deny that she'd looked over the fence daily, just in case he'd been in his garden. Ella watched Will. He stared into the fire beacon. Every emotion seemed to travel through his face and for a moment he looked as though his worst nightmare was about to happen. He must have sensed her looking at him be-cause he turned, and for a short time he caught her eye and a smile lit up his face, before he turned back to the beacon and stared back into the flames. Ella looked at the pile of wood and hoped that there would be enough to keep the beacons burning. After all, the beach would soon be very dark without the glow and the cove had been known to be dangerous at night.

She took the opportunity to study Will. He leaned against the cliff wall, where he'd now pulled his blanket up behind them both. It cushioned them from the cliff and provided a little comfort from its coldness. He was well dressed and tall, or he would be if he were standing up. Ella had noticed the night that he'd leapt over her fence without a shirt on that he had a good, solid frame. He was well built but not overweight. Will was a good-looking man; his face was symmetrical, angular and glowed in the firelight. Yet at that moment, he looked terribly sad and just a little more than vulnerable. She just didn't know why. He rubbed the stubble on his chin with one hand, while his eyebrows moved up and down, in and out of a frown. Tears filled his eyes and Ella could tell that he was deep within his own disturbing thoughts.

Eventually, Will forced himself to turn away from the flames. He closed his eyes momentarily and then opened them to stare out to sea again. He turned to his left and looked towards the town of Filey, where it stood in the distance with its tiny twinkling shore lights.

'Have you been to the cobbles in Filey?' Ella asked quickly. She felt the need to lighten the mood, and stood up to stare at where the deep shadows of the Filey houses stood. She looked down at her boots, picked them up and banged them against the rocks, rubbed the sand from her feet and pushed them into the warm sheepskin interiors.

Will stood up to join her. 'Yes, I went up there to have a look round when I first got here. It's really pretty.'

Ella walked along the beach and Will followed her. 'Back in the old days it was full of atmosphere and fishing boats. The boats used to stand on the cobbles, each one painted a different set of colours making them recognisable from the shore. You see, the wives would stand up there.' She pointed to the cliff tops. 'They used to see the colours of the boats and know when their husbands were safe and coming home. Each man risked his life day after day to bring the fish in. But without a jetty, their boats would get stuck in the sand. They had to be pulled in and pushed out by a tractor, which stood on the cobbles waiting for them every morning and night.'

'That's a beautiful story.'

'Ha. No, it's not. It used to be a beautiful story. Most of the boats have gone; only seven remain and they can only fish for six months of the year. So, their true story, the story of a full and active fishing village, has died. The EU restricted their quotas; they couldn't make a living and most of the men had had enough of getting stuck in the sand, risking their lives and fighting to get both in and out to sea on a daily basis.'

* * *

Will stared at where the fishing town stood in the distance. Even though they were probably a mile or two away, he could just make out the lights that still lit up the shape of the harbour wall. The town was large, full of tiny terraced houses and he suspected that fishing had supported many of the local households for years. After all, other than tourism and chip shops, what else did the town have?

'Life sucks. It must have really changed for the people up there,' he said as he thought of how much his own life had changed during the past year. Of course, he hadn't lost his livelihood. But one minute he'd had all the people around him that he loved and, quite literally, the next minute everything changed. He'd lost everything and everyone; they'd all gone.

'It does,' Ella muttered. 'I remember interviewing one of the fishermen on his last day at sea. We did a double page spread about it. He couldn't carry on fishing as there was no money in it any more, yet he had no idea what else he would or could do. It's all he'd ever known, you see. Fishing had been his life for as long as he could remember, and his father's life before him. They'd taken out loans to buy the boat and, as far as I'm aware, the boat's standing in dry dock and sadly the family are still paying for it, month after month.'

'But as a reporter, you could have made a difference, brought attention to the industry?' The words were more of a statement than a question and Will watched as Ella swallowed hard and then took small tentative sips of the lager from her can.

'Yes, I'm a reporter and I did try, but it was just before, you know, and my injuries changed everything,' she whispered, before once again turning and staring out to sea. 'I haven't worked since the accident. But my job's being held open for me and I am planning on going back to work soon.'

Will walked over to the beacon, threw a log into the cage and then made his way back to stand by her side. He was beginning to understand why she felt so angry. There were three sides to almost every article. First you got the reporter. He'd look for and find the story. He'd get to the bottom of the facts, he'd write it, and be responsible for putting it into print. Then you got the reader. The person who would buy the paper. They'd read it, and digest it. Some articles would stay with them, but most would be forgotten within the day. And then, finally, there was the victim, there was a person like Ella whose whole world had been turned upside down by a single incident. Their lives would be exposed for the world to read and they'd be the type of person who everyone thought they knew, just because they'd read what the papers had said.

God, she looked so vulnerable, so beautiful, yet so very defenceless.

They returned to where Will's blanket lay on the beach. He placed his barely drunk lager can in the sand, concentrating on it as he turned it round and round to ensure it wouldn't fall over, then he rested his knee against a rock and clasped his hands tightly together. He had an overwhelming urge to hold Ella, to pull her close, to keep her safe and to tell her that everything would be okay. He wanted to prove to her that not all men were cruel, barbaric or evil. But instead, he closed his eyes against the sea breeze, forcing himself to stay where he was, knowing that to move towards her, or to hold her was the last thing he should do. She barely knew him and he knew that any sudden action from him would most probably terrify her – as it had the night he'd first met her – and the last thing he wanted was to send her running vertically up the cliff face in fear.

'... yeah, really wish I could get out of it.'

Will's thoughts came back to the present, and he realised that Ella had been speaking but he had been so deep in thought that he hadn't heard anything but the 'get out of it' part.

'Sorry, I missed that...' He now looked directly into her face as she spoke, searched her eyes and noticed tears forming in their corners.

'I wish I could get out of the job. I feel I need to do something else. I thought about becoming a photographer; it's kind of what I do anyhow. I do take the pictures that go with my articles. So it wouldn't be too much of a change in direction.' She was focused, adamant and determined. 'And, if I'm honest, I think I could cope with that. I like taking photos, I love capturing a single moment in time. It's something to remember the past by.' She took a tentative sip from the can, then looked away from his face and into the burning embers of the fire beacon. 'I never really saw how hurtful it all was before, not till I was on the receiving end. So now, now I have two choices: I need to be a better reporter, or I need to do something else.'

Will nodded in agreement. 'I think being a photographer could be fun. Just think of all the weddings you'd get to attend.'

Ella slapped Will's arm. 'I'd most probably take photos in refugee camps, warzones or the Arctic.' Her hand rested on his arm for a moment too long, but she quickly snapped it back to rest back upon her own knee.

Will rubbed his arm. Not that the slap had hurt; it hadn't. But he'd enjoyed her touch and wished she'd left her hand there a little longer. He thought about his life since Ella had returned home. He'd seen her pottering in her garden on so many of his days off. She'd been tending, nurturing and sometimes just staring at a plant for what seemed like forever and, only yesterday, he'd watched as she'd sat for hours on the bench with a book on her knee. She hadn't looked at it once. She'd just stared endlessly into space, deep in thought and, if he was totally honest, there were so many days when he'd happily have sat there with her.

'I think you'd enjoy being a photographer, but I'm so sorry you want to leave the reporting industry. It should have been kinder to you.' Will spoke the words and meant them. He was annoyed with every reporter that had ever written anything about her case. For all the articles that had upset her. For the untruths that had hurt her. It was very obvious that she still had no idea what he did for a living. And he wondered how she'd feel when she finally found out that he was the Editor of the Scarborough Star. He looked at his beer can that was partially buried in the sand and shook his head. He knew he should have told her what he did on the first day they'd met. He'd had the chance in the garden while they'd drunk the wine. But he'd been hungry and the thought of pizza had preoccupied his mind. He knew she'd spotted him in the court and, for a while, he thought she'd have mentioned it. She had probably thought him to be a nosy neighbour who'd popped along to listen in. His stomach twisted inside; whether he told her now or not, she'd think the worst. The last thing he wanted was to lose the small amount of friendship they'd now developed, but he had no choice. He had to tell her the truth.

He stood up and walked to a more desolate area of the beach. He bent down, picked up stones and skimmed them towards the sea. He noticed Ella paying attention to his technique before collecting a handful of stones of her own. She took her position beside him and began skimming them much further than he had; a silent but competitive challenge began.

'Ella, look... I – I need to tell you something...' he began, just as a huge, radiant smile came over Ella's face. She dropped her handful of stones and ran past him to hug Sarah, who stood before them.

* * *

'You have some explaining to do,' Ella growled. She then looked at Josh, who'd crept up behind where Sarah stood. 'And you too.'

'Come on, Ella. Don't get grumpy with me. It's not like I left you, is it? I'm a copper, I was sitting up there, watching and protecting you. I could see everything you were doing,' Sarah murmured as she once again pulled Ella into her arms and began whispering in her ear. 'I must admit though, I did think about going. You did look kind of cosy there with your gorgeous neighbour friend, hun.'

Ella sighed with relief, then looked up and caught the mischievous look in Will's eyes. The earlier comments of playing Sarah and Josh back at their own game came back and she remembered how Will had offered to take her home. Could she really trust him? Could she really get in a car with him, alone?

'Honey, why don't you just do that?' Ella suggested. 'Josh looks like he'd rather be anywhere else in the world than here, babysitting me. Will here has offered to take me home. He does live next door, so it kind of makes sense, doesn't it?'

Sarah looked from Ella to Will. 'Oh, right, okay. Are you sure?' Sarah cheekily ran her tongue across her teeth and leaned in close. 'Honey, don't do this if you're not ready.'

'Sarah, Will's my friend. I'll be fine.' She linked arms with Will, pulled herself into his side and glanced up to catch his eye.

Sarah stood, open-mouthed. 'But—'

'Sarah, honestly, she'll be fine,' Will chipped in. 'It's not like you don't know who I am. You know where I live, you know where I work and I'm sure that within half an hour of our leaving, you'll be on the phone to Ella asking for the low-down.' He picked up the can of lager that was still wedged in the sand. 'And I've only drunk around half an inch out of this can, so I'm perfectly safe to drive.'

'Ella, are you sure?'

Ella felt Sarah's glare as she held her shoulders and searched her eyes for any indication that she wasn't happy. But Ella nodded. 'Honestly, you two get off. Go and enjoy yourselves.'

Sarah shuffled on the spot. 'Well, we do kind of have some unfinished business that we'd really like to take care of, if you know what I mean... So...' She continued to hug Ella and a laugh came from somewhere deep within her. It started soft, but turned dirty, making Ella know exactly what the unfinished business was.

10

Will dropped his keys into his desk drawer, slammed it shut, switched on his laptop and stared into the screen which illuminated his office. It was dark outside and over an hour since he'd dropped Ella off at her house.

The journey back from the beach had been quite tense. Even though Ella had chatted quite openly, he'd glanced over to where she'd sat and had felt his heart reach out to her as she'd practically clung to the car door during the whole journey home. Her nails had dug into the vinyl and he'd noticed how, at one point, she'd opened the window, just a fraction to allow the breeze to waft her in the face. He knew she'd been nervous of getting in a car with a man she barely knew and rightly so, especially after what she'd been through. He'd watched the fear as it tore through her face, just as it had that night in her garden and once again he had wanted to reach across, pull her into his arms, erase all the bad memories and take away every inch of her pain. But just as he'd realised on the beach, he knew that he couldn't. It would have been the worst thing he could have done. What's more, it was obvious that she didn't want to be touched, comforted or looked after. To do any of these things could have had her leaping from the vehicle whilst still in motion.

The only thing that made him feel just a little better was the fact that she'd have probably acted exactly the same way if she were alone in a taxi.

He looked up at the clock. It was now well past midnight. The office was closed and the only journalists still working would be typing up reports from home, not sitting behind a desk in a dark and empty office block. But he'd been unable to sleep. After dropping Ella off, he'd gone into his house and paced in and out of the newly-fitted kitchen, before taking himself to bed, where he'd tossed and turned, his head full of Ella. The things that she'd told him had gone around and around in his mind. She'd told him about what she'd gone through first-hand.

She'd repeated her dislike of reporters and once again he'd tried to tell her about his job. But Ella had begun to sneeze repeatedly, and once again the moment had been lost. He knew that he had to tell her, he just didn't know how.

Somehow, he had to prove to her that he was different. She'd told him that there had been just one reporter she'd trusted, just one that she'd allowed to help her, which meant that there was hope of getting her to trust him too. He just didn't know how without her considering that he might just be one of the vultures that had hurt her so badly before.

He knew she'd seen him in court. He'd sat there for the duration of the trial, hiding at the back of the gallery, listening to the evidence, yet at the time even he hadn't understood why he'd gone. He'd had another reporter covering the case, writing a story that he knew he'd eventually edit. So, there was no real purpose for him being there. Except for the fact that he cared. He'd wanted to make sure that Ella was okay. He'd wanted to see the man accused of attacking her, but most of all he'd wanted to see her get justice.

But her case had fallen apart and her 'so called' attacker had been set free, and he'd moved mountains to ensure that his paper had stayed impartial.

The last thing he'd wanted was for Ella to look bad, but he knew that by writing the truth, Rick Greaves would have got the sympathy vote. After all, he'd been a man who it appeared had been falsely detained for six months, only to be set free at the end of the court case. The defence barrister had blown the whole case apart and Will had seen the torment that Ella had gone through. In his eyes she'd been through enough already and the last thing she needed was for him to plaster her face all over the front page of the Scarborough Star, so he'd carefully positioned the well-edited story on page six with a short headline that he hoped would gain no attention.

He began hammering at the keyboard, writing full sentences and then deleting them again with the ferocity of a jackhammer. He slammed his fist down on the desk, making cold coffee jump out of a mug and splash over the sides. He then pulled a tissue from his drawer and began to dry up the mess.

He had to find a way to prove to Ella that not all reporters were bad. He closed his eyes and clasped his hands together. He knew that Ella felt as though the system had failed her, felt as though her attacker had walked free, that justice hadn't been done and, in her own words, she wouldn't rest until she brought her attacker back to court and sent to prison for what he'd done.

Will opened his eyes and stared back at his screen. If only he could help her, if only he could find out what really happened that night. If only he could unravel the clues, find out who Rick Greaves really is. Surely if a man of his size and physique had attacked Ella, he would have easily killed her. So why hadn't he? Why had he left her for dead? Why hadn't he finished the job? Had he been disturbed? Had he had second thoughts? Had something happened to make him flee the scene? And why, after he must have known that Ella had seen it, why had he been so stupid to put the hoodie in the gym's dustbin? But then, on the other hand, what if the jury had been right? What if Rick was innocent? What if... A host of possibilities swirled before him. Will was determined to find the truth. After all, it was his job to dig into things that didn't appear right. It was his job to get to the bottom of things and, if he could, he'd make sure that Rick Greaves was brought to justice not only for Ella, but also for his two wives that had previously died in suspicious circumstances. Had their deaths been a horrid coincidence? Had Rick Greaves really been so unlucky that he should lose two wives so quickly after marriage, and both before they were thirty-five?

He knew he had to find a way to give Ella peace of mind. It was the only way she'd move forward with her life. And only when she began moving forward would she start trusting again. After doing the job for so many years, deep down she must realise that not all reporters were bad. She cared about everyone and everything and it must occur to her that others cared too.

A noise in the corridor startled him. He looked up, stood up from the desk and walked to the back door of the building, and opened it at speed.

'Josh, what the hell are you doing here?'

Josh fell through the door, his trousers undone and hanging around his knees. Both he and Sarah landed heavily on the carpet, with Sarah still practically attached to his anatomy. At the sight of Will, Josh forcibly pushed Sarah away, fastened his trousers and looked around as though he hoped, for some bizarre reason, that Will hadn't noticed what they'd been doing or that Sarah was now comically crawling on hands and knees towards the back door.

'Boss, you gave me a fright. It's after midnight.' He looked at his watch as though confirming the time. 'What the hell are you doing here?' It was more than obvious that both he and Sarah had drunk far too much since leaving the beach and they both began to giggle.

'Sarah, it's time to go home. Josh, phone a taxi and put her in it,' Will growled. 'Right now!'

Josh stopped laughing and nervously pushed his glasses up his nose, before staring at the floor. 'But, Will, come on, don't be so grumpy, we're not hurting anyone... Are we?'

'NOW,' Will shouted as he walked back into his office and slammed the door behind him. He didn't have time to listen to Josh's excuses, nor did he really want to hear them. He had too much to do, too much to think about. He sat down and once again began tapping at the keyboard. He searched his own newspaper archives for Rick Greaves, flicked through several pages of data and then clicked on the image icon that appeared at the top of the page. Numerous pictures popped up and he moved slowly through them, one by one.

Rick Greaves stared back from each of them. All had been used by his newspaper in the past, but most had been years before. Will scratched his head, wondering why there were so many. He seemed to be with many different women and Will recognised one or two of them from the courtroom. 'Quite the lothario, aren't we?' Will whispered, and continued to flick forward until he came to the ones from the time Rick's first wife had died, then the second. He quickly took note of the article numbers. Rick's first wife, Julia Greaves, had died when she had fallen into a cesspit while out running. His second wife, Patsy Greaves, had been an estate agent and she'd fallen down the stairs while giving an evaluation on an empty property. Both were strange ways to die, but both could have been legitimate accidents.

Will listened for sounds of Josh, but heard nothing. He sighed and then flicked backwards until he came to one of Rick's wedding photographs. For a few moments Will looked at the bride who was looking up at Rick with a look of pure love. But Rick's face told a different story.

Why did he glare at the crowd? Who was he glaring at? 'What are you still doing here?' Will asked as Josh fell back through the door and into the office. He dropped haphazardly into the chair by Will's desk and slouched into an almost laying down position.

'I can explain, you know, about...' Josh blushed and stared at the floor.

Will sighed. 'Do you know what, Josh? Don't. Don't explain, because I really don't want to hear it.

She's in the force, for God's sake. Can't she get dismissed for that sort of thing?' He waved an arm around in the air. 'You know, in a public place?' He tapped his pencil on the desk, wondered how he was supposed to deal with Josh, shook his head and tried to calm down. Josh was young, was ruled by his libido. In the short time that Will had known him, he'd quickly worked out that Josh's sole purpose for living was to get to his next lay, preferably within a single day of the last.

'It's hardly a public place, is it?' He looked around, over his shoulder and then back to where Will was sitting. 'And she wouldn't really get sacked, would she?'

Will looked up. 'I have no idea, Josh. I think the cockle sheds might have been a bit public, don't you? And if you hadn't been too busy trying to get into her knickers, you might have thought about how many people were enjoying the view.'

'Come on, boss. We didn't do anything on the beach. We were trying to give you and Ella a bit of space. But me and Sarah, well, there was no trying about it, we really would have got laid if you hadn't been here.'

'Enough. I really don't need to know. Is she safe? Did you put her in a taxi?'

'Yes. She's on her way home.' He overempha-
sised the nod, wheeled the chair further away from
the desk, crossed his legs and nervously began
poking his ear with a finger.

'Good. Now, for God's sake, Josh, don't do it
again.' Will stood up and walked round the desk to
perch on its edge. 'This is an office, it's where we
work, it's not a goddamned knocking shop. Is that
clear?' Will sighed. 'Besides, she has her own house.
Why don't you go there next time?'

Josh continued to stare at the floor. 'Yes. Sorry. I
guess we didn't think of that,' he said, with a glazed,
drunken look.

'Good, now I'm going to make you some strong
coffee, help sober you up, and while I do so I want
you to look at that photograph on my screen and tell
me what you think.' He moved away from his desk
and walked towards the kitchen.

Josh looked up, sighed and then stood up to walk
around the desk, where he stared at Will's computer
screen. 'That's that bloke's wedding day, isn't it?' His
finger touched the screen. 'For a man who just got
married, he doesn't look very happy, does he?' He
picked up the cold coffee and took a sip. 'Yuk, this
coffee's cold.'

'Of course it's cold. That's mine from earlier,'

Will shouted from the kitchen. 'Who is Greaves looking at in the photo?'

'Isn't that the guy that got done for fraud?' He tapped at the screen. 'We did a story on it. He used to be Rick's business partner, but now he just works for him.' Josh laughed and leaned closer to the screen, caught the stapler and sent it flying off the desk, where it broke open, spilling staples all over the floor.

'Shit, sorry.'

'Ex-business partner, that's interesting,' Will's voice shouted as he came through from the kitchen. 'What've you just broken?'

Josh looked puzzled as he took the coffee from Will's outstretched hand. 'Err, just a stapler, I'll clean it up. But can you rewind a bit? Why do you care about who Rick Greaves is looking at? I mean, fill me in, I'm totally lost.'

Will paused and wondered whether it was worth carrying on. Josh could barely focus, never mind make a sensible assumption. 'Go home, Josh, we'll do this tomorrow.'

'No, not yet. I'm intrigued. I want to know what you're thinking.' Josh had now switched into work mode. He studied the picture.

'Well, this photo is from our archives, not from

the internet. Which means we used it in a story.' Will wrote the reference number down. 'Here, I want all the details about this story. I want the headline and the facts.' Will's finger tapped at the screen. 'I want you to find out as much as you can about his former business partner. I'm sure it's him that Rick is glaring at.' Will paused and enlarged the picture. 'And on Monday morning, go down to the register office. I'd like to get hold of a copy of the death certificates.'

'Whose death certificates?'

'I want to see the death certificates of both Patsy and Julia Greaves. I want the hospital report, the coroner's report. I want everything. And, above all that, I want to know who the business partner is, what went wrong and what he's got on Rick Greaves.' He once again used a finger to stab at the screen. 'I've got a feeling that something isn't right and I think he's at the centre of it.' Will picked up his coffee. 'We're going to get to the bottom of this, Josh. Even if it kills me.'

11

Ella couldn't sleep. It was almost daybreak and she'd tossed and turned for hours. Her body ached, her mind spun and she'd sat up, pumped up the pillows and thrown herself back at the mattress so many times she'd lost count. She'd tried every technique she could think of, yet she was still wide awake and for the past two hours she'd literally counted the tiny red rose buds that were embroidered on her curtains.

Eventually she stopped counting and stopped trying to get back to sleep. She sighed, wriggled around and finally tossed the duvet to one side. After opening the curtains, she sat back down on the bottom of the bed and stared out of the window across to the farm and to where Bobby's tractor stood by the side of his barn. The sun was just beginning to rise. Its amber glow looked all hazy, giving the fields a misty yet ambient look.

Her mind had been going over and over what had happened the night before, what had been said and how she'd felt. Her trip to the beach had been fun, but not what she'd been expecting. Sarah and Josh disappearing on her had set her on edge and, even though Will had been great company and Sarah had assured her that she was still watching, the whole evening had made her just a little bit anxious. She thought about how she'd have handled the situation three or four months before and came to the conclusion that she wouldn't have coped at all, and with a nod of her head she decided that progress towards her recovery had definitely been made. She cast her mind to Will. He was so good looking. He appeared to be reliable and, deep down, she was sure that she trusted him. But despite all that, the drive home had given her palpitations. Her stomach had been turning, her heart had been pounding and she'd felt so nauseous that she began wishing she could get out and walk. She'd eventually resorted to opening the window a little to allow the wind to blow in her face, while all the time she'd gripped the door handle of the car as though her life had depended on it.

Walking down the stairs, Ella allowed her hand to press against the wall, knowing that Will's staircase stood to the other side. His cottage was a mirror image of hers, identical in every way except for the conservatory she'd added the year before. She whispered a silent apology to him through the wall. He'd done nothing wrong, yet when they'd pulled up outside, she'd scarpered into her cottage like a frightened animal. And now she really thought about it, she'd been rude and hadn't even thanked him for bringing her home.

Ella stepped into the kitchen and switched on the kettle. She felt the need to speak to Will. She wanted to sit with him, chat to him and share food with him. She laughed. 'Why do I feel the need to share his food?' She opened the fridge door, pulled out the milk and poured it into her coffee, before walking through to the conservatory where she stood for a moment with the door wide open.

She'd already watched the sunrise and now from where she stood at the back of the house, she saw the day was promising to be warm. She pulled her dressing gown tightly around her, picked up a magazine from the hallway table and headed for the garden bench with her coffee in hand, where she sat and stared at the garden.

* * *

It was just after seven o'clock in the morning when Will pulled the car up onto his drive. He slumped in his seat, too exhausted to move. He'd spent the whole night at the office. He was tired, couldn't wait to climb into his own bed and felt relieved that it was Sunday. A day when he could curl up for hours, without any good reason to get up.

The time spent at the office had been useful. He'd been pleased with the information he'd dug up on Rick Greaves and more than that, he'd now worked out who Rick had been glaring at in the photograph, as well as all the relationships he'd had, hadn't had and had almost had. He'd been quite a guy in his time and not always for the good. All of that knowledge was moving around his mind, like a production line where one piece of jigsaw after the other was zooming along and dropping heavily into place. He just wasn't sure which piece of information fit where or whether there would be gaps in the jigsaw once he'd finished throwing it all together.

Will stretched in the car seat. Ella's kitchen light was on and he stared at the amber glow, wondering if she'd left the light on for safety or whether, like him, she was either already up or hadn't slept.

The thought that she might be so close made him smile. She could be standing in the kitchen right now, making coffee. He contemplated going around, knocking on the door, and checking that all was okay. Realistically he hoped that she might make him some tea and toast and that they'd get to sit together on the bench, chatting.

Climbing out of the car he crept over to the fence that separated his and Ella's garden. He crouched down to peep through the same hole that he'd looked through just a few weeks before. But instead of spotting Ella through the kitchen window, he could clearly see her, fast asleep on the bench. She looked beautiful, peaceful with a magazine clutched in her hand and her dressing gown pulled tightly around her. Will noticed an abandoned coffee mug on the small wall, which meant that she'd probably been there for a while.

Once again, he found himself staring through a fence, feeling uneasy and wondering what he should do next. Should he shout, wake her or sneak away and allow her to sleep? Would she be embarrassed if she knew he'd been there? He stood up and stretched, deciding that it would be better if he never mentioned that he'd seen her.

He looked back at his own house, to where his own bed waited, to where he'd finally get some sleep and, after a few moments, he made the decision to leave Ella be.

* * *

Ella stirred. The sun had warmed her face and she moved her shoulders in an attempt to get cosy, but couldn't. She was uncomfortable; confused she stretched out her leg in an awkward movement. A sudden crashing sound made her jolt and she opened her eyes to see the broken mug where it had fallen from the wall and landed with a bang on the patio. 'What the...' She suddenly remembered the night before. The memory came back to her, along with the long sleepless night she'd endured before she'd made her way out to the bench. She sat up, pulling the dressing gown around her body.

There was a noise. The gate flew open and she

jumped up from her seat. 'Hi, Miss Ella. How are you today?'

Ella froze on the spot.

'Bobby, what the hell are you doing here?' she asked as he trotted past her and into the garden.

Her breathing became erratic, her heart pounded and she began to inch her way towards the back door as she weighed up the situation. Bobby had made his way to the bottom of the garden with a huge smile on his face, while all the time pushing a lawn mower across the grass.

'It's Sunday, Miss Ella. So I thought I'd cut the grass for you.' He laughed. 'I don't think God will miss me at church, not for one week.' He suddenly stopped in his tracks, looked Ella up and down and then spun around to face the other way. 'Oh... Oh no. I'm so sorry. You're not dressed.' He shuffled on the spot and kept glancing over his shoulder. 'I should go. I'm sorry.'

Ella had already reached the back door. Her whole body shook and she hesitated, took a deep breath and tried to keep her voice calm. 'Bobby. Please. You really don't have to cut the grass.' She clung to the door handle and watched as Bobby stood with his back to her. His head suddenly dropped and he looked down at the path. 'I mean,' she continued, 'I really appreciate that you did this for me, but I can do it myself now.'

'But I like doing it for you, Miss Ella. You're my friend and I like to look after my friends.' The words were heartbreaking; he sounded so sad. But Ella couldn't cope. The anxiety was too much and she really didn't want anyone invading her personal space. Her eyes closed, but then flashed open again. 'Bobby. You have to stop. We're not friends. We barely know each other and as for cutting the lawn, I can bloody well do it myself!' She shouted at him, then slammed the door, locked it and slid down to the floor behind it. Images of axe murderers crossed her mind and, in her panic, she quickly grabbed the phone and moved to the stairs, where she sat halfway up, shaking. Her whole body shook. She couldn't breathe and her fingers stumbled over the numbers as she searched for Will's number.

A loud, sporadic knocking at the door made her jump. Tears were streaming down her face and she moved further up the stairs. 'GO AWAY, I'll call the police,' she screamed, while wiping her eyes on the sleeve of her dressing gown. 'You can't keep coming here, I've told you, I don't want you here.'

Then there was a second knock. 'Ella, Ella, it's

me. It's Will. What happened? Are you okay? Please, please, open the door.'

Ella moved quickly down the stairs, opened the door and fell into Will's arms. 'I know I shouldn't have, but I just shouted at Bobby.' A huge sob left her throat. 'I know he was only helping, but... but...'

'I know, I know,' Will whispered as he held her in his arms. 'He scared you, didn't he? Don't worry, he's gone.'

* * *

I walk up and down, pacing, thinking of what to do next. I thought that things would be better but they are not. There's nothing to brighten my mood and no one to care. I have no friends, no one likes me.

All I can think of is what I have done. Of who I have already disposed of. Of who will be my next victim, of who has recently got in my way and of how I will kill them. There are so many possibilities, but only one person really sticks in my mind. One person monopolises my thoughts and I know that you will be next.

I'm tired, I need to sleep, I need to get the image of you out of my mind. I don't want to be alone with my evil, twisted thoughts and I make my way to bed in the hope that I might find comfort in my sleep. I enjoy the feeling of falling into the darkness like an abyss and I wonder if this is what it's like to die, if this is what my victims feel just moments before they are gone, or if there is more. Is there a bright light at the end of a tunnel or a rainbow to run beneath? I think for a moment and hope for the darkness as I slip into a deep, yet troubled sleep.

12

For the first time in months the gym was overcrowded. People queued for the equipment and the ones that were exercising pulled, danced and moved in rhythm to the music that boomed throughout the main room.

Michelle's eyes were everywhere, all at once. She pushed a hand through her short, blonde hair as she strutted across the gym to where the water coolers stood. She caught her reflection in a mirror and smiled. Her recent weight loss was showing and the Lycra was looking good. She twisted to check out the new, cute shape of her backside, just as one of the male members walked past and whistled.

'Behave,' she shouted as she made her way to look through the window of the studio, where at least thirty women were dancing around all in perfect time to Zumba. The sound of dance music seeped from the room and into the gym where the grunting and clanging could be heard as the male members picked up weights that were far too heavy for them and then resorted to dropping them on the mats with loud and resounding thuds. 'If it's too heavy to put down, it's too heavy to pick up,' she shouted out loud. 'I'm sure the floor will fall through one day.' She pulled at the paper towel dispenser and reached up to wipe a mark from one of the mirrors.

It had been a long time since there'd been such a buzz in the air. It was good to see that everyone was smiling, laughing and joking again. All the people who'd previously stayed away were back and Michelle smiled at the prospect of business picking back up. 'Nothing like your boss being banged up to kill the flow of customers,' she whispered. Again, she studied the activity around her. It was her job to ensure the members stayed safe, that none of them injured themselves whilst working out and she was also there to instruct, should she be needed.

Michelle thought of the court case. It had been a whole week since Rick had been released, but today he'd messaged to say he was back from the holiday he'd gone on to get over his prison experience and he'd be back at the gym later. The message had filled her with a mixture of nerves and excitement. She looked forward to seeing him, but knew that things would be different between them than they had been before – their relationship had changed and they were closer now than they'd ever previously been. She danced on the spot; it was a relationship she really wanted to develop further. A relationship she'd nurtured and a romance that had begun many years before. They'd worked together for years and on one or two occasions in the past they'd had brief encounters, especially after he'd lost both of his wives. She'd been there for him, so much more than anyone else and blushed at the thought that this time, he might just fall for her. This time, she'd be the one and this time she'd have the chance of love and a future with him, something she'd wanted for a very long time.

Michelle took a sip of water from the water cooler. It was all she could think to do to quell the flip-flopping of her stomach, which seemed to do a somersault every single time the door opened and another member walked in. Picking up her mobile, she re-read the message, taking special notice of the kiss he'd left at the end.

Home from holiday. Be in later, looking forward to getting stuck in. Rick x

Once again, she glanced at her watch and took in a deep breath. 'Soon, he'll be here soon,' she whispered to herself. Spotting a random towel left by the cross trainer, she walked across the gym and picked it up, before heading back to reception where she dropped it in a box by the desk.

'Come on, come on, you can't be long now, can you?' She stood by reception, nervously tapping her foot up and down while scanning the whole room. She tried to decide what Rick would think of the changes. She hoped he'd like the new layout, and the new colours. They'd painted the walls and the reception had been moved closer to the door. After all, all the staff had had a lot of time on their hands over the past few months, and with the lack of customers they'd used the time wisely by decorating, moving the equipment around and creating spaces for each type of activity. Clear, defined areas could now be seen and Michelle liked the idea that the big weights, where the men grunted and growled, were now as far away from the light weights and aerobic mats as possible. At least now the members could use the mats and meditate or stretch without worrying that a thirty-kilo dumb-bell would crash to the floor beside them.

'Nina!' she shouted. 'Where are you?' She listened and waited for an answer, but when no reply came, she shouted again, her voice now slightly raised. 'Nina!' She flung open the door to the staffroom to see Nina's tiny frame sitting in a corner, her mobile pressed tightly to her ear. 'Nina, I won't shout again,' she urged, 'please, the place is heaving, and the mirrors, they still need polishing.'

Nina shrugged and turned back into the corner. She flicked her long, dark hair over her shoulder in defiance and whispered into the handset. She finished the call, dabbed at her tear-filled eyes so as not to smudge her thick, black eye make-up and grabbed a handful of polishing cloths. 'Okay, okay. I'll do them now.' She paused and sniffed. 'Only reason I didn't do them before was because old Joe was on the cross trainer, you know, doing his stuff. I didn't want to disturb him.' Her voice held a note of belligerence as she pushed the mobile in her pocket and stamped towards the mirrors.

Michelle didn't like her attitude. Nina had changed. Her moods were all over the place, one minute happy, the other minute sad to the point of devastation and on other days she seemed to have an air of defiance about her that no one could control.

'Nina, are you okay? Because...' Michelle stumbled over her words. Was it her job to control Nina's moods? Was she expected to be a psychoanalyst on top of everything else? She looked Nina up and down. Her frame was small, her features petite, and she looked and acted more like a teenager than a woman in her twenties.

'Nina, you do know you shouldn't be on your phone, don't you? Not during work time.'

Nina stopped in her tracks, and turned. Tears now fell down her face. 'It was my stepdad. You know what he's like. I can't ignore him. You know that.' She wiped her eyes on the back of her sleeve. 'So please don't start on me. I've had a horrible day.' She stared directly at Michelle who passed her a tissue from the box on reception. 'I don't want to live there, or with him, but I can't afford to move. Not on what I'm paid here and he says that if I can't contribute more, I have to get out.' She blew her nose on the tissue. 'Did you say Rick was coming in later? I need to see him. I need more hours.' She tipped her head to one side waiting for an answer.

Michelle nodded. 'He'll be busy though. Don't you go bothering him about hours, not on his first day back.' The truth was that Michelle wanted Rick to herself and didn't want to share him, not today.

'But, Michelle...' Again, she sobbed. 'I'll be homeless.' Nina was still young. Her mother had died years before and she'd been left to live with a stepfather she hated.

'Okay, you can ask him when he gets here. Just don't jump on him the minute he walks through the door. If anyone gets to do that, it'll be me.' Michelle smirked.

'Wow. Why the hell would he want you jumping all over him?' Nina responded sharply with her hands on her hips. 'You're not his type, are you? You're far too, you know, butch.'

The words hit Michelle like a sledgehammer and she turned and walked rapidly towards the staffroom. 'Just go and make those mirrors sparkle, will you? And don't stop till they do,' she added as she swung open the staffroom door. She had no idea why Nina had been so cruel. No idea why she'd been more than happy to hurt her feelings, or why she would call her butch. Michelle sighed and once again checked her phone for messages. She wondered if Rick would text again or if he would just walk in like he'd never been away. Either way, she was determined to look good, determined to look feminine and sexy so that Rick would want to spend time with her, although she knew that her time with Rick would be limited, especially today. She looked towards the office where the office manager, Tim, had been hiding since before breakfast. Tim used to own the gym, alongside Rick. But money had been laundered. Tim had dug a hole so deep that he couldn't get out and eventually Rick had worked out the truth. Walls had been punched, whole mirrors had been smashed and equipment had been thrown. But, when the crunch came to the crunch, Tim was still family. He was the brother of Rick's first wife, and once he'd calmed down Rick had used his own money to pay off Tim's debt. He'd saved him from going to prison and in return Rick had taken complete control of the business. But all the time Rick had been in prison, Tim had been running the place, acting all weird again and Michelle knew that whatever was going on behind that door, Rick wasn't going to like it.

Michelle picked up her handbag, rummaged through it to find her make-up and sprayed herself with perfume. She smiled at the thought of seeing Rick again, but now her mind was clouded with doubt. Could Nina be right? She looked at herself from all angles in the mirror. Come to think of it, her hair was short. It was practical for work, but Michelle thought of Rick's wives and girlfriends. All had had either long or shoulder-length hair. All had been slim, like her, and all had had perfect smiles. She smiled at herself in the mirror. 'Not bad,' she whispered. 'Not butch.' She shook her head but frowned with doubt. 'Definitely, hopefully not butch.'

She'd been to visit him in prison, on the pretext that she wanted to keep him involved in the changes at the gym. She'd taken colour swatches with her and had discussed the décor and the movement of equipment, and it had quickly become apparent that over the past few months he'd warmed towards her. She'd always made sure she looked her best. She'd worn make-up and she'd purposely worn the per-fume he'd commented on previously, and on one occasion he'd hugged her when she'd arrived and kissed her on the cheek as she'd left. That had to be a good sign, didn't it?

The memory filled her with a warm glow. But she wasn't stupid. She knew that Rick was a ladies' man. She knew he chatted up anyone in a skirt, but she also knew that he'd been hurt in the past, and that he'd allowed himself to love before. He'd been more than happy to settle down and it hadn't been his fault that on both occasions he'd been dealt the cruellest of blows. With each blow, Michelle had had another chance, another opportunity to win her prize; she'd been there for him, allowed him to cry on her shoulder. But on both occasions, she'd lost out to others and had to stand by and watch as he romanced other women. This time she intended to win.

Dropping her handbag back down to the floor, Michelle wiped the sink and the toilet around with a wet cloth, and polished them off, before once again studying her appearance in the mirror. Satisfied that she looked the best she could, she glanced over her shoulder to see Nina, just standing with her arms dropped by her sides. She was watching her. Studying her. And Michelle didn't like it.

'Nina, haven't you got anything to do?' She put

both her hands on her hips. 'Go see if Tim wants a coffee, he's in the office no doubt cooking the books before Rick gets back.' She laughed at her own joke, but deep down knew how close to the truth that joke was.

Michelle once again grabbed her handbag and pulled a lipstick from within. She studied the colour; it was a deeper red than she normally wore, but she felt mischievous. She was determined not to look butch in any way and touched it lightly to her lips. Pleased now that her appearance said come and get me, she pulled her fingers through her short hair. 'There you go, you look amazing, he'll love you,' she whispered to herself with an appreciative, but cunning smile. 'Who'll love you?' Nina asked. 'I hope you're not thinking Rick will, cause Rick loves no one, only himself.' She'd walked up behind Michelle and was now standing in the staffroom doorway. 'And why are you wearing lipstick? You never wear it for work.'

'None of your business. Now, why don't you go and speak to Tim about your hours, give you something to do rather than bothering me.' She looked Nina up and down. 'No point in bothering Rick, is there?' If truth be known, Michelle had seen the way that Nina looked at Rick, she knew she liked him and wanted to keep her as far away from him as she could. There had already been too many women who'd got in her way and she was sure as hell that Nina wouldn't be the next.

'I'll be asking Rick, not Tim,' Nina growled. 'Besides, we have some unfinished business to clear up. Business that doesn't require bright, whore-like lipstick.' Once again her words stung, but she smiled sarcastically before turning away, walking across to the office and bursting in through the door, without knocking.

'Michelle sent me to ask if you need coffee,' she asked through the open door and Michelle could see Tim, looking like a frightened rabbit in the headlights, his hands full of paperwork. It was a sight that made her close her eyes with dread.

'Yeah, coffee would be great.' He stood motionless. His arms were lifted high, his biceps bulged and the T-shirt he wore looked as though it were about to burst at the seams. 'And, Nina, close the door behind you.' His voice was more of a growl. 'And when you come back, try knocking.' The whole scene was suspicious and Michelle just knew he was up to something. She crept to the office window, stood to one side, and peered through while holding her breath.

As she thought, Tim was quickly scanning every piece of paper on the desk and throwing them into one of two piles. Once the desk was clear, he picked up one of the piles, opened the bottom drawer of the filing cabinet and dropped them inside. Michelle stood back, the doubts and the worries spinning around in her mind. She didn't want it to be true, but if Tim was up to his old tricks again, why had he waited so long to cover his tracks and why would he hide the evidence where Rick could easily find it?

* * *

'Is this it?' Rick questioned as he looked up from the books.

'What can I say, it's been slow.' Tim stood with his back to the grey metal filing cabinets. He was smirking with nerves, while all the time carefully watching every turn of the page that Rick made. He looked as though he was trying just a little too hard to remain calm; his apparently calm demeanour was belied by the way he was constantly twisting his hands together as though he were wringing out dishcloths, and Rick wondered why a man twice his size with biceps the size of tree trunks would look quite so worried, unless once again he was up to something that he shouldn't be.

'You going to prison didn't go down too well around here,' Tim said. 'Everyone thought you were guilty.' He bit down on his bottom lip, cocked his head on one side and winked, in a slight attempt to lighten the mood.

Rick stood up and walked to the door. 'Did you think I was guilty?' He stood for a moment looking through the glass, taking in the atmosphere and noted that Tim didn't answer. He'd only been back an hour and it felt like when you'd been away on a holiday; everything looked different when you returned. The gym had had a makeover. It looked all new and fresh and he wanted to stand for a while and take it all in. He wanted to see what he'd missed. He closed his eyes just for a moment while he listened to the surrounding noises. If the losses were as bad as he'd initially thought, he could be about to lose it all. It was a thought he couldn't bear. He'd grown up here; he knew every nook and cranny, every sound, and every noise, all of which he'd loved for many years. He vividly remembered the days when he'd happily mooched around the place as a child. He'd spent hours watching his father training boxers in the ring. It was a ring that still stood there to this day, his father's picture hanging on the wall beside it. Rick held his breath for just a moment, while once again he listened more carefully to the sound of metal banging against metal, the grunting, the panting, the distant and repetitive music that came from the aerobics class, along with the continual whirring of the cross trainers, rowing machines and the perpetual sound of spinning that always surrounded the air bikes.

'This gym is my damned life, Tim. You need to tell me what's going on, cause I thought you'd look after things properly, especially after last time.' His hand slammed into the wall. 'How the hell could you do this to me, again?' He spun around on the spot, his eyes accusing. 'According to the books it looks like you've sat on your arse the whole time I've been away. God damn you, it looks as though you've let it all go, but then I look out there,' he said, tapping on the window, 'and I see people. I see members, all working out. I see the aerobics hall full and do you know what that tells me, Tim?' He glared at his brother-in-law who stood before him, shoulders hunched, lips pursed. 'It tells me that these books have been manipulated, and in a big way. Am I right?'

'Look, I can explain.' Tim edged towards the

desk. His huge, solid frame towered above Rick's and for a moment Rick stepped backwards, in order to put the desk between them both, while he weighed up his options.

'Do you know what, don't explain. I don't want to hear it. You've got twenty-four hours to make this right.' He threw the file towards where Tim stood. 'You got that?'

'Twenty-four hours?' he growled. 'I can't... You know I'm no good at books.'

Rick slammed his hand on the desk. 'Obviously.'

Both men stood and glared. Their eyes locked and both took in a deep breath as though trying to work out what the other would do next. Eventually Rick spoke. 'Tim, listen to me. You can't bullshit me. We're family.' He rubbed at his chin. 'I was taught how to do the books by the best and so were you, so don't tell me you don't know how to do them.'

'Pft.' Tim turned his back on where Rick stood. 'Why couldn't you stay away?' he demanded. 'Things were okay while you were inside.'

'Really?' Rick felt his temper rising. 'Really, is that what you think?' He was furious. He scanned the piles of paperwork that were spread all over every surface. 'There's no wonder the books are a mess.' He pointed to the desk. 'I'm amazed you have any idea where anything is.' He pulled his wallet from his pocket and pulled out an old, tatty photograph. A picture of his first wife, of Tim's sister, Julia. 'Do you see this? Do you?' He waved the picture in Tim's face. 'This is your sister. God damn you. She was the only person that gave you a chance. You were a waster, you ended up inside, but she tried to look after you and all I can think is it's a good job she isn't here to see you now. I bet she's doing a frigging somersault in her grave.'

Tim turned, opened the top drawer of the filing cabinet and pulled out a file. He smirked and forcefully threw it towards the desk. 'I don't give a toss what she'd have thought; why would I?' He pushed the file towards where Rick stood. 'It's all in there: the takings, the lack of takings. Make of it what you will.' He leaned across the desk, and his muscles flexed and almost burst through the arms of his T-shirt. 'And Rick, don't ever bring my sister into this again. You might have loved her, but I wouldn't give a toss what the bitch thought.' His hand skidded across the desk; the lever arch file flew off and landed on the floor with a thud. 'She's in the best place, if you ask me. Now, if you've finished, I've got work to do.' Once again, he locked eyes with Rick. And both knew that it was now a battle of wills and one of them needed to back down. Both were capable of anything. Both had been known for their sudden violent outbursts and for a moment it was a close contest as to who would hold out the longest. In fact, Rick knew that Tim's temper could easily match his own, especially when provoked.

13

Ella had had a quiet morning. She'd woken, changed the bed and cleaned the house. The washing machine had just finished and she had stepped out into the garden and was walking to-wards the washing line, when the gate opened, making Ella jump backwards. 'What the...?' She held her washing basket in her arms, and let out a sigh of relief once she realised that it was her mum that had walked in and not Bobby, as he had a few days before.

'Oh, Mum, it's you. You made me jump.' Ella looked puzzled. 'What are you doing here? Let me just hang this lot out and we can have a proper chat,' she said as she grabbed the pegs. The line stretched between two poles, one at either end of the garden and already she had her quilt and pillow cases hung on it. She bent over, picked up a pair of trousers from the basket and hung them upside down on the line, just as her mother had once taught her.

Once finished, she walked back to where her mum stood and held her arms out for a hug. 'Ohhh-hhh, it's so good to see you. Where's Dad?'

'Oh, he's in the car, dear.' Her mother seemed nervous. She was staring at the ground, and Ella immediately knew that something was wrong. Her father never stayed in the car. He was normally the first in through the back door, switching on the kettle and helping himself to the biscuit tin. So why was today different?

'Mum, what's going on? Why doesn't he come in? Is he okay?' Ella rambled, stopped hugging her mum and walked to the side of the house in order to see the car and make sure her father was indeed sitting inside. He waved, and then looked over his shoulder and into the back seat. 'What the hell is he up to?'

'Oh, darling. He's not up to anything, but...' She paused. 'Well, actually, okay, he is. I've done something. I really did think it was a good idea at the time, but your dad got mad with me. He said I was interfering and should have asked you first. So, he's told me that I should come and face the music, you know, tell you by myself. He isn't having anything to do with it. Not unless you're happy.'

Ella looked puzzled. It was very unlike her mother to do anything unusual. She was normally a creature of habit; everything had a time, a place and an order in which it should be done. 'Mum, you're scaring me, what on earth are you talking about? What the hell have you done?'

Carol waved to her husband, indicating that he should come in. Her arms were suddenly wrapped tightly around her daughter. 'Please keep an open mind; I really did think that I was doing the right thing. But if you hate it, we can always take her back.'

'Her? Take who back?' Ella looked over her mum's shoulder to see her dad slink out of the car. He reached into the back seat and then walked up the drive holding a huge fluffy pink blanket like it was the most precious thing he'd ever carried.

'Don't blame me. It wasn't my idea,' her father whispered as he leaned forward and kissed Ella on the cheek. 'Good morning, darling.' The pink blanket was still held protectively in his arms. Then, from nowhere, there was a wriggle and a whine. Ella jumped back as the pink blanket began to move, and then a tiny golden ball of fluff poked its nose out and let out a full-blown howling cry.

'What the hell?' Ella's eyes opened wide with shock as she tried to weigh up what her parents had done.

'She's probably thirsty or hungry,' Patrick said as he stroked the puppy's head. 'She's had a long journey and she's thrown up in my car. Twice. Your mother insisted we set off at five this morning, just so we'd get there and back early. She wanted her to have the full day to settle in before bed time.' He raised his eyebrows and indicated to where her mother stood. She was looking more and more nervous and still appeared to be holding her breath.

Ella looked from her mother to her father and then back again. Her hand automatically reached out to comfort the crying puppy. 'Seriously, am I right in thinking that you bought me a puppy? Isn't that something you should have done when I was eight?'

Her father looked uncomfortable and nudged his wife. 'Your mother had the idea that you might like some company. Apparently, you'd said you wanted a dog, you know, because of the one that found you.'

Ella looked towards where her mother stood. 'Really? Shit, you really did buy me a puppy, didn't you?'

'If you don't like her, then...' She paused and looked up at Patrick. 'Well, I guess we'll take her back. But I thought it would give you something to love, to cuddle and ultimately something to bark and keep you safe if anyone was around,' her mother rambled. 'We searched and searched for one that doesn't moult; it's a Cockapoo. Apparently, they're really great pets and—'

'Mother, enough,' Ella cut in. 'Stop justifying it. I love her.' Ella's arms went out to take the bundle from her father. The puppy nuzzled into the nook of her neck and immediately stopped crying. 'Oh, you like that, don't you? Do you want some water? I bet you're really thirsty after that long drive, baby girl,' Ella said as she pushed her nose into the puppy's fur. Breathing in deeply she closed her eyes. It was the same smell that she'd noticed that day in the field, the same smell that had been on the Springer puppy as it had snuggled into her and had given her the hope she'd needed to survive. In that moment, when that puppy had lain beside her, she'd known deep inside that she was going to live and that she was going to get her life back.

A sudden, overwhelming feeling of gratitude came over her. Not only for the man and his dog who'd found her, but also to her mum and her dad for buying her the puppy and reminding her that against all the odds, she really had survived. Blinking back the tears, she went into the kitchen, grabbed a dish from the cupboard and went to fill it at the sink.

'We're going to be okay, me and you. You'll see,' Ella said, still snuggling the puppy, which happily lay in her arms. She crouched down to place the bowl of water on the floor, before placing a kiss on the puppy's head and then laying the blanket on the tiles, just as a curly, golden fluff ball fell out of her arms. Its little legs suddenly free, it made a dash and began running wildly around the kitchen, making Ella laugh. 'Oh, wow. She's like a mini whirlwind.'

'I'm sure she'll settle down, love.' Her father walked through the kitchen, stepped over the pup and took up his normal role. He switched on the kettle and opened the cupboard, and waved a cup in the air. 'You want a cuppa?'

Ella shook her head. 'No, not for me. I'm off to the shops. Going to have to go to the village as I need dog food, a bed, dishes, toys, blankets. What else? I've never had a puppy before. I have no idea where to begin. What does a puppy eat?' She paused and gasped. 'And… What if I don't know what to do, what if I'm the first person in history who fails at looking after a puppy?'

Carol looked towards Patrick and smirked. 'You'll learn. It isn't hard, it's a bit like having a baby. It's all new to her too.' Carol leaned against her husband. 'Do you remember that first night, Patrick, when we took our Ella home? We were totally in awe, we just sat and watched you with wide open eyes. We were terrified if you slept too long, terrified if you woke and more than that, terrified to sleep ourselves. We took it in turns for days.'

Patrick made the coffee. 'How could I forget. We got a bigger instruction manual when we bought the blooming kettle, thirty pages in twelve different languages. When we got our Ella, the doctor handed me a tiny bit of paper that gave us a few helpline numbers should we have a problem.' He laughed. 'Anyhow, you don't need to go shopping. Your mother bought everything. I'll go and get it all out of the boot.'

Carol's hand went to Ella's shoulder. 'We got you all the essentials. Kind of bought everything that the pet shop had – you name it, it's in the car. It's probably enough to last her for the next five years. All you have to do is choose a name.'

Once again, Ella looked between her parents. 'But where will she sleep?' She walked from kitchen to conservatory and sighed. 'If I leave her in the kitchen, she might get too hot, and she'll be making her way upstairs without permission.' She went back in the kitchen, picked up the water dish and walked back into the conservatory. 'I think we'll call you Millie.' Ella nodded, satisfied with the choice. 'And you... you'll get to sleep in here.'

14

Will turned over in his bed, rubbed his eyes and looked at the clock. The blue luminous light lit up the room, while digital numbers shone back at him in a hazy, blurred manner; he eventually worked out that it was still only two thirty in the morning. Just twenty minutes after he'd last looked. It was still dark and, for June, it felt unusually cold.

Picking up his pillow, he beat it with his fist, punching it over and over and then threw it back towards the pine headboard, before watching it fall off the edge, where it landed with a thud on the floor below. He sighed in defeat, couldn't be bothered to pick it up and climbed out of bed to pad out of his room and across the landing for what felt like the tenth time that night.

He hated the nights that were like this. Some nights he'd toss and turn for most of it, some nights he'd sleep for just an hour at a time; on others, he'd get no sleep at all. These tended to be the nights when the flashbacks came and went.

It had been his sister's eighteenth birthday, a night when all her friends and family were gathered to celebrate. He was looking forward to the party, but work called; a story had beckoned and he'd had no choice but to go even though his mother begged him not to. But the story was one of the biggest he'd ever worked on. He'd been on the fringes of it for months, yet now, just a couple of years later, he couldn't even remember what the story had been about.

It had been very late when he'd returned home. He'd been driving back and the traffic had slowed, which was unusual for the time of night. He could hear the sound of fire engines long before he could see them. And then he'd watched as they'd flown past the line of traffic at speed, their sirens blaring out, one after the other. He'd known they were heading in the direction of where he lived, but he thought they'd be going to some other house, some other destination. But how wrong he'd been. He'd been so tired, so sick of waiting in the traffic that at one point he'd thought about just pulling the car over and curling up to sleep. But something had kept him going and it had only been when he'd rounded the corner of his street that the full horror of what was happening unfolded before his eyes. His home had been ablaze, with three fire engines all at work to stop the flames. The adrenaline had hit him and he remembered jumping from the car and running towards the house. He'd clawed his way through the crowd, and had felt himself being pulled back by firemen who shouted words he couldn't or didn't want to hear. The only noise was that of the fire, of bangs and explosions, all coming from within his home.

Nothing seemed real and he scoured the crowd looking for his parents and sister. He'd felt the need to get to them, to tell them that all would be okay, that he'd look after them, that a house could be replaced. But then each face had blended into one, and when words of sympathy came from neighbours he'd never met, the thunderbolt hit him. His home was burning and within it had been his whole family; they had all died together at a time when he should have been with them, protecting them.

A candle had been left burning. The party jovialities had ended, the guests had gone home, and the candle was forgotten. His parents and sister would have been asleep when it started and all he could hope was that they had died from smoke inhalation before the flames reached them. Sometimes the nightmares were too powerful. He'd wake up, hot, sweaty and screaming. Sometimes, it was easier just to give in, to stop trying to sleep, to go downstairs, take a shower, wash away the heat from his body, make a drink and watch television until exhaustion took over; quite often he'd find himself lying on the settee the next morning, shivering and uncomfortable. But at least on those nights he'd finally managed to sleep and the nightmares were kept at bay.

Will walked through his cottage in the darkness, down the stairs, past the bathroom and into the kitchen. He stood there for a moment and admired the new units. The glossy white doors reflected back at him, and in contrast were the jet-black surfaces which shimmered with glitter, like shiny twinkles that reminded him of tiny diamonds waiting to be mined. He'd chosen the surfaces with his sister in mind. Deborah had loved everything that sparkled. He missed her, but it was important to him to have things around him that would uphold her memory.

Just as he'd planted red robin trees in the garden for his parents; they'd both loved the tree and their garden at home had had lots of them spread around in every border. 'They keep their colour all year round,' his mother had once told him. 'The reds and golds brighten your day no end, especially on a cold winter morning.' So the trees had been planted, along with the conifers, the magnolia and the cotoneaster that they'd loved so dearly. He stared through the darkness towards the shed. Now painted in a deep green it looked better than it probably had in years. Next to it stood his apple, pear and cherry trees, his very own fresh fruit Müller corner.

He missed Kent. He missed his parents' house and he missed the place he'd called home. But selling the house, after it had been refurbished with the insurance money, and moving far away had been the right thing to do. And now there was nothing left for him in Kent. No memories, no house, nothing. His family had gone, and not a memory or picture remained after the fire. He felt for his wallet, opened it and pulled out the picture of Deborah, the only one he'd managed to salvage. He stroked the photograph. 'I'm so sorry,' he whispered. 'I should have been there. I should have saved you all.'

A sudden noise made Will spin around. A loud and continuous banging came from the house next door.

'Arrrrghhhhhhhhh, nooooooooooooooooooo! Heeeeelllllpppppp! Nooooooooooooo!' The scream came from Ella and Will immediately panicked. He ran out of his cottage and began banging on Ella's door. 'Ella, you okay? Ella, please, open the door.' He slammed his fist against the small glass panels.

Another scream came from Ella and Will knew he had no choice but to get in. 'Ella, I'm going to break the door down. If you're near the door, cover your face.' Again his hand went up and, without thinking, he punched the glass. 'Ouch' he screamed as the glass broke.

Will studied the glass, pulled the shards out of the small panel, reached through, turned the Yale and slowly opened the door, peering around it as he did.

'Ella, Ella! You okay? Where are you?'

* * *

Ella whimpered, pulled her pyjama top down to cover her dignity with one hand and held tightly onto her ankle with the other. She could see Millie, the puppy, through the conservatory door. She was sitting with woeful eyes, waiting to be fussed.

'Will...' She sobbed. 'In here. My ankle... Oh my God, it hurts so much.' She moved slightly to one side, screamed and then stretched her foot out before her. Ella's whole body shook. She held onto the steps, hoping that she could save herself from the nauseous feeling that had begun to take over her body. 'I heard the glass break. Did you really break the window on my door?'

'I'm sorry. I heard you scream,' Will explained, but the thought that someone had broken in so easily terrified her. She knew that Will had used minimal force, but still, within seconds, there he was making his way through the darkness of her lounge. There was a bang, the shrill noise of the telephone, followed by a curse, which indicated that Will had fallen over the coffee table and the telephone had now hit the floor. Then there was another noise, something else hit the floor and Ella guessed it would have been the wine glass that she'd left there the night before. She tried to remember if it'd had any wine left in it, but felt sure that she'd emptied the vessel, knowing that without it, she wouldn't have slept at all.

She waited. She knew she needed his help and

felt grateful that he'd responded the way he had. She inched her way off the stairs and pulled herself towards the door behind which Millie sat.

'Is it broken?' she asked as Will fumbled his way through the kitchen. She caught sight of his face in the moonlight and just a fraction of a second later he landed in a heap beside her. Ella gasped as she noticed his partially naked body and blushed as she thought about looking away. 'I'm so sorry. I can't believe I woke you up.' She tried to smile. 'But you really could have got dressed; I kind of don't think I was going anywhere.'

'And I kind of didn't know that, did I? The fall sounded quite dramatic. I was worried you'd, well, I knew that you'd hurt yourself, cause of the scream. But I didn't know if you were alone or whether you had company.' Ella knew he was thinking of Bobby, of how terrified she'd been of him the last time Will had turned up to save her. 'Look, never mind, I'm here now, aren't I?'

Ella cringed as pain once again tore through her ankle. 'Well, as you can see, I'm sort of alone and still alive, just.' She pointed to his bare chest and feet. 'So if you'd like to go back next door and put some clothes on, I really don't mind.'

Ella watched as Will looked down at his bare feet

and held out his arms in resignation. If she were honest with herself, she really didn't mind the view, even though she'd never have admitted it to Will. His body was taut, he obviously worked out and she liked the way ginger curls randomly covered his chest.

'Well, as you said, I just love to make a big entrance.' He stood up and began tapping his hands across the wall in search of a light switch.

'Did it break?'

Will shook his head. 'Sorry, I've no idea if you've broken your ankle or not, let me put a light on and I'll take a better look.'

Ella kept tight hold of her ankle. 'No, silly, I meant the wine glass. I heard you fall in the lounge; the glass, it fell off the table. Did it break?'

Will seemed to catch up with the conversation and Ella could just about make out his shape as he found the light switch. 'Okay, light's going on, watch your eyes.' She waited for the intensity of light, but Will had caught the wrong switch and only the faint lights that shone out from under the kitchen units came on; a soft glow lit up the area. She'd moved herself off the stairs and into the small hallway that separated the stairs, the kitchen, the bathroom and the conservatory.

Ella looked at her ankle and smiled. It looked red and swollen but didn't look as though anything was pointing in the wrong direction, and she let out a sigh of relief. She looked up at where Will now stood over her, as a scream left her lips.

Will screamed with her. 'What – what now?'

'Your wrist, Will, you're bleeding!' Her eyes searched around the faint light of the kitchen. She could see bloodstains all over the wooden floor where he'd crawled through from the lounge on his hands and knees. 'Quick, there... on the unit, there's a tea towel.'

Will did as he was told, grabbed the tea towel and wrapped it around his wound. Ella propped herself up against the bottom step, watching as Will clicked on a second light, which lit up the whole kitchen while he tried to clean the blood from the walls with damp kitchen towel. 'You need to go to hospital.' She lifted herself up to perch on the bottom step and yelped. Pain had seared through her foot, yet she tried her best to put on her brave face. It was the face she'd learnt to use almost every day while she'd lived with her parents. It had been the same face that she'd used for reporters, doctors and physiotherapists when they too had told her to try harder, walk further and to pull against the huge elastic bands that they'd issued her with to help with the exercises. A loud howl came from inside the conservatory and Ella began to laugh at the way Will spun around on the spot. His eyes locked with Ella's as he stared at her and she knew he was waiting for her to make the noise again.

'That wasn't me.' She giggled and moved across the floor on her bottom. She turned onto her belly to look through the glass door of the conservatory. 'I think you need to meet Millie.'

Ella noticed Will take a huge step back. He tried to look around casually, walked into the lounge and picked up the glass that had fallen from the table. Luckily, it had remained intact, which was more than could be said for the telephone, which now lay in two pieces on the floor. Finally, he spoke. 'Okay, Ella. Now I'm worried. You're talking to or about imaginary people and I really do think we need to get you to a hospital.'

Ella began to laugh uncontrollably. 'Will, seriously. Do you really think I have an imaginary friend?'

She pointed at the door and to a puppy who now jumped up and down at the glass waiting to be let in. 'Look, Millie is a puppy. My parents bought her for me.'

'Oh, oh wow.' He looked relieved and knelt down beside Ella. 'She's so beautiful.' He stopped for a moment, his hand held to the glass door. 'I really want to cuddle her, but first I need to look at your ankle. I need to see how badly you've hurt it.'

She smiled, sat back upright and moved her leg. She gave out another moan as Will moved to put her foot on his knee. 'Ella, let me see.'

'It'll hurt, won't it?'

'Ella, I promise you, I won't hurt you, but I do need to know what we're dealing with.' Will placed his hands on hers. Her whole body trembled and she physically held her breath. 'Ella, please believe me. I promise I won't hurt you,' Will whispered the words for a second time and Ella noticed how he looked directly into her face as he spoke. She caught his eye. It sparkled in back at her, and it occurred to her that it was the first time she'd noticed how blue his eyes really were. A blue that was so beautiful, so very pure. She tried to think of a comparison and the only thing she could think of was her mother's sapphire ring. She remembered the day that her father had bought it and placed it on her mother's hand. It was exactly six months after their twenty-second anniversary. He'd known how much she'd loved the stone but had never been able to afford to buy her one before. When they had got engaged they'd bought the cheapest ring they could find and, for once, her father had wanted her to have the best. He'd given her the ring exactly halfway to their forty-fifth, halfway to their sapphire anniversary; he thought it best that she should wear it for the next twenty-two years and six months, rather than wait until they got there.

'Ella, can I?' The words interrupted her thoughts and she reluctantly moved her hands, lifted them up and held them over her eyes as though afraid to look at the damage she'd done.

'It's the same ankle I hurt before.' Her voice shook and she held her breath. Will hesitated before carefully rolling up the leg of Ella's pyjama bottoms. He looked at the ankle from what appeared to be every direction and then reached out gently to pick her foot up from the floor.

'Sorry, my hands are cold,' he said as he manoeuvred her ankle gently from side to side, up and down. 'Can you feel this?' He pressed her toe and watched her face for a reaction.

Ella nodded. 'That's fine.'

'Okay, press your foot down against my hand.'

Ella pressed down and once again yelped. 'Yes, yes that hurts. You promised it wouldn't.'

Will rolled her pyjama leg back down. 'I didn't promise it wouldn't hurt. I promised that I wouldn't hurt you. There's a difference.' He laughed. 'I think it's a bad sprain, but I'm no expert and, after what happened before, I think I'd better drive you to the hospital. Get them to check us both out properly,' he said as he held up his wrist, just as Millie once again let out a howl. 'But first, I need to clean up the broken glass, and then I'm going to take a look at your new buddy.'

15

Will unloaded the last of the turf and began the laborious task of carrying it from the front to the back of his house. There were fifty rolls, all of which needed laying that day. The garden had been prepared, the bushes had all taken root and the whole lawn area had been levelled with the precision of a flat iron. It was all ready for the lawn.

'No, Millie. You do it out here. I won't tell you again, you don't pee in the house. Peeing in the house is bad. Peeing out here is good, do you get it?' She paused. 'Of course you don't get it, but you will.'

Will listened intently as he heard Ella's voice go from normal to high pitched in one sentence and then back to normal again. 'That's it. Yeah. Good girl. Clever, Millie Moo, now you get a treat.'

Crouching by the fence he peered through. From his position he could see Ella as she balanced precariously on the crutches. Her auburn hair was tied back in a simple band and after the night before, her normal pristine look appeared slightly dishevelled. Millie was totally unfazed by the situation. She raced around the garden and looked up in hope that Ella would chase her.

'Hey, Ella. How's it going? You need a hand?'

He saw Ella's face light up as her eyes turned in the direction of the fence. 'That'd be great. Do you have time?' Will climbed onto the bench and leaned on the top of the fence. 'Of course, I can make time,' he lied as he looked behind him at the rolls of turf. 'Besides, I'd love to come see the puppy; I mean it is a whole six hours since I last saw her.'

He watched as Ella perched on the bench, putting the crutches beside her; the worried look on her face told Will that she was fully expecting him to vault the fence.

'Okay, you're allowed. So long as you use the gate and don't, you know, fly over the fence like a banshee,' she shouted as Will jumped down, ignored the pile of turf and for the second time in twenty-four hours, ran from his house to Ella's.

* * *

'I don't know what my parents were thinking. Don't get me wrong, I love her, but I have no idea what to do,' Ella explained as she watched Will pick Millie up, place her on his knee and stroke her until she flopped into a deep sleep. 'I mean, how am I supposed to know what she needs?' Ella shrugged. 'Good job I know what I need.' She looked back at the house. 'Do you want a coffee? I'm sure I could manage to make some.'

 'I'd love a coffee, but I'll make it. You sit there.' He pointed to the bench on which she was already sitting. 'Besides, the hospital said to rest.' He walked into the kitchen expecting to see the bloodstains all over the walls, but every mark had gone. The kitchen was pristine. He shook his head, wondering how she'd managed to clean it all on crutches and with a puppy underfoot. He put the kettle on to boil. 'Now then, without moving, shout and tell me which cupboard the sugar is in and – I take it that one of these cupboard doors will be the fridge.'

Ella laughed. 'The fridge freezer is under the stairs,' she shouted.

'Okay, okay, I should have seen that,' he retorted as he opened the fridge door, pulled out the milk and then turned to make the coffee, pouring milk into each mug. 'I could have done with a mug or two of this at the hospital this morning,' he said as he walked back to the fridge and replaced the milk. 'I don't know about you, but those waiting rooms really don't have any added comfort, do they?'

Ella thought of the waiting room and the hours they'd sat waiting to be seen. The whole night had dragged and she'd been terrified of what the doctor might say, as her ankle had been badly injured during the attack and the last thing she'd needed was to damage it further. But Will had been there. He'd sat with her, talked to her and helped her in and out of the hospital, even though he'd been hurt himself. She remembered glancing across to his bandaged wrist and seeing how the over-attentive nurse had looked after him while cleaning and gluing the cut. The nurse had continually smiled at him and had made the longest job of bandaging the wrist. But Will had shrugged off the attention, and had ignored the advances.

'Wow, how long does it take to make coffee?' Ella

asked as she made her way into the kitchen. 'Come on, we should sit in here.' She used a crutch to point into the lounge.

'Come on then, Mrs, go sit down,' he joked, and Ella hobbled into the lounge and smiled as she sat on the settee. She liked having him around, liked the attention, and loved the fact that someone was there for her. What's more, she really appreciated the fact that Will had promised he wouldn't phone her mother. Ella knew she'd have rushed over at breakneck speed and, right now, it was the last thing she needed.

Millie had crawled up and had snuggled herself into a comfy position on Will's knee.

'She certainly loves you. She's not fallen asleep on me like that yet. All she's done since she arrived here yesterday morning is run around like a lunatic, squeak her toys and pee in my house.' Ella's hand reached out and stroked the sleeping puppy. 'As I said earlier, I have no idea how to look after a dog.'

'Well, I'd get used to the peeing.' Will laughed as his hand continued to stroke Millie, who now lay inverted on his knee. 'It's simple. Make sure she has enough food in her dish, enough water in the other and then give her lots of love. She needs to feel content and wanted. Dogs are part of a pack.'

'Pack, a pack of what?'

'She's a part of your pack, silly. A dog is a pack animal. They hate to be alone.' Once again, Ella's hand reached out to the puppy. Her hand momentarily rested on his and he felt a sudden rush of warmth. He caught her eye. He wanted to kiss her so much. Wanted to hold her, but didn't dare. For some reason, he still thought it just a little too soon. The last thing he wanted to do was scare her off. He purposely turned his attention to the front door and jumped up. 'Right, I'm going to pop to the glaziers, get some glass and repair that door. I'll be back soon.'

* * *

Will leaned against the spade, looked at the huge pile of turf that was now lit up by his floodlights, pulled on a long, yellow, rubber glove to cover his bandage and, one by one, began laying the strips of grass down the length of his garden.

It was late and dark. He'd spent the whole day with Ella. He'd repaired the door and played with Millie for what seemed like hours, and it wasn't until he returned home that he'd remembered that he had a pile of turf that he still needed to lay. Now, to spoil what had been a great day, it began to rain. Not just a pitter-patter of tiny drops, but giant button sized drops that fell repeatedly, drenching him within minutes of it starting. But it didn't matter. He began to laugh at the irony, looking up at where Ella's spare bedroom window lit up at the back of her house and saw the shape of her silhouette through the closed curtains. He thought of being up there with her, of holding her in his arms, but then shook the thought from his mind. 'Oh boy, it's time you did some work,' he whispered to himself as he turned away, pushed all thoughts of Ella from his mind and patted the first roll of turf into place.

16

'Josh, it'll be fine,' Will said into his phone. 'I'm just going in for an induction. Pretending to be a customer and all of that. People do it every day.' Will locked the car and walked towards the gym. 'And no, I don't need back up. It's the middle of the day, what the hell do you think is going to happen?' He pushed the car keys into his pocket. 'I know,' he responded to Josh. 'But Ella sure as hell thought there was something going on here and...' He paused and tried to look through the frosted glass. 'Well, I want to find out what it is.'

Will stood listening as Josh ran through the names of the people who worked at the gym, what their relationships were to Rick Greaves and how long each of them appeared to have known him. 'So, you think the brother-in-law is up to something, do you?' He nodded in agreement to what Josh was saying. 'Okay. I'll call you back later, give you an update.' He went to push open the door. 'And, Josh, go look into that story in Filey I told you about. Find that fisherman and let's see if we can get him some publicity.' He clicked the phone off, pushed it into his pocket and walked into the gym.

'Hi there, how are you doing? I'm Michelle,' said a woman with short blonde hair as Will dropped his gym bag to the floor.

'Yeah, I'm good, thanks.' His eyes were scanning the room. 'I'm here for my induction and I'd be up for a bit of a work out.' He smiled, but then held up his wrist. 'Except, I might have to take it a bit easy.'

Michelle walked around the reception desk. 'Looks nasty. How long is it since you did it?' Without waiting for a reply, she picked up a clipboard. 'Follow me.' She walked him over to the male changing rooms. 'If you get changed, then we'll take all your details, including how you managed to do that.' She pointed to his wrist, but her eyes were staring across the room to where Rick Greaves stood chatting to one of the other staff members. They looked close, but were constantly looking over their shoulders at what was happening in the gym. The woman was shorter than Rick and had long dark hair. Will went through the list of employees in his mind and came to the conclusion that the woman would be Nina.

He went into the changing rooms, threw his bag on the counter and pulled his shorts, trainers and T-shirt from the bag. It had been a while since he'd been to a gym, but it was the only way he could think of to get close to Rick Greaves. He wanted to see first-hand who this man was, how capable he looked of hurting someone and, if Josh's suspicions were right, he needed to find out who Rick's ex-business partner and brother-in-law was too.

Will threw his bag in a locker and then entered the gym. He stood waiting by the door as he noticed that Michelle had stomped over to where Rick and Nina stood, still chatting. She towered over Nina and it was more than obvious that Michelle was listening in to the conversation. Nina obviously had a bee in her bonnet about something and Will watched as Rick rubbed his head with both hands. He stared at Nina with apologetic eyes and gently shook his head.

'Not here. It's not the place.' Rick looked uncomfortable. 'Go do some work, we'll talk later.' He gently touched her on the shoulder, but Michelle was standing right behind her.

'Don't be stupid, Nina. You know that didn't happen.' She looked from Nina to Rick. 'Rick, tell her.'

'Sod off and mind your own business, Michelle. This is between me and Rick.'

Michelle stood her ground. 'Rick, tell her what you told me. Tell her you don't remember.'

Rick pursed his lips. 'Look, Nina. Things are... complicated. It's true, I really don't really remember that night.' He seemed to withdraw into his own body. 'A lot has happened. I mean, I do remember you being there. I just thought you'd given me a lift home or something.' He chewed his bottom lip. 'What can I say?' He looked from one woman to the other but stopped on Nina. 'Sorry,' he whispered, before turning his back and walking over to the cross trainer.

Then, in a burst of temper, Michelle threw the clipboard she'd been carrying at Nina. 'Now, as Rick said, go and do something useful. Try doing some bloody work for once.' The words were spat from her mouth before she turned and practically ran to Rick's side. Will then saw the resigned look on Nina's face as she turned and walked in his direction with eyes full of tears.

'Okay, William. Are you ready?' She came to a stop before him. 'I'm Nina and I'm going to take you through a few of the machines and test your general fitness.' She picked up a bag and walked ahead. Will followed. 'You completed the medical form online before booking your induction and it looks like you're normally quite fit and healthy. Always a good sign, we don't like our clients popping off in the middle of a session.'

'Wow. Does that happen often?' he asked seriously. He realised that Nina had been forced into taking over his care and he wanted to make an effort to put her at ease.

'Does what happen often?' She pulled a tissue from her pocket, wiped her eyes and glanced back to where Rick now stood chatting to Michelle.

'People popping off, of course.'

Nina shook her head. 'Don't be silly. Of course not. I'm going to attach these sticky things to your chest, is that okay? It measures your heart rate while you train.'

Will took a deep breath, sat down and took his T-shirt off. 'So, what was all that about?' he asked as Nina attached the sticky pads to his chest.

She looked up and caught his eye. 'Nothing, it's personal.' She once again glared in Michelle's direction and sighed. 'We were, you know, together. But Rick's conveniently forgotten.' She moved to sit on the bench. 'But I don't understand how he can forget. You don't forget things like that, do you?' she questioned as she leaned across him and patted the pads down. 'Okay, this belt goes around your waist and holds the monitor in place,' Nina said as she stood back up and put her arms around Will's waist to pass the belt from one hand to the other. She stopped mid-pass and looked up into his eyes, lingering for a moment before coyly looking away. 'That should do it. You can pop your T-shirt back on now. And, look, I'm sorry, you shouldn't have to listen to my personal problems.' She smiled, walked to the treadmill and began pressing buttons. 'Now, if you want to start on here at a fast walk for five minutes, then we'll check your heart rate as you finish.'

Will stepped onto the machine and began to walk, slowly at first, but then sped up just a little. He wanted to take the first piece of equipment steady; he didn't want to embarrass himself and end up in a heap on the floor, nor did he want to lose concentration on the real reason he was there. He used the time to look around the gym. Rick Greaves was at the other side of the room. He leaned against a cross trainer, chatting to Michelle who had now jumped onto the machine and was working her legs. They were both laughing. Rick was pouting his lips and every so often he'd say something and then pull up the arm of his T-shirt to flash a bicep, or lift his shirt to show off his abs. Michelle was tall and extremely thin, with short blonde hair. She seemed to laugh in all the right places, and Will noticed her look directly into Rick's eyes on a number of occasions, while he appeared to go into full-on poser mode and began picking up weights the size of small cars in a futile attempt to impress. In fact, his whole chat up routine would be laughable and amusing except for the fact that Will could see how upset Nina looked. She stood and watched the whole performance he seemed to be laying on for Michelle's benefit, all the time with a look of thunder on her face and tears in her eyes. Yet, on the other hand, he admired Michelle's stamina; not only was she having to climb the piles of bullshit that Rick was piling up, but also, to Will's knowledge, she'd been on the cross trainer since he'd begun running, yet still didn't look as though she'd break a sweat any time soon.

Will took note of the time. It'd been ten minutes since Nina had set the machine going and he pressed the treadmill's red button, making it grind to a stop. He looked over his shoulder, but Nina hadn't noticed. She stood leaning against the reception unit, Styrofoam cup between her teeth as she chewed down on the plastic. Her eyes were fixed on where Rick stood, still chatting and still periodically flashing his muscles at Michelle, who had finally stopped the cross trainer and climbed down. Michelle had picked up her towel and was smiling at Rick. Her hand went up to his cheek in a soft, loving gesture, but Rick quickly turned away as he realised that Nina was watching.

'Hey, you're not even out of breath,' Nina commented as she lifted Will's shirt to take a reading from the tiny monitor.

Will winked. 'Of course not, it's hardly hard work, is it?' Nina lifted her hand to the pads that were stuck to his chest as though checking them and pressed them firmly against his skin. Her hand lingered on his shoulder, and then moved to his bicep, before allowing her fingers to stroke his forearm, making Will tense up. Her touch was more than just professional. When she looked over her shoulder in Rick's direction, he realised that she was just trying to make Rick jealous.

'I like a man with stamina,' she suddenly said. 'I like a bloke who can give me a run for my money; has to be a good thing, right?' Her eyes lifted to his and Will purposely looked away. The last thing he wanted was to create an atmosphere at the gym, or for Nina to try chatting him up. He was here to do a job. He thought through his options as quickly as he could.

He needed to keep Nina on side and find out more about the gym, and about the people who worked there. Ultimately, he needed to find any clues that might lead to what had really happened to Ella. But there were also the deaths of both of Rick's former wives. Surely a man would have to be really unlucky to lose two wives so tragically and then to have a third female friend almost killed – or would he?

'Your fella over there looks like he'd have a bit of stamina. Don't want him getting the wrong idea, do we?'

Nina began to laugh. She pouted and gave him a small wave. 'Darling, you're right, he has amazing stamina, but you can't call him my fella, not when he conveniently forgets we were together. Isn't that right, Rick?' She said the words just loud enough for Rick to hear and look in their direction. Another attempt to gain his attention.

'Isn't what right?' There was amusement in his eyes as he walked over in their direction.

'William here thought you were my fella.' Her hand went up to touch his arm. 'Fancy that when you pretend to forget the nights we spent together?'

Rick jumped back as though Nina had scalded him. 'Nina, I've said—' He paused and took in a deep breath. 'We need to talk about this in private.' He smiled and Will saw the sparkle return to Nina's eyes. Rick moved away.

'Oh my God. I'm so sorry,' Will said as he tried to smooth over the situation. 'I hope I haven't caused a problem?' he lied and followed Nina to the cross trainer.

'We've always had a bit of a relationship. I hoped it'd be more. But, it's been on and off for years. But...' She pointed to the machine. 'We were together the night before he was arrested.' She began pressing buttons on the cross trainer, then indicated to Will that he should climb onto the foot pedals and clicked the start button. 'Go on, begin to stride.'

Will was glad she'd given him something to do. He began to press one foot down and then the other, soon getting into the constant rhythm of the machine. The machine had picked up speed and he worked as hard as he could to keep up the pace. 'The night before he was arrested? Wasn't that the night that woman got attacked?' Nina sidled up to the side of the machine, pressed her body against it and fluttered her eyelashes in Will's direction. 'That's right.' She looked down as she said the words and Will actually began to feel sorry for her. It was more than obvious that she still liked him. 'We seem to just get together and then he meets someone else.' She shrugged her shoulders. 'He's been married twice, you know.'

Will smiled. 'Twice, wow. He doesn't look old enough.' He paused. 'He sure as hell gets divorced quickly, doesn't he?'

'Oh, he didn't divorce them. They both died.' Nina's voice was barely a whisper; it was obvious she didn't want Rick to hear what she was saying. Her hand waved in the air as she indicated to Will that he should step down from the cross trainer and move over to the rowing machine. 'Here, have a go on this next. Set it up like this.' She set the tension on the wheel and passed him the handles. 'You only need to do a few minutes on each piece of apparatus today and then I'll check your statistics, see how fit you are.'

Will began to pull on the machine. 'Am I doing this right?' He knew he wasn't, but he needed to keep her attention. He smiled as Nina stood behind him, pulled the handles over his shoulders and lifted his elbows to position them higher.

Will leaned forward and moved the tension up. 'I'm intrigued. Are you going to tell me what happened to his wives?'

Nina sighed and perched on the rowing machine beside him. She looked over her shoulder and began to whisper. 'Julia, the first one, she worked here, did the accounts. She was obsessed with personal fitness, went out running all the time. But they lived in the sticks and the houses nearby all had septic tanks, you know, for the waste. One of the neighbours had left the lid off his and she fell into it in the dark.' She pulled a face. 'Straight in and couldn't climb out. It was the next morning before they found her. She'd probably drowned.'

To say they'd been work colleagues, Nina didn't look particularly sad about the woman's death and Will noticed that her eyes were constantly watching where Rick worked out. He now lay on a bench press and lifted huge, black weights as easily as though they were big pillows on a stick.

'So what happened to the other one?' Will needed to know more and stopped rowing to listen. He leaned forward, grabbed his towel and wiped his face.

'Patsy, she was an estate agent. They'd only been married a couple of weeks when she fell down a flight of stairs.' She shook her head. 'One of the empty houses she was trying to sell. No one knew she was there and, again, it was hours before they found her. She went into a coma and died two days later.'

'Didn't anyone think it a bit suspicious?' Will watched as Nina stood up, picked up the medical bag and looked over her shoulder to where Rick still lay.

'No, of course it wasn't suspicious. What the hell are you trying to suggest?'

'Sorry... I was just, you know... thinking out loud?'

'Look, it happened. It's over. Rick is back here where he belongs. If you want to know any more, you'll have to ask him.' As she stepped back, Will could practically feel her build a wall between them.

'I just mow lawns for a living; I'm a landscape gardener,' he lied. 'And I know I shouldn't have asked those questions, but I don't normally get to talk to many people; just plants, bushes, trees, you know...'

Nina glared at his hands. They didn't look like they'd been used for manual labour and for a moment he thought his cover was blown. But then she physically softened. Her whole body calmed and her face lost the tight, calculated look that she'd had just a few moments before.

'AAARRRGGGHHHH!' The scream came from the far side of the gym where Rick was working out. Nina didn't waste a moment. She immediately dropped the medical bag and ran over to where he lay pinned beneath the weight bar. He'd been on the bench press. The strength in his arms had obviously failed and the bar was now tipped to one side, pressing heavily against his ribs. But Michelle had got there first.

'I've got it, it's fine,' Nina shouted at Michelle, as in one swift movement she pushed Michelle out of the way and grabbed at the bar. 50k hung on each end and she lifted it in one swift movement, without flinching. She dropped it on the floor beside where Rick lay, allowing him to sit up as his hand grabbed at his bicep.

'What the hell?' Michelle growled from where she'd landed in a heap on the floor.

Nina hovered over Rick. 'Are you okay? Do you want some ice?' Her hands immediately went to his shoulders; her eyes looked up and fixed with his and Michelle jumped up to stand by his other side.

'I'm fine.' Rick looked embarrassed and Will tried not to stare. The bar must have been heavy and he doubted that many women would be capable of lifting it, yet Nina had tossed both it and Michelle aside as though they weighed nothing at all, leaving Michelle with a look of thunder in her eyes.

'Nina, go and look after your client,' Michelle ordered. 'Get back to work and leave Rick alone. I've told you before, he doesn't want you slobbering all over him.' She stood up tall, her whole frame towering over Nina's, but Nina didn't move.

'Who are you to tell me what to do? I take my orders from Rick, not you.' She crossed her arms, but then her hand went to Rick's shoulder. 'Are you okay?'

'Nina, I'm fine. Now, please, as Michelle has asked, go and get on with your job.' He sounded stern, but not angry and he sat for a moment, nursing his pride.

With the need to do something, Will walked back to the cross trainer that faced towards where Rick sat. Once again, he climbed aboard and began using his stride to gain some speed. He carefully watched Nina; she'd reluctantly moved back in his direction, but had stopped short. She pulled a mobile from her pocket; it hadn't rung and Will presumed she'd had it on vibrate.

'No, not yet,' she said with a sigh. 'I'll ask him later. He seems to be in a really bad mood right now.' She paused and listened while all the time watching where Michelle and Rick sat, side by side. 'Yes, I've promised that I'll ask, haven't I?' Her words were just a little more than a whisper, but loud enough that both Will and Rick could hear.

'Ask me what?' Rick shouted and Nina placed a hand over the phone. She sighed as she padded across the floor and back to where Rick sat.

'My stepdad. He needs me to pay more rent, and I was wondering if I could work more hours?' She shuffled her feet. 'And, well, I think you kind of owe me.' She smiled, a practised smile that lit up her face. 'Another ten hours a week should do it.'

But Rick shook his head. 'No can do, Nina. This place is on its arse. Ask me again in a few weeks, but only if things pick up.' He looked towards the office, where Tim would be sitting, watching. 'And, Nina: first, I don't like bribery and second, you've been told before about the phone. Either put it away or go and tell Tim that I just fired you.' He held her gaze. 'Do you understand?'

Nina nodded, turned and as loudly as she could,

she spoke into the handset. 'He said no, you heard him, right? Well, now I'm probably out of a job too.' She paused and listened to the call. 'Yes, yes, I know what you're capable of, but he won't like you threatening him.' Again she paused. 'Yes, all right. Look, I have to go.' She hit the off button and with tears in her eyes she pushed the phone back into her pocket.

Will shook his head. Nina was obviously a lost soul and he felt for her. But he'd seen enough internal politics for one day and climbed down from the cross trainer. He headed for the showers, but glanced back momentarily to see Nina hiding behind reception, where she sat sobbing and dabbing at her eyes, watching as Michelle prowled around Rick. She smirked in Nina's direction and Will began to wonder what it was about Rick Greaves that got women so interested. And if there were a magic answer, would he really want to know what it was?

* * *

I hate being watched. I hate everyone looking at me as though they know me, as though I'm nothing. I would much rather be the one who watches, the one who finds those vulnerable moments when I can make those who have hurt me suffer. It's then that I have the control, it's then that I feel empowered and it's then that I'm happy, knowing that for once it's someone else who's suffering, rather than it just being me.

Everyone wants answers, everyone wants to know the truth. They think finding the truth is the right thing to do, but they have no idea how many people will get hurt in the process. Everyone needs to walk away and do the smart thing. Before I hurt someone else.

17

Tim slammed the main door shut, thrust the lock into position and stamped across the gym and into the office.

'I'm in so much trouble,' he whispered to himself as he pulled open the bottom drawer of the filing cabinet and dug out the pile of paperwork that he'd hidden. He leafed through each sheet, studied some and screwed up others. None of them made sense, not to him and he began opening and slamming drawers and cupboards.

He resented Rick's words and tossed the screwed-up pieces of paper in the bin, before pulling a bottle from the filing cabinet drawer and pouring himself a large glass of whisky. He took a long slurp and then lifted the bottle again. 'Time for a top up.' He slushed the liquid into the glass and laughed as droplets splashed up and over the side, landing on some of the receipts. He slammed his fist down on the desk and watched as the whisky once again jumped in the glass.

'So, maybe I did spend a bit too much. Nothing wrong with that, is there? After all, why the hell shouldn't I have some perks? It was me that spent every hour here, wasn't it? Me that looked after things and had no bloody life while he was in prison.' He thumped himself on the chest gorilla style. 'Was me that kept the doors open and the bloody place afloat, wasn't it?' He nodded with exaggerated movements, laughed at himself and then once again picked up the glass. He studied the golden fluid before drinking it down in one gulp and slamming the empty glass back down on the desk.

He flopped down in the chair and stared at the safe. He knew how much money was in there. He knew how easy it would be to take it, start a new life and escape the whole rat race that had become his life.

'Would it be worth it?' He got up and his hand skimmed the safe's door. 'I could leave; I could go away, start again. Rick would never find me.' He looked up at the world map that covered the office wall. 'Where would you go?' He stared at the islands: the Maldives, the Caribbean. He could easily go to any of those places. After all, he was fully qualified; everyone needed good instructors and he could easily get a job in any of these countries.

Tim looked back at the glass, filled it once again with whisky and drank it down in one. Then, without a second thought, he opened the safe, reached inside and felt for the pile of notes. Placing them on the desk, he simply sat and stared. He had no money of his own, not any more, and he thought of the possibilities that this money would bring. It'd serve Rick right if he took it. His fingers reached out and stroked the notes.

'Tim, what the hell are you doing?' Michelle's voice rang out as the door burst open and Tim jumped back in his seat.

'Michelle, what – what the hell are you doing here? I thought everyone had gone.' He nervously looked from the money to Michelle and back again. She'd seen him with it. She'd seen him contemplating what to do and she'd probably heard every word he'd just whispered. He stood up, stepped towards the door and looked Michelle directly in the eye. 'I asked you why the hell you were still here?' he bellowed.

Michelle stepped back and turned towards the door. 'Look, Tim, I don't want any trouble. I was just using the showers. I have to go. I have a date.'

Tim saw that she once again looked around him and at the money. She knew what he was about to do. He spun around on the spot, grabbed the money and pushed it back into the safe. 'I was just counting it, right?' He slammed the safe door shut, walked out of the office and across the gym and unlocked the door. 'Time you were gone, isn't it?' He studied Michelle as she left the building. He knew how close she and Rick had been getting lately and he guessed that any date she might be going on would be with him. His heart rate quickened. Would she tell Rick what she had seen? He knew he had to do something to stop her talking, he just didn't know what.

18

Rick placed a dozen red roses in a vase, stood back and admired them. The vivid red colouring against the white walls of the hallway looked stunning and he silently congratulated himself on the choice. He spun around. 'Candles,' he whispered to himself. 'Light them now, or later?' He thought for a moment but then picked up the matches and, even though it was summer and still daylight, he decided to light them in the knowledge that by the time he'd finished serving dinner, it would be dark and the romantic amber glow of candles was always preferable to harsh electric lighting.

Rick walked to the hallway mirror, looked himself up and down to check his appearance, shook his head and ran up the broad oak staircase.

'Should have worn the white one,' he muttered to himself as he flung open the door to his dressing room and rummaged around in the wardrobe for the white linen shirt that he had in mind. 'That's better,' he said as he pulled on the shirt, walked out of the dressing room, back onto the landing and across to the bedroom which stood at the front of the house.

He nodded in approval. The room looked fresh, flowers had been placed in several vases around the room, the sheets were crisp and clean and the music system had been programmed to play soft romantic music, just as he liked it. He silently hoped that his evening with Michelle would end up in here.

The shrill sound of the phone echoed through the house. 'Hello, Rick Greaves.' He balanced the handset on his shoulder and walked from the bedroom onto the landing.

'What do you want, Nina?' He moved the phone from one ear to the other, walked over to the dressing room and pulled the door closed.

'Rick, it's my stepdad. Seriously. He's threatening to throw me out if I don't pay more rent. And, as I said earlier, you owe me and I could really do with the extra hours.'

Rick sighed. 'Nina, do you know what time it is? I'm busy and, what's more, your housing arrangements are really not my problem. I'm amazed I've still got my own house after all that's happened.'

Nina went silent and Rick heard her sigh.

'Nina, is there anything else?' Rick was growing impatient; he wanted to make sure the food was organised and really didn't want to continue this conversation, not at home and definitely not tonight.

'But, Rick.' A sob left her lips. 'I thought we were a team.' Again, she paused. 'You have to help me, Rick, you just have to. I'm scared of what he'll do next. I've tried talking to him, honestly, but you know how unpredictable he is. And he hates you.' Her voice was now racing with panic and the words were an obvious threat.

'Nina, what do you mean he hates me and he's unpredictable? What will he do?' Rick was losing his temper. Nina was always talking about her stepfather, how cruel and dangerous he was and the threats he apparently made. He thought back over the years. There had been threats before, back when Julia was alive. Threats about wages, hours and always over how Nina needed more.

'Rick, he knows we slept together.' The words were barely a whisper. 'I told him. He's not happy and you know he'll do anything to protect me, don't you?' The words were all too clear.

'And I've told you never to threaten me. Getting mixed up with you was a mistake. Got it?' Rick thought of Nina. Of the night she kept reminding him of and of how he must have been so drunk that he couldn't remember any of it. Her being in his bed the next morning was as far as his memory stretched, but he had no idea how she'd got there or what had happened between them.

Rick had had enough. He really didn't care what had or hadn't happened between them. It was simple: he wouldn't be bribed, he didn't owe her and there wasn't enough money in the business to pay for more staff hours, no matter how much she wanted them. 'Nina, as I said before, the gym can't afford the hours. Please don't phone here again.' He slammed the phone down and checked his watch. The last thing he needed was threats. Especially tonight. Tonight he had everything planned with precision: the evening, the meal and the sensual entertainment that followed. He took in a deep breath, knowing that Michelle would arrive soon. He just had time to pop down to the kitchen, check the dinner and choose one of the many white wines he had chilled and ready to go. He needed something crisp and rich, that would go well with the salmon. He thought for a moment, remembered the case of Stellenbosch that he'd brought back from South Africa the year before and nodded his approval.

'On with the starters,' he announced as he bounced down the stairs and into the kitchen where he opened the fridge to reveal the two plates of smoked salmon, prawns and horseradish. He just needed to add the vinaigrette, which he lifted from the fridge. He stirred it and then tasted it with the spoon, then looked across the room to where the fruit bowl stood. 'More lemon,' he said as he walked across, chose one of the lemons, cut it in half and squeezed just a few drops into the liquid. Stirring it one more time, he took another taste. 'Perfect,' he said, just as the doorbell rang.

* * *

Michelle stood outside Rick's house and took in a deep breath. She was still alarmed by what she'd seen at the gym. She rummaged in her clutch bag for a mirror to check her appearance. It was the first time she'd been to Rick's home and a nervous excitement ran through her whole body; she had to look perfect, but Nina's words kept spinning around in her thoughts. She stared at her image. Did she look butch? She really wanted to look feminine, she wanted to have sex appeal and, more than anything, she finally wanted to get the chance to be with Rick.

She tried to think of the positives; he had finally asked her out to dinner and tonight was a real date. She tried to smile, but couldn't help feeling just a little disappointed that he hadn't taken her out to a restaurant, wined and dined her publicly, but after all that had happened, she'd understood the reasons he'd given for staying home and keeping a low profile. To be seen out would have attracted too much attention, and although he'd been cleared as an innocent man, there were some that still thought him to be guilty.

But, she knew differently, and a huge smile crossed her face. Rick couldn't possibly have attacked that woman. She shook her head. 'Not Rick, it wasn't Rick, it just couldn't have been,' she whispered to herself as she put the tiny mirror back into her bag.

She thought back over recent months. She'd been to visit him in prison, had gone over all the changes at the gym and for just a few moments at the beginning or end of each visit, he'd held her hand, or kissed her on the cheek. Everything before that had just been work. There had always been a mutual spark of attraction between them and she'd often hoped that he'd take the relationship further. But things had happened; other women had always fallen into his path and each time she'd taken a back seat, watching from a distance. But not this time. This time it was her turn to have Rick's full attention and even though she suspected that Tim was up to something, she wasn't ruining tonight for anyone. There would be plenty of time to speak to Rick about him tomorrow.

She stepped forward, rang the bell and waited for the door to open.

'Michelle, how are you? You look amazing.' Rick stood before her in a white linen shirt. It was paper-thin and through it she could make out the shape of his perfect abs. She nodded in approval. He was looking pretty amazing himself. 'Did you find me okay?' His voice cut through her thoughts.

'I did. You're further into the countryside than I thought, but once I'd worked it out, I was fine.' She stepped through the door and inhaled. The whole house was fresh, clean and smelt of lilies. 'Wow, Rick. Your house, it's beautiful. I love it,' she managed to say as Rick took her jacket, opened a closet and placed it inside.

'Well, thank you. The food is this way.' He swept his arm in a motion that indicated she should walk towards the kitchen. 'I've just finished making the vinaigrette that goes with the starter. Actually, I should have asked, you do like fish, don't you?' he questioned and Michelle smiled and nodded at the same time to show her appreciation. She was impressed. Not only had he cooked the food, he'd gone to some considerable effort to make everything fresh. 'It smells fantastic.' Michelle looked around the dimly lit kitchen. It was made of a light carved oak, had black granite worktops and looked brand new. She watched Rick as he added the vinaigrette to the two plates of food, quickly followed by a small handful of fresh salad leaves. 'I made a tomato, garlic and chilli sauce. Just the pasta and a little Italian sausage to add and it should be perfect.'

Michelle felt a rush of excitement as Rick walked towards her. His hand lifted up and caught her by the waist. He then stared deep into her eyes before lifting his fingers to her cheek. He had the lightest touch, sensual with just a hint of dominance. She felt him lift her chin up towards him before moving the fingers to weave themselves gently through her hair.

He then smiled and moved away, but his eyes were constantly fixed upon hers. He was teasing her and she liked it. 'Shall we eat?' she heard him say as he opened the fridge, and she watched as he lifted a bottle of wine from it. 'I hope you like a good Stellenbosch?'

Michelle nodded and followed Rick as, carrying two plates, he walked through the vast hallway. She smiled at the candles and looked up the staircase to the galleried landing beyond. She closed her eyes, just for a moment, and wondered if she'd end up walking up those stairs before the end of the night, but then as she opened them again she caught the reflection of something through the window. She turned, moved closer to the door and stared out.

Rick looked over his shoulder. 'All okay? The dining room is this way,' Rick said as his foot pushed open a door to reveal a beautifully decorated room.

'Sure. Sorry, I thought I saw something outside,' she said as she walked into the hallway, looked through the hallway glass, then dismissed the thought and followed him into the room.

Again, the room was all white with a solid oak table that would have seated at least twelve people.

Leather chairs stood all around its edge, but Rick had set the table just to one end and had placed a vase of flowers as a barrier to give the table a more intimate look.

'Thought it'd be friendlier this way.' He leaned forward, picked up an igniter and lit the tall church candle that stood central to the table before turning out the lights. 'You know, both of us together at one end of the table, rather than sitting at opposite ends shouting, "Send down the salt".' He laughed nervously at his own joke and made a sweeping gesture with his arm as though pushing the salt from one end to the other. His arm then once again caught her around the waist and Michelle took in a deep breath as his lips carefully brushed hers.

Rick pulled away. He didn't want to rush things, not tonight. Tonight was all about showing Michelle how special she was. She'd been there for him when no one else had. She'd visited him in prison, brought him news of the gym and supported him on the days when he'd felt as though he were losing his mind.

'Would you like wine?' Once again, his lips

grazed hers in passing as he leaned forward, picked up the wine bottle and without waiting for her to answer, half-filled the glasses. He picked them both up and handed one to her. 'Here's to tonight,' he said as his glass touched hers.

They both sipped the wine and, without losing eye contact, they both sat down at the table, where Rick had placed the plates of food.

The phone rang.

'Bloody phone,' Rick sounded aggrieved. The noise of the phone had broken the mood and he stood up from his chair, walked into the hallway and turned off the ringer. 'That should help.'

Michelle laughed. 'Don't you think you should have answered it? It could have been important.'

Rick returned to his seat and lifted a piece of salmon onto his fork. 'Nothing is as important as you are, not tonight.'

* * *

Michelle finished her starter. 'Wow, you certainly can cook, Mr Greaves.' She lifted her glass to her lips and sipped at the wine and it occurred to her that if she drank much more she wouldn't be in a position to drive home; surely Rick would know that.

Rick stood up. 'I'll just go and finish off the pasta. Would you like to join me in the kitchen?' He picked up his glass and Michelle did the same, following him out of the room.

'So, how long have you lived here?' Michelle was curious; the house looked brand new on the inside, but the amount of trees, bushes and landscaping outside told a different story.

'Just over a year. I sold the other house after Patsy died.' He turned away and stirred the sauce. 'It held too many memories, with Julia and then Patsy. I needed a fresh start.'

Michelle nodded. 'I can understand that. I doubt I'd have stayed there either.'

She spun around as her mobile began to ring. She hesitated. 'Agh, what is it with phones tonight? Sorry, do you mind?' She walked to where her bag lay on the worktop. 'It's my mum's ringtone.'

Rick smiled and Michelle walked into the hall to take the call. 'Hi, Mum. All okay?' She paused. 'Okay, okay, slow down. Who told you this?' She walked back into the kitchen and picked up her bag. 'Mum, okay, take deep breaths, I'm on my way to pick you up.'

Michelle pressed the off button on the phone. 'Look, Rick. I'm so sorry.' She closed her eyes and a single tear dropped down her face. 'Mum just had a call from North Yorkshire Police. It's Dad, he's been in an accident.' She swallowed and then continued. 'He's a long distance lorry driver and his wagon just left the road. The police told Mum that he's all right, but he's been taken to the hospital.' She fiddled with her bag. 'I have to go collect Mum and, you know, take her to him.'

Rick immediately switched off the range. 'Give me a minute, I'll come with you.' He began heading towards the hall, but Michelle shook her head.

'Rick, no. You've never met my mum and it's hardly the right time to introduce you, is it?' She walked towards the door. 'I'll call you later. Let you know what's happened.'

He held out his arms and pulled her into a hug. 'Okay. But if you need me, just call.'

Michelle climbed into the car and picked up her phone to send a text.

Mum, I'm on my way. Just leaving Rick's. Will be home in twenty minutes. x

Michelle turned the engine on and began driving at speed. It was still summer, the nights were light, but even though she knew most of the roads in this area well, she kept an eye on her mirrors as she took the car swiftly through the lanes that led from Rick's to the main roads.

She glanced down at her phone to see if her mother had replied and wondered if she should phone her instead. 'Shit, no signal.' She held the phone up and over her head, wound down the window and held it outside; still nothing. A car sped up behind her and she slowed down to allow it to pass. But then, without warning, she felt her whole car jolt. She lost control of the steering and she automatically hit her brakes as hard as she could. There was a squealing of brakes, followed by a loud thud as her car skidded off the road, went over the grass verge and headed towards the fields at speed, stopping just short of a deep and water-filled ditch. She felt her stomach turn as she leaned backwards, afraid that the car would tip into the water and, for a moment, she just sat. She closed her eyes, swallowed hard and took in short, sharp breaths as she tried desperately to slow her heart rate that pounded with the intensity of a bass drum. Her eyes were fixed on the ditch and she realised just how close she'd come to plunging into the depths of the water. She felt bile rise in her throat at the thought.

She looked over her shoulder. The other car had

now turned in the road. 'At least you stopped, you moron.' She pushed at the door that didn't want to open and ended up kicking at it with force. She then stepped painfully out of the car and into the mud that covered the embankment. Every inch of her hurt; her shoes sank into the mud and she closed her eyes as the tears began to fall. This was the last thing she needed tonight. First her dad and now her. She thought of how her poor mum would feel when she got yet another call telling her that her daughter had now been involved in an accident. Her neck hurt, her shoulder had been pulled back by the seat belt and the strap of the shoe cut into her toes. An involuntary sob left her lips. She looked up to the sky as raindrops began to drop, one quickly followed by another. She looked down at the dress she'd bought specially for tonight, paid for on her credit card, along with everything else that she couldn't afford and now, even before it was paid for, it would be ruined by the mud and the rain. She looked at the mud-covered straps on her shoes and bent down to pull at the leather, before slowly beginning to walk towards the other car. But then she stopped walking. The other car hadn't moved. The driver hadn't emerged and she stared at the dark blue Golf, and at the driver, as its engine revved and it drove directly at her.

* * *

I'm sitting looking at your prone body as you lie in the dirt. You're on the grass verge, to the side of the road. But your shoe has travelled. It flew through the air and it's now lying on the white line in the centre of the road. I feel the need to put it back on your foot, but I can't. I'm shaking with the adrenaline that pumps through my body, I feel frozen in time and I have to wait for the moment to pass. Eventually, my hands hit the steering wheel so hard that the horn blasts out and I look around to ensure that the road is still empty. Then, I smile. The road is quiet, and I sit back for a moment and stare. I'm so angry with you but there's no time to think about that now, and I start the car in the knowledge that I took back the control. And now, now you've paid the price.

19

Will turned over in bed, woken by the shrill sound of his phone ringing. He opened his eyes and for the second night in a row, it was still dark, cold and far too early to be woken up.

'What?' He balanced the phone between one hand and the pillow and tried to move into a position where he could see the clock. He covered his eyes with his arm, shielding them from the glare of the luminous numbers.

'Will, you need to get down here. We've got a body on the top road. Woman, it's a hit-and-run. I can't get close enough to get a shot.' Josh sounded disturbed and excitable all at once. 'Will, bring the big camera, we need the zoom to get a picture of the police activity, they're everywhere.'

Will knew that the story must be big for Josh to have phoned in the middle of the night. Normally he'd have attended the scene, taken the photos, written up the report and had it on his desk by the time Will got to the office next morning.

'Josh, for God's sake. I'm knackered. Can't you handle it?' He sat up and knuckle rubbed his eyes.

'Normally I would, Will, but...' Josh sounded as though he were running. Again, it was unlike him. The last time Josh had done anything that would have broken a sweat it had involved Sarah and the cockle shed.

'Okay, Josh, I'll come out. Try and get the exclusive. Do we know who the woman is?' Will fumbled for the light, turned it on and stepped across the room, realising that after he'd finished laying the turf the night before, he'd only had two hours' sleep.

'Course I do. You remember Sarah, don't you, the one you kicked out of our office?'

Will butted in. 'Oh my God. She can't be dead, Josh, she's Ella's friend.'

'Catch up, Will, Sarah isn't dead. But she did phone me. Like you said, she's a copper, was first on the scene and she called me while waiting for the emergency services to arrive. Which means I get the exclusive. The woman's called Michelle Everett and as I said it looks like a hit- and-run. Bastard killed her outright.' The words made Will stop in his tracks. He stood for a moment before opening the wardrobe door and looking along the line of identical crisp white shirts. He pulled one out and began to get dressed.

'I've heard that name before.' He couldn't think where from, but was sure it had been mentioned recently. Will searched his mind. 'What does she look like?'

Josh paused. 'Well, I'd like to say she's beautiful, tall and blonde, but right now I'd say that her beauty may have been a bit of a previous feature.'

Will cringed at the thought. He rushed down the stairs, out of the back door. The door slammed as he ran down the drive to where his car was parked by the kerb at the front of the house. He automatically looked up at Ella's front bedroom window. A light glowed and he noticed her peep from behind the curtain, then texted whilst waving.

Sorry, did I wake you?

She responded straight away.

Not at all. I was reading. Heard your door, worried you might be about to break in again. Lol!

Go back to bed. I'll pop and help with Millie in the morning. Hope your leg's a bit better?

He'd have liked to keep the conversation going, but knew that time was of the essence and if he wanted the story, he really had to go.

Thank you, the leg's ok ish xx

Ella's reply came just as Will saw the light go out and Ella's house was left, like his own, in darkness.

* * *

Will pulled his car up on the top road. He grabbed his notebook, camera bag and jacket from the back seat and abandoned the car. He could see the blue flashing lights in the distance and knew that he was as close to the scene as he would get without being stopped by the police. Besides, he knew that he'd get closer on foot. He had to find Josh and, if he guessed correctly, Josh would be as close to the police and body as he could possibly get.

He jogged towards the flashing lights of the emergency vehicles.

'Now then, what do you know?' Will asked as he caught his breath and dropped the camera bag at Josh's feet.

'Not much. I've been digging around on the internet. You know you said you'd heard the name before? Well, can you remember where from?'

'I did say that, but no I can't think where from.' The truth was that Will had thought of nothing but Ella during the drive over. He'd thought of the night they'd sat together in the hospital waiting room, how they'd chatted for hours before going back to Ella's cottage. He'd been shattered, but had spent the whole of the next day running in and out of the house in an attempt to teach Millie that peeing outside was good. There had been an accident or two, but at least he'd had the opportunity to stay close to Ella. She hadn't seemed to mind him taking up residence on the settee in her cottage, nor had she seemed to mind feeding him breakfast, dinner and tea which had saved him a trip to the supermarket. Then he had begun thinking about food and of how he'd repay the debt.

He rubbed his eyes; two hours' sleep was never enough, but after doing this job for the past five years, he'd learnt to cope. He knew that at some point during the day complete exhaustion would take over and then he'd collapse in a heap, normally in the back of his or one of the other reporters' cars.

'Really, come on, try and think where you've heard the name before. You'll kick yourself when I tell you.' Josh perched on his car bonnet, tapped his pen on his notebook and waited for Will to reply.

Will shook his head. 'I have no idea.'

'Oh come on, Will. Play the game. Are you sure?' Josh pulled a face, raised his eyebrows and jumped down from the bonnet.

'Josh, do you know what time it is?' He looked at his watch. 'It's one in the morning and if you hadn't already guessed, I'm too tired for games. Just tell me who the hell she is.'

'Michelle Everett.' Josh paused. 'The gym, Will. She works at... No, she worked at Rick Greaves' gym.'

Will stared at Josh, his eyes wide like saucers. 'Get away.' The words slipped from him mouth. They had no meaning but it had been all he'd felt capable of saying as he looked to where the blue flashing lights continued to light up the moors and he could see men erecting a small white forensics tent. He'd watched this scene so many times before and still couldn't get used to it. He looked up at the sky and then down at the ground, which was wet. He knew that the rain must have already fallen and it threatened again. The team only had a short period of time to erect the tent, preserve the scene and collect any samples or evidence from along the road. If the rain came down heavily, any evidence that they might have retrieved could be washed away and the identity of the hit-and-run driver lost forever.

'Has the coroner arrived yet?' He set off running towards the blue and white police tape that now stretched across the road. 'Josh, give Sarah a call. If we're going to get the best story we need to get to the other side of that tape and we need to speak to that coroner.'

* * *

The roads of Ugathwaite were quiet. Sleepy even, with street lights dimmed and most of the houses still in darkness. But daylight was just about to break and the birds had already begun their morning chorus.

Will pulled his car over to the side of the road,

turned off the engine and closed his eyes. He listened for just a moment. The noise was beautiful, pure and natural and he could have sat for hours just listening to the birds, but knew that if he did, he'd be asleep within minutes. There was still a lot of work to do and he needed to get moving in order to stay awake.

'Come on, sleeping beauty, shake a leg, we're here.' He nudged Josh, who in return grunted from the passenger seat and turned over like a petulant child. 'Josh, come on, work to do.'

'Where are we?' A miserable sounding whisper came from somewhere beneath the anorak, as one arm at a time began to move in an outward stretch.

'We're at Greaves' house. Come on, we need to bang on his door and get the interview before either the police or the rest of the press get here.' Will thought long and hard about what Ella had said, that journalists really were vultures, and he had to agree. He even included himself in that statement. He watched the house. All was in darkness and he felt sure that Greaves was inside, sleeping. Just like Josh, who once again had begun to snore in the seat beside him.

Will nudged Josh. 'Come on, I've had no sleep either.

The sooner we're done, the sooner we go home.'

'But you never want to go home,' the voice murmured. 'What's changed?'

Will thought of Ella. How he wished that right now he was curled up on her settee chatting to her, Millie sitting between them, playing and fussing till she fell asleep in an exhausted heap. He sighed. That's where he'd like to be, but he was tired, so very tired and felt as though if he stopped, he'd sleep for a week.

'JOSH,' he shouted and Josh jumped up from his prone position and sat upright in the front of the car.

'Jesus Christ, Will. You didn't have to scare me half to death, what's that all about?' Josh pulled the coat on that he'd been using as a blanket and zipped it up.

'Go and interview Greaves. See what he has to say and get a picture. I'd go myself, but he'd recognise me from the gym. Can't blow my cover, not now they think I'm a landscape gardener. And I still want to be able to go into the gym and see what's happening.'

Josh turned and reached into the back seat for his camera. 'Okay, five questions max. Then you take me home, right?'

* * *

Josh opened the car door, jumped out, stretched and walked over to the detached house. Trees and bushes surrounded the property, giving him ample time to look around. There were no cars on the drive, no sign of life, meaning that the house was either empty or Rick Greaves was tucked up, fast asleep in bed.

Josh's fist banged on the door with a thunderous knock and then he stood back and waited before banging again.

A light went on upstairs and the silhouette of a man came into view as he stumbled down the stairs. 'What the hell, who is it?' The voice bellowed and a second light went on in the hallway. Rick Greaves ran his hands through his hair as he peered through the glass in the front door.

'Rick Greaves, I'm Josh Bates, Scarborough Star. Could you tell me what you know about the murder of Michelle Everett?' Josh watched for Greaves' reaction. He held his camera at the ready and waited for the full impact of the question to sink in.

Rick stopped in his tracks. He looked down at the floor and then reached forward, turned the key in the lock and pulled the door open to the flashing lights of the camera.

'Stop that flashing, for God's sake.' Rick held his arm up to cover his eyes. 'Now, tell me again, what the hell did you just say?'

Josh smirked. 'You heard me, Mr Greaves. Michelle Everett is dead. I'd like to know what you know about her murder?'

Rick appeared to grab hold of the door frame. He swallowed hard, and then looked behind him and into the house. His legs looked as though they were about to buckle as he swayed back and forth. 'Dead? What the hell are you talking about, she – she was just here?'

Once again Josh began taking photographs. But Rick's hand swung out, narrowly missing his face. 'I've told you to stop flashing that bloody thing.'

Josh managed to bounce out of the way as Rick made repeated attempts to grab at the camera. Josh once again sidestepped. He felt like a gazelle dodging a lion and smirked as he jumped out of the way. 'No you don't,' he said. 'This camera was expensive.'

'Then stop shoving the bloody thing in my face, you asshole!' Rick screamed. 'You said murder, but that can't be. She was here, she left just after ten. As far as I'm aware, she went to collect her mother, something about her father having been in an accident.'

'So, she was here, was she? Why was that, Mr Greaves?' Josh clicked away on the camera.

'I've told you, she left at around ten. Her mother called and said that her father had had an accident. I offered to go with her, but she refused. That's the last I saw of her.'

'Well, I'm afraid she didn't get there. She was found on the top road, hit-and-run.' Josh paused. 'Don't you think it's a horrible coincidence how everyone associated with you ends up dead or seriously injured?' He paused and stood back. 'Why do you think that happens, Mr Greaves?' Rick looked visibly shocked and Josh wondered how a man could continually manage to act hurt, each and every time one of his loved ones seemed to die.

'Get out of my face and get off my drive. I'm saying no more until I've phoned my solicitor.' Rick's voice was getting louder and louder, and decidedly more aggressive.

Josh looked back to where the car was parked. He knew that Will was waiting and he heard the engine rev up, which was probably Will indicating to him that he still had his foot on the accelerator, just in case they needed to make a fast retreat.

'What happened, Mr Greaves? Didn't she like your advances? Is that why she left?' Josh pointed at the spent candles. 'Because if you ask me, it looks like you were all set up for a romantic night.'

Rick stepped back into his house, grabbed his mobile phone and began tapping a number into the pad.

'Were you and Michelle a couple, Mr Greaves? Did you argue, is that why she left?' Josh continued. The question was simple and was intended to gain a reaction. 'Seriously, it seems quite amazing that most of your former wives or partners end up dead or dying, doesn't it?' Josh saw Rick's hand fly out towards him and felt himself falling backwards. The camera flew towards the bushes and he landed heavily on his bottom, just as the click and flash of Will's camera came from behind him.

20

Ella checked her reflection in the mirror and admired the new shape that her body had become. After the attack, she'd barely eaten for months and had become far too thin, but now the curves had returned in all the right places. She approved. The new jeans hugged her, along with a Bardot style T-shirt which seductively hung off from one shoulder and she nodded appreciatively. She sat down at the dressing table and pulled the straighteners through her hair, making sure each strand was perfectly flat. Sighing, she picked up the nude lip gloss and carefully applied a thin, but perfectly shaped layer.

'Millie, Will's coming round soon. Are you excited?' she asked as the puppy trotted into her bedroom and made an attempt to jump up onto the bed. Her front paws reached up, while her back legs did an over-excited scramble in an attempt to get a foothold, which made Ella laugh before reaching down to put a hand under Millie's bottom. She helped her up and then watched as she began to snuggle herself down in the quilt. 'Hey, don't you start getting any ideas, little one. This is not your bed.' She looked down at the ball of fluff that simply turned onto her back and waved her paws around in the air until Ella conceded and sat beside her, tickling and rubbing her stomach.

The noise of the postman pushing letters through the door sent Millie bouncing up. She fell off the bed and then ran as fast as she could down the stairs, yapping as she went.

'Hey, silly. Slow down, you'll hurt yourself,' Ella shouted and then sat back down at the dressing table, checking her appearance once again. It was just eight thirty in the morning and even though she'd had a restless night, she felt excited that Will had said he'd call round.

The day before had been fun. He'd spent the day playing with Millie. They'd both monopolised his time for the whole day without a thought and Ella had then felt guilty as she'd peeked out from the bedroom window and watched him laying turf until late.

But then she'd heard him go out. It had been the middle of the night and she'd lain awake wondering where he'd been going. To her knowledge men only went out that late for one of two reasons and both normally involved a woman.

Could Will have a girlfriend? It was something she hadn't thought of before and the idea not only startled her, but for some reason it actually bothered her that he might. He hadn't mentioned a girlfriend, but then again, why would he?

Ella sat down on the floor and moved herself towards the stairs. Her ankle was still painful, so she began to make her way down one stair at a time on her bottom, while Millie sat in the hallway, looking up, her tail waving from side to side, before she suddenly ran up the stairs and jumped on Ella's knee, licking at her face.

'Hey you, I can't go down the stairs with you on my knee,' Ella laughed, grabbing at her crutches, which stood in the corner of the hallway. Swishing Millie off her knee and onto the floor, she used the crutches to propel herself forward.

'Go on, get out and play for a while,' she said as she opened the conservatory door and watched as an excited Millie ran down the garden. A female blackbird had dared to land on the grass and Millie was suddenly more than determined to chase her off.

Ella picked up her mobile and flicked the screen across to check the clock. Eight forty-two. It'd been hours since Will had gone out, hours since he'd texted her. She pressed the message icon on her phone to check what Will had said.

I'll pop and help with Millie in the morning.

She read the words over and over. He'd definitely said he'd call in. But was he going to be calling in to see her, or to see Millie?

Ella watched Millie as she ran up and down the lawn. Ella laughed at the puppy when she stuck her nose in a bush, only to pull it back really fast, as another blackbird swooped out at her and chirped wildly as though telling her off for the disturbance.

Leaving Millie to her antics, Ella made her way to the front of the house. She noticed that Will's car had returned and she felt her stomach twist in excitement. It hadn't been there ten minutes before, which meant that Will had definitely been out all night.

So, the question remained: where had he been? And, realistically, was it any of her business? Ella shook her head. She knew it shouldn't bother her, but it did. She walked back into the kitchen and switched on the kettle.

Ella sighed. The thoughts of Will and another woman swirled around in her mind. After all, after midnight was hardly a time when you nip to a shop, to the pub or to visit an elderly relative. He'd only just gone to bed a couple of hours before, or so she'd thought, and he'd gone out in what looked like a suit, a white shirt and a tie. All clothes that she'd have thought a little smart for doing any of the above visits. She scratched her head, and poured the coffee. Will's movements were affecting her far too much. Ella shook her head. She barely knew anything about him. She couldn't remember him mentioning any relatives; in fact, she really couldn't remember Will mentioning anything about his private life at all. The conversations between them had never been on a personal level. They'd been more about Millie, the garden, the news, the weather and how Josh and Sarah were or were not getting on. Come to think of it, they'd completely avoided any subject that would have meant disclosing any personal information about him, or about her. She felt a little puzzled, and wondered if they'd both done that intentionally.

Ella stopped in her tracks. She nodded and sighed. He must have a girlfriend. Of course, that's where he'd have gone. She mentally kicked herself; how could she be so stupid? It was obvious that Will would have a girlfriend. He was, after all, a red-blooded male... Or was he? She pondered the thought; maybe he was gay, maybe that was why he'd never mentioned a partner. But if there was a partner, why didn't he or she come and visit Will at home? 'Arrrghhhhhhh!' she screamed, moving her hands through her hair and over her head, ruffling her hair. 'Why, why did you make an effort? He's calling to help with Millie, not to see you.'

'Ella, hello,' Will's voice shouted through from the conservatory door. 'Ella, you there?'

Ella's hands went back up to her hair. She looked across to the mirror that hung over the fire and began smoothing her hair back down at speed, losing the grip on her crutch; she watched in slow motion as it fell against the chair, bounced and propelled itself towards the television, just missing the screen.

Ella went to grab at the crutch, put her foot to the floor and squealed as the pain shot through her ankle. Lifting her foot up quickly, she lost her balance, began falling towards the settee and in a movement that couldn't be stopped, landed in a heap, just as Will bounded through the door.

'Bloody hell, Ella. What happened? It's okay.' His arms were around her. 'I've got you,' he said as she happily sank into the warmth and security that was Will. The television had turned itself on and the noise coming from it had made her jump. She bit her lip, determined not to cry.

'What happened?' Will asked, his arms still around her. Ella had no idea where she'd begin and decided to stay quiet rather than try and explain how she'd ended up in a heap. Besides, how could she tell him that she was making herself presentable for him? Tidying her hair up and checking her lip gloss in the mirror and hoping that he hadn't spent the night with another woman, or man.

She felt stupid and for no good reason, she finally felt the forbidden sob leave her body.

'Hey, come on. It can't be that bad, can it?' Will's hand lifted and she felt his fingers stroke her face. She gasped and then held her breath as Will tilted her face towards him and she found herself staring into those vivid blue eyes.

'The TV... I might have broken it,' was all she

could think to say. Her heart began beating heavily in her chest; her breath caught in her throat and she managed half a smile. Every part of her began to tremble. Will's sapphire eyes looked deep into hers and, for a moment, she saw the pain and need behind them.

'Ella, the television is fine.'

Will's lips were so close that Ella could feel his breath on her face. Her eyes could only see his and she knew that they searched hers for permission. 'Ella... Can...?'

She blinked, nodded and reached forward to feel his lips touch hers. Just a graze at first, a tease and then he began gently surrounding her mouth with soft, gentle, tender kisses. The scent of his aftershave was a soft, musky smell that stimulated every sense. She felt alive for the first time in months as his lips left hers momentarily and began to follow a path down her neck. She closed her eyes, enjoying the sensation as Will's lips kissed every part of her neck, making her moan with desire. She allowed him to take control. His lips returned to hers, capturing them in a more demanding way. This time his tongue teased hers, sending shivers racing through her body. With each kiss the intensity deepened and she felt his fingers move over her shoulder, down her back and trace their way down the curve of her spine. Ella gasped and closed her eyes just as the door flew open and Sarah barged in.

'Oh, wow. Sorry, my dears, am I disturbing something?' Her voice had a hint of amusement and she disappeared out of the room as quickly as she'd burst in. Ella could hear her opening and closing the kitchen cupboards. 'I'll put the kettle on, shall I? Give you two the chance to, you know, part the waves.'

Ella swallowed hard. But Will continued to hold her close. He pressed his forehead against hers, looked into her eyes and then pulled away to kiss her gently on the lips. 'This isn't over.' His eyes searched her face. 'Can we, you know, carry this on later?' It was a question and a promise, making Ella nod and smile in agreement.

'You just finished work, Sarah?' Ella shouted through as Will stood up and began pulling at his trousers, tucked his shirt back in and ran a hand over his head as though tidying the hair that he didn't have.

'Doesn't she ever knock?' Will whispered, his hand doing an imaginary knock in mid-air. Only to catch Ella under the chin, pull her back towards him and once again press his lips tenderly to hers.

Ella shook her head and continued to blush and giggle. 'I've never been so embarrassed,' she whispered, feeling like a schoolgirl who'd just been caught out by her parents.

'Yeah, I've had a bad night. I needed coffee,' Sarah shouted back. 'Bloody long night it was too. We had a hit-and-run on the top road. That's why I've called in. I wanted you to hear it from me, before anyone else. But I guess Will has already told you.' She paused and they heard the kettle come to the boil. 'Looks like she worked at the gym.' Again she paused. 'Sorry, Ella, but we've had to drag Rick Greaves in for questioning.' There was a banging of drawers, followed by a clatter of cutlery. 'You got a teaspoon? Actually, don't worry, I've got one.'

Ella stood up. The giggles had disappeared and been replaced by a stomach twisting anxiety. The sheer mention of Rick Greaves' name sent her heart racing, her stomach into knots and her body into a continuous trembling that once again started deep within her and didn't stop.

'What... what happened? And tell me the truth. Don't flower it up. I need the truth,' Ella questioned, not really wanting to hear the answer, but knowing that whatever had happened, she needed the unedited version.

Will grabbed hold of her. 'Don't ask,' he said as his arms surrounded her and he led them both back to the settee. Sitting down, Ella cuddled into the safety of Will's arms. For a moment the trembling stopped and for a few seconds she allowed herself to enjoy the comfort that his arms brought.

Sarah returned to the room carrying a pack of biscuits. 'Found these in the cupboard, you don't mind if I munch, Ella, do you? I'm starving.' She dropped the open pack on the table, pulled two biscuits out of the packet and pushed one in her mouth whole, then disappeared back into the kitchen.

Ella smiled. It had been a standing joke for years that Sarah was always hungry, and she'd learned to always keep a stock of goodies in the cupboard, just in case. 'There are some crumpets in the first cupboard, help yourself,' she shouted through the wall, while her hand casually rested against Will's leg. She caught his eye. A warmth travelled between them and for the first time in months, she felt a deep happiness that she hoped would stay forever.

'Hey, Will,' Sarah shouted, 'where did you and Josh disappear to?'

Ella felt Will stiffen. She looked at him, a puzzled look on her face. 'How does Sarah know you were out with Josh last night?'

* * *

Will jumped up from the settee and opened the kitchen door. 'Milk in my coffee, please, and if you don't mind, make it strong. I'm knackered.' He pulled a face at Sarah and held a finger to his lips, but she was too busy placing crumpets under the grill.

'Ella, do you want tea or coffee?' Sarah shouted as she pulled the sugar from the cupboard, grabbed at the teaspoon and placed a heaped spoonful into one of the mugs. 'That's for me. It's needed. I'm knackered too.'

Will needed to find a way to stop Sarah talking about the case. He needed time to tell Ella what he did for a living, but he had no idea where to begin. Too much time had passed, too many opportunities missed. He'd tried over and over to tell her that he was a reporter, but each and every time something had happened to stop him and, in the end, he'd wrongly avoided the subject.

'Sarah, I really don't think Ella needs to know the details about last night. You can see she's upset,' he whispered, once again holding a finger up to his lips.

'What are you hiding, Will Taylor?' Sarah whispered back. She stared over his shoulder and towards the door behind which Ella sat.

'Look, let me talk to her first, you know, about the job.'

'Oh my God, she doesn't know you're a reporter, does she?' Sarah whispered, pushing her way past Will. 'Why the hell haven't you told her, it's not like you're an axe murderer, is it?' she asked as she carried the mugs into the lounge, giving one to Ella and passing the other to an anxious looking Will.

Sarah looked around before sitting down. 'Ella, where's Millie Moo? She's normally all over me by now.'

21

Will ran out of the cottage, down the length of the garden and began clapping his hands together in an attempt to attract the puppy. 'Millie, come on girl, Millie.'

He searched every corner of the garden and looked under every bush. He then looked towards the garage and the gate, the road and farm beyond. The gate was closed, but he couldn't remember whether it had been when he'd arrived. He'd been tired and on automatic pilot. He tried to think back over his actions. He remembered jumping out of the car. He'd gone into his house, dropped off his laptop, his camera and his phone. But then, without a second thought, he'd headed straight for Ella's.

Could he have left the gate open? Had Sarah? She'd arrived after him and normally anyone touching the gate would have the puppy scurrying towards it in the hope that it was a friend carrying food or treats. But that hadn't happened. Millie been there when he'd arrived. Which probably meant she'd already been missing when Sarah arrived. His reporter's mind threw every question up in the air and he watched them all land in a heap without an answer.

He shook his head and tried to think. Where would an inquisitive puppy have gone?

Will hurried towards the road. His eyes searched each door along the street, and each garden in the hope that one of the neighbours would run out clutching the puppy escapologist. He watched a car as it slowed down, went past and headed up the lane, towards the moors. Could someone have stopped their car and taken her? No, no, no, that can't have happened. Ella would be distraught if Millie was gone. He searched his mind. Had Ella taken Millie to the vet's, had she been microchipped? He was sure that she hadn't. After all, she'd only had her a few days and was on crutches and now, now the dog was missing and it was probably all his fault. He stood in the street shouting,

'Millie, Millie, come on, puppy! Come to Will!' He didn't know what else to do but try and find her and began to run helplessly up and down the road.

'Millie, come on, girl.' He ran in the same direction as the car, and to the end of the road, where Sarah already stood talking to someone. 'She's small, golden and fluffy, around eight weeks old?' he could hear her saying as she questioned the neighbour, who shook his head, promised to keep a look out and headed off in the opposite direction. 'Millie, come on, baby. Millie...' Ella yelled from the front door and Will could hear the desperation in her voice. He knew he had to do something to make things right, but what?

Where do you even begin to look for an escapologist puppy?

He ran to the farm opposite, shouting and clapping as he went. A tractor stood abandoned to the side of the lane and Will quickly checked around in case Millie had climbed into the cab and fallen asleep, or worse she could be hiding underneath. But then Will stopped in his tracks and looked at the height of the cab. She could barely climb on the settee without help and he realised that there was no way she'd have climbed into a tractor. No. He had to think sensibly. She was small. She had to be somewhere where small things could get. He ran into the farmyard, into the hay filled barn. Climbing up and over the bales he looked down from above. 'Come on, Millie, where are you? Come on, girl.' He fully expected to see the fluffy ball of fun fast asleep in the middle of the bales, or bounding towards him and jumping into his arms. But he didn't.

Sarah ran into the barn behind him. 'Millie, Millie,' she shouted continuously and then turned to Will. 'We're going to have to draw up a plan, search separately, cover as much ground as possible. We need to get help, call Ella's parents. Millie could be anywhere by now.'

Will rubbed the top of his head with both hands. 'Okay, phone Ella's parents. Have you got their number?'

Sarah nodded.

'Okay, I'll go back to Ella. We'll sync phones, the first to spot her, calls the others.'

They both set off back towards the cottage, to where Ella could be seen frantically shouting for Millie.

'Sarah, wait a minute. I have to tell you something.' His hand touched her shoulder and she spun around to face him. 'You're right, Ella doesn't know I'm a reporter. I've tried to tell her, honest to God I have, and I will. But she made it very clear to me that she thinks of us all as vultures and I kind of want to prove to her that we're not before I tell her. Besides, it's not like she isn't one herself, is it? She is going back to work soon.'

Sarah glared. 'I know she's still a reporter, Will, but even so, she's still not fond of them and you know that.' She smiled. 'You've got till Saturday. If you don't tell her, I will. Can't be fairer than that, can I?' She glanced in his direction and smirked as Will reluctantly nodded in agreement.

But then a noise made them both stop in their tracks. It was a whimper, followed by a 'Shhh...'

Sarah began walking around the hay bales, edging her way past one stack and then the other. She lifted a finger in the air. 'Behind here,' she mouthed, and then rounded the corner to see Bobby sitting in a corner, between two hay bales, with Millie fast asleep in his arms.

'Okay, Bobby. What are you doing?' Sarah spoke with authority. Her normal chatty personality had been replaced with her professional one and she took a step towards where Bobby sat.

'I didn't hurt her, and I wasn't going to keep her, I promise.' His eyes were filled with tears. 'I wanted to see the puppy, but Ella shouted at me.' A sob left his throat. 'I was only trying to help her and she shouted. Said I couldn't go over any more.' His hand continually stroked Millie who had now stirred from her sleep. She'd spotted Will, and in her excitement was now trying to escape Bobby's grasp.

'So, how come you have Millie over here?' Again Sarah took a step forward. Her voice was calm, her mannerisms slow. She crouched down, making her body seem less imposing as she moved slowly forward. 'Can you let Millie go please, Bobby? I think she wants to go to Will.'

A tear dropped down his face. 'I thought Ella was my friend.' His eyes looked longingly down at Millie. 'I don't have many. And now, now Ella don't like me any more. But I wouldn't hurt the puppy.' He shook his head. 'She was out there on the road.' He pointed in the direction of Ella's house. 'She ran over to me and, well, I just wanted to play with her for a bit.' He looked down at Millie, lifted her to his face and took in a deep breath. 'She smells really nice. But once she was over here, I knew you'd think I took her. I was a bit scared.'

'She does smell really nice, doesn't she?' Sarah spoke calmly. She quickly turned to Will, indicated that he shouldn't move and then once again she spoke to Bobby. 'Ella's probably really sorry that she shouted at you, Bobby. She's had a really tough time. You know she was badly hurt, don't you? And that day you walked in when she wasn't expecting you, she wasn't even dressed, Bobby, and you really scared her. You do see that, don't you?'

Bobby nodded. His whole attention was on Millie. 'Am I in trouble?'

Sarah shook her head. 'Not if you give Millie back now. You might have to promise that you won't take her again though. And I'll tell Ella how sad you are, that you'd like to make friends and that you were just looking after Millie for a minute. Okay?' Sarah held out her arms and slowly lifted Millie from Bobby's knee, just as a loud and piercing scream filled the air.

'That's Ella!' Will screamed as he spun around and sped towards the cottage.

22

Ella had wandered back and forth along the road, all the time looking and shouting for Millie. She could feel herself being drawn inwards, every part of her felt numb as she feared the bad news that would soon follow. It was the story of her life. Something good would happen, and then something bad. Her energy levels had dropped, her shoulders slumped and she walked slowly towards the cottage, all the time worrying about Millie, wondering where she was, whether someone had got her and whether she'd ever be found.

Ella stared across the miles of fields that were opposite the front of her home. A deep longing overtook her mind. Millie had only been with her a couple of days and already she'd proved to be the worst dog owner in the history of mankind. How could she have lost her?

Millie had brought her and Will together and, right now, all Ella wanted was to once again feel the tenderness of Will's kiss, the warmth of his mouth on hers, as Millie playfully sat on the settee between them.

'Millie, come on girl, Millie.' She'd shouted and shouted for what seemed like an eternity and now, now she appeared to have lost both Sarah and Will too. They'd disappeared in the direction of the farm around ten minutes before and Ella had stood by the cottage since, not daring to move. It was only right that one of them stayed home, just in case Millie came back.

Ella wrinkled her nose. What was that smell? She wandered back alongside the cottage. If it had been a hot sunny day, she'd have thought that one of the neighbours might have started a BBQ or a garden fire. But the weather had been cool for the past few days and she doubted that anyone would be too bothered about sitting outdoors.

'Hi, Peter,' she called as Peter and his Labrador, Cookie, walked along the lane. 'You haven't seen my puppy, have you?' She held her hands out before her, indicating her size. 'She's a Cockerpoo, about this big. With golden fur.' Ella fussed Cookie, but Peter shook his head.

'I've only just come out, but I'll ask me mam. She was out with the pram earlier, she might have seen her.' He walked up the drive alongside her. 'Do you want me to check round the back garden for you?' he asked as he stood back and then, with a questioning look, said, 'Ella, what's that bloody noise?'

Ella turned and let out a loud scream. The fire alarm could just be heard coming from her house and she suddenly remembered Sarah's talk of being hungry and her offer of crumpets.

Ella froze on the spot. 'What... what if Millie's still in there?' she shouted as every millimetre of air was suddenly sucked from her lungs. Panic set in. She held onto the fence and screamed as loud as she could for Will.

'Peter, here,' she tossed her mobile phone at him. 'Do you know how to call 999?' She paused and watched him nod, 'Good, call the fire brigade. Tell them to come quickly.' Ella counted to ten, dared herself to enter and then ran into the cottage. Her ankle stabbed with pain, but her instincts told her to ignore it. She had to save her home, save what she'd worked for and she had to protect the only real place other than her parents' house where she'd ever felt safe.

Without any real thought of the consequences, Ella ran through the conservatory and into the kitchen. The whole room had filled with smoke, flames lapped upwards and she found it difficult to see where she was going. She coughed repeatedly, grabbed at a tea towel and wafted it in the air. And then, without warning, Will was there. His hands were on her shoulders and he moved her back towards the door. 'Ella... go back outside, now. I'll sort it.' His words were stern, and Ella stepped back but didn't leave; she watched as, with fire extinguisher in hand, Will pushed himself forward and aimed it directly at the grill.

The fire was out and suddenly his arms went around her and she felt herself being pulled out of the house and into the garden. 'Oh, Ella, don't you ever do that again, do you hear me?' he gasped as he spoke. 'Running into a burning building was stupid and dangerous and you can't ever do it again. Promise me. Promise me now!'

Ella could hear the mixture of anger and fear in his words and she swallowed hard and nodded.

'I can't do it, Ella. I won't do it.' He paused and his whole body heaved with emotion. 'I won't lose you too.' His lips captured hers. The kiss was deep, meaningful and Ella became lost in the moment, even though somewhere in the back of her mind she knew that at some point soon he'd have to tell her who else he'd lost, and when.

* * *

Will shook from head to toe. Both he and Ella were outside and had taken refuge on the grass while the fire brigade checked the house to make sure it was safe.

He felt physically shaken, inside and out and his hands still visibly shook with terror. The last time he'd seen a house fire, it had killed everyone he loved. He knew what it could do, and how quickly it could kill. His heart had dropped into his boots the moment he'd seen Peter hopping up and down on the drive. He was shouting and screaming all at once; the words, 'Fire, Fire, there's a fire,' had hit Will's ears and he'd immediately pulled open his car door and grabbed the extinguisher, grateful that this time he'd had one.

The days after his parents and sister had died came to mind and he remembered how much he'd kicked himself, wishing he'd had either an extinguisher, or something else that might have helped. Although in his heart he knew that he couldn't have done anything that fifteen firemen hadn't, he'd vowed never to feel that helpless again. Even though he'd bought the extinguisher two years before, it'd still been wrapped in the same box that he'd bought it in, so he'd had to quickly unpack it as he'd run towards the cottage.

He stroked Millie, who now sat beside him on the grass, and for a time he closed his eyes, knowing that running into a burning house had probably been the single most stupid thing he'd ever done. But he hadn't thought for himself. He'd thought about Ella; she'd been inside, and his whole being had screamed out to save her, to protect her. Besides, there was no way he was going to lose her too. Not if he could help it.

23

'Keep going, there you go, nearly there.' Will breathed in deep and watched the cross trainer's clock until it finally clicked over to fifteen minutes. 'And you did it.' He climbed down and wiped his face on a towel, picked up a water bottle and sipped at the liquid. He needed to burn off some steam. He looked around, choosing his next piece of equipment, which wasn't an issue because the gym was practically empty. The staff appeared to outnumber the customers and Nina had patrolled her way around them all like an overbearing hyena.

Only three people seemed to have been in during the past hour. Two had walked in and walked

out again without training and the other had
worked out on one of the cross trainers for around
ten minutes before giving up and leaving the room.
Will noticed he'd headed for the steam room, only
to be followed a few moments later by another
scantily dressed man. Neither seemed to have reappeared, making Will smile and raise an eyebrow,
vowing not to follow them. After all, there were
some occasions when people really didn't want to be
disturbed and after he and Ella had had Sarah burst
in on them that morning, he fully understood when
one of those moments might be. A frown crossed his
face. If only Sarah hadn't burst in. If only Millie
hadn't got out and if only they hadn't all ended up
running around looking for her. At least then the
grill wouldn't have set on fire. And even though the
fire was small and had extinguished easily, he still
never wanted a loved one of his to find themselves in
that situation ever again.

Will raised an eyebrow. Was that what Ella was?
Was she a loved one? Was she his loved one? A deep
breath in brought a smile to his face. He puckered
his lips and thought of the kiss, of how beautiful and
sensual she'd felt in his arms. Shaking himself from
his thoughts, he moved to the stepper machine.

'Quiet in here today,' he said as Nina once again patrolled the outskirts of the room. He had to stay focused. He wanted to know what she knew about Michelle and needed to see if she'd give anything away.

'Yeah, wonder why?' Her face was tense; she'd barely smiled all the time he'd been working out and, for the first time, she looked directly at him. 'Doubt all the bloody reporters parked outside the door are helping.'

'What's with them?' He could see through the glass, and saw where Josh stood, shoulders slouched, obviously tired, camera in hand.

'Didn't you hear? There was a hit-and-run on the top road last night. The woman that died... well, that was Michelle. She worked here. You'll remember her; tall, short blonde hair, I think she was here the last time you were in.' Nina looked away as she spoke, pulled off her tracksuit jacket and threw it on the floor.

'Seriously? That's awful.' He thought for a moment, knowing that his next question had to be worded just right. 'Do you know what happened?'

'As I said, it was a hit-and-run.'

Will rubbed his chin and then put a hand on Nina's arm. 'Wow. There's no wonder you look a bit out of sorts. Are you okay? I mean, were you two close?'

Nina took a drink from the water fountain. 'Not really. Obviously, I knew her. But I wouldn't call us friends.'

'So, where is everyone else?' Will glanced around, looking for assistants.

Nina shrugged. 'Rick is once again being harassed by the police and Tim hasn't turned up for work today. No one seems to know where he is. He isn't answering his mobile. So today, until Rick gets back, it's just me.' The words were sad and Nina stared into space as she said them. 'But at least now I get the extra hours I wanted.'

Will was taken aback. 'Wow.' He paused and wiped his brow. 'So, where has Tim disappeared to? Has anyone tried his house?'

'Do you think we're stupid? Of course we've tried his house. There was no answer. No one was home.' Nina pouted and walked towards the rowing machine. 'Anyhow, let's talk about something else. Do you want a rowing challenge?' Nina's voice was suddenly enthusiastic. She smiled, walked back towards him and allowed her hand to pat him on the shoulder where it lingered, before slapping him heavily on the back. 'Come on, I need to burn some energy.'

Will nodded. He needed the challenge just as much as she did. He needed to get rid of the frustration that was eating him inside. His thoughts were of Ella. He could still feel her pressing against his skin. He could still smell her perfume. And that kiss. That kiss had been amazing. Once again, his mind drifted to the few moments before everything was spoilt, to the tenderness they'd shared in that single moment before Sarah had barged in through the back door. The kiss had made him feel as though every inch of him had suddenly been awakened from the deep and sleepy coma he'd been in since his whole family had died.

He walked over to the set of perfectly positioned rowing machines. Twelve in total, all empty. He took a seat on one, made himself comfortable and watched as Nina took a seat on the machine next to his. 'So, why didn't you close today, you know, out of respect?'

Nina ignored his question, positioned her feet under the restraints and looked over at him. 'Okay, five minutes, longest distance wins.' Nina pulled on a pair of gloves, pulled the chain towards her and looked to her right where Will sat, waiting.

The challenge began with long, hard pulls. Will pushed out with his legs, making sure that each pull counted and watched the digital counter begin to move in an upward direction. But Nina also pulled hard. She dug deep and her focus was fixed on the dials.

'Come on,' she screamed. 'You can do better than that, give it some... PULL.'

Will grunted, and began pulling as hard and long as he could.

'Keep going,' Nina shouted as she began leaning further forward, pulling further back and somehow, flying past Will's score with ease.

'How did you manage that?' Will asked as he stopped rowing, gasping for breath. He picked up the water bottle and began to sip at the fluid. He wiped his forehead on the sleeve of his T-shirt and spun around on the seat. Nina just sat there, staring at the dials. Her long dark hair hung loosely down her back, her make-up still looked perfectly posi-tioned and annoyingly she hadn't even broken a sweat. 'Stamina, baby, and a good leg action.' She pouted as she spoke, looking him up and down. She'd turned towards him, her knees almost touching his. Her hand reached out and took his hand in hers. Will froze. He didn't know what game she was playing, nor did he really want to get involved. But then, as quickly as she'd turned to him, she'd moved away and Will noticed her look around the gym, presumably to ensure that no one else was listening. 'Look. You were right, I need to lock the doors, you know, out of respect.'

Will felt apprehensive. If Nina locked the doors, the only people that remained in the building would be himself and the two men who still hadn't emerged from the steam room. 'The woman who was killed, Michelle, was she Rick's girlfriend?'

'No, no more than I was.' Nina stood up, grabbed her towel and began drying off the sweat that had suddenly appeared. 'You have to realise, Rick was into everyone and so long as Rick is happy, that's all that seems to matter to him. And you, you ask too many questions.'

Nina turned her attention to the machines and began switching them all off at the mains. 'If you want a shower, be quick. I'm locking the doors in ten minutes.' Her words were dismissive and she continued to walk around the many machines in order, ensuring each one was off.

'Hey, I didn't mean to offend.' Nina kept her back to him.

'You must know him better than anyone, you

know, being a friend of his and having worked here so long?' Will knew he needed to dig, he needed to get a reaction. 'Seems like all of his wives or friends end up dead. Do you ever get worried? I mean, I'd take a wide berth of him, if I were you.'

'Seriously, why would you think I'd be in danger?' She raised her eyebrows. 'I'm not. You can be assured of that.' Again, her words were abrupt.

He pushed for more. 'But how can you be sure, Nina? Two wives dead, that girl who was beaten and now one of his employees has been killed. Bit of a coincidence, don't you think?'

Nina physically froze on the spot. 'I don't think; that's what makes us different. And, to be honest, you've asked one too many questions. I want you to leave. Now.' She turned to stare directly at him. Her eyes looked deep and fierce and Will knew it was time to go.

* * *

For the first time since she'd bought her car, Ella was grateful that it was an automatic. Her foot was still painful and the thought of pressing it down on a pedal would have been all too much. But she'd needed to get out of the house, needed to escape the fire damage and, what's more, she needed to do some shopping. The cooker was ruined and she'd already ordered a new one online, but she needed to buy some food for the next few days that didn't require cooking – although she smiled at the thought of the pizza she planned to throw in the basket. She had every intention of asking Will to cook it for her, just as he had asked her on the first night they'd met.

She drove into town and past the gym, where she saw the commotion of reporters that were all camped outside. Some sat in their cars, others had stepladders, long range cameras and looked as though they were ready to camp for the week. Once again the circus that seemed to constantly surround Rick Greaves had begun.

Ella paused for a moment and then turned the car around. She didn't need to see the commotion, nor did she want to be a part of it so she decided to drive the extra few miles into Scarborough. For once, she'd go to the shops there, even though the parking wasn't as easy.

* * *

It was still before lunch. The shopping had been done and Ella drove her car past the Sea Life Centre, where she parked. She wound the window down and breathed in deeply. The sea air was refreshing and, using just one of her crutches for stability, she climbed out of the car and took a seat on a bench to admire the view. There hadn't been many days since the attack that she'd done this; she could count on one hand how many times she'd allowed herself to be totally alone with nature and even though she still felt nervous of everyone and everything, she knew that moving forward and taking little steps was the right thing to do. After all, hadn't it only been that morning that Will had kissed her and hadn't he promised that he'd call in to see her again after work today? A smile crossed her lips and an expectant shiver ran down her spine.

Would he kiss her again?

Half of her hoped that he would, but the other half still needed an answer to the obvious questions: where had he been with Josh the night before? Had they been out clubbing with friends and were those friends of the female variety? Sarah had obviously been with them, so that just left Will. Had he been out with another woman? But then, Sarah had been at work, so they couldn't have been in a club, could they? Not knowing really bothered her and she wondered if she was reading more into Will's outing and the kiss than there actually was.

A dog barking made her jump and she realised that her thoughts had turned into dreams; she'd been so relaxed that she'd actually fallen asleep on the bench where she sat. She shivered and wrapped her arms around herself, and it took her a moment or two to become conscious of how cold the sea breeze had become.

Climbing back into the car, she threw the crutch into the front seat and drove back out of Scarborough and towards her home. But as she drove closer to home her reporter's curiosity overtook her. There were two ways she could go; one way would pass the gym and the crowd of reporters, and the other way would completely avoid them. Her thoughts went into overdrive; there was something about this story that didn't add up, just like her accident and the two wives that had died so suspiciously before she'd been beaten. The spiralling thoughts got the better of her and she found herself not only driving down the same road as the gym, but parking close to the crowd of reporters that still stood outside.

It wasn't the first time she'd parked and watched the gym. She used to do it before she met Rick

Greaves, before the disastrous date that had left her for dead and before her whole life had changed. Back then she'd been one of the reporters too. Back then she'd been hungry for the story, adamant that there was one and convinced that Rick Greaves had been guilty of murder. Now, everything was different. Now she hoped she'd see something that would prove he'd hurt her, see something that would prove he'd killed his wives, and ultimately lead to the reasons why Michelle was now dead too. All she needed was one tiny clue that she could use against him, bring him back to court and see him sent to prison for what he'd done to both her and them.

She tried to stay outwardly calm, but felt anxious on the inside. She knew that he'd been questioned. But that didn't mean he was still with the police. He could have already been released, which would mean he was either already inside the building, or that at any minute he could drive past, pull his car up near to hers and walk right past her.

Her stomach turned and Ella physically shrank in the car seat. Only her eyes glanced out over the edge of the door and she watched the reporters, who all stood, laughing and joking. All of them wanted that perfect story and the perfect picture to go with it, but at the end of the day, they were all there to do a job and ultimately it was easier for them to be friendly than to act as rivals or enemies. Ella remembered the comradeship that she used to feel. She'd actually loved being a part of the group. She'd always felt the safety in numbers. And even though some had kept the bigger stories for themselves, most of the time the smaller stories were shared.

She wanted to hate them. They'd hounded her, but she missed them. She missed the adrenalin of finding a new angle on a story and she really missed the thrill of seeing a photograph that she'd taken, along with her words, on the front page of the Filey Chronicle.

She sighed. Should she have gone back to work sooner? Had she allowed the accident to cloud her judgement? Were the reporters really as bad as she'd thought? Or like her, had they just been doing their job and searching for the perfect story?

Had she made it worse for herself by hiding away, by not giving them the story? And by doing so, had she created her own crazy circus?

Ella crouched down further in her seat and closed her eyes for just a few moments, enjoying the sun as it came in through the car window. Her mobile buzzed, and she opened her eyes to glance down at the phone.

A message from Sarah.

Hey hun. Bad news. Scumbag's been released.
Thought you'd want to know xx

Even though she expected his release, the anger
once again tore through her. Another woman he'd
been associated with had died and, once again, it
had nothing to do with him. She shook her head,
slammed her hands onto the steering wheel and
took in a deep breath. Looking across at the crowd of
reporters she saw one or two look at their phones,
followed by an excitement that sped through them.
They too must have heard the news that Rick
Greaves had been released and Ella could see that
they were gearing up, getting ready in case he
turned up at the gym.

Ella looked back down at her mobile. She
needed to do something positive. She needed to
get herself back to work. The only way she could
make a difference was by being there, by getting in
the middle of it all and by writing the story in her
own words. And like it or not, she needed the
backup of the other reporters. She searched
through her phone, found her editor's number and
dialled.

'Alan, it's Ella, Ella Hope. How's it going?' She paused, waiting for him to reply.

'Hey, Ella. I'm good. How are you doing?' He sounded genuinely happy to hear her voice, but then the paper had been covering her sick pay for months and she guessed that he'd rather be paying her to work than to sit at home. 'Well, I kind of thought I'd like to come back to work. If that's okay?'

'Well, that's the last thing I expected you to say, but, do you know what, Ella? Times are hard. We've got around twenty stories to cover and only ten reporters to do the work. And now, we have a big one. That girl on the top road, the hit-and-run and no one to cover it.' Alan suddenly seemed to realise what he'd said. 'Not that I'd ask you to cover that story, obviously, I'd send you on something else.'

Ella smiled and looked across to where all the reporters gathered. She could see Daisy, the reporter from the Filey Chronicle standing outside the gym with her camera in hand.

'So, what do you say, can I take my desk back, you know, part-time to start with?' Again, she smiled as Alan rushed in.

'That'd be great, Ella. You'd be really helping me out. I'm having a bit of a nightmare, to be honest, and your desk is still empty, none of the others want to sit at it.' He laughed. 'I guess everyone knew you'd be coming back. So, when are you starting?'

'How about tomorrow, first thing in the morning?'

'Ella, that'd be great. I'll even go and buy you a new mug for your coffee. You know, by way of cele-bration.'

Ella laughed. But something caught her eye. It was Will; he was wearing his sweats and he walked out of the front door of the gym, bag over his shoulder and heading towards the car park. Inquisi-tively, Ella leaned forward and watched where he went. She saw his car, parked to one side of the building, hidden from where the reporters stood.

'Oh you sneaky thing, what are you doing in there?' she whispered. She knew that Will went to a gym. It was more than obvious; she'd felt his mus-cles. They were firm, sculptured and perfectly pro-portioned. But she didn't know that he worked out here. He knew her history and she wondered why he hadn't mentioned that it was this gym that he went to.

'What?' Alan was still on the phone. 'Who you talking to, Ella?'

'Sorry, Alan, talking to myself. I'll see you in the morning and thank you.' She looked back to where

Daisy now stood, leaning against a wall with a man standing in front of her. She looked closer. The man looked familiar and she felt herself laugh out loud. 'What are you doing here?' she whispered as Josh turned and then bent down to pick up a camera. Her mouth dropped open; it wasn't often that anything shocked her, but the sight of Josh with the reporters did. It explained everything. Josh was a reporter, and Will... Well, Will was his boss.

24

'I saw him, Sarah. He was there. Josh was there too, he was obviously one of the reporters and, by deduction, Will is Josh's boss, which makes him a reporter too, but you already knew that, didn't you?' She paused and watched as her friend began to squirm. Ella picked up her coffee. 'Am I right?'

Sarah sat on the floor. For once she was on the other side of the questioning and she didn't look too happy. Her uniform had now been changed for tracksuit bottoms and a sloppy T-shirt, her hair was loose and hung around her shoulders and she gripped a coffee mug and allowed Millie to jump all over her legs, while fussing her with her spare hand.

'Ella, I thought we were going to be decorating

the kitchen. I came all dressed for it.' She pointed down at her clothes, obviously trying to avoid the question.

'Sarah. Come on, tell me the truth. You've known all along that he's a reporter, haven't you?' Ella watched Sarah fidget. She looked everywhere in the room, except at where Ella sat. 'Why didn't you tell me?'

'Ella, okay, look.' She lifted her hand up from tickling Millie and shrugged. 'I promised him that I wouldn't. Besides, since you're a reporter too, it's all a little irrelevant, isn't it?' Sarah tried to look smug and Ella wished she'd kept the information about taking her old job back to herself.

'Wait a minute, what do you mean you promised him? Why would you do that? You're supposed to be my friend, not his. How long have you known?'

'I've kind of always known... as you say, he's Josh's boss. You know that I've been seeing Josh and, well, we've been getting a little close. So we've kind of bumped into Will once or twice, seen him around, you know what I mean?' She recounted the story of going back to the office, falling through the door and Will throwing her out, demanding that Josh put her in a taxi.

'And you didn't think I'd want to know any of

this?' Ella tried to hide her emotions. She didn't know whether to be angry or amused; she could just imagine how Sarah would have reacted, or how embarrassed and annoyed she'd have been when Will had caught them.

Sarah stood up from the floor, sat on one of the chairs and pulled her knees up under her chin. 'Oh, Ella, for God's sake, you've got eyes. You're supposed to be a reporter. In fact, you're the best reporter I know. I honestly thought you'd have worked it out. They hardly hid it and you overheard what I said that morning, you know, about the girl getting killed on the top road. You're still off work, so I rang Josh to tip him off. Thought it'd be a good exclusive for him and he got to the scene before everyone else. He rang Will, who arrived around ten minutes later. It didn't occur to me that you didn't know, not until I asked Will where he and Josh had disappeared to... you know, right before Millie disappeared. Will's face was a picture, he almost crawled under the settee and it was only then that I realised that you didn't know.'

'And yet you still didn't tell me, because...?' Ella pushed her tongue into her cheek; she was enjoying watching Sarah squirm as she tried to wriggle her way out of giving the answers. It was more than obvious that she preferred to be the one asking the questions, rather than the one answering them.

'Oh, come on, Ella. You know I would have. But Millie disappeared, everything went mad and we both ran over to the farm looking for her.' She paused and thought. 'I did challenge him about it though and he said that he'd tried to tell you on a number of occasions, but then you'd come out with the "I hate reporters" campaign and he didn't know what to do. As far as I'm aware, hun, he's been working overtime to try and put Rick Greaves away. He's even paid to be a member of his gym. Only way he could get close while trying to gain some information there and, what's more, he was the first reporter at Rick Greaves' house yesterday morning.' Sarah smiled at Ella. 'He's trying to prove to you that reporters can be good people too. Give him a chance.'

Ella looked shocked and put her coffee mug down. 'Are you sure he's doing all of that for me? Why would he?' She knew that Will must care; the kisses hadn't lied, nor had the constant texts full of promises and affection that had been sent since.

Sarah nodded, held out her hand and grabbed hold of Ella's. 'He really cares about you, babes.

Please don't let him know that you worked it out. He will tell you, it might just take him a while.'

Ella shook her head and began to laugh. 'Okay, you're off the hook. I won't tell him. Besides, it's been fun watching you squirm and I might just enjoy watching him squirm too.' She threw a paintbrush at Sarah. 'Come on, we have a kitchen to paint. New cooker comes at the weekend and Will's promised to take the old one to the skip. Which means that we have to get that and the other burnt stuff outside and ready to go.'

Sarah walked into the kitchen, sighed and looked at Ella's hockey stick that had hung above the cooker. 'Can it be repaired?'

Ella shook her head. 'Nah, it's time to get rid of it.' She reached up and lifted the stick from the wall. 'Don't know why I kept it so long anyhow.'

25

Ella brushed her hair and at the same time managed to fuss Millie who sat beside her on the bed. 'Grandma Carol is coming to let you out later. I'm sure she'll play with you for a bit and give you some food.' Ella looked down at the puppy, who was lying back with her legs akimbo, her eyes closed and waiting for Ella to tickle her belly. Ella had no doubt that the words had gone completely over her head, but continued talking anyhow. 'I'm going to work today, baby dog. Something you'll have to get used to, but do you know what?' Ella tickled Millie's ears. 'Just think of all the doggy biscuits I'll be able to buy you when I get some real wages. No one can live forever on sick pay, can they?'

Ella stood up, tied her hair up in a messy bun and checked her appearance in the mirror. She'd thought she'd have felt more nervous than she did. She thought that by now the anxiety would have kicked in and she actually began to feel guilty for feeling so calm. Would the nerves kick in later? She hoped not, the last thing she'd want to do was make a fool of herself, especially in front of the other reporters. She hopped down the stairs and into the kitchen where she perched on a chair to take the pressure off her foot. Maybe she'd made a mistake. Maybe it was too soon to go back to work. She could walk short distances now, but still needed the crutches to go any distance. She pulled on a tubular bandage, thick socks and high ankle boots to give her more support.

A tap on the window sent Millie yapping towards the door, right up until the point where she recognised Will and the yap turned into a high pitched and excited yowl.

'Hey, how are you?' Will asked and Ella watched as he looked her up and down before moving towards her, pulling her into his arms and dropping a soft tender kiss on her lips. 'Wow, you look nice. Did you miss me?' he asked, still looking puzzled. It was more than obvious that he hadn't expected her to be all suited and booted and the look of surprise on his face made Ella smile.

'Yeah, I guess I missed you.' She held two fingers together indicating a really small amount. 'This much, but don't get big headed, because I have to go out.'

Will's arms encircled her. 'Hey, not so fast. I wanted to talk to you. I've something to tell you.'

Ella knew that Sarah had given him the ultimatum the week before and that, once again, Will was probably going to try and tell her about his job.

'Can it wait, hun? I've really got to rush.'

Will looked disappointed. He closed his eyes, took in a deep breath and nodded. 'No worries. Can you keep tonight free for me?' He raised his eyebrows. 'I really need to talk to you about something. All will be explained later, okay?' He kissed her on the end of her nose, making her wrinkle it up. He was teasing her and she liked it. She also knew that she could tease him back and intended to do so, right after she'd done her first day at work.

'Right,' she suddenly said, jumping up from the stool. 'I have to go out, you know, people to see, things to do.' She was purposely being evasive and knew that he'd be wondering why. But then again, he'd been evasive for long enough about being a reporter. Come to think of it, he'd never once spoken of his job, of his day at work or about any of his colleagues. Which kind of meant that he'd been secretive rather than lying about it.

Will followed her to the door. 'Where did you say you were going?'

Ella smiled and bent down to stroke Millie one more time. 'I didn't.' She grabbed at her crutch, held the key up in the air and pushed him out of the door. 'See you later.' She followed him out, locked the door, hobbled down the path and jumped into her car. 'Oh, and can you cook tonight? I don't seem to have a cooker,' she shouted before she blew him a kiss and waved.

* * *

I don't want to get up. I'm lying here, in my bed, wishing I could lie here all day. My mind rotates continuously; a million thoughts fly through my mind, jumping sporadically from one thought to the next with no natural start or end. It's like flicking through old black and white negatives projected onto a screen. It's exhausting, and I want it to stop. It's as though I can feel the walls closing in, every second that passes the world feels as though it's getting smaller and smaller. I spend my days looking for ways to run, ways to escape the life I live. I try to keep busy, I try not to think of what I have done. I know that it was wrong. I know that no normal person would do this, but something deep inside me wants to do it again. I feel the need to murder and I terrify myself over who will die next, because no one is safe.

26

Ella pulled up at the gym. Her car was suddenly surrounded and she took in a deep breath as she watched with keen interest how the other reporters dashed towards her.

'Ella, how do you feel about Rick Greaves being released?' a reporter shouted. His microphone flew forward and almost hit her in the face. She stepped back, unbalanced, fell backwards and grabbed at her car for support.

'BACK OFF!' she screamed, her voice angry but controlled. 'I'll say this once. I'm here to work, not to give you a damn story. That ship has sailed. Now, get out of my face and let me be.' She felt her stomach turn, but held her nerve and grabbed the crutch from the front seat, along with her camera bag and notebook, and made her way to the side of the gym, where the other reporters stood. One after the other they nodded, smiled and acknowledged her without saying anything further.

For a few moments she stood, used her crutch to steady herself and watched the gym with eagle eyes. She'd been right to worry about the anxiety that she might feel. Earlier she'd been okay, but now the tension had built itself up and she hadn't realised quite how bad it would be. She could feel her stomach turning, her mind spinning and a thick mist drifted in front of her eyes. She knew that the first interview would be the worst, especially if she had to face Rick Greaves, but she also knew that all eyes were on her, that every reporter in Yorkshire was waiting to see what she did. It occurred to her that if she could only get through today, tomorrow would be easier and the day after that would be easier still.

'Daisy, are you ready? Bring the camera.' Ella inched her way to the front of the crowd. Her stomach lurched forward as Rick Greaves' Outlander screeched to a halt outside the gym. He hesitated before climbing out. He still didn't know she was there, he still hadn't seen her, and certainly wouldn't be expecting her. She felt an odd sense of excitement to see the shock on his face when he did.

'Don't miss this, Daisy, for God's sake. Are you ready? Rick Greaves,' she jumped in quickly, before the other reporters could do so, as he opened his car door. 'I expect that I'm the last person you expected to see today?' she asked and saw the look of dismay in his eyes. 'I'm here today, Mr Greaves, to find out why you tried to kill me and, what's more, why another friend of yours, Michelle Everett, has been murdered.' She swallowed hard. 'Were you driving the car that hit her, Mr Greaves?'

Rick's feathers were obviously ruffled. He pulled on the lapels of his suit jacket as he tried to step away from the car. Ella saw what he was trying to do and brought her crutch up, slamming it against the car window, blocking his exit.

'You need to get of my way.' His words were strong, but his eyes jumped from reporter to reporter as each one held up a camera, making him lift his arm to cover his eyes as the flashes began to go off like mini explosions. 'I said move.' He grabbed at the crutch and pushed it out of his way.

'I'll ask you again, Rick, why did you attack me? Why did you leave me for dead? Why is another of your associates dead and is it just a coincidence that two of your wives died in suspicious circumstances too?' She steadied herself, using the crutch and followed him towards the door. 'Do you think you can keep getting away with it? Do you think that beating women within an inch of their life is acceptable? Or is it just a hobby of yours?' As Ella stood between Rick Greaves and the door, she could feel her stomach doing somersaults as if an orangutan was jumping inside it over and over.

Rick stared over her shoulder at the gym's doorway. 'I won't ask you again, now move out of my way.'

'I'll move when I get an answer. You can't even look at me, can you? I need to know why. I need to know why you did that to me.'

Ella could see him trembling from top to toe. He stared directly into her eyes. 'I did not hurt you. I swear to God, I did not attack you and, believe it or not, I actually liked you. IS THAT CLEAR?'

Ella shook her head. 'You liked me? Jesus, I'd hate to be one of your enemies.'

'Look.' He pulled her to one side and whispered, 'You have no idea how sorry I felt when I heard what had happened. I saw the news report the next morning and I couldn't believe it. But then you blamed me, you seriously seemed to think that I'd hurt you. I did months on remand. Jesus Christ, woman, have you got any idea what that's like? I'd done NOTHING wrong.' His eyes searched hers. They were deep, dark and Ella could feel herself holding her breath to a point that she suddenly gasped and began to cough.

'But... but... it had to be you.' Once again she swallowed hard. The interview was going all wrong. Everyone could hear, everyone would believe him. 'You were there, we were together. It had to be you.'

'We were together that night, but you left. That doesn't make me a woman beater, does it?' Rick reached for the door.

'But...' Ella looked around; all the reporters were waiting for her to speak, the flashes of the cameras still exploding in her face. Everyone was watching the exchange. They watched every move and she suddenly felt a new and frustrating confusion. What if he was telling the truth?

Cameras flashed and the reporters moved forward, all shouting questions of their own. Ella looked back to where Daisy had been standing. She needed reassurance, needed to see a friendly face, but saw no one except a blur of faces disappearing into a mist.

27

'It's okay, you're okay now.' Ella heard a man's voice come from somewhere in the distance. Nothing felt real, her head and eyes felt heavy and an annoying waft of air repeatedly went across her face. It was cool and intermittent and she felt a certain amount of gratitude as her body went from boiling hot to a cooler and more bearable temperature. She was lying down, on her side with her hand under her face. It was a flat surface, hard and not very comfortable. But at least it felt safe. A cool, damp soft cloth was dabbed across her forehead and a second one was pressed against the back of her neck. Her body began to cool and slowly she began to feel more and more alert.

Another waft of air hit her square in the face. It suddenly began to annoy her and Ella opened her eyes, just a little at first, and peered out cautiously.

A desktop oscillating fan stood before her. She could see the blades spinning around as it twisted from side to side. It stood close to the floor, which meant that she must be on the floor too.

'What – what... Where... What happened? Where am I?'

'You're fine. You're in the gym. I've called an ambulance.'

The voice of Rick Greaves spoke and Ella felt herself jump on the spot in an attempt to see his face. Panic rose within her and her eyes darted towards the door.

'Door's locked. Sorry, had no choice or all the world's press would've been crawling all over the place.' He was dipping the flannel in a bowl and then wringing it out. 'Here, this'll help.' He placed the flannel back over her forehead.

Ella looked across the room and out the window to where she knew the crowds of reporters would still be gathered. They'd wait all day if they had to, cameras still in hand, waiting for their one opportunity of a front page photo, and the one they'd end up with would be her leaving Rick's gym in an ambulance. She shook her head. It was the last thing she needed.

'You can't keep me here.' Ella once again began to look around. 'I... I want to leave.'

'So leave. I'm not holding you here and, if I'm honest, I'd have preferred you to collapse on any other doorstep in Scarborough, except for mine.' He looked concerned and Ella lay back down. 'I had no choice but to bring you in here. It was much against my better judgement, I might add. Half of that lot probably think I'm murdering you as we speak, the other half are waiting for you to accuse me of something else I didn't do.'

Ella sat up and then held onto the floor. She still felt dizzy and her legs felt like marshmallows. They'd gone all soft and squidgy and she knew it would be impossible to stand, making her watch Rick Greaves with nervous eyes. He moved away, sat on the rowing machine, leaned back and watched her intently for a few moments.

'Look, would you like some water, or something?' he suddenly asked without moving.

Ella looked from him to the water fountain and then back again. The last time she'd drank with this man, she'd ended up drugged and she had no intention of that happening again.

'Bloody hell, I'll drink from it first, if it would make you feel better.' He smiled tentatively as though reading her mind. He stood up and took a plastic cup from the side, filled it and drank the water. 'See? It's not poisoned.'

Ella nodded her head. 'Then, yes please. I'd like some.'

She took the cup from him and sipped slowly, while Rick returned to perch on his seat. His hands were clasped and held under his chin, his white T-shirt stretched around his biceps and his legs were crossed. He looked nervous, and Ella knew that she might never get the opportunity to get him alone and speak to him like this ever again.

'Can I ask you a question?'

He frowned and nodded. 'Ask away.'

'What happened that night? I mean, what really happened?'

* * *

Rick closed his eyes. He'd known bringing her in here alone had been a gamble, but he hadn't had much choice. One minute she'd been challenging him about the night she'd been attacked, the next minute she'd been falling towards him and had landed in his arms, in a faint. He'd quickly weighed up his options and finally, and without too much thought, he'd dragged her into the gym to escape the continuous glares and cameras of the reporters. He looked towards the windows and felt happy in the knowledge that he'd had them all fitted with the etched manifestations, making it impossible for the reporters to see in.

'Please... I need to know... Please tell me what happened?' Her eyes pleaded with his as she repeated the question.

He thought for a few moments before answering. After all, she'd already heard everything he'd previously said in court, and he had no idea what more he could say to convince her of his innocence. He hadn't attacked her. He had no idea what had happened himself, but he wished to God that he did.

The last thing he remembered, he'd been looking into her eyes, the lamp light had made them sparkle and for just a few moments he'd thought he should kiss her. But then, something had caught his eye; he couldn't remember what, but when he'd looked back at Ella, the moment had gone. Then he'd begun to feel ill. The room had started to move all by itself and he'd had an overwhelming feeling that he was about to pass out. He'd excused himself, headed for the bathroom and had felt sure he'd been about to publicly embarrass himself. He remembered splashing cold water on his face, holding onto the sink and steadying his feet. He'd locked himself into a toilet stall, put the seat down and sat with his head in his hands. The next thing he remembered he woke up leaning against the wall.

When he'd returned to the table, Ella had gone. He'd paid the bill, driven home, collapsed in a heap and the next thing he'd known Nina had been there. He remembered her being at the house, making him coffee and... and... Had she been in his bed? He couldn't remember. It had been the middle of the next day when he'd been woken up by the police. Nina had gone and he'd been arrested. After that, he'd spent the next few months in custody. The nightmare had begun and, for the life of him, he had no idea what had happened to either of them.

'I didn't do it. I know you don't believe me, but I honestly didn't attack you,' he whispered. He held his hand out for the cup, refilled it and passed it back to her. 'I swear to you I didn't do it. I went to the bathroom, I felt so ill, thought I'd got food poisoning. You know the scallops, I thought they'd affected me and I must have passed out. When I eventually came out, you'd gone.'

'But... What did... I... I don't... I don't understand.' Ella moved awkwardly, pulled herself up and onto a chair. She sat forward, stared at the floor and seemed to grip onto the gym equipment as though her life depended on it. She shook her head from side to side and rubbed her face with her hands as though shaking off cobwebs. Her eyes searched his. 'If it wasn't you...' A sob left her throat. '... I don't... If it wasn't you, I don't know who... who it was... Why... why did they do that to me? He... she... they almost killed me. I didn't deserve that. What did I do to deserve that?'

Rick simply shook his head. 'I'd give everything I have, every single penny to answer that question. Seriously, I've already lost so much and want nothing more than to clear my name.' He paused, grabbed a second cup from the water fountain and sipped. He trembled, tears sprung to his eyes and he felt close to breaking down. He was a man, he was supposed to be strong and the last thing he wanted to do was to cry, especially in front of Ella. But he knelt down before her, placed a hand on each of her shoulders and stared deep into her eyes. 'Ella, can I tell you something?' He shook with nerves. 'I'm terrified. People keep dying around me. It seems that everyone I care about or love, they die, and I'm so scared and I'm so, so sorry. I know you were hurt and your life since has been a nightmare, but my life's a nightmare too and I have no idea how to escape from it.' Rick turned away and discreetly wiped his eyes. 'I'm an amorous person, Ella. I like women, I like being with women, I find it easy to love them and I love being loved in return.' He choked back the tears. 'That shouldn't be too much to ask, should it?'

* * *

Ella shook her head. She had no idea how to react. The whole situation was totally surreal. She was here, sitting in the gym, with Rick Greaves and he was pouring his heart out to her, at a time when he had no need to lie. No one else was here. No one could hear him, no one except for her.

She'd hated him for so long. She'd felt so much anger towards him, yet, even after all that, it still made her really sad to see him so emotional. He was muscular, strong, a great looking man that had been reduced to tears, and the sudden reality of the situation hit her.

She believed him.

Rick Greaves was innocent and with that

thought, Ella gasped for breath and began to retch repeatedly.

'It's okay, I've got you,' Rick's voice once again calmed her as a wastepaper basket was thrust into her hands and the cloth was once again dampened and placed on the back of her neck. 'You're okay, let it out.' He held one hand against the flannel; the other had pulled her long auburn hair to one side, where he held it from falling back into her face.

They sat quietly, waiting for the moment to pass. No words were said, needed, or asked for. Ella closed her eyes; she didn't feel any danger. She felt safe, looked after and what's more her heart went out to Rick. He'd obviously been through as much as she had. Of course he hadn't had the broken bones, but he had had his heart broken, over and over again.

Ella looked up, caught his eye and held his gaze. A silent word of forgiveness passed between them. And then, without warning, a banging on the door spoilt the moment, making both Ella and Rick jump and look up.

'Who the hell?' He ran to the door.

'North Yorkshire ambulance, sir, did someone call for us?'

28

After her episode at the gym, Ella decided it might be a good idea to work from home for the afternoon and spread newspaper clippings all over the dining table. She'd gone to her newspaper office and collected all her old files that contained a full itinerary of Rick's life for the past four years, and she intended to revisit it all. She'd collated clippings from when he was at school. She'd found announcements for his first and second marriages. There were obituary notices about the two wives that had died, along with newspaper reports that had seemed to fill the front pages for days. She'd found articles that were related to the gym, the fifty grand Outlander, and the house purchase that had cost over a million.

She'd downloaded pages from his Twitter and Facebook accounts, sayings and messages going back years. There had been the talk of his business partner, Tim, who'd been the brother of Rick's first wife. Rick had dug him out of a hole and saved him from prison, and had subsequently taken full control of the gym. The circus surrounding Rick was huge and all of this had happened before her attack, before all of her own medical reports along with the articles that had covered Michelle's death. She'd been an employee of Rick's too, and another coincidental death that seemed to surround his life, just like both of his wives.

Ella stood back and sighed. She was satisfied with her collections. This was reporting at its best, gathering the evidence and spreading it out to make sense of it. It was just a shame she didn't have everything. Original copies of his wedding certificates, divorce papers, death certificates and coroners' reports, all would need to be collected – she'd applied for them but knew they'd take time. However, it was important that she had them so that the whole picture would appear before her. Rick Greaves' whole life would be laid out on the table and for the first time nothing would be hidden.

Sarah burst in through the door, shook an umbrella, placed it back outside, kicked off her bright pink wellingtons and passed a box of doughnuts to Ella who had been watching her entrance with amusement. 'I brought us midday sustenance as it's raining,' she said as she walked through the conservatory and into the kitchen, switched on the kettle and pulled mugs from the cupboard. Ella followed her, picked Millie up and began rummaging in the fridge. 'You want some treats?' she asked Millie, as she placed her down on the floor and dropped pieces of left over chicken into her bowl.

'What are you doing for the rest of the afternoon?' Sarah asked as she poured the boiling water into the mugs. 'I need to go shopping. Do you want to come?'

Ella shook her head and thought of how to answer. She couldn't go shopping with Sarah, not after passing out that morning. Besides, she already had plans, but didn't know how to tell Sarah what those plans involved, nor how to get rid of Sarah quickly.

'I'm a bit busy today, sorry.' She looked over her shoulder and towards the door as she said it. 'I've kinda got someone coming around.'

Sarah began to smirk. 'Oh my, you've got a hot date with Will, haven't you? It's about time you got back in the game. Is he coming around to give you a good sorting out, girl?' Her eyes were open wide as she waited for Ella to answer. 'Or have you two already, you know?' Her hands moved to her hips and made a rotating movement that made Ella smirk.

Ella carried the doughnuts back into the conservatory. 'Sarah! Not everyone jumps straight into bed, you know. Relationships are built on so much more than that. Besides, it's not Will that's coming around.'

'Okay, so spill the beans. If it's not Will, who is it?' Sarah asked as she walked back into the conservatory, two mugs of steaming hot coffee in her hand. She passed one to Ella, then pulled open the doughnut pack and took one, nibbling at the pink icing on one edge. 'What's all this?' She pointed to the table.

Ella began putting the clippings into some sort of order. 'Just stuff. I'm working from home today. I got out all my old files and to complete the picture, I've just downloaded all of this.' She pointed to the new pile of printing.

Sarah leaned forward. 'So, you're digging up your case again, are you?' Her eyes scoured the table. 'The police are still looking into it, you know, and I'm sure they won't let it drop, not till you get some justice.'

'Sarah, I really think Rick Greaves is innocent. Actually, he is innocent. I just know it. It wasn't him that attacked me. Don't ask me how I know, I just do.'

'My God, have you been on the bloody happy pills? How come you've changed your tune?' Sarah picked up one of the articles and then caught Ella's eye. 'Are you sure?'

Ella nodded and watched the cogs begin to turn in Sarah's mind. 'I saw him this morning and he looked me in the eye and swore it wasn't him, and do you know what, Sarah? I believe him. His eyes didn't flinch, not once. If anything, he looked as terrified as I've been.'

'Have you spoken to the police?' She sat down and pulled Millie up and onto her knee, immediately feeding the pup small lumps of iced doughnut. 'Brought them up to date?'

'What will the police do, Sarah? I know you say they're still looking into it, but he's already been cleared. What I need is to find who the real attacker is, and hey – stop feeding Millie or you'll be cleaning up the mess when she gets the runs.'

'So, where do we start?' Sarah asked as she put Millie back on the floor and leaned forward to look at the table. 'I have no idea.' Ella began to move the clippings around. 'But I know it wasn't Rick. You should have seen him, Sarah; he really didn't need to say what he did. He was so emotional, so very broken and he had nothing to lose. No one else could hear; he could have said anything, but he didn't.' She picked up one of the articles. 'And what's more, Sarah, he looked after me. Jesus, he even held my hair back while I threw up in his rubbish bin. Which is why I'm working from home this afternoon rather than being back at the office.'

Ella saw Sarah pull a face and stop in her tracks. 'You went back to work then?'

Ella nodded. 'Yes. Part-time.'

Sarah didn't look up. Instead, she began picking up the newspaper clippings and looking at them one by one. 'I've always fancied being promoted to detective.' She leaned back in her chair and studied a clipping.

'Well, here's your chance. Rick's going to be here in about twenty minutes. We're going to look over all the evidence and hopefully find some clues.'

Sarah dropped the half-eaten doughnut onto the table, rubbed her hands down her jeans and stared at Ella. 'Hello. Seriously? Are you off your stupid goddamned trolley?'

Ella continued to sort through the clippings. 'Sarah, he didn't do it.'

'He might not have, Ella. But you have realised that everyone he gets mixed up with seems to end up either almost dead or very dead, haven't you? He's hardly someone your mother will approve of you being around, is he?'

'Mum won't know.' Ella looked defiant. 'I'm determined to get to the truth, Sarah. Whatever I have to do, I will find out what happened.'

'Your mum will find out, especially if I tell her. Jesus, Ella, what if you're attacked again, or worse? What if you get killed?' She suddenly stood up, walked around the table and pulled Ella into her arms. 'I couldn't bear it. Not again.' She choked back the tears. 'I sat there, Ella, day after day, by that hospital bed. I hated Rick Greaves, I cursed him and I prayed for you. I really prayed. I actually thought we'd lost you.'

'That's why I'm meeting him here. No one can drug me here. The drinks are mine. I make them and, what's more, no one can make me go anywhere that I don't want to go. Anyhow, if you're so worried, stick around. As I said, he'll be here soon. You can make the coffee and play detective if you like.'

29

'That's right, a big bouquet with really bright colours.' Will pulled the money from his wallet. 'I take it you can deliver?' His hand rested on the counter, while he looked up and down the small rack of gift cards. There were ones with love hearts, ones with flowers and others with rainbows and he wondered which he should choose. He really liked the one with a love heart on, but couldn't decide if it'd be too much, too soon. After all, they'd only shared a kiss or two, albeit passionate ones, or the first would have been passionate if Sarah hadn't burst in and completely spoiled the moment.

'Definitely, of course I could.' She pushed a pad

towards him. 'Write down the address. Now, do you want to include a cuddly teddy? The ladies love them,' the florist asked, with a hopeful look on her face, as she pointed to a shelf full of furry bears. They all stood, sat or lay. All were of varying size, shape and colour, had different faces and appeared to peer down at Will with beady eyes.

Will shook his head. He wanted the flowers to speak for themselves. He'd asked Ella to keep the evening free and he was determined that, for once, he was going to do things right. First, he had to tell Ella about his job. It was something he should have done before, and he just hoped she didn't hate him or think him to be any sort of a vulture. 'Are they for your girlfriend?' the florist asked as Will's mind wandered to picture Ella's face, her smile, the way she curled the side of her mouth up when she was teasing and then, then he thought of her kiss. A warmth spread through him and he knew that tonight was all about making the right impression. And once he'd got over the stumbling block of his job, he would wine, dine and romance her, right from the beginning. Ella deserved it. But was she his girlfriend? Was that something he could call her? He cautiously nodded his head, while deep down hoping for it to be true.

He pulled the money from his wallet as the florist began pulling stems of lilies out of a vase and arranging them into a bouquet. 'I take it you'll want roses in here too?' she queried, almost apologetically. 'They're good for the romance.' She sang the words in an Italian accent, which made Will frown – he was sure there hadn't been an Italian accent there before, and it suddenly occurred to him that she was trying to ease the tension.

He took a deep breath and smiled. 'Yes, roses are good.'

'Okay, my dear, I can do that. That'll be forty-five pounds, and you want them delivered today?'

'Yes, please.' He passed the money to the assistant and closed his eyes momentarily as he imagined Ella's face when the flowers arrived. He knew she'd be happy, knew she'd feel pampered, but most of all he wanted her to feel loved. 'Can I leave it with you? I wrote the address on your pad.' He turned towards the door and opened it, looked back, smiled and winked. 'Thanks.'

Will stood by the kerb and waited for the traffic to slow. It was market day. The whole town was alive with activity. The road was busy with cars, taxis and buses all fighting for their position on the road. Men, women and children all pounded the pavements to the sound of market stallholders shouting out loud, selling their wares. Will looked up and down, searching for a better place to cross. But then, he stopped in his tracks and ducked behind a fruit and veg stall. His eyes were fixed on Nina, who stood on the opposite side of the road screaming and shouting into a mobile, which was making people turn and stare.

'Don't you dare do this. You just can't! I won't let you, we had a deal.' She turned away from a group of women who'd stopped to listen. A sob left her throat and she suddenly threw the mobile against a wall and then stood back as it landed on the floor in a hundred pieces.

'What on earth are you up to?' Will whispered to himself as he inched further along the road. He wanted to get in a better position. Somewhere he could see what she was doing. His journalistic instincts kicked in and he began looking for a vantage point, somewhere he could take a picture from. He watched as Nina dropped to her knees and made a futile attempt to push the pieces of the mobile back together.

Will felt around in his pocket for his phone, but Nina had her back to him. Her hair hid her face and Will tried time and time again to get a picture, but then managed to catch a button on the phone and watched in dismay as it switched itself off. 'No, you can't do this, not now.' He began flicking at the screen. 'Come on, I need you to work.'

'Will. What are you doing here?' Nina's voice rang out making Will jump. He once again looked down at the phone, waved it in the air and then pushed it into his pocket. 'I was talking to a friend and the damn thing cut out,' he lied, but couldn't think of anything else to say. 'Are you okay?'

Nina sniffed back the tears and smiled. Her hand immediately went out and held onto his arm. She hooked her arm through his. 'I'm okay. I could use a drink though.'

Will had to think quickly and decided that the truth would be best. 'I... I've just been buying some flowers.' He pointed to the florist shop.

'Oh, okay.' She looked down. 'I could really use a friend, someone to drink with. Are you coming?' Her arm was still hooked through his, and she twisted around to allow her fingers to squeeze his bicep.

Will tried to think of an excuse, looked at his watch and hesitated. 'I could have a quick one. But I really don't have long. I'm on my lunch break.' He tapped the watch. 'Besides, shouldn't you be at work?'

Nina pulled him towards a bar. 'No. Rick's closed up for the day.' She looked up at him with huge eyes, pouted and put both hands together as though praying. 'I just hope he hasn't closed for good.'

Will was puzzled. 'Why would he close?' Nina's hand had grabbed his and she pulled him into a wine bar, where she navigated through a crowd of people and made her way to a pair of empty bar stools.

'Gin and tonic please, large one.' She sidled up to the bar, pulled herself up on the stool and turned to Will. 'You want the same?'

Will shook his head. 'No, not for me. Just a Diet Coke, I'm driving.' He sat on the stool next to Nina. 'So, you say Rick's shut the doors?'

'He did,' Nina said as the barman passed her the drink. 'Oh, Will. Everything's gone so very wrong, again.' Nina looked visibly upset and she reached for a napkin from the bar and blew her nose. 'I just don't know what I'll do.'

The bar was full of customers who were busy chatting, either showing off the purchases they'd made in the town or simply sitting, smiling at one another, texting or people watching, while drinking vast amounts of alcohol. Everyone was interacting noisily and Will wished for the bar to empty. He wanted to hear what Nina was saying without having to lean in quite so close.

'So, what's gone wrong?' Will asked outright. He caught her eye and smiled. In reality, he wanted to get the meeting over with as quickly as possible, and decided that by getting to straight to the point he might just get Nina to give him the story he'd been wanting for weeks.

Nina sighed. 'Shall we order?' She picked up the menu and began to study it, turning it over and over, until Will was sure that she'd read every single inch twice.

'I thought you just wanted a drink?' Will took in a deep breath and waited for a few moments until Nina eventually spoke.

'I'm a bit hungry. I'd like something to eat.' She picked up the gin and tonic and shook the glass. 'Especially if I have a couple of these. The food will soak it up, don't you think?'

Will took notice of the smirk that followed her words. She was working the situation, playing him. She was amused and he knew it. Once again, he looked at his watch. 'I'm in a bit of a hurry. As I mentioned, I'm on a lunch break.' Will shuffled around in his seat.

'That's a shame.' She paused. 'But I think you'll make time for me, Will.' Nina pulled at another napkin and dabbed at her eyes. 'You do want my story, right?'

Will hesitated before answering. 'Nina, I have to get back to work, so unless this is really important...'

She looked him up and down and Will knew she was taking in the look of his expensive suit. 'That's what you wear to mow the lawns, is it?'

Will closed his eyes. He knew she'd worked him out and he watched her carefully as she glanced down at the floor, before she looked up directly at him. Her dark eyes pierced straight through him in her defiance.

Will sat and thought about what to do before speaking. 'Okay. I take it that I'm busted. But seriously, I wasn't just after a story. I really did like working out there. And I'm sorry Rick has closed the doors. Are you okay?' He smiled politely, but deep inside he was getting impatient.

Nina sipped at her drink and completely ignored the question. Will didn't want to be impolite but knew that if she didn't respond soon, he'd have to leave, even though by doing so, he'd lose the chance of the interview. The one story he'd been chasing for weeks. And because of Ella, this was the story he just couldn't let go. He needed to know what Nina was up to; he had to know what had gone wrong, what her views were on Rick Greaves, what she knew about the wives that had died, but, most of all, he wanted to know if she knew anything about Ella's attack. If he left now he'd lose the chance of it all and since Nina had worked him out to be a reporter, this could be the last chance he got.

'Now, come on Will, indulge me. Do you want to order a sandwich or not?' A false smile crossed her face as she nudged the menu towards him. 'The beef and horseradish sounds amazing,' she advised, pointing to the list.

Will backed down and took the menu from her. Maybe if he calmed down, acted relaxed, and pretended that he wanted to be there, she'd relax too, and then he hoped she'd answer his questions.

'Okay. The beef and horseradish sounds great. Can we get two of those?' He passed a twenty-pound note to the barman. 'Please.'

Will listened to Nina's small talk while they waited for the food. She'd talked about Michelle, about the upcoming funeral and about how she had needed more hours at the gym, not less.

The food arrived and Will struggled to eat. He knew that Nina was watching him. She seemed to be enjoying the power she thought she had over him. She knew that he'd lied, that he wanted her side of the story and she'd made it very obvious that she'd worked out what he really did for a living.

'It's the gym that's the problem,' she finally announced. 'I think Rick will close.' She picked up her sandwich and began to nibble at its edge, biding her time. 'If he closes us down, I'll lose my job and that wasn't the deal.'

Will moved uncomfortably in his seat. He was going through the motions of eating the sandwich while silently listening to what Nina had to say. He hadn't responded to anything she'd said so far and was hoping she'd just continue.

'Rick's arrest and court case hit us hard. Members were just starting to come back, but then Michelle died. We were hit again, people stopped coming and now Tim has disappeared. Not only has he disappeared, he's taken all the money that Rick had. All of it. Thousands. Why would he do that? He was family,' she said between tiny bites of her sandwich. 'But then, he did disappear right after Michelle was killed.' She lifted an eyebrow.

He stopped eating and looked at the floor, thinking. 'It is a bit of a coincidence. So, surely the police are looking for Tim, aren't they?'

Nina looked uncomfortable. 'I... I don't know.'

'Okay, Nina. Now, think carefully. Did Tim have an alibi when Michelle died?'

She held onto the bar for support. 'I don't know.'

Will weighed up the situation. 'So, Tim had no alibi that we know of.' He paused. 'How about Rick, did Rick have an alibi?'

'He's innocent.' Nina looked around; she smiled at one or two people that she recognised, picked up her gin and tonic, realised the glass was empty and indicated to the barman that she'd like another.

'Are you sure about that? I mean, come on, Nina, everyone around Rick seems to either die or get hurt. Unless...' A thought crossed his mind. '... unless Tim was involved.'

'I haven't been killed or hurt, so you can't say everyone, can you?' Nina's voice had turned from polite to irritated. She picked at the sandwich, pulled the pieces of beef from within the roll and nibbled.

Will put a hand out to rest on the bar beside her. 'Nina. You weren't a wife or a girlfriend, were you?'

She looked up. 'I was sort of a girlfriend. Rick used to take me out, we'd end up in bed and then he'd move onto the next girlfriend, or wife. Besides, that Ella Hope, she walked away too, so your theory is kind of flawed.'

'Nina, come on, she hardly walked away, did she? I'd say that Ella is the innocent one in all of this, and she was terribly hurt. According to the papers they only just found her in time, ten more minutes and she'd have been gone too.'

Nina purposely slowed her words. 'Would that be the same Ella Hope who caused all the trouble and identified Rick as her attacker that night? Would it be the same Ella Hope who ruined Rick's life? And, is she the same Ella Hope that's still best friends with Rick?' She sat back on her stool and watched his reaction. 'Oh, sorry, you didn't know they were still friends, did you? Silly me.' She pulled a final piece of beef from the roll, pushed it into her mouth and chewed with a smirk crossing her face. 'That's right, she still sees him.' She nodded. 'She still spends time with him on the quiet, but without the papers knowing, of course.' She paused and stared. 'You really didn't know, did you?' She looked amused. 'What's wrong, Will? Wasn't your team of reporters there this morning? Didn't they see what happened?' She shrugged her shoulders. 'It's going to be all over the newspapers tomorrow. Your girl, Ella Hope, was outside the gym with a photographer. She approached Rick directly. She even managed to do a fake swoon to get Rick to catch her. He carried her inside where no one else could see. It'd obviously been something they'd planned. Don't you think?'

Will stood up. He'd heard enough. He put his napkin down on the bar. 'I'm really sorry, but as I said earlier, I really do have to go back to work.' He saw the shock in Nina's eyes and knew that she'd fully expected him to stay and listen to her stream of lies.

'But, Will, don't you want to know the rest?' Nina goaded him. 'I thought you wanted a story? After all, your next-door neighbour, your girlfriend, is most probably screwing Rick as we speak.' She sat back, looking pleased with her accusations.

But Will stood firm.

'How do you know she's my neighbour?'

'Oh, Will. For a reporter you're a little bit stupid, aren't you? It really didn't take much to look up your address on the computer. Brings up other members in the same road. I knew on that first day you came to the gym that you lived next door to Ella Hope.'

Will breathed in and out as deeply as he could. He was slowly losing control. He'd had to listen to Nina for far too long and now he needed to leave.

But before he did, he took one step back towards where Nina sat and with his nose practically touching hers he growled, 'You're wrong, Nina. Ella might live next door, but that doesn't make her my girlfriend, and if she is screwing Rick, as you put it, then good for her. She's a free agent and entitled to do whatever the hell she likes.'

30

'I need some Blu-Tack,' Sarah said as she picked up another piece of paper and moved it into a position amongst the others on the table, like a small piece of a jigsaw puzzle, before rearranging the other pieces and laying them before her in date order. She stood back, looked down and studied the pattern for what seemed like an eternity. 'Do you have some? Oh, and a writing pad.' Sarah looked around her, clicked her fingers and fully expected the Blu-Tack and pad to appear like magic and drop into her hand. 'Ella, come on, this is important!'

Ella turned to a cupboard, opened a drawer and pulled out the Blu-Tack and a pad. 'Hey, isn't it me that's supposed to be working today, not you?'

Sarah picked up an article, pulled off a piece of Blu-Tack and stuck the article to Ella's wall. 'Ella, this is research. I'm helping you. Now listen, let's put these in order. Rick was born in 1983, that makes him thirty-five,' Sarah said, writing the information down. She then looked around at the other pieces of paper. 'So, when did he meet his first wife, what was she called?'

'Julia, he married her in November 2010.' Ella looked puzzled. 'Was that on the twenty-first?'

'It was.' Sarah scribbled on her pad, creating a timeline. 'And she died in the November of the following year; he'd only been married for a year when she died.'

'That's right.' Ella picked up the laptop and began tapping away on the keys. 'She'd been out running. It was dark, and she fell into an open septic tank, banged her head on the way down and, by the time they found her, she'd drowned.'

Both Sarah and Ella looked up and towards each other and pulled a face. 'Yuk, what a way to die,' Sarah said as she continued to scribble on her notepad.

Sarah picked up a note and did a double take. She looked back down at the timeline. 'His second wife, Patsy. She died in November too.'

Ella patted her knee and smiled as Millie climbed up onto her lap and curled up to sleep.

'Ella, don't you think that's a bit of a coincidence?'

Ella shrugged her shoulders. 'One in twelve chance I guess, you know, of the month being the same. Wouldn't have thought it too much of a coincidence. It's not like they planned their own death, is it? We covered the story at the Chronicle. At first, we all thought it was Rick, that he'd killed them both, and I was still convinced of that when I met him for that drink. But now, now I'm not so sure.'

Sarah nodded and sighed. 'Well, if you're not sure then you need to think about it, and do you know what helps you think?' She paused and rubbed her throat.

Ella shook her head. 'I would have no idea.'

'Well, I'd say a nice brew, a yummy chocolate Hobnob and a bit of play time with a puppy dog.' Sarah grabbed Millie from Ella's knee and curled up on the sofa. 'Come on, Ella, it's your turn, I made the last one, didn't I, Millie Moo? Besides, you don't like me playing in the kitchen since the fire, do you?'

* * *

Hope you're going to be home this afternoon. Keep
an eye out for a surprise delivery xx

Ella felt her stomach flip as she picked up her
mobile and read the text from Will. A delivery
sounded exciting, but why was he making sure she'd
be home? After running out on him that morning,
she'd texted him to say that she was back and would
be around as and when he got home.

You've got me all giddy. Give me a clue, what's the
delivery? xx

Ella responded and watched the screen, hoping
for a reply. She looked for the little dots moving
around to indicate that Will might be typing something back, but there was nothing and Ella felt a
wave of disappointment travel through her. She put
the phone down, walked back into the kitchen,
pulled mugs from the cupboard and began to make
the coffee.

'Will just sent me a text. I have to watch out for a
surprise delivery,' she said, walking back into the
conservatory. She passed the coffee to Sarah. 'Sorry,
no Hobnobs.'

'Maybe tonight's the night, honey.' Sarah giggled.

'Ohh la la, he's probably got something real special planned.' Millie had settled back down on her knee, but woke up as the coffee was passed, realised that Sarah had nothing more to feed her and jumped down from her knee and ran to the door.

'Hi there, is all okay, or am I interrupting something?' Rick's voice made them both jump as he held a hand up and knocked in mid-air at the open door. Sarah continued to giggle as he stood before them, tall, muscular, tanned and handsome. His white shirt emphasised the muscles that poked out from underneath and his jeans hugged him in all the right places.

'No, not at all. Rick, this is Sarah.' Ella's voice trembled as she stared at Rick; she couldn't help it. The mere sight of him still made her feel anxious, vulnerable, and even though she'd convinced herself that he was innocent, her breath still became laboured and shallow. Her eyes fixed on him, on the way he stood, the way he looked and the way he clutched hold of the energy drink in his right hand. 'Jesus, Ella. You okay? You've gone really pale,' Rick's voice wavered. 'You're not going to go and faint on me again, are you?' He stepped into the conservatory, placed the drink on the windowsill and held out an arm to where Ella stood.

Ella just managed to reach out. She grabbed hold of his arm, but couldn't move. She just stared, transfixed on the bottle for what seemed like an eternity. The bottle was made of plastic, clear plastic with bright blue liquid, which looked almost luminous in the daylight. There was something about the bottle that made her nervous, but what? What was it about the liquid that caught her attention? Why did she suddenly have a feeling of déjà vu? And why was the sun's reflection on it so important?

'Wow. What is it about you and passing out? Err, can you get her some water?' Rick looked at where Sarah still sat, gawping.

Ella felt herself being shepherded towards a chair. She sat down with a bump and her gaze went to Millie who jumped up on her knee. It was as though she knew that Ella wouldn't be in the mood to play and settled down to snuggle into her lap. Ella continued to stare at the bottle; her stomach turned as she realised that the daylight had the same effect as the street lights had had, the reflection of light on liquid, just as it had been on that November night, the year before.

'Here, sip this.' Rick pressed the glass to her lips. She obeyed and sipped. Her hand rested on his shoulder and she looked directly into Rick's eyes.

'That's... that's what you said. I remember... that's what you said – that night.'

Rick knelt down before her. 'Ella. What do you remember? Please, it's important, try and think.'

Ella gulped in air and closed her eyes. The whole night came flooding back. 'I was waiting for you, where we'd arranged, outside that pub. I'd been at work all day and I was hungry. The only food I'd had since breakfast was some toast. But then, while I was waiting, I remembered the half bag of midget gems I'd got left in the bottom of my bag. I pushed one in my mouth. But then I saw you pull up, and I swallowed it whole. It... it made me choke. You passed me a bottle, like that one, it was an energy drink, bright blue, the same colour as that.' She pointed to the bottle. 'It'd been in the door pocket of your car. You said, "Here, sip this," and I did. I took two or three big sips. The choking stopped and, for a short while, I felt okay. But not long after, almost as soon as we'd finished our starters, that's when I began feeling a bit groggy.'

Rick stood up, stepped back and sat in the tub chair opposite. 'I drank from that bottle too. I'd been working at the gym. I ended up staying later than I'd planned. I'd showered and changed at the gym and came straight from there to meet you.' He pulled his hand through his hair. 'It was the only thing we both drank from. I hadn't thought about it before; it didn't seem important. You didn't drink that much, certainly not as much as I had. I finished off the bottle before I put it back in the car.'

'I know. I'd forgotten it too.' She stroked Millie. 'Why didn't I remember it before? If there had been any dribbles left, they could've tested it, they could have found out what was in it. Traced it back, looked for fingerprints.'

Sarah picked up the bottle and held it up to the light. 'If anyone's interested in my opinion, I'd like to know who else had access to your bottle during that day, other than you?'

* * *

Will walked up Ella's path, stood in the conservatory entrance and took in the scene before him. Both Ella and Rick were sitting in tub chairs, Rick's hand was holding Ella's and Sarah stood with a bottle in her hand, staring at them both.

He stood. Shook his head and cursed. He'd dismissed all that Nina had said to him, hadn't believed a word of it, had been so sure she'd been lying. Damn it. He'd left her sitting in the bar and had rushed to see Ella. But now, now it looked as though she'd at least been telling him some of the truth.

Will turned back. He didn't think that he'd been noticed and wished he hadn't come. He'd been so sure of Ella, of the affection, the cute texts, the laughs they'd shared and the intimate moments they'd created. All of that had been real, or so he'd thought, and he'd wanted to come to her, hold her in his arms and ask her what Nina had meant by her accusations. But now, now he'd seen it all for himself.

Millie suddenly stirred, realised he was there and bounced down from Ella's knee to race excitedly to where Will stood, making the others look towards him.

'I'm so sorry. I'm obviously disturbing something; I shouldn't have come.' Will stepped backward and almost fell over Millie, who'd launched herself at his ankles. 'All right, Millie Moo, there you go.' He tickled her stomach as she rolled over at his feet. 'Will has to go home, puppy dog. Go on, go back to Ella.'

Ella's eyes connected with Will's and she suddenly came back to life. Will watched as her whole body reacted at once and she jumped up from her seat and along with Millie, she launched herself towards where he stood. 'Will, come in, please, please come in.' Her arms were around him. A sense of relief passed through him and he responded by pulling her close. He'd wanted to hold her so much, wanted to believe that she wanted him too. He breathed in deep and took in the scent of a fresh shampoo that was overshadowed by a soft musky perfume. He closed his eyes, took a moment to think and immediately knew that he shouldn't have doubted her.

Sarah ran across to him with the bottle. 'We've just worked it all out. Rick turned up with this and Ella remembered everything. She was drugged and, just now, she worked out how. She drank from Rick's bottle. One just like this was in his car and he gave her it to sip when she had a choking fit. So all we have to do now is work out who wanted to drug her.'

Will shook his head. 'No... no, we don't. What we have to do is to work out who hated Rick enough to drug him. The drink wasn't aimed at Ella, was it? It was aimed at Rick. I think Ella just got in the way, drank from the bottle accidentally and got attacked because she was seen with Rick.' He moved further into the room and Ella sat down in the chair.

'But how did they know? How did they know that I'd had some of that and that I'd get sick?'

Will thought for a moment. 'I'd say they were watching. Whoever drugged you must have followed Rick. They saw everything, and when you left the restaurant looking slightly worse for wear, Ella, they took their chance.' He knelt down in front of her and looked her in the eye. 'I know it doesn't help, but you were not the target. Rick was.'

* * *

Ella pointed to the articles that were now stuck all over her wall, and quickly talked her way through the timeline. 'Rick, your first wife, Julia, she died in November. I was attacked in November too and Michelle died in June. How much would I bet right now that you married your second wife in either June or November?'

Rick shook his head. 'Sorry, I married Patsy in October of 2012.' He ran a finger over the timeline that Sarah kept adding to. 'Do you really think they were killed?' A look of horror passed over his face. 'I really believed they were freak accidents. The thought that someone could have actually murdered them is unbearable. I mean, why would they be killed? What could anyone hope to gain from their deaths?' He ran his hands up his neck and then through his hair, while Millie continually tried to jump up on his knee.

'Well, I certainly wasn't an accident. Whether I got in the way or not, the attack was very real. I didn't imagine it, nor did I imagine the months of recovery that I had to go through afterwards.' Ella picked up the glass of water and spun the liquid round and round.

Rick held his head in his hands. 'Oh my God. I feel so guilty. All of this is my fault. You got hurt, and they all died because of me. Someone hates me enough to do all this. But why, and who?'

* * *

I want to hate you. There would be nothing I'd like more. I used to think we were friends, I used to think we were close and that you'd tell me everything. But you didn't. You just kept taking up with those other women, taking them out and you even went as far as to marry them. Well, I stopped all of that, didn't I? And now, now you're afraid to love. You're afraid that someone else will die, and so you should be.

I watch you all the time. I watch everyone around you and I plan what to do next. I plan how to make you suffer for what you did and I spend the minutes and hours just staring into space, considering my revenge. You see, I thought I had it all. I really did. But you, you took it all away. You hurt everyone around you, but mostly you ended up hurting yourself, over and over again. And now, now I see you, looking around, wondering who did all of this to you and why. But you'll never work it out. Not until I'm good and ready for you to do so.

31

'Five more minutes,' Will whispered to himself as he picked up a bottle of red wine and pulled the cork to allow it to breathe. He kept one eye on the back door, nervously waiting for Ella's arrival. This was the first real date they'd had. He knew that by now the flowers would have arrived, and excitedly hoped that Ella had loved them. He wanted their evening to be faultless and, once again, checked the roast potatoes, which were browning to perfection.

Will walked around the dining table that he'd taken into the lounge. The ambience was better in there with the softly dimmed lights and it felt preferable to sitting in the kitchen looking at a pile of dirty pots while they ate. He looked at the back door and the garden beyond. Next year, if he could afford it, he'd build a conservatory, one to match Ella's on the other side. It would be a perfect place for the table and, if all went to plan, maybe they'd get a connecting door that went between.

He smiled and thought of how much his mother and sister would have loved Ella. They'd have probably all gone shopping together, done girly spa days and would have teased both him and his dad at every chance they'd got. He could see them all now, laughing, colluding together and mischievously mocking. He sighed, realising how much fun they'd have had, and how unfair life was that they had never got to meet.

But Ella falling into his life had been more than he could have wished for. His mother would have loved her, just as much as he did. The thought made Will jerk back to reality. Did he love Ella? Was that how he felt? He tried to be objective, tried to rationalise, but the more he considered it, the more he realised that Ella was the first person he thought about when he woke up each day and the last person on his mind before falling to sleep.

'Knock, knock. Can I come in?' Ella stood at the door in a black, fitted, off the shoulder dress. The soft curls of her auburn hair hung loosely around her shoulders, framing her face. It was still daylight and Will had thought about eating in the garden, but now, looking at Ella, he was pleased he hadn't decided to. She was hardly dressed for al fresco dining. He stood for just a moment to take in the view. 'Is it too much? Sarah made me go shopping.'

Will shook his head. 'Not at all. I've... I've made roast beef, roast potatoes and greens. Is that okay?' The nerves once again escalated through his body and he turned around to pull the potatoes out of the oven. 'It's almost ready,' he said, shaking the tray, before putting them back inside. He stood and looked her up and down. She looked amazing.

Ella stepped towards him. 'The flowers are gorgeous, thank you,' she whispered as her arm went around his neck. She pulled him towards her and her lips grazed his, as she glanced into the lounge. 'Wow, the table looks great.'

Will led her into the room where the wine already stood on the table. 'Here, I'll pour.'

'Actually, wait. There's something missing. Wait there.' Ella ran from the room, out of the door and into her own cottage. Two minutes later, she was back. 'Candles, we need candles.' She held a box of candles in her hand and Will felt the colour physically drain from his face.

'Ella—' He stopped abruptly; how on earth did he tell her about his family? 'Ella, please. I don't like candles. Please don't light them.' He knew the words were weak, and knew that Ella had no way of understanding.

She looked at him with puzzled eyes. 'Don't be silly. They're lovely. I have candles everywhere, all the time.' She began to pull one out of the box, making Will grab at it.

'Ella, I said no. I don't want them in my house, nor do I want them in yours.' He took in a deep breath, knew he sounded insane and pulled Ella to a seat on the settee. With tears in his eyes, he began to explain.

Ella listened intently as Will recounted the night his whole family had died. She closed her eyes and felt tears drop down her face as she saw the vulnerability in his. Now, everything made sense. She thought of the day at the beach, the way he'd looked into the fire beacons, how sad he'd been and how she'd wondered even back then what his story was. It also explained to her why he'd come to live up in the north.

She held him close. She now knew what she wanted and Will Taylor was at the top of her list. She knew he'd gone to the trouble of cooking, but she wasn't hungry. Since seeing him today, standing at the door looking in at Rick Greaves, with all that doubt on his face, she'd thought of nothing else but convincing him that he was the one she wanted and had no intention of wasting another moment.

'Will?' Ella grazed her lips with his.

A look of uncertainty flashed across his face and Ella held her breath with anticipation, but then felt him pull her towards him. His lips touched hers once, twice and then with a passion she'd never known, he parted her lips. He was strong and demanding. His tongue sent shivers racing down her spine, making her moan with desire.

Ella took in a breath; the soft undertones of his aftershave roused her senses as for a moment his lips left hers and began working their way down her neck. Ella gasped. She knew that this, tonight, here in this cottage was more than just a kiss. And she responded eagerly as the desire engulfed them both.

'Ella...' Will stopped. His breathing was laboured but he searched her eyes. The word was simple. One word, one tiny question that meant so much.

But Ella had no doubts and she nodded without

hesitation. 'Will, take me to bed.' Her eyes locked with his. 'Ella. Are... are you sure? I need to know that you're sure.'

Ella pulled away, suddenly doubting her actions and began to turn towards the door. 'I'm sorry. I shouldn't have...' Ella felt tears spring to her eyes. She'd been too forward and embarrassment flooded through her. But Will's arms went around her waist. 'Don't... Ella... Don't go. Please.'

Ella could hear the nerves in his voice. His hands gripped her hips and lingered there for just a moment, before he turned her around. 'Don't go.' His eyes implored hers. 'Because, Ella, if you go, I don't know what I'd do. You're everything to me... You're so beautiful and I, well... right now, I really want to kiss you.' She felt his lips touch hers. His mouth moved slowly, sensually and his hands pulled her hips closer to his. She could feel his arousal, could feel his need and once again she responded urgently to his kiss. Ella lifted her hands up and ran them over his shoulders. She could feel the muscles flex beneath her touch. She began to unbutton his shirt and the urgency between them increased. Will picked Ella up, her legs wound around his waist and he moved them both toward the bottom of the stairs, his eyes continually searching hers.

Ella felt him take two of the steps. She knew the staircase was steep and she had no intention of allowing him to carry her the whole way up. Her hands tore at his shirt, her tongue teased his and she felt herself being lowered to the steps, where his hand began to unzip her dress.

'Shall we?' She pointed up the stairs and smiled seductively, pulling Will up the stairway behind her.

She caught the deep, sensitive sparkle in his eyes and thought carefully before she spoke again. 'Will. I really want this, I want us,' she whispered as her arm hooked him behind the neck and pulled him into the bedroom. His shirt immediately dropped to the floor and once again she kissed him. Slowly this time, sensual, and at an unhurried and gradual pace. Every touch was one of meaning, every kiss one of passion.

'Oh, Ella, I want you so much. But please, I... I have to tell you something first.' He once again searched her eyes. 'Please... you have to understand that I've wanted to tell you this for ages.' She saw the panic in his eyes.

'Will...' She wanted to stop him, wanted to tell him that she knew, but she realised that this was something that he needed to do. Her eyes closed and she waited for him to speak.

'Ella, I should have told you before. There can't be any more secrets, not between us, not if...' He sighed and then purposely took a step away from her. His hands went to his head, obviously struggling with his thoughts. 'Ella, I'm a reporter. No, damn it. I'm the Editor at the Scarborough Star.' He closed his eyes, before opening them to search her face. 'I swear to God, I've tried to tell you before. So many times.'

'Will, I know.' She teased his lips with hers. 'I've known for ages and it doesn't matter. What does matter is that right now, all I want is for you to make love to me.' She looked into his eyes, saw the relief and laughed, before pulling him onto the bed. Her lips were crushed against his, as the strong, muscular contour of his body pressed passionately against hers, his arousal now fully apparent.

'Ella, you're so beautiful.' His words were a whisper as his lips began to work their magic. 'Please let this be true. Please want me.'

The words were soft, gentle, yet heartbreaking all at the same time. Ella had never wanted anything so much in her life. Her heart pounded like a bass drum. Her hands moved to his jeans in a single silent answer to his question. She pulled at them with urgency as she lifted her face back to his. Their mouths and tongues moved together in a unison she'd never previously known and their hunger grew with each moment that passed.

'I want you so much,' Will whispered, between kisses. He skimmed her hips and thighs with one hand, as the other moved up her spine sending currents of desire spinning through her entire body.

Instinctively, Ella arched towards him. Her dress had long since been removed and as she lay beneath him she heard the last piece of her underwear drop to the floor. She gasped as Will pressed against her. His deep eyes once again locked with hers and she gently nodded, giving him all the permission he needed. Will slowly began to explore her. He took his time to arouse, to give pleasure and to show the affection that she desperately needed. Ella lay back to surrender to his touch as Will's hands carefully touched her with a pleasure that was explosive and pure, and then the deep sparkle of his eyes caught hers. His mouth once again descended and their bodies became one. They moved together in a deep, rhythmic motion and Ella allowed herself to shout out with desire as her body responded with the intensity of an erupting volcano.

'I love you,' Will whispered as he supported himself above her. 'I loved you from the first moment I spied on you through the fence.'

Ella's eyes lit up. 'Did you really spy on me?'

He nodded. A cheeky grin crossed his face and his hands moved down and he began to tickle her.

Ella giggled. 'Stop tickling. I'm too busy thinking of what you've just said!' She slapped his arm and then immediately rubbed it better. 'So, you were watching me that day, before you leapt over the fence and frightened me half to death?' Ella poked him in the ribs as he curled up behind her. His arms protectively enveloped her body and for a few moments they lay together in silence.

'Are you sleepy, Ella?' he whispered gently, closing his eyes, just as Ella jumped out of bed, grabbed Will's shirt and pulled it on.

'Not a chance, Mr Taylor.' She limped towards the door. 'My ankle still hurts, but I'm hungry and, as far as I'm aware, there's roast beef downstairs.' She began to hop down the stairs. 'I'll race you for it.'

32

Will stared at the laptop and at the picture that glared back at him. 'Damn it.' He shook his head. 'It's so damned obvious.' He stood up, paced up and down and then grabbed his jacket. 'Why didn't I see this before?' He leaned forward, pressed print and waited for the picture of Nina, with her mother and stepfather, standing next to a dark blue Golf to emerge.

Will hesitated. Ella was still sleeping upstairs. But he had to go. The fact that Nina or her stepfather owned a blue Golf was far too significant. He had to see if they still had the car, especially after the night he'd spent with Ella. He'd lain awake watching her for hours. He'd held her and comforted her through disturbed sleep. She'd had nightmares and he'd watched her pain as she'd tossed and turned with the torment. The memory and emotion of that night was more than obvious. He hated that her dreams were so vivid and hated that on most nights she went through them alone. Well, that wouldn't happen any more. From now on, provided she wanted him, he was determined to look after her, determined to be there for her and determined to find out who had attacked her that night. He wanted them brought to justice, in the hope that seeing them locked up for good would help Ella sleep.

He looked at his watch and hesitated. 'Can I do it? Can I get there and back before Ella or Millie Moo wake up?' After eating dinner the night before, Ella had gone back to her cottage to bring Millie over to Will's for the night. He was amazed that Millie hadn't already bounced down the stairs and he silently gave himself permission to go. 'I won't be long and if I find the car, I'll phone the police. By tonight we could have justice.' It was what he wanted more than anything. He headed out through the back door, closing it carefully behind him.

Will jumped into his car. 'I won't be long,' he whispered to the bedroom window behind which Ella slept. He looked across to the farm. The morning sun began to creep up in the sky and Bobby was already sitting on his tractor, waving enthusiastically. Will smiled and waved back. He felt sorry for Bobby. He was lonely, and only the week before Will had explained to Ella about how Bobby had been cuddling Millie on the day of her fire. How he'd been upset that she'd shouted at him and that all he'd wanted was to be friends. He was sure that Bobby was harmless and Ella had agreed that the next time she saw him she'd speak to him.

The mere thought of Ella put a smile on his face. 'A new sun, a new beginning,' he whispered as he thought of the night before. Of how he and Ella had tenderly made love. Of how cautious, yet demanding their bodies had been and then of how they'd fed each other the roast dinner and laughed. It had felt like years since he'd laughed so much and then, once the laughing had turned back into passion, they'd moved back to the bedroom, where they'd made love repeatedly right through the night until every millimetre of his body had been on fire with desire. But then, as he watched Ella sleep, she'd screamed. She'd grabbed hold of his arm in her sleep and he'd been so full of adrenaline that he tossed and turned for hours. In the end, it had been easier to go downstairs. To make a drink and open the laptop. He began scanning through social media, through images and through any data that he could find in the hope that something would jump out, something new, something of value. He looked at anything and everything that might point to Ella's attacker. He'd flicked through many pages over and over again. And then he'd seen it. A photograph that had been sent to Nina's social media two years before. The words, 'Hey, do you remember this day?' beside it. And there it had been. The car, a dark blue Golf, her family and the fairground behind them.

Will had stared at the teenage Nina. He thought of how petite and vulnerable she'd looked. Yet now, even though she was still petite, she came over as strong and capable, albeit a little in need. Was this your family car? Did it belong to your stepfather? Will quickly looked back at his notes. Nina's stepfather was Harold Hannigan. Was that whose car it was?

And the main question was, if it had been his car, did he still own it? Or was it just a huge coincidence that he'd once owned a blue Golf? Will knew from the phone conversations he had heard Nina having that her stepfather was controlling. But was he capable of murder? And if so, why? A million questions flew around Will's mind. Will had seen the way Nina had looked at Rick. She'd told him of their one-night stands, of how Rick would take her to his bed and then a few days later he'd move onto the next woman, girlfriend or wife. Had Nina told her stepfather what had happened? Had he taken revenge on her behalf, or had he been protecting her interests? Looking after his little girl? But if he had, why had he killed Rick's wives or Michelle? Why attack Ella? There were so many unanswered questions and, from what Will surmised, all of them could probably be answered by Harold Hannigan.

Will pulled the car to a stop. He looked down at the address he'd written down and then back up at the farm. This was where Nina was supposed to be living, but the house looked as though no one had been there for years. To say it looked run-down was an understatement. Trees and bushes were overgrown, the hedges hadn't been cut in years and the five-bar gate was broken and rusty. Will slowly pushed it open. He listened for signs of life, for livestock or dogs. And, after a few minutes, he took a tentative step forward, and then another. The farm was quiet, far too quiet, and Will's eyes searched his surroundings constantly as he crept towards the outbuildings. They stood to one side of the house and had no doubt been where the livestock had been housed. But now nothing looked used. Even the house didn't look lived in. It looked old, disused and possibly haunted, just like those houses he'd seen in films and he felt pleased that he'd come here in daylight and not late at night. He stared up at the property. He'd never seen anything like it. The windows were beyond dirty. Most of the curtains were closed; some hung in pieces like rags, with nets so dirty they obviously hadn't been washed in years. If he didn't know better, he'd have thought it derelict, forgotten and unloved. But this was Nina's home; this was where she and her stepfather lived. Or was it?

Will stepped to one side. What he'd come to find wouldn't be in the house, and he turned his attention to the outbuildings, which were in a worse state of decay than the house. Most were derelict and others had fallen into complete disrepair. There were either holes in the roof or no roof at all and Will wondered how much maintenance Harold Hannigan had actually done over the years.

'What kind of a man are you?' Will whispered as he crept from one building to the next. He looked through holes in the walls or doors, but saw no sign of life, no livestock, no machinery.

Will then made his way towards the only barn that didn't have a door. He stepped forward cautiously and peeped inside. 'Okay, what have we here?' he sang out as he pulled at the edge of a tarpaulin. It looked as though it had been quickly thrown over a dark blue vehicle. Will pulled his phone from his pocket and took pictures from different angles. He then pulled at the tarpaulin until it fell to the floor to fully reveal the dark blue Golf, its bonnet still damaged and bloodstained.

'Oh, boy.' Will looked down at his phone. His hands were shaking so much he dropped it; he knelt down to catch his breath. 'I really have to phone the police. No, Sarah. No, the police,' he whispered to himself as he looked down at his phone, picked it back up and began to tap at the screen. 'Sarah, yes, Sarah, she'll know what to do.' He pressed the icon and watched as Sarah's name flashed up on his screen as it began to call.

There was a noise. It came from behind him and for a moment he froze on the spot, glancing down at the screen. 'Come on, answer,' he whispered, but then a torturous pain suddenly surged through every part of his body.

33

Ella woke and stretched. She could hear Millie whining and for a moment she felt disorientated and just a little confused. She turned over against the white duvet and pillow and caught the shaft of sun that had found its way between a gap in the white curtains. She sat up to see Millie bouncing around on the floor, waiting to be let out. 'Morning, puppy,' she said as she smiled and then laughed as the memory of the night before came flooding back. She climbed out of bed and began to search the floor. She had no idea where her clothes were, and, worse than that, the bed beside her was empty. Will had gone.

'Morning,' she called out as she picked up her

bra. 'Will, are you there?' She padded around the bedroom, slowly retrieving her articles of clothing that seemed to have been thrown in every direction. 'Will, could you call Millie? She really needs to go out and I'm having a bit of a problem here finding my knickers.' She listened for an answer, but when one didn't come she threw on her clothes and made her way down the stairs, one at a time. Her ankle still hurt, and she hopped down them on one foot using the banister for support.

'Come on, Millie, find Will.' Millie scrambled past the door, through the kitchen and into the lounge, where she doubled back and ran to the back door, waiting. Ella opened it. 'Will, where are you? Come on, stop hiding, this really isn't funny.'

Ella took in a deep breath as the realisation hit her. The cottage was small and it was more than obvious that it was empty. She stood for a moment and just stared out the front window at where Will's car normally stood.

Okay. So, he'd gone out. He'd left without telling her. Why would he do that? She tried to be rational. Tried to think of the places he could have gone and the reasons why, but she felt abandoned, alone and disappointed. A thought sprang to mind. Milk? She quickly opened the fridge, but a full four-pint carton stared back and her disappointment turned to anger. Why had he left her alone? Why hadn't he been there, to wake up with her, especially after the night they'd spent together?

Ella once again looked at her watch. It was just after eight; it was still early. Would he have left her a message, a note? She smiled. 'Of course. He'll have left a message. He always sends messages.' She began searching for her mobile and finally found it down the back of the settee, where they'd sat the night before, eating, feeding one another and laughing until they'd cried. She immediately swiped the screen and checked it for messages. Excitement seared through her and she smiled when she saw the red indicator show the number two. 'I knew it,' she said, but her words were premature.

Darling. Don't forget, your new cooker comes at nine. I tried to call but you're not home. Where are you? Mum x

Morning. It's Michelle Everett's funeral today. Midday. Any chance you could cover it? I wouldn't ask but Sally phoned in sick. Alan.

Two messages. Both wanting her attention. Neither of them from Will.

Ella glanced at a calendar that hung on Will's wall. 'Friday. It's Friday.' Relief spread through her. 'He'll be at work,' she thought as she called his mobile. It went straight to voicemail. Not to be defeated, she tapped on the office number he'd given her last night.

'Hello, Will Taylor's phone,' a female voice at the Star sang out. 'Can I help you?'

Ella stumbled on her words. 'Will... Will Taylor, I'd... I'd like to speak to him, please?'

She listened as the woman at the other end chuckled. 'Yeah, you and half of Scarborough, dear. He hasn't shown up yet. Shall I get him to call you when he comes in?'

Ella put down the phone and stared at it. 'Something's wrong. But what?' Her mind spun as she continued to gather her things, knowing that Will wouldn't be so cruel. He wouldn't walk out on her like this. She was sure that he wouldn't leave her to wake up on her own, not unless he couldn't help it. He was a reporter, after all. Maybe he had been called out on a job, but then his office would have known about it. Deep down, disappointment took over her senses and she had no choice but to leave, go back to her own cottage and hope that he got in touch soon.

'Come on, Millie. Let's go home.'

* * *

Ella stamped around her kitchen. Her mother's text saying that the new cooker was coming today had reminded her that she still had things to do. Which meant putting all the decorating trays and brushes in the shed and all the smoke damaged items that were still piled up next to the conservatory in the boot of her car. Like it or not, no one was going to do it for her and they were becoming unsightly and needed taking to the tip. The old cooker had already been dragged outside and Ella tried tugging at it some more, but failed. It was simply too heavy. She resorted to pulling open the oven door and emptying it of its shelves, baking trays and the grill pan. After the fire, it was all covered in a thick black carbon that dirtied everything it touched and she dug around for a bin bag and placed them inside. She then began pushing items from the pile into the bin bags. She picked up her old hockey stick. It wouldn't fit in the bag and was the last thing she wanted to throw away. It reminded her of school, of times when she'd been happy and part of a team, but it had been burned in the fire and with a heavy heart she placed it in the boot, ready to go.

Satisfied with her work, Ella walked back to the front window and looked out. Will's car still hadn't returned. Her heart felt heavy with disappointment. Today should have been a happy day. Today should have been full of fun, of more love-making and of her and Will getting to know each other properly.

A tear fell down her face. 'Where are you Will? What made you leave?'

34

Nina stood motionless, looking down at the dry, arid earth. It had been a while since she'd been to this exact spot and she stood with her back against an old oak tree. The leaves created a canopy over the woodland and the light twinkled through the spaces as the sun broke through like shiny diamonds. It was the same tree she'd stood against years before, but now it stood much taller and broader than it used to.

Nina closed her eyes and tried to remember how the woodland had looked seven years before, and then she opened them wide to scan the terrain. Everything was different. Everything had grown randomly and nothing seemed at all familiar. She strode forward, taking twelve strides from the tree. Saplings, bushes and weeds had grown haphazardly and where once she'd had a direct route, she now had to step to the side, over and around the growth that had sprung up before her. She tried to ignore them. They were not important, not today and she moved around them as though they hadn't grown at all, as she continued to count her steps.

It was early, just before nine. The sun was already warm, and the promise of heat brought a haze that surrounded the woodland. Nina watched as the sun rose between the trees, but then she noticed the black clouds far in the distance. Deep inside, her stomach fluttered with nerves as she paced nervously up and down. 'Where else could I hide?' She cursed under her breath and kicked at the ground.

She looked to her right, to the lake. She stared at its fertile edge that rippled as tiny fish came up to eat bugs that hovered around at its surface. The last time she'd been here had been seven years before after a week of torrential rain. The ground had been soft, spongy and easy to dig. She thought of the sound that the spade had made as it had hit the ground. The way the mud had squelched as she'd dug deeper and deeper. With each spade of earth that she'd dug, another had slipped back into the hole, making the night long and arduous, but satisfying.

Nina looked around. She hated herself for what she'd done here. She hated every image that her mind still created and gazed longingly at the woodland's beauty, feeling grateful for its protection.

Nina looked over her shoulder as a truck sped past, making her duck behind the tree. She held her breath. The new road was now located just a few yards from where she stood, much closer than it used to be. Years before it had been a dirt track, only used by the locals. A simple, yet private place where she'd been able to hide for hours, totally uninterrupted. But now, since the diggers had been to work, a new road had been constructed that was used as a short cut from one village to the next or as a through road to the motorway.

Nina glared at the ground and breathed a sigh of relief. If the road had been created just fifteen feet closer to the lake, the diggers would have exposed her twisted secret and everyone would have known what she'd done.

She kicked at the earth and stamped her feet as tears began to fall.

'I hate you so much. It's all your fault.' She continued to kick at the tufts of grass that grew above where her stepfather had been buried deep below. Nina took in gulps of air, steadied herself against a tree and then inched her way down, until she lay on the parched woodland floor as though listening for signs of life beneath its surface. 'They all think you're still alive, do you know that?' She laughed, a deep hysterical laugh. 'I pretend you see. I pretend you call me when I'm at work. Rick tells me off all the time. But at least it gets his attention. At least on those days he knows that I exist. I tell them how cruel you are, how awful my life is.' She nodded and then kicked out at the tree. 'I told them how you'd throw me out if I didn't pay more rent.' Her hand went up to her dark, greasy hair and pushed it back from her face. 'But it was all a ruse, you see, I just wanted more hours at the gym, more hours to spend with Rick.'

'This is your new daddy, Nina.' The memory of her mother's voice rang out and Nina remembered her five- year-old self looking up to see a big man who wore jeans, but no shirt.

'I certainly am,' Pete had said. 'You'll be fine with me, poppet. I'll look after both you and your mammy from now on. Don't you worry.' He'd looked at her with a smirk, a leery tone that even at such a young age had immediately made Nina feel afraid and awkward.

Nina turned onto her back and looked up to where the canopy of trees stood above her. She wiped away the tears that ran down her cheeks. She could see his face, the smirk, the sparkle in his eyes and the joy he'd taken in hurting her, abusing her.

Again her head shook from side to side. Nina closed her eyes as tight as she could. It helped her remember, helped her hone in on the memories of her mother, her childhood and the time before Pete. She liked to remember the time when both her mother and father had been alive, a time when she'd felt loved and protected and that she belonged. Life had been simple back then. She'd been allowed to be a child. But then her mother had died, she'd been left alone to live with Pete and everything changed. And now, now she had to cover her tracks. This was a day she hadn't planned. She had to think on her feet but she was good at that – she'd had to be. Her mouth was dry and she desperately needed a drink. But there wasn't time. A sudden feeling of nausea hit her. She couldn't remember the last time she'd eaten and she thought back to Will, to the sandwiches they'd shared. 'You just had to interfere, didn't you? Why? Why did you do that? I liked you. You were nice. But now, now I've had to get rid of you too.' She closed her eyes as she waited for the feeling of nausea to pass and then opened them wide to listen and watch the road beyond.

'So many people speeding past, all with someone to go home to. Do you hear them?' Nina stood up. Her sobs turned to a hysterical cackle as she began to trace the ground with her steps. Four steps in one direction, two steps the other. She traced the edges of the grave with her foot, tried to recall the exact position her stepfather had been in and the way he'd looked when she'd pushed him over the edge and into the hole she'd dug. He'd been drugged, bound and gagged, but his eyes had lit up like candles in the darkness. They'd stared at her, pleaded with her and had filled with tears as she'd thrown the first shovel of dirt over his body. He'd been terrified, just as she'd wanted him to be. But she'd felt no remorse. She'd wanted him to suffer. She'd wanted him to panic, to pray for mercy, to wonder when the torture would end and she'd wanted him to feel that sensation of suffocation as the last of the dirt had fallen on top of him. Just as she'd felt on so many occasions in the past, when he'd drugged her, forced himself upon her, held pillows over her face while she'd gasped for breath and then, once it had been over, he'd promised her the world, if only she kept quiet.

Nina sat back down and stamped her foot at the ground and thought of all the people she'd killed. 'If only he'd loved me. If only he hadn't loved the others. They'd all be alive and me, I'd be happy. Someone would love me.' She began to shake. She'd known that using the car as a weapon had been a mistake, that it would only be a matter of time before the police or the reporters would put one and one together, before they matched the paint, the car and the fragments from the hit-and-run. She'd known they'd come for her but hadn't realised that today would be that day. She began to laugh nervously. 'But I have no regrets... Her death was justified.' She once again stamped on her stepfather's grave. 'And you... you were my first, in so many ways, and you got exactly what you deserved.'

35

Ella stood at the gate with Millie in her arms. She watched the deliverymen pull away, just as Bobby pulled into the farm opposite on his tractor. He lifted a hand and cautiously waved, making Ella feel guilty as she waved back. Will had explained what had happened, that Bobby felt lonely. That he was upset and confused that she'd shouted at him. He'd been trying to be helpful. Besides, Ella had noticed that since that day he'd looked very sad, lost and alone.

She walked across the road with Millie in her arms. 'Hey, Bobby. Are you okay?' She still felt a little nervous, as she did of all men. Will leaving without a word had proved to her that all men were capable of anything, even the ones she thought she could trust. But Bobby had done nothing wrong except for in her own imagination. She was sorry she'd shouted and felt the need to try and move forward. If nothing else, she felt the need to apologise.

Bobby looked excited. He jumped down from the tractor and ran to where Ella stood. 'Hi, Miss Ella. Can... can I see the puppy?' Ella nodded and watched how he carefully lifted Millie from her arms and gently hugged her to him. 'She's so pretty, isn't she?' He snuggled her close to his face and kissed the top of her head, while his fingers tickled her under the chin. 'She's grown, haven't you?' he said to Millie as he continued to tickle her, the look on his face one of pure love. 'I'd like a dog. I'd like one to run around with me on the farm.' He passed Millie back to Ella. 'But I can't. I'm the only one here, there's too much to do and I don't have time to train one.'

Ella smiled. 'Well, if you promise not to sneak up on me, you can come and see Millie sometimes if you like.'

Bobby almost bounced on the spot with excitement. 'Can I? Can I really?' He paced back and forth. 'I didn't mean to scare you that day, I was—'

'I know.' Ella reached out and touched his arm. 'I

know you were trying to help, Bobby, and I'm sorry. I didn't mean to shout at you.'

He smiled, reached out and stroked Millie one more time. 'I saw Will this morning. He went out really early.'

Ella looked back at the spot where Will's car had been parked, just as a police car pulled up in its place with Sarah, in uniform, in the driver's seat. 'Hey, Sarah, what's up? I was just going to work.' Ella saw the stern look on her face, and ran across to meet her.

'Is Will home?' Sarah asked and began making her way down the side of Will's house, scanning the gardens.

'Sarah, what's wrong?' Ella knew that something wasn't right. Sarah's tone was all official, she was in work mode and not her normal bubbly self. 'Sarah, you're frightening me.'

Sarah shook her head, tried the back door and walked in. 'Will, are you home?' She walked from kitchen to living room and then doubled back and made her way up the stairs, all the time shouting.

Ella just stood, watching and wondering what Sarah was up to. 'Do you want to tell me what's happening?' she asked when Sarah reappeared.

But Sarah shook her head. 'I don't know what's

happening. All I do know is that at 7.45 a.m. I had a call from Will and just as I picked up the phone, I heard a noise and then... then it went dead. All attempts to reach him since then have been unsuccessful.'

She thought about what Bobby had said. 'He went out really early. Have you traced the call? Looked into where he is, or was?' Ella felt her legs begin to shake. 'Could... could he be in trouble?'

Sarah took her friend by the shoulders. 'That's why I'm here. I need to decide if he's in trouble or not. He might have just called by accident. Can you tell me how he was last night?'

Ella shook her head, then sat on the settee and told Sarah everything about the night before, including how she'd got up to find Will gone, the messages from her mum and from work, and then she repeated what Bobby had said while Sarah made notes.

'Ella, look. It's probably nothing and I probably wouldn't have even looked into it, but Josh said he hadn't turned in for work, so now...' She tipped her head from side to side. 'No worries. Did you say you had to go work?' Ella shuffled on the spot. 'I did. But I can't go... not if Will's in trouble, can I? I... I need to call him.' She picked up her mobile and began searching for his number. 'Ella. Don't. If he's in trouble, the sound of the phone ringing might make it worse. If I have any news at all, I'll call you.' Her eyes caught Ella's. 'Now, you go, go and work, and by the time you get home, all will be sorted.'

36

It was midday. Rain had begun to pour relentlessly and showed no sign of stopping. Globules of water bounced like huge gobstoppers from the dark grey sky. They made it difficult to see the other side of the cemetery, never mind recognise anyone that stood more than a few feet away, and Ella found herself holding her hand up to shield her eyes from the water as she peered between the gravestones. A priest stood at the head of the grave and, regardless of the weather, was speaking calmly and slowly to a congregation that appeared to be shuffling their feet in anticipation of leaving, going to the club and drinking away the afternoon, all courtesy of Michelle's parents. Hundreds had turned out to mourn, some who knew Michelle, many who probably didn't. Most had been members of the gym and had felt the need to attend as a mark of respect. All were dressed in black, all drenched by the rain, and almost everyone appeared to be sinking into the mud with every second that passed.

Ella tapped Josh on the arm and indicated over to Rick, who was standing around ten feet behind the rest of the crowd. Michelle's parents glared at him, as they both sobbed uncontrollably. It was more than obvious that Rick wasn't welcome. He looked stern, cold and almost as though he was lost in a nightmare that he had no chance of waking up from. His eyes were not fixed on the grave, but on a figure that stood in the distance. A figure that looked like Nina, but from this far away and with the driving rain, Ella couldn't be sure, because the figure was partially hidden.

'Look.' Ella pointed. 'Over there. Is that who I think it is?' she asked Josh, who stood by a tree, discreetly taking as many photographs as he could. He carefully pulled the camera away from his face and looked in the direction Ella had indicated.

'Who is it?' he queried. He picked the camera back up and pointed it in the direction of the gravestone beside which she stood. He zoomed in and clicked. 'Is that—' He stopped, looked at the digital display and enlarged the picture. 'What the hell is Nina doing here? I thought she hated Michelle. I remember Will saying so.'

Ella shrugged. 'How should I know why she's here? Besides, have you seen Rick's face? He looks absolutely furious.' She tapped Josh on the shoulder. 'Look, he's walking towards her.'

They both watched Rick. He walked past the head of the grave, briefly looked at the coffin, and then walked through the graveyard to where Nina stood.

* * *

'Where the hell have you been?' Rick grabbed hold of Nina's arm, spun her around and paraded her away from the funeral. 'You've been missing for days. You do know that you can't just do that, don't you?' He paused. 'With both Michelle and Tim gone, I've been doing it all on my own. Do you think that's fair?'

'Go to hell, Rick. I thought you were closing the place down.' She looked up and spoke with tear-filled eyes. 'I didn't think you needed me. You always seem to need everyone else, rather than me. Now, I told you to get off me,' Nina growled, pulling her arm from his.

'Nina, of course I need you, God damn it. But remember I also pay your wages, which means that you turn up when the hell you're supposed to. Do you get that?' He looked her up and down and took notice of how she was dressed. Of how her coat was uncharacteristically dirty. She was drenched, her boots were covered in mud and her hair was wet, and greasy; she didn't look as polished as normal and Rick suddenly felt concern. 'Nina, are you okay?'

'Get off me,' Nina shrieked as Rick once again held onto her arm and practically dragged her across the cemetery to where his car stood.

'What the hell are you doing here, Nina? You and Michelle, you were hardly friends, now, were you?'

'I came to pay my respects. Not against the law, is it?'

'No it's not. But I am surprised you came at all. Now. Where's your car?' he asked, looking up and down the street.

'I got rid of it.' She looked down at the floor as she spoke. She suddenly seemed to notice how muddy her boots were and pulled a tissue from her pocket, crouched down in the pouring rain and began to wipe them clean.

Shrugging he pulled her to her feet and marched her across to his car. 'Here, get in there. You can polish your shoes later.'

* * *

Sarah paced up and down Will's lounge, checking her phone for the twentieth time that minute. She stared out the window and through the driving rain that bounced on the pavement. She was waiting for her colleagues to arrive. Waiting for someone to confirm that what she'd seen on Will's laptop was not just a coincidence and that, like it or not, Will Taylor was in some kind of trouble.

She felt the need to ring Ella, to tell her what she'd seen, but protocol forbade her. Right now, she had to do her job. Stick to the rules and follow the evidence.

Sarah had been working all morning. She'd borrowed Ella's keys before she left and she'd sat for over an hour in her conservatory collating all of Ella's evidence. She'd lifted one document after the other and studied it. There had to be a link. She was sure that there was something that connected all the deaths together. After all, could one person be so unlucky that almost every woman he'd ever cared about could die in so many strange or unexplained ways? Which left the question: was the person who'd killed Michelle responsible for killing both of Rick's wives? And how the hell was Ella connected to all of this? Why had she been beaten and how had she lived, when all the others had died? The questions spun around her mind like a fairground ride.

All that Sarah could really see was that if someone had hurt or killed them all then they'd ruined Rick's life, just as much as if they'd killed him too. But that triggered the most obvious question, the one question she didn't really want to ask: had Rick killed them and had he beaten Ella? It was a theory that went around and around her head, a theory that offered her no answers, especially after a jury had acquitted him.

Another thought crossed Sarah's mind. Was it possible that Ella's attack wasn't related at all? The MO was different. No one else had been beaten. No one else had lived. 'If Ella's attack wasn't related, then there could still be someone out there. Someone that still wants her dead,' Sarah spoke out loud. The thought made her tremble and even though it was twenty degrees outside, she suddenly felt cold.

Again she thought of the evidence. Of how Nina's face had tormented her from the newspaper clippings and now, back in Will's cottage, she'd seen the picture on his laptop of Nina with her mother, stepfather and the car. Something wasn't right. Sarah shook her head. 'It couldn't be, could it? What on earth would be his motive?'

37

Nina paced around the edge of the lake and waited for darkness. She'd been standing there for what seemed like forever, not knowing where else to go. She looked down at her watch and knew that she'd have to wait for a few more hours before darkness would fall. She looked across to where Rick's Outlander was parked between the trees with Rick, now unconscious, on the back seat. Another night, another victim.

She thought of the Golf, now burned out and dumped. She pulled at her hair and tore at the roots. She'd gone too far. Things had gotten far too messy. But then she thought about Will and felt an overwhelming sadness, followed by relief. She'd had no choice but to dump his lifeless body in a roadside ditch. She'd had to get rid of him. He'd seen too much. He was a reporter, after all, and she knew that without a doubt he'd have gone straight to the police. But then, she'd realised that it was the car that would lead to her downfall, not Will, and she'd had no regrets when she'd set the fire and the flames had finally taken hold.

She thought about her options. She had a plan. She had to convince the authorities that her stepfather was responsible. After all, the car did still belong to him, and no one knew that he was dead. In fact, by answering the fake phone calls, she'd kept him very much alive. Everyone would think that he was responsible. That he'd killed them all. He'd be blamed for everything and then, to top it off, he'd never be found. They'd presume he'd taken his own life and she, she would play the grieving daughter. She nodded. Yes, she could do that, she could sob for the cameras, beg him to hand himself in and then pretend to search for him herself.

A deep sense of ending took over her mind. She knew she was out of control. She was panicking too often, making too many mistakes and killing without thought and yet... a sly smile crossed her face, followed by a deep and evil laugh as she walked back towards the Outlander and peered inside. Rick lay on the back seat, his face pale grey, his eyelids fluttering.

It hadn't taken much to drug him or to convince him to drink from her bottle, a bottle she'd pretended to drink from herself. After all, she couldn't risk him fighting back. Not with what she had planned. He'd already ingested enough of the fluid to down an elephant and all she really needed to do was wait until he passed, and then... then she could bury him in the woods, right beside Pete. She'd got away with it before; she could get away with it again. Couldn't she?

She was tired. She'd been awake for days. She was surviving on adrenaline and wondered if she'd have the energy to dig the hole. Leaving the Outlander behind, she walked back into the woods and stared longingly at the spade, wishing it were magic and would dig the hole itself. But then she began to laugh hysterically. The spade was old, it was the same one she'd used before and now it leaned against the tree, worn and battered with; for a moment she wondered if driving the Outlander into the lake would be easier. At least then Rick would be with her and finally they'd be together in death, as they should have been in life. She yawned and wondered what to do. She needed to sleep.

Nina looked up at the sky. 'Come on darkness, we're waiting.' It was now late, but dusk still hadn't fallen. She walked back to the car, to where still Rick still lay. She pulled open the door, climbed in the back seat beside him and rested her hand on his forehead.

'If only you'd loved me, I wouldn't have to do this, would I? And you do know that all of this is your fault, don't you?' She stroked his face. 'We had a plan, me and you. It was all organised. All you had to do was love me, but you didn't.' Nina curled up beside him. 'They all had to die, didn't they? And then we... we were going to be happy together. But you couldn't do it, could you? You never loved me. You kept looking for 'The One' and those other girls, when you could have just had me. So, you made me kill them. Don't you see that?' She smiled a half smile and stroked his face.

'And Tim, he thought he could get away with taking all of our money too. But he didn't. I got all the money back and the police, well, they'll most probably find his body sometime soon.' A deep throaty laugh left her. 'I drugged his whisky. The whisky he hid in the filing cabinet, the whisky he thought no one knew about. Oh, he'll have got home. He'll have been so tired he'll have curled up in his bed and I expect that is where they'll eventually find him. So, no one wins, you see. All because you couldn't love me as I love you.'

She searched around in the centre console of the car, found a pound coin and tossed it in the air. 'Okay, heads, we drive into the lake. Tails, you go in the woods.' She caught the coin, turned it onto the back of her hand and stroked his face. 'Are you ready, my darling? Are you ready to hear your fate?'

A groaning noise came from somewhere deep within Rick and his eyes fluttered open and then closed. His mouth drooped to one side and Nina stared into his face. 'Not your best look, my love,' she said as she wiped his mouth free of drool with the back of her hand.

'H-he-lp... me, pl-pl-leeeeeease,' Rick moaned. His voice was faint and distant and Nina moved her ear close to his mouth to listen.

'Of course I'll help you, darling. That's my job; that's what people do when they love each other.' She reached into a rucksack and pulled out a bottle. 'Here you are, take a drink of this.' The bottle was pressed to his lips. 'I know you're not feeling too well right now. But, I promise, this... this will help you sleep.'

She poured the cloudy liquid into his mouth. The more he drank, the drowsier he became and once Nina was satisfied that he'd had enough, she lay him back down and once again she curled up by his side. 'That's right. Cuddle into me.' She closed her eyes. 'We'll wait here together, until it's dark.' She pulled a blanket over them both. Nina once again stroked his face with her hand. 'If I can't have you and if you won't give me the chance to love you, then I won't let anyone else have you. Is that clear?' Nina closed her eyes, snuggled into Rick and waited for his breathing to deepen, before finally allowing herself to sleep.

* * *

It was dark and eerie in the back of the car when Nina woke. She looked at her watch. She took a few moments to enjoy the closeness that she shared with Rick and spent a short time just holding his hand, touching the finger where his wedding ring had been and tenderly stroking his face. He felt cold. Colder than she'd ever known and she listened carefully for the sound of him breathing. But there was nothing. She couldn't hear his breaths and she jumped out of the car and gasped for air.

'No, no, no, no. You have to breathe. Just one breath, please!' She marched up and down, tearing at her hair, not knowing what to do. 'You're not supposed to die. Not yet. The coin said that we were going to drive into the lake. We were going to be together even in death.' She looked at the spade and swallowed hard, just as a deep sob left her throat. She didn't want to die. But what choice did she have? Nothing was left. Rick was gone and there was no one else in the world that loved her.

38

Will tried to open his eyes, but couldn't. They were heavy, like lead. A bleeping noise began to annoy him and the smell of antiseptic filled his nostrils.

'Where am I?' He struggled to speak; his throat was sore. His breathing got faster and faster as panic set in.

'Okay, Mr Taylor. Stay as still as you can. You're in hospital. You were found by the side of the road in a ditch; it's a wonder you didn't drown.' He felt his hand being lifted, his wrist being touched. 'You've suffered a head injury.' The voice was soft, gentle, and that of a woman. 'It's not too bad, don't worry.'

'What road... what...' He tried to think back.

Tried to work out what had happened, but all that filled his mind was Ella; he could see her face, her smile and, most of all, he remembered her kiss. 'We were... I was... Ella, I have to get to Ella.' His breathing once again began to accelerate, and he purposely concentrated on slowing it down. He was in a hospital. But the nurse had spoken of a road-side. Had he been in a car crash? Surely not; if the car had crashed, how would he have ended up in a ditch? All he knew was that being in hospital wasn't supposed to be the plan. Not today. Today... today he should have been with Ella. So, why wasn't he?

'Shhhh, try and relax.' The voice came again and Will forced his eyes to open. He could just make out the woman, a nurse. She smiled down at him, while all the time looking at a monitor. 'Now, your next of kin? We've tried to contact them, but the phone numbers are not recognised.'

Will once again closed his eyes. He could see his mother's face, the flames that had engulfed his home and then... then he was standing by the grave-side, where all his family had been buried together, and tears began to fill his eyes.

He tried to shake his head. 'They're dead. They're all dead.' He moved his hand to wipe the tears, but felt the nurse restrain him.

'You have a drip in the back of your hand, Mr Taylor. We sedated you a little when you first came in, to monitor how bad the injury was.' She gently held his hand down by his side.

Sedation? That explained the way he felt. The heavy eyes, the numbness and the need to sleep. But he couldn't sleep. Not now. Now he had to re-member what had happened. And then suddenly, like a flash of lightning, he saw the Golf. It was standing right there before him. He mentally turned around, visualising all that stood around the car. He saw the tarpaulin, the bloodstains and then... then he turned and saw... Nina.

'Jesus...' He could feel his heart pounding in his chest. Adrenalin coursed through him and, without a thought, he sat up on the bed. 'I... I have to go.'

The nurse jumped back, and pressed a buzzer. 'Can I get some help in here?' she called as the room lit up with red flashing lights.

Will held up his hands. 'Please. I'm not danger-ous. I just really need to go.' He looked down at his hand. 'You said my injury wasn't so bad... so you can take this out, right? Or shall I pull it out? I'd really prefer it if you did it for me.' He held out his hand to her as four other nurses ran into the room. They stopped in their tracks as though weighing up what to do, all waiting for instruction, all waiting to pounce.

'Mr Taylor,' came the first nurse's voice, 'I'd strongly advise that you lie back down. The sedation you had should have begun to wear off, but to be sure, I'd give it another hour before you try and move.' She stared into his eyes. 'Please?' She looked over at the incoming nurses, shook her head and watched them retreat.

But Will shook his head. 'What time is it?' He glanced through the room and to a window beyond.

'It's nine o'clock,' the nurse confirmed. 'You've been here most of the day. But I can see you're deter-mined to leave.' She reached out, lifted his hand and took his pulse. She then sighed as she pulled the cannula from the back of his hand and wiped the area clean. 'You're not allergic to plasters, are you?' She pulled a small plaster from a pack and as Will shook his head, she attached it to his hand. 'Now you shouldn't drive, operate machinery or make any life changing decisions, not for twenty-four hours. Do you understand?'

Will nodded in agreement. He did understand. But that didn't mean he'd comply.

* * *

An hour later Will was unlocking his car. It was still hidden in the trees near Nina's farmhouse and he stepped through the long grass to pull open the door. After locating his wallet in the glovebox, he paid off the taxi driver. And then, without thought, he jumped into the driver's seat. His mobile had died some hours before and he plugged it in, only to watch it light up like a Christmas tree with messages and missed calls. Everyone in the world had been trying to get hold of him. He looked for Ella's name. It was there, just before eight and then nothing. He knew she'd be angry and kicked himself for having left her alone. He should have told her where he was going. He should have left a note, a text or made a call. But he'd been so sure he'd be back, so sure she'd still be sleeping once he returned and after he'd watched the nightmares she'd suffered, he hadn't wanted to disturb the only peaceful sleep she'd seemed to have had. But right now he owed her one hell of an apology.

He glanced back at the farmhouse as he drove away. He was still unsure what had happened there, of what Nina's involvement was or how he'd ended up in the ditch where he'd been miraculously found. What he did know was that none of that had hap-

pened by accident. Someone knew the answers and
he was determined to find out what they were.

39

Nina drove the Outlander at speed. It was a big vehicle and one she wasn't used to driving, but she was terrified and needed to get to a hospital quickly.

She swerved around a corner, raced through a hairpin bend and then glanced over her shoulder. The colour had completely left Rick's face and her whole body shook with the fear of what she'd done.

'It's too late. I... I know it's too late.' She slowed the car to a halt. Her eyes filled with tears and huge, soul- wrenching sobs took over her body. A scream left her throat and she began kicking at the pedals of the car.

But then, as quickly as they'd begun, the sobs stopped and she stared into space. Her mind became clear. A hospital was not going to save him. Which meant that she now had only two choices left: did she aim for the water, or did she bury him with grace and dignity in the woods?

'I could say a prayer for you,' she whispered as she turned the engine back on and once again began to drive.

The road twisted and turned in all directions. One minute she'd be driving uphill, the next she'd be going down. She reached across to a box of tissues, pulled one from the box and wiped her eyes. She lost concentration, just for a moment. A car's headlights were aiming directly at her and she found herself swerving the vehicle violently to one side. 'Oh my God.' She cursed, slowed down and pulled back onto her own side of the road. She realised how close she'd been to crashing. And for just a split second she wondered what the police or the fire brigade would have made of a vehicle with two dead bodies in it, one that had died some hours before the other. She slowed down as she neared the lake again, pulled the Outlander over and stopped.

* * *

Will slammed his foot on the brake, swerved and stopped. The hospital had told him not to drive and that... that had been why. But he shook his head. He was sure the near accident hadn't been his fault. He was sure the car had aimed for him, but he hadn't been sure whether it had swerved on purpose or by complete accident. He just felt relieved that the collision hadn't happened.

He thought for a moment. The car had seemed familiar. Outlanders were not common in this area and he tried to think back to where he'd seen it before. He looked down at his phone, now fully charged, and with trepidation he pressed on Ella's name.

'This had better be good.' Ella's voice was calm, but angry. And without a doubt, Will didn't blame her.

'Ella, listen. I'm so sorry.' He paused. He could hear her breathing, and even though she barely said a thing, he could feel her temper. 'Ella. I'll explain everything later. But I know who attacked you. I know where the Golf is. I found it.'

'I know. Sarah saw it on your computer. She's had a team searching the farm all afternoon. The car's been found, burned out, and Sarah and the police are trying to find Nina so that they can question her, especially now that they suspect that Harold Hannigan could be dead. The police have looked into his finances etc. He's had no bank activity for years. So... thanks for the information, Will, but you're about ten hours too late.' Her voice was flat, and without emotion. 'Is that all, Will? Because I really have to go and let Millie out.'

Will felt his heart sink. Ella was furious. No, from the way she sounded, she was more than furious. 'Ella, I swear to God I thought I'd be back before you woke. I really did.' Will wiped his forehead. His skin was cold, clammy. He still felt drowsy, and he knew he shouldn't be driving. 'If I could have got to you, I would have. But I was attacked. I've been in hospital, sedated. Tell Sarah that Nina attacked me. And then she dumped me on the side of the road, in a ditch. She left me for dead.'

Will listened. Ella made no sound and for a moment he thought she'd hung up.

'Ella?'

'I'm here.'

'Ella? I...'

'Oh my God, attacked? Will, are you okay, because... I really thought... I thought you'd walked out on me.' The words came between sobs and broke Will's heart. He knew how badly Ella would have felt, how much emotion she'd have gone through.

'Ella. I swear. I would never do that to you. I'd never intentionally hurt you. Jesus, Ella, I love you.' He swallowed and realised what he'd just said. He knew he'd said it before, but now, now he knew it was true, he really did mean it. He really did love Ella Hope. 'If I could have got back to you today, I swear to God, I would have.' He paused and restarted the car. He had to get home. He had to get to Ella.

'Will, I want to trust you, I want to believe that you love me, but after what happened with Rick, with the attack—'

'Ella, that's it. The car, it was Rick's car.' He suddenly remembered where he'd seen the Outlander last.

'Will, what are you talking about? What car?'

'An Outlander. Rick drives a Mitsubishi Outlander, doesn't he?' He didn't wait for her to reply. 'Ella, I've just seen it. He's just gone flying past me at speed, almost run me off the bloody road.'

Once again Ella went quiet. 'I saw them earlier. They were at Michelle's funeral.'

'Who?'

'Nina and Rick. They left together, in his car.

Shit, why didn't I remember this?' Ella paused. 'Will, where are you?' Will had begun driving and looked around. 'I'm about five minutes away from you, between you and the gap, near the lake. Actually, I can see the Outlander. It's parked up ahead. He's pulled up. I'll call you back.'

40

Will slowed his car as he drove past where the Outlander was parked, just as the rain once again began to fall. He was about to pull over, but saw Nina and changed his mind. She had tears streaming down her face, and after what Ella had just said about her stepfather, he wasn't taking any chances.

Will parked further up the road, out of sight. He sat for a moment before he climbed out and quietly closed the car door. He then stood and caught his breath. The rain dropping on his face was refreshing, but his head still spun, his legs still wobbled and he felt as though he were walking in a cartoonish and unusual way as he crept along the roadside. His hands held onto anything and everything he could grab hold of and he used the trees and bushes as camouflage until he was close enough to try and see what Nina was doing.

He felt a sense of relief as she disappeared into the woods. She was now out of his view, but the Outlander was close. He could almost touch it and, using the vehicle to hide himself, he crept to its side and peered in through the window.

'Oh, no. Oh my God,' he whispered as he saw Rick's lifeless body laid flat on the back seat. He peered around the vehicle, tried to see where Nina had gone. The rain now fell persistently; it blurred his view and he could only just make her out as she seemed to pace up and down, deep within the woods, spade in her hands.

His hand lifted to the door handle and, as quietly as he could, he pulled open the door.

'Okay, Rick. Okay, let's check you out.' He felt for a pulse. Again, and again, his fingers felt along his neck, and he sighed with relief when he felt the faintest of throbs. Again, he looked into the woods. Nina had vanished. The last thing he wanted was for her to come back now, knowing that if she could incapacitate Rick, she'd have no issue with doing the same to him. Besides, she'd already tried to kill him once and there was no way he was about to give her a second chance.

'Hold on, mate. I'm going to try and help you.' Using every ounce of his strength, Will pulled Rick out of the car. They both collapsed in a heap and Will used his foot to gently close the door behind him. He tried to stand, but his foot slipped on the wet grass and he sat for a moment trying to decide what to do. He had two choices: he could try and get help or he could drag Rick's body along the verge, one inch at a time. 'Damn it,' he whispered, 'Bloody sedatives.' He knew what he'd normally do, what he'd normally be capable of. But his strength was failing and his body felt weak. He took in a deep breath. He had to get Rick to safety and, with Rick's head resting in his lap, he hooked his arms under Rick's and pulled as hard as he could.

'Shuffle, pull, repeat, shuffle, pull, repeat, that's the way,' he chanted over and over again, as he inched his way towards where he'd parked his car. He could feel the raindrops dripping down his forehead; his clothes were soaked, but his mouth was dry and he felt desperately in need of a drink. With his strength so much more depleted than normal, it was only the adrenaline that kept him going and, with one final surge of effort, he once again tried pulling Rick to safety.

Every few pulls he looked into the woods. He had to know where Nina was at all times. Had to ensure she wasn't about to spring upon them both. He'd already seen her handiwork and how he felt right now, he really didn't fancy tackling her, not when she had a spade in her hands. He looked over his shoulder. His car was still too far away down the road, the rain wasn't helping and he made the decision to pull Rick behind the trees and bushes. They formed a line between the road and the lake and Will knew that they both stood more chance if they were camouflaged by the waterside.

Once there, Will finally felt able to check out Rick's condition more thoroughly. 'Come on, Rick. Breathe.' Rick was struggling and, without hesitation, Will placed his mouth over his and blew into his lungs. 'Come on.' Again he blew. Will pulled his phone from his pocket.

'Ambulance, and the police. Fast. Please, tell them to come fast.'

* * *

'You say Will's been sedated and he's doing what?' Sarah screamed down the phone with a voice loud enough to break glass. 'Ella, she's dangerous and Will, what the hell is he thinking? He shouldn't be driving or confronting Nina!'

Ella's heart began to pound. Sarah was right. Nina was dangerous and if Will challenged her in his condition, there was no telling what she'd do next. 'Sarah, meet me there. Meet me at the lake.' She slammed the phone down without waiting for an answer, ran from the house, ignoring the pain in her ankle, and jumped into her car.

Turning on the windscreen wipers, Ella followed the road, followed the twists and turns. Then, finally, she spotted the Outlander at the roadside, swung in beside it and, without thinking, jumped out of the car. Her door slammed. She'd expected to see Will, expected his car to be right there, but something was very wrong.

'Couldn't help but interfere, could you?' came Nina's voice from behind her. Ella spun round to see a large object aiming at her, and then heard the sound of Will's scream as he launched himself forwards.

'Noooooo!' His voice and then body appeared

from nowhere and the object dropped to the sodden ground, and so did Nina.

Ella looked down at the ground, at where the spade had landed. She threw herself forward, but the ground was slippery and Nina moved quickly. Once again the spade was in her hands. Will jumped to his feet but wobbled. He grabbed at Nina, missed and then once again propelled himself at her.

And then, as though in slow motion, the spade went high above Nina's head and spun out of control. It flew in Will's direction and Ella heard an agonised scream, before Will dropped to the ground, clutching at his side.

Ella's mind spun. This wasn't happening. This couldn't happen. She couldn't allow Nina to win, not again. Turning quickly, Ella opened the boot of her car, grabbed at the burnt hockey stick and swung it as hard as she could in Nina's direction. The stick connected with Nina's head and snapped in half before Ella saw Nina drop to the ground. For a moment Ella froze. She couldn't breathe and felt her legs go weak. 'Is... is she dead? Oh my God, I... I killed her!' she screamed as she dropped to her knees. She hurriedly wiped the rain from her face and gasped for breath as she looked from Will to Nina and then back again. Should she check Nina?

Should she see if she was alive? Or did she look after Will?

She chose to look after Will and scrambled through the wet grass until she knelt by his side. She could see the blood oozing from a huge gash in his side and she quickly moved into action, pulling off her cardigan and pressing it hard against his skin. 'You'll be okay. I saw this on telly, it'll help. It'll stop the bleeding.' She bent her head down to his and their foreheads touched. 'You'll be okay. I promise.' Their eyes locked and her lips momentarily grazed his. 'I'm so sorry I thought badly of you... I thought you'd left. I... I should have known you wouldn't.' A slight half smile crossed her lips and then she sat up and began fumbling in her jeans pocket. 'The ambulance, I have to call the ambulance.'

But Will lifted his hand to her face and wiped the rain from her cheek. 'I called them,' he said, his voice just a whisper as he twisted to look behind him. 'Rick, he's over there, he isn't looking good.' He pointed to the bushes.

Ella gasped and jumped up. But Will's sudden movement made her spin on the spot.

'Where is she?' Will shouted as he lifted his head to look at the ground where Nina had lain. His eyes opened wide. 'Where the hell did she go?' The question didn't need to be answered. The Outlander's engine fired up and the car suddenly sped towards the bridge but turned abruptly before it got there, and in one swift movement, it left the road and flew through the air. Ella's hands went up to her face as she watched the Outlander hit the water with force. Then, as though time had stopped, she felt the breath leave her body as she watched the car slowly disappear below the surface of the lake.

Ella jumped up. 'We... we have to get her! She'll die! She... she can't die!' Ella scrambled on her hands and knees to the water's edge. 'Will, she has to pay, she has to pay for what she did to me... to you... to us! To all of us!' Will reached out and grabbed hold of her hand. His grip was weak, and Ella knew that he was suffering. She looked along the road. The ambulance still couldn't be seen, but from somewhere in the distance, sirens could be heard. 'Will, I can hear them. They're coming.' She gripped his hand, but her eyes went back to the lake.

'Ella, please, it's over.' His voice was barely a whisper. She could hear the pain in his words and held a finger to his lips.

'Shhhh, try and save your energy.' Again, she looked up, 'I can hear them, Will... they're coming. I promise. They won't be long.' She knelt by his side as his eyes searched hers.

'Ella, promise me...' He struggled with the words and Ella lowered her face towards his.

'Shhh... It's okay, my love... They'll... they'll be here soon.' The words came between sobs. She knew he was losing far too much blood and she held her hand tightly over the wound, but she gasped as the colour left his face and she could physically see the life draining from him.

'Ella,' he whispered. 'Leave the job, promise me.' His body began to shake. 'No more danger.' He gripped her hand. 'Go... go take photographs... weddings, dogs... anything.' He smiled. 'Something nice, on sunny days.' He tried to lift his face closer to hers. 'Stay home when it rains.'

Ella nodded. 'I will. I swear... Weddings. Yes... I'll do weddings...' She wiped the tears on her sleeve. 'I'll do anything, anything you say, just don't you dare leave me, not now. Not now I've found you.' The words tumbled from her mouth just as Will's head tipped to one side, his eyes closed and the hand that had held onto hers fell away.

* * *

I was blinded by tears when Ella Hope rose up before me. She was the one who'd lived, the one who'd caused all the trouble. And now, now she was here, interfering. She was watching me. She knew what I'd done and I had to get rid of her. I had to stop her from talking and swung out with the only weapon I had, my old, rusty spade. But then like a vision, a ghost appeared before me. Will Taylor was there, although he couldn't be there, could he? He was dead. I'd disposed of him, but now... even the dead are coming back to haunt me, and all I can wonder is who will come next? I can't bear to see them, their opaque, eyes staring at me, screaming at me and accusing me for taking their lives. I know I'm crazy. I know I've gone too far and that I can't go on. I know that if the dead come back, if they come back to haunt me, it's one part too many of crazy. I feel myself crawl to the Outlander. I pull myself inside and start the engine, and then I smile knowing that my final journey is about to begin.

41

TEN WEEKS LATER

Ella walked up and down the garden. It was still early, before breakfast, yet already the sun was warm and Ella smiled, knowing that later in the day it would get warmer still. She breathed in a mixture of aromas. The scents of tomato plants, roses and lavender were all jumbled together, but Ella didn't mind. Every single smell, bird, bee or butterfly made her smile and it was mornings like this that made her thankful to have survived Nina's rampage. Others hadn't been so lucky, and she was more than aware of how easily she could have joined them.

'Here you go, Millie. Fetch.' She kicked a ball down the garden and towards the cottage as Millie happily scampered after it. But a noise in the house sent her racing inside and Ella ran in behind her in her daily race for the post. It was a race she almost always lost.

'Millie, come back with that!' Ella shouted as Millie sped past her and down the garden, a copy of today's newspaper firmly grasped in her mouth. 'Sit down, Millie, stop.' Ella stood still, shook her head and watched as Millie mischievously made her way as far down the garden as she could. But then as quickly as the game had begun, it ended, and the paper was dropped as yesterday's marrowbone caught her attention.

Picking up the paper, Ella made her way back to the garden bench, where the morning sun shone down on the pages as she began to turn them. She glanced over the headline and sighed. It was the headline she'd always known would be there and a picture of Rick jumped out from the page with the headline 'Murdered business owner finally laid to rest' written above it. A tear dropped down her face. Rick had been in a coma for six weeks before his family had made the heartbreaking decision to turn off his life support. She thought of the funeral and the sense of sadness that had surrounded the day. After all, everyone had blamed him for the murders and her attack. Everyone had thought him guilty, even her. Yet, finally he too had become one of Nina's victims. He too had lost his life, and for what?

Diaries at the farmhouse had told of Nina's obsession. Of how she'd been abused by her stepfather. How she'd killed him, then searched for love and had latched onto Rick's kindness, mistaking it for affection. Jealousy had driven her. But her motives had been clear and following the inquest, Ella had actually felt sorry for the person that Nina had become, knowing that if she'd had a loving home, with the love of a mother and a father, if she'd had the family time, the Christmases and birthdays that Ella had had, then Nina's life would have almost certainly turned out very differently.

Ella sighed, turned the page and smiled as Will's face stared up at her. She read the headline with pride: 'Local Editor brings life back to Filey.'

'Hey, what are you up to?' Will's voice came from the kitchen. 'I'm making coffee, do you want some?'

Ella turned and smiled at Will who stood in her cottage doorway. He'd lost weight since the injury, making his shorts hang loosely around his waist. His T-shirt was held in one hand, while his other arm was stretched above his head. The wound that almost killed him was still clearly red, puckered and visible. He caught Ella's eye, saw her studying the scar and quickly pulled his T-shirt on to hide it.

'Don't hide it. You're still here; that's all that matters.' She walked towards him, kissed her fingertips and held them to his skin as his arm surrounded her and pulled her against him.

'So, what are you up to?' His lips teased her neck as his hand traced the curve of her spine.

'Oh, I was just reading about how you set up the social media page, how the crowdfunding was arranged and how the Filey fishermen now have boats and hydraulics to get them in and out of the sea. And all because of you.' She put her arms around his neck and kissed him hard on the lips. 'You're a local hero.'

Ella felt herself being pulled towards the stairs. 'Mmmmm... But I just want to be your hero,' Will whispered as his mouth moved gently over hers. His arms tightened around her and she could feel every inch of him as he pressed himself close to her body. 'You know, you could always take me upstairs and—'

Ella began to laugh. 'Hey, stop it...' She pointed to her equipment bag. 'I have a wedding to photograph today and I have to be with the blushing bride in just under an hour.' She looked down at her watch, at the luminous hands that continually ticked by and her mind flew back to that day on the moors, of how she'd wished for more time, of how many bargains and promises she'd made, of how she'd felt her life slowly slipping away, and of how she'd kept her eye on the time, on the seconds and minutes, determined to live.

Now she appreciated everything she had, made every second count and genuinely tried to make the best of every single day. If nothing else, the last few months had taught her so many valuable lessons. She now knew how slowly time could pass when you're watching the clock, how precious life was and how in one single moment it could so easily be lost forever. She thought of how she'd almost lost Will, of how she'd sat by his hospital bed night after night and of how she'd promised to love him, and to do everything she could to make him happy, if only he too survived.

She took in a deep breath and smiled, turned back to him and allowed her eyes to lock with his as she took off her watch. 'We have time,' she whispered as she laid her watch on the sideboard, and between kisses she pulled him up the stairs behind her. 'We'll always have time.'

THANK YOU!

Dear Reader,

Thank you so much for reading *The Fake Date*.

I really enjoyed writing this book, although I did find it challenging.

I hope that you loved the story and enjoyed following Ella's story. I'm sure you'll agree that right from the beginning, she had quite a battle on her hands and went through a really tough time before finally finding the happiness she deserved with Will.

As an author, I still find it surreal that I now have 8 published novels. With that in mind, I'd love to know your thoughts and I'd be delighted if you'd take just a few moments to leave me a review.

If you enjoyed The Fake Date, then please take a

look at my other titles, which include The Sister's Next Door, The Serial Killer's Girl and The Weekend.

Please feel free to contact me anytime. Either at @Lyndastacey on Twitter, Lyndastaceyauthor on Facebook or on my website at www.Lyndastacey. co.uk

Once again, thank you for reading, it was a pleasure to write this novel for you..!

With Love Lynda x

ACKNOWLEDGMENTS

Firstly, I'd like to thank the lady who this book is dedicated to, Kathy Kilner. I've lost times of the hours that we've sat in her conservatory, staring at the cottage next door. We'd often discuss how sad it was to be empty, and we'd constantly wonder who would next move in and once they did, whether they'd ever tame their unbelievably overgrown garden. It was Kathy's cottage that gave me the idea for Ella's cottage, along with her puppy Millie who I just had to bring into the book.

I'd also like to thank my wonderful friend, and fellow author Jane Lovering, who is my constant support. Her critique service is amazing (www.janelovering.co.uk). We often have very long brainstorming phone calls to discuss plot, characters and story arcs. She often helps me pull the story apart and put it back together and somehow by the end of the call, we always come up with the answers.

Thank you also to my husband, Haydn. He's supported me in everything I've ever done and puts up with the rollercoaster that I constantly seem to be on. The last thirty-two years have been quite a ride, but I'm so pleased we've taken it together.

Finally, thank you to my publishers Boldwood Books and to my wonderful editor, Emily Ruston. Thank you for everything. xx

ABOUT THE AUTHOR

L. H. Stacey lives in a small rural hamlet in Yorkshire, with her 'hero at home husband' Haydn, and her puppy 'Barney'. In 2015 her debut novel won a prestigious publishing contract.

Sign up to L. H. Stacey's mailing list for news, competitions and updates on future books.

Visit Lynda's website: http://www.lyndastacey.co.uk/

Follow Lynda on social media:

f facebook.com/LHStaceyauthor

twitter.com/Lyndastacey

instagram.com/lynda.stacey

BB bookbub.com/authors/lynda-stacey

ALSO BY L. H. STACEY

The Sisters Next Door

The Serial Killer's Girl

The Weekend

The Fake Date

The Safe House

The House Guest

The Fake Date

THE
Murder
LIST

**THE MURDER LIST IS A NEWSLETTER
DEDICATED TO SPINE-CHILLING FICTION
AND GRIPPING PAGE-TURNERS!**

**SIGN UP TO MAKE SURE YOU'RE ON OUR
HIT LIST FOR EXCLUSIVE DEALS, AUTHOR
CONTENT, AND COMPETITIONS.**

SIGN UP TO OUR
NEWSLETTER

BIT.LY/THEMURDERLISTNEWS

Boldwood

Boldwood Books is an award-winning fiction publishing company seeking out the best stories from around the world.

Find out more at www.boldwoodbooks.com

Join our reader community for brilliant books, competitions and offers!

Follow us
@BoldwoodBooks
@TheBoldBookClub

Sign up to our weekly deals newsletter

https://bit.ly/BoldwoodBNewsletter